THROWAWAY GIRL

AN AUGUSTINE FLOOD NOVEL

THROWAWAY GIRL

DAVID HEINZMANN

FIVE STAR
A part of Gale, Cengage Learning

GALE
CENGAGE Learning™

Detroit • New York • San Francisco • New Haven, Conn • Waterville, Maine • London

LIBRARY OF CONGRESS CATALOGING-IN-PUBLICATION DATA

Heinzmann, David.
    Throwaway girl : an Augustine Flood novel / David Heinzmann. — 1st ed.
       p. cm.
    ISBN-13: 978-1-4328-2550-8 (hardcover)
    ISBN-10: 1-4328-2550-X (hardcover) 1. Private investigators—Fiction. 2. Child trafficking—Fiction. 3. Chicago (Ill.)—Fiction. I. Title.
PS3608.E38T48 2011
813'.6—dc23   2011031289

First Edition. First Printing: November 2011.
Published in 2011 in conjunction with Tekno Books and Ed Gorman.

For Francis and Andrew

CHAPTER 1

No clue what her name was.

Augustine Flood peeked again at the smooth skin of her arms. Once more, it told him he had made a mistake. The word *teen* formed in his aching mind as she lay motionless, her bare back to him.

The sun was already high over the lake and pouring blistering light into the bedroom, and Flood did not have the head or the stomach to do anything but close his eyes and play possum. He lay there for ten minutes thinking up reasons not to roll over and beg the naked girl's pardon.

Finally, he faced facts and sat up. His head stung with pain, dry like all the blood had been drained out of him. She didn't move. He touched his forehead, half expecting to find a hole. He decided to pretend she wasn't there. Steeling himself against the nausea whirling through him, he stood up, prayed it would flow past, and then tilted blindly toward the kitchen to start coffee. A glass of water was next, but he thought it might not stay down.

The coffee started dribbling into the pot as Flood hobbled back down the hall to the bathroom. The apartment was a mess—newspapers on the floor and unwashed glasses everywhere. The place smelled faintly of stale whisky. At least there was no rotting food lying around. He wasn't eating much. Books and CDs were all in their places because, other than the habit of opening the daily papers, he had not read or listened to anything in months.

Still no idea about this girl.

The spray of the shower stripped away the film of secondhand smoke and firsthand drunkenness and gave him a little hope. But then, standing in front of the mirror with his face lathered and a blade raised, the freshness proved fleeting as he got a look at himself in a bloodshot close-up.

This was no way to begin another day. But it was routine, lately. Except for the girl; she was a twist. Since Jenny left him Flood had slid this way, a little further every week. The split from the firm had compelled him to hang out his own shingle. At the time that had been a good thing, his name was in the press for a while and that had brought in clients. But now he was in trouble. Nobody to fall back on. Nobody with any common sense making sure the bills got paid. Maybe he should have been patient and hooked on with another firm. He had no idea how he would meet expenses this month, including paychecks for Jamie and Veraneace.

He stumbled back toward his bedroom to dress and there she was again. Flood reeled through the last hours once more, and a fragment came into focus. A whiff of perfume, a smile, the playful hip nudging him as he teetered on a barstool. He did not remember bringing her home. He certainly did not recall sex. But maybe a few words of conversation. Something he said had gotten a laugh, made him feel for an instant that he had his feet back on the ground. But the strain to remember exactly what had happened was crowding out the guilty thoughts of why it had happened. Why was he sitting by himself at the corner of the bar at the Palmer House at whatever time it had been? Late. That's right, the call to Jenny's voicemail. Sober, but pointless. Afraid to say anything that he actually felt. Afraid to say that he just wanted to hear her voice.

Anyway, what was this girl's story? Traveling on business.

Selling or buying, he couldn't remember. Whatever it was must have been a lie, he decided. She was too young. But last night, Flood was thinking he had no one to be faithful to, so what the hell. Now he looked at her bare back, firm bottom and trim thighs and he prayed she was more than twenty. For Christ's sake. She still looked dead to the world, so he tiptoed to his rumpled, discarded suit and searched the pockets for money. He would offer her cab fare, if he had it. He found a ten and three ones in a pocket and laid them on the chest of drawers before stepping over a pile of dirty clothes into his closet. He dressed in a suit that, while not clean, had at least been hanging properly. He put on his last clean shirt and a tie and walked out, kicking through the loose clothes on the floor in search of his shoes. When he was finally dressed, Flood poured a cup of coffee and sat down at his dining table and looked out his windows to the west, away from the glare of the sun off the lake. He couldn't stomach looking at the papers, so he had left them outside his front door. Thoughts he had set aside earlier now seemed a soothing alternative to the question of the girl in his bed.

His last client wrote a check that bounced. The one before that didn't even claim to have any money, but at least he had known that going in. One thing had not led to another this summer and Augustine Flood and Associates was running through his rainy day fund so fast that he was not sure whether there was five thousand or five hundred dollars left.

This is what happens, Jamie said, and Flood had nearly punched him in the face for saying it. *Post-traumatic stress,* Jamie said. Flood told him to fuck off.

Jenny had moved to Washington. The job at the Corcoran Gallery was a dream, and she would be close to her mother in Baltimore, she said. She emphasized the mother part, as if duty called and she had to set her own feelings aside. But she didn't have much else to say about it. Flood had argued, but at the same time his head was saying, *I'm the one who took away everything and anything you ever felt about safety and security. I'm the one who put you in a deep, dark hole filled with demons, I killed the bad guys and don't regret it, and told you I loved you and meant it, but there was no amount of sunshine or slaughter to undo the evil that happened to you. I'm the one who taught you everything you never wanted to know about Chicago.* He didn't blame her for leaving. If she was smart, she'd never come back to this medieval place.

Jamie said she needed her space, and finally Flood did lay hands on him. He shoved him against a file cabinet. He was drunk and Veraneace came out of her chair with a stapler, of all things. But by God, she found his funny bone with the thing and it made him howl and then she kicked him out of his own place of business. He marched right back down the street to Miller's Pub and had a beer.

A nice chunk of the rainy day fund was Jamie's law school tuition. One of the fringe benefits of working for Flood, but he wasn't thinking about that when the girl in the bedroom finally spoke up.

She was standing in the doorway to the living room, wearing the little black dress from last night, but her dark blonde hair was now loosely gathered in a pony tail. Flood looked at her fresh, young face and he was afraid.

"You don't look so hot," she said, waiting.

He didn't get up, and he wasn't sure if he could get up, but he asked, "Can I get you some coffee?"

She smiled and walked into his kitchen on her own and, from the sound of things, found a dirty mug, washed it, and then filled it with coffee.

"You want a refill?" she said.

"I'm fine," he said. "Tell me again, what do you do for a living?"

He heard a laugh. She came back into view, crossed the living room slowly, taking things in and seeming to enjoy his anxiety, and sat down next to him. The apartment was a two-bedroom with a dining area outside the kitchen. But Flood had a smaller table in the dining area, and had put his large oak farm table here by the windows, looking out on the river twenty-four stories below and Wacker Drive on the other side.

"Do you think I'm jailbait?" She spoke slowly and deliberately. He was being teased, and didn't respond. "What did I tell you last night?"

"You told me you were a buyer or in sales or something. I can't remember."

"I can't remember, either," she said, taking a sip. She looked around. "Your apartment used to be nice but now it's a mess. Your coffee's still good."

She was amusing herself and making his head worse. He was counting downward in years as he studied her unlined face and slender, smooth throat.

"So?"

"So, I don't have a job. I go to school."

She could tell he felt sick.

"It's OK," she finally said. "Remember, we were in a bar. I'm of age. I'm twenty-three. I'm getting an MBA at DePaul. Sorry, I lied, Mr. Suddenly Has a Conscience. Sometimes I get bored and dress up and go see what happens in a hotel bar."

"Jesus," he said. "That's terrible."

That pissed her off, but she wasn't quite sure what to say first, so he kept going.

"I'm forty and an asshole, but I won't hurt you. You could have ended up with some sociopath."

She rolled her eyes in a way that suggested she'd already

been down that road, deciding he wasn't questioning her virtue so much as voicing a misplaced concern for her well-being "You're not an asshole," she said. "Your girlfriend left you, and you thought she was it, so now you don't know what to do next."

"Did I tell you that last night?"

"Part of it. That you got dumped."

He looked away from her with a grimace of self-disgust. That made her laugh again. Someday she was going to do serious harm to herself, he thought, looking back and finding her smiling eyes on him. She was cute as hell.

"Well, then. I was fairly honest with you," he said. "Meanwhile, you made a bunch of shit up."

"Which you happily bought," she said. "And you were drunk."

"Vulnerable, and you took advantage of me," he said and tried to smile. For the first time this morning the notion crossed his mind that he might actually be able to eat something later in the day. More of the evening came back to him.

"We didn't have sex," he said.

"Right," she said gleefully, like a teacher pleased with her pupil. "Actually, I got a wonderful night's sleep. My bed sucks. Yours is nice."

He almost apologized but caught himself. He couldn't remember if he had fallen asleep or if she had. They had both been naked. It was better left unknown.

His cell phone rang, thank God. From the screen he saw it was his office calling and he picked it up while she sat there next to him. He still had no idea what her name might be.

"Lawyer named Philip Swain called," Veraneace said. She was already cranky and barking at him. It had been a week since the stapler incident but she still had an edge. Jamie had taken a vacation and Flood did not know whether he would come back. Through the fog of thoughts, the name finally registered.

"Philip Swain?"

"You know him? Actually, wasn't him. Was his secretary. First she said he wanted you to call. Then I asked what it was about and she said he wanted you to come to his office after lunch today for a meeting, and I said you'd be there because it sounded like real money. Who is he?"

"He's a lawyer."

"I know that, fool. I told you that."

"What time?"

"She said one-thirty; I said you'd go."

Flood said OK and hung up on her as she asked again who Swain was. If you made a list of the four or five biggest big-shot lawyers in the city, Philip Swain would probably drop in around number three. In fact, he was beyond being a big shot. He was the sort of lawyer you heard about and never saw, with a legend that meandered from Chicago through Washington and New York and back to Chicago again. He had been a deputy attorney general under somebody—Johnson or Nixon. That was after clerking for a Supreme Court justice. He'd maybe been a diplomat. Flood couldn't remember, and had never had any reason to know. Swain was rumored to be a sort of liaison for the mayor, providing him access to leaders around the globe, despite the fact that he was North Shore born and bred and wouldn't be caught dead in Bridgeport. The firm was old and carried his name, or rather his grandfather's name. Swain was old, too. At least he must be.

His laptop was sitting on the table. Flood opened it and did a quick search for Philip Swain. Sears Tower, or whatever they called it now. The website for his firm boasted more than three hundred lawyers, doing everything from mergers and acquisitions and telecommunications regulations to property tax appeals and personal injury. It was hard to imagine what Philip Swain would want with Flood.

"You OK?" the girl said.

He looked up and she was looking at his phone, trying to sort out what had pushed him from the depths of hungover lethargy to agitation so quickly.

"I'm OK. Um, what is your name, please?"

"You don't remember?"

"Yeah, sorry. I'm bad with names."

"You were calling me Miss Lyons from Winona last night."

That rang a bell, actually. "Winona, Minnesota?"

"Of course."

"Lovely town."

"A jewel."

"Well, Miss Lyons, did you tell me your first name?"

"I believe I did."

"Care to repeat it?"

"Maybe next time."

No mood for games. "Perhaps. It's time to go to work. Come on, I'll walk you back to your dorm."

She rolled her eyes.

"I don't live in a *dorm*. Jeezus."

"Well, it makes me feel worse to think that you do, and I need to make an impression on myself this morning."

"You poor, sad man."

"Finish your coffee."

Chapter 2

It took two elevators and nearly ten minutes to get from the lobby of the Sears Tower to Swain's office on the ninety-somethingth floor. The receptionist summoned Swain's secretary, who led him down a sleek, glowing hallway lined with large offices. They turned the corner at the office of a former governor, who was immediately recognizable to Flood, tall and paunchy in there, leaning back in his chair and gazing at the airspace over the Loop as he prattled away at his speakerphone. Swain's own corner office looked east and north, offering a dizzying view, towering above the rest of the tall buildings and the endless vibrant blue of the lake. It made Flood feel like he wasn't in an office building at all, but hovering above the city in a dirigible. Flood would never get any work done up here. He was much better off on the second floor of a dusty old Jewelers' Row cave on Wabash. He didn't care what anyone said, this was still the tallest building in the world.

When Swain's secretary led him into the office, he found the old man, distinguished, tall, trim and gray all over, standing in front of his desk, which, like all the furniture, was in the Mies-inspired Modern style. On the sofa, standing up and offering her hand was a woman who introduced herself as Jane Ash. She sat back down.

Swain had a manila folder resting on top of a leather portfolio on the glass coffee table. He picked up the folder and handed it to Flood. Inside there was a photograph portrait of a strikingly pretty young woman with shoulder-length brown hair, which was loosely parted and hanging elegantly over her forehead. She had piercing hazel eyes and wore a tepid smile, as if this formal pose, with a strand of pearls, was a concession to someone for whom she cared deeply. Probably her mother. In addition to the portrait, there was a photocopy of a short obituary, without a photograph, in the *Tribune*. Jane Ash was named as the dead woman's mother. Flood could feel her eyes on him as he perspired a little. The percolation of adrenaline was crowding out his hangover but it also was making him a little breathless.

The obituary for Alice Jane Ash did not mention a police investigation. And while it gave an incomplete explanation of her death, its recitation of her life raised more questions than it answered. With a couple hundred words the reader learned little more than that she was twenty-five and worked as a project coordinator for the Chicago Initiative on Homelessness. The obituary noted that she had grown up in Winnetka, attended Phillips Exeter Academy but graduated from New Trier Township High School, and then Georgetown, and that she was survived by her brother James of New York, and her parents, Jane of Chicago and James Sr. of Winnetka.

Almost as an afterthought, the article acknowledged that she'd drowned in Lake Michigan on the first Thursday night of June. The cynical eye would size up a rich kid, do-gooder who probably got drunk or stoned and fell off some other rich kid's boat. Alice Jane Ash was begging to be dismissed in the published account of her passing.

As he sat on Philip Swain's exquisite sofa and met Jane Ash's glance again, he realized the other glaring omission of the obit. The name Ash had struck him as slightly familiar, and as he mulled it over, finally her father's name brought her identity more clearly into view. James Ash was a Heidecke. The obit never got around to mentioning that Alice was a Heidecke. She was stupendously rich, an heiress to one of Chicago's great industrial fortunes. How carefully the information had been controlled, he thought.

Flood scoured his memory for any fragment of information he held on this family. Perhaps only that they were quietly rich, not the sort who sought the spotlight of society-page coverage. The Heidecke name was on the wings and additions of a few hospitals and museums, but it had been so for decades. They did not make headlines anymore. Nonetheless, these were very rich people and one would have thought the media would have taken note of the passing of one of them, especially a young and beautiful one.

"I'm sorry about your daughter," Flood began, and Jane Ash nodded.

Nobody was saying anything so Flood surmised he was supposed to turn his attention back to the folder for a moment. He did. Underneath the obituary was a medical examiner's report, which he scanned quickly just to see that the manner of death was drowning, and cause of death was "pending police investigation." He saw that her blood-alcohol content was .11. Drunk, but not very.

Jane Ash sat with her arms crossed in ongoing judgment. She looked about fifty, an attractive woman with shoulder-length blonde hair accented with a few thoughtful strands of gray. She was dressed in a cream-colored linen suit and white blouse and had that clubby middle-aged athletic look of a woman who played tennis, or walked golf courses, or swam, or all three. She wore a gold bracelet and small gold earrings that matched. There were no rings on her fingers and her wristwatch had a brown leather band.

"Did Philip explain what I want?" she asked in a tone that did little to warm the atmosphere.

"No, but I gather you want a private investigation of your

17

daughter's death. One that parallels the police investigation."

"Parallels?" She raised her eyebrows a little.

"Well, whatever you think of the police department, their detectives will do things that I have to do. If I take this case, I would be running into them frequently, at least at the beginning," Flood said. "Anyway, it would be foolish to try to ignore them."

She nodded and thought for a moment. Flood saw some evidence of grief, but she had put it on hold for this meeting. There was something terribly strong about her, he thought. He wanted her to like him, but that did not necessarily mean she would be a good client. Not that he was in a position to decline it, whatever it paid.

"Was Alice—" Flood began, only to be cut off.

"A.J.," her mother said, making Flood feel that he had sat in the wrong chair. "No one called her Alice."

Flood nodded and quietly repeated "A.J." It was curious that the obituary had not mentioned the name she used, if her mother's immediate reaction was any guide to how people felt about her given name. He smelled a broken family's bitterness in the mix.

"Was A.J. having any problems? Personal problems or conflicts with anyone? I mean—and I don't want to suggest I believe this, but it's the first thing that needs to be ruled out— was there any indication she might have suicidal thoughts?"

"Not at all," Jane Ash said, clearly ready for the question. Her dislike for it seemed to bring her back to the police. "The detectives appear to be nice, competent men," she said. "But they seem to believe my daughter was an alcohol and drug abuser who killed herself, either on purpose or by accident. And in the meantime they have many drug and gang murders to investigate."

Flood didn't know about the first part, but she was right about the second part. The city's detective bureaus were sectioned into five "areas," and Area Four had been assigned the case. It was unclear why, because the Loop and downtown lakefront, which had one of the lowest violent crime rates in the city, were part of Area Three, which ran along the lake and North Side neighborhoods, covering mostly middle-class and affluent areas of the city. Area Four, on the other hand, was probably the messiest, most violent detective assignment in Chicago. The heart of Area Four was the West Side, abysmally poor neighborhoods like Lawndale and Garfield Park, most of which were controlled by competing factions of the Vice Lords street gang. But the area also included Little Village and Pilsen, Mexican neighborhoods that were ruled by the Latin Kings, 2-6, Satan's Disciples and several other, smaller gangs. Together, they made for the most concentrated violence in the city, and kept the homicide detectives headquartered at Harrison and Kedzie, five miles from the spot where A.J. Ash drowned, very busy. Area Four detectives were responsible for investigating more than one hundred murders a year, and they solved fewer than half of them.

And her death was not their typical brand of investigation. They were used to turning one gang member against another, bartering drug charges for information in a desperate and hopeless landscape where the narcotics trade was the only viable means of survival. A.J. Ash's world could not be further removed from the nightmare that was Chicago's West Side.

Flood did not know offhand the names of any of the current crew of detectives in Area Four, but he figured whoever caught the case would have a bit of a learning curve. And if Jane Ash's daughter was an alcoholic and/or drug addict, they could hardly be criticized for suspecting her death was not a homicide.

"I want to pay for a proper and thorough investigation of my daughter's death, by someone focused solely on her case," Jane Ash went on. "And I believe, or I have been led to believe, that you're the right man for this."

Flood marveled at her polish. Philip Swain, one of the most prominent and revered lawyers in Chicago, just sat in his leather club chair across from where she sat on the sofa and silently monitored the conversation.

"What do you think, Mr. Flood?" she asked.

Flood wondered if Swain would ever jump in, or if he was just there for show, to demonstrate her enormous resources. She could afford to take over Phil Swain's office in the clouds and have him just sit there and say nothing. Flood found it slightly difficult to think about her question.

"Well, I don't know anything about it other than what I read in the obituary, Mrs. Ash. Why don't you tell me about your daughter?"

She looked at him for a moment, and then asked, "What do you want to know?"

"Well, the obituary doesn't say much other than that she went far away to a very exclusive prep school but graduated from the public school close to home, and she worked for a homeless organization. And you tell me the detectives have jumped to the conclusion that she was an addict and probably died accidentally. I need you to fill in some gaps. Let's say they do think that, is there any reason they should? You said you don't believe she was suicidal, but did she have reasons to feel particularly disappointed, or had she gone through a traumatic breakup? Did she have a problem with alcohol and drugs? I know it may be difficult, but I'd like you to just talk a bit about A.J., and why you have suspicions about her death."

She sat silently for a moment taking in the questions, and then just glanced at Swain. Finally, he had something to do. He cleared his throat in a way that made him sound older than his seventy years, and hunched forward a little, hugging the fine worsted fabric of his tailored glen-plaid suit.

"A.J. had been through a lot, frankly," he said. "She was twelve when her parents divorced, and that was difficult on everyone. But, as you might imagine, it was particularly hard on a girl of that age. She was a bright girl, but she didn't take to school very well in those days. She didn't like Exeter, and she was her own worst enemy at New Trier. Quite a bit of drinking, and some fighting. Jane and I made a few late-night trips to the Winnetka Police Department in those days. But—" he said the word hard and loud, as if he was signaling a watershed transition in A.J.'s short life. "She was, as I said, quite bright, and she tested very well, and a few people may have put in a good word, and she got into Georgetown. The independence did her some good, and she really turned the corner out there. She studied history and sociology and became very interested in the well-being of others. It was quite remarkable. After college she joined an organization in New York for a year working with runaway girls who lived on the streets. She decided to come home to Chicago and continue that sort of work, and she was studying for the LSAT, and I believe she would have made a fine public-interest lawyer."

Flood nodded. He had stopped looking at Swain after the recitation of the difficult high school years and kept his eyes on Jane Ash as he heard of her daughter's metamorphosis in Washington. But Swain had left the key question unanswered, and Flood addressed Jane Ash with it.

"The report says she was tipsy, but that doesn't really indicate a problem. Why would the detectives have any reason to suspect that behavior was still an issue?"

Jane Ash seemed to want to handle this question herself, and Swain was clearly reluctant.

"She stopped using cocaine and marijuana when she was eighteen. I am sure of that. But she continued to drink, Mr. Flood. I think she mostly drank wine at dinner, but she would often drink too much of it."

"Does alcoholism run in your family?"

"A bit. My ex-husband drinks more than he should, and his parents were the sort who always had too many cocktails too early in the afternoon, mostly out of boredom. They had nothing to do."

"But you are skeptical that her drinking played a role in her drowning?"

"Skeptical," she said, picking at the word unhappily. She looked like she wanted him to use a blunter word, but her closed lips finally bore what looked like might someday become a smile. "Yes, I am skeptical, Mr. Flood. I'm not saying it's impossible. And I'll admit I don't want to believe it, but I also think it's a conclusion that no one should jump to too soon. And I'm afraid that might happen."

She stopped speaking and let Flood study her face for a bit. She was making carefully persuasive statements that she had perhaps rehearsed, at least in her head. Nonetheless, she seemed sincere. It suddenly dawned on Flood that she was a lawyer, although no one had told him so.

"Do you still practice law?" he asked.

She smiled, understanding that he was guessing based on the way she presented herself.

"No, not for twenty years. My license lapsed ten years ago. But I worked here, you know, at this firm."

He didn't, obviously. She said it with pride, almost a sense of ownership.

With the sky-high view and the bright light flooding into the office from the two walls of floor-to-ceiling windows, the room had a surreal quality and Flood had to remind himself this wasn't some game—and that he was still dealing with a woman who had buried her daughter a week before.

"Mrs. Ash, what do you think might have happened?"

She sat a long time showing no expression. Finally, she moved her body as if to talk, but it appeared she was unable to get any words out. She took a breath and looked at Swain again.

"We don't know," he said. "But there is something. A.J. cashed a couple of five-thousand-dollar checks last year. It was very unusual. She lived modestly, paid for most everything with a credit card and typically did not withdraw more than a hundred dollars in cash every week. And we cannot find this money."

Flood found that his pulse was accelerating a bit. It was something, though it was months ago.

"Did you tell the police?"

"Yes, it's why they think drugs might have killed her, actually."

Flood's eyebrows arched. They weren't telling him something, so he waited.

"They found a small amount of heroin in her apartment," Swain said. "None in her system, though."

He glanced up at Jane Ash. She was the one who had firmly declared that her daughter had not touched drugs since she was eighteen. "Why did you say she was clean if drugs were found in her apartment?"

"I can't explain why they were there, Mr. Flood," she said. "But I can tell you that it wasn't like A.J. She wasn't that person anymore, she had grown up. And the fact that it was there makes me very, very suspicious. A.J. had been fairly candid with me about her drug use, and she said she never used anything but cocaine and marijuana. I had asked her about heroin, and she said she had always been afraid of it. She was a rebellious teenager, not a desperate addict. So this doesn't make sense."

Flood flipped through the pages in his file. He turned back to the mother.

"Five thousand dollars is likely too much for a user to spend in one buy," he said. She nodded eagerly back at him, and he went on. "And if she was using a lot it's unlikely you would see just two large withdrawals. Over time, there would be more."

"I'm telling you, she wasn't using heroin," she said.

Jane Ash's voice was steady, but her eyes were pleading and wilting. Flood tried to move on.

"Well, tell me about the last time you saw her. Was she herself?"

"I hadn't seen her in two weeks, which was unusual, but not—" she stopped.

"Not what?"

Jane Ash shook her head apologetically. She was overcome. When she spoke she sounded exhausted, suddenly, and near tears. "I'm sorry, it's just that I sound so clinical. I just—"

Swain started to unfold his long limbs to get up, but she raised a hand without looking at him. He sat back down and looked at Flood, and neither of them said anything.

"I was going to say it wasn't particularly alarming. It was unusual, but not *alarming,*" she said, her eyes rimmed with tears. "It's just an awful thing to say now. She's gone and I'll never see her again. Never talk to her again. Never hold her in my arms."

Flood waited another moment and then said, "There's no easy way to talk about this."

She nodded but didn't say anything more. Flood made up his mind but kept asking questions.

"Was she seeing anyone? A boyfriend?"

She shook her head dismissively. "There was a young man I think who was pursuing her, but she wasn't interested. It was nothing."

"Was he aggressive in any way? Or was she troubled by his interest in her?"

"I don't think so. His name was Warren something. Investment banker just out of Kellogg. He really wasn't her sort of thing."

"How'd they meet?"

"Um, I think a charity ball for the Initiative. His firm probably bought a table. I don't really know. She mentioned him a couple times. I think she had dinner with him once and he was smitten. But I really don't think he was trouble. My daughter was a beautiful girl, Mr. Flood, and she drew a lot of attention from men, but she didn't spend enough time with any of them to develop a relationship that could sour."

"And you're not concerned that one of them might have grown overly frustrated that she wouldn't spend more time with him?"

She shrugged, without a ready dismissal for the possibility. Flood could tell Philip Swain was watching him closely, trying to read his face and separate it from the questions he was asking. He decided it was time to end the uncertainty, but he had a disclaimer to throw at them, not that it would matter, he figured.

"Well, I'm a lawyer, and you already have Mr. Swain. Are you sure you don't want to hire a private investigator instead? You're looking for a purely investigative job."

"I know what you are. I read all about that casino thing with those mobsters. You seem to me to be dogged and resourceful, and Philip has said nothing to dissuade me."

She was talking about the debacle involving an estranged suburban couple who'd tangled with the Outfit over a scheme to control a casino development. Flood had been working for a small Loop firm then and became entangled in the case, and unraveled the whole thing and almost got himself, Jenny, and a few other people he cared about killed.

"I didn't lose my law license, if that's what you mean."

"You looked smart," she answered, sounding like she didn't mean to flatter him. After all, she said *looked*, not *were*.

"Well, I typically charge an hourly rate as an attorney."

She looked a little annoyed, but she had been ready for this and glanced at Swain. He slowly leaned over and opened the leather portfolio. Inside were a fresh blank legal pad, a nice fountain pen and a check. Swain slid the check across the table toward Flood. It was written on the firm's account and made out to Augustine Flood and Associates in the amount of $50,000.

Swain cleared his throat and spoke: "There will be another check in the same amount if you can provide a clear and proven explanation of what happened to A.J. If someone is responsible for her death and you can establish that, there will be a bonus."

At his hourly rate, two full weeks of work would add up to under $16,000. He couldn't calculate the math quickly enough, but guessed that he had just been handed a check for a couple of months working overtime exclusively to figure out what happened to A.J. Ash.

"Expenses handled separately, of course," Swain went on. "If your hourly rate exceeds this amount, the difference will be paid."

"What if the investigation only takes a week?"

"The offer is on the table," Jane Ash said. "Let's move on."

Flood was in no position to refuse.

"I'll need access to everything she had," he said.

She shrugged and looked at Swain, who said of course, but clearly had a couple of questions about what that meant.

"Bank accounts, her phone voicemail, cell phone records, credit cards, passwords, email, all that stuff."

They both nodded.

"Recently I've been using a retired Chicago police detective to assist on cases. He'll be able to help deal with the Area Four detectives handling A.J.'s case."

Swain cleared his throat and stood up. "You can have

anything you need, Mr. Flood."

"One more thing, Mrs. Ash. I'd like to know whether you've discussed this with your ex-husband before I contact him."

"He knows," she said. "He's been in Europe on business for a week and isn't due back for a couple more days. The trip was pre-arranged and I encouraged him to go. If he's grieving, there's no one for him to grieve with here other than his second wife."

She left it at that. It gave Flood a precise impression of what she thought of the second wife, but not really much of an idea what she thought of her ex-husband.

"I'll need to talk to him, of course."

"Good luck," she said. "We'll give you Skiddy's number."

"Who's that?"

"He's sort of vice president of my ex-husband's life. You'll have to go through him."

"Is he helpful?"

"Skiddy? Much more so than James." She shrugged.

"So, I take it this investigation wasn't his idea, as well?"

She shook her head. "He thought it was a foolish idea. He figures the police are right, and this will just embarrass everybody in the end."

CHAPTER 3

Billy McPhee was tied up all day down in Joliet.

Flood had called and left a voicemail message for him as soon as he left the massive lobby concourse of the Sears Tower. He carried a corned beef sandwich from the Berghoff bar back to the office and was eating it and scouring the Internet for information on Swain and the Ash family when McPhee returned the call.

"Who you working for?" Flood asked.

"None of your business."

"Well, I need you."

"Be a couple days."

"Hmm. How about I buy you dinner tonight and we can chat about it."

"OK, well, I'll see you at Lem's at seven o'clock. I gotta go," he said and hung up.

"Um," Flood started to protest, but McPhee was gone.

Lem's was a barbecue stand on the South Side, just east of the Dan Ryan Expressway. The rib tips were just about perfect, but he would have to cross nine miles of highway under construction to get to East 75th Street. Not to mention, the place had no bar and no tables. But it was pointless to call back and argue.

Veraneace had been gone when Flood returned to the office. With no clients and little to do, she spent most afternoons taking long lunches with her old City Hall coworkers and then running errands and shopping. When she finally returned to the office, Flood informed her they had work and money. She looked at him for a moment like she didn't believe him, but then he sent her to the bank with the $50,000 check.

"This is Philip Swain?" she asked, holding up the check that bore his firm's name.

"And then some."

"All right, then," she said, heading out.

Flood was out of string for the moment. He needed whatever documents Swain was gathering together for him from A.J.'s life, and he needed McPhee to grease the skids at the cop shop.

He slumped down with the printouts of tidbits he'd found on the Internet, but he'd already gleaned the information that was there. His eyes grew heavy for a moment, and he closed them.

Anytime he slept sober these days, he risked having a dream. In this one, there were no police around to hold him back and he calmly walked in silence to the trunk of Nuccio Beppo's black Town Car and opened the lid. Jenny was not laying there bound with duct tape and freezing. Opening the empty trunk led to a room. She was sitting on the floor of the room, her back against its wall. Flood extended his hand to touch her but he couldn't quite reach. She said nothing and looked at him like she did not really know him.

Veraneace put her hand on his shoulder and shook him awake. "What the hell you doing? It's four o'clock in the afternoon and you're screaming in your sleep."

Flood sat up and rubbed his eyes. "What was I saying?"

"I don't know. It was just a bunch of wailing through the door. You need counseling," she said, then briskly hustled back to her desk muttering, "It's like running a nursing home around here."

When Flood pulled into the parking lot on 75th, McPhee was

standing there leaning against his black Explorer, his muscular forearms crossed on his chest, a toothpick in his mouth. He watched Flood roll in and park next to him, studying him with a smile on his face the way he always did. They had some history and it never ceased to amuse Billy McPhee that he'd retired from the Chicago Police Department only to go to work for an ex-fed a dozen years his junior.

McPhee had a short, bulldog body, belly, powerful legs and arms, and muscular hands with stubby fingers. His summer uniform was a brightly colored golf shirt, black or navy dress pants, and polished black dress boots. He wore a gold wristwatch and a single gold chain that always seemed to cast a slight reflection on the dark brown skin of his neck. There was usually a toothpick tucked between his lips when he wasn't dealing with clients.

When Flood got out of his car, McPhee stood up straight and they started to walk across the parking lot toward the barbecue joint.

"How long did it take you?"

"Twenty minutes. I thought it would be worse."

Behind the large floor-to-ceiling windows Flood could see the hulking black steel smokers. Firewood was stacked on the floor along the windows. A smokestack poked through the roof, leeching a blend of wood smoke, pork aroma and spice into the night air. The smell of what McPhee called "actual, *gen-u-wine* barbecue" was irresistible. Flood wanted to get to the task at hand, but he knew McPhee had been toiling all day with few breaks.

"How'd the thing go?" he asked as they reached the side entrance.

"Just fine. Copper down there took me to a pretty good taco joint for lunch."

If Flood wanted specific details about the work McPhee did,

he would have to ask pointed questions. But if the work went well, McPhee would talk about where he ate lunch. If it went poorly, he would grumble that private detective work was a general pain in the ass.

"Which one?"

"Place called Vela's."

"Yep, it's good. There's a Los Comales down there, too, on the street that runs past the old prison. It's just like the one on 26th Street."

McPhee grunted. "Los Comales on 26th is right behind County. That one out by the prison? Why they want their restaurants close to inmates, I wonder?"

"I don't know."

"But they have them little tiny tacos I like. I'll keep that in mind when I go back down."

Flood opened the door to Lem's and the smell intensified.

"If you're going back, do it tomorrow," Flood said, "because I'm going to need real help on this."

Under the dingy fluorescent lights of the vestibule they stepped into a short line behind a large woman in a dirty t-shirt and an old man in a baggy suit that looked moth-eaten and stained at the pant cuffs by years of sloshing through Chicago winter sludge. Behind the wall of plastic security windows, two big women in white aprons filled orders, tucking paper liners into red and white baskets and then plunking rib tips and wings—few people splurged on slabs of ribs—into the containers on top of slices of cheap white bread. They bundled the orders into brown paper sacks that quickly began to spot with grease.

When it was Flood's turn, he stepped up and asked for two small orders of tips, sauce on the side. Lem's didn't serve drinks from behind the counter, but there was a soda machine that vended cans of Diet Rite, a couple flavors of Crush and A&W.

Flood bought two cans of root beer.

"So what is it?" McPhee asked.

Flood laid it out briefly as they ate over the tailgate of McPhee's Explorer. A very wealthy woman drowned off Navy Pier and her mother wanted to pay for them to give it a very hard look.

"What do you really think about it?"

"I don't know enough. If I'm in a really cynical mood, which I'm not, I'd say she got drunk and had a stupid accident. One of her rich, spineless friends witnessed it but is hiding from the fact, and none of that squares with her mother's delusion that her daughter's wild partying days had been ended by an overwhelming sense of noblesse oblige."

McPhee dipped a plump rib tip into a cup of sauce and chewed off the meat, leaving the nub of white cartilage in his greasy fingers. He discarded the bone into the crumpled brown bag and reached for another. A police car zoomed by going east on 75th, its monotone claxon squawking down the block and the rack of blue strobes lighting up the sides of the buildings. The light caught McPhee's face and turned it a ghostly silver-gray for an instant. McPhee didn't even glance at the squad car. Nothing could be more commonplace in this part of the South Side.

"What about the money she took out?"

Flood shrugged. "We'll see. That's my first stop. She probably has easy access to a hundred times that much cash, but they said she never used it. Didn't spend money to begin with, and when she did, used a card."

McPhee was thinking, looking deep into the rib container as if it contained wisdom.

"So why you need a short black man to investigate a bunch of rich, white folk?"

Flood had a mouthful of pork and grinned, trying to keep his lips closed as he said, "Why do you think?"

McPhee nodded. "Who's got it, Area Three?"

Flood shook his head. "Four."

McPhee frowned. "Why Four?"

Flood shrugged. "Need to find out."

"I take it this is a well-paying job?"

Flood grabbed a bunch of thin napkins and destroyed them wiping his greasy fingers, then nodded. "This, Billy McPhee, is what we call a well-paying job."

"All right, sounds like fun. You want me to call over there and set something up for day after tomorrow?"

Flood swallowed and smiled again. "You know, they found her body on midnights."

McPhee winced. Flood wanted to go see the detectives tonight; the team assigned to it would have been working the overnight, 11 P.M. to 7 A.M. shift. McPhee looked at his watch and saw that it was just 8:15 P.M.

He sucked his fingertips, then wiped his hands on napkins and fished his cell phone out of his pants pocket. He scrolled around while tucking a fresh toothpick into his teeth and hit a speed-dial button and then put the phone on speaker so Flood could hear, too.

"Dickens," McPhee said as the phone rang. "He's lieutenant over there now. Used to be my sergeant in Area One."

The voice of a middle-aged white man came on the line and grumbled, "Dickens."

"L.T., what's going on?"

He recognized the voice immediately. Flood figured he had to recognize the voice because every cop he knew had his cell phone set up to hide his number on caller ID. McPhee was no different.

"I'm good, Billy. How're you? Been months. You don't call, you don't visit. You still working for that nut, Flood?"

Flood smiled, even though he didn't know Dickens. An ex-FBI agent who made the news for a bloodbath that got one cop wounded and a handful of wise guys killed could have been called much worse by a CPD detective.

"Yeah, now and then. Bought me tips at Lem's tonight, so, you know, I don't complain."

"Well, what's up?"

"Me and the *special* agent got a new job, involves coming by and talking at some of your boys on midnights, I guess." McPhee often called Flood the "special agent" to tease him, emphasizing the *special*. "You got a file open on a rich, white floater named Ash?"

"Oh, yeah. I know a little about it. That's a *death investigation*, you know," Dickens said. Death investigations were what the department called bodies when they hadn't officially made up their minds that they were murders. "Been open more than a week; ain't going anywhere fast. Tally and Fitzpatrick caught that one. I think they think accidental."

"That's the one," McPhee said. "Why the hell you got an Area Three case you don't want, anyway?"

"Lucky us, we were covering for Area Three that night cuz of Johnny Di Buona's retirement party. You remember Johnny D?"

"Hell, yes, I remember Johnny D. I was at that party—back room of the Napoli Tap. I didn't put two and two together."

"Yeah, so that's why. Anyway, the family hired you?"

McPhee glanced at Flood, who nodded it was OK.

"Yep. Momma wants us to nose around."

There was silence on the other end while Dickens thought about it. McPhee kept the conversation moving.

"Brother Tally I know. Who's Fitzpatrick?"

"Smart kid. Came from special operations a couple months ago. Listens to what Tally tells him to do most of the time."

McPhee made a little face, trying to read what Dickens was telling him.

"Cowboy?"

"Not too bad. He'll be OK once we get him programmed."

"A'right. Well, I'll come by and check him out."

"OK, Billy. I don't mind, but just don't surprise me with anything, OK?"

"We find something, we'll bring it straight to you, L.T. We ain't got no badges anymore."

In the neighborhood, the Area Four Detective Headquarters was known more commonly by its cross-streets—Harrison and Kedzie—even thought that entailed more syllables. It was a squat but sprawling brick building set up on the edge of the wide, deep trough of the Eisenhower Expressway, which cut through the West Side of the city like a great, rapid river. The building was surrounded by small parking lots overflowing with police cars. In addition to housing Area Four, the building also served as the Eleventh District patrol headquarters. In police parlance, "busy" meant lots of violent gang crime. Harrison and Kedzie was probably the busiest place in Chicago.

Flood had to park across Kedzie in the poorly lit overflow lot. McPhee had simply pulled his Explorer to the curb in front of the front door and made sure he stopped and said hello to blue shirts he recognized at the front desk. The lobby of the building was poorly lit and dingy, with some litter on the floor and some old, torn crime-prevention posters tacked to the walls by the vending machines, which were out of just about everything. A couple of vagrants lingered, pretending they might have official business to communicate but really just taking refuge from the cruel streets on the benches in the corner. At a side table along the wall, a young reporter from the City News Service typed into his laptop with a cell phone lodged between his shoulder and ear. When Flood walked up to the front desk to join McPhee, the reporter perked up and watched them closely, trying to decide if they looked like a news story that he'd get screamed at for missing.

McPhee said so long to the old sergeant doing paperwork at a desk behind the counter and they headed for the stairs. The first floor was all patrol division, and the second floor belonged to the detective division. The architecture and layout was nearly identical at each of the five area headquarters across the city. Flood had a passing familiarity with this building from his days working gang money-laundering cases with the FBI, but he was more familiar with Homan Square, the giant converted warehouse several blocks west where the Narcotics and Gang Investigation Section worked. Most of his contact with cops had been the NAGIS investigators, not detectives.

Billy McPhee had been a homicide detective for fifteen years in Area One on the South Side. When he made sergeant a few years before retiring, he had transferred to NAGIS and ran drug investigations. He had a string of informants and gang members that grudgingly respected him. Flood had led McPhee's team on a task force group on a couple of cases before leaving the Bureau. He liked McPhee's bluntness and humor, and respected his street instincts. McPhee also had an unflappable sense of right and wrong, and he was rarely compromised by the situational ethics of being a cop.

When Flood had blown the whistle on a corrupt officer who was taking payoffs from the Latin Kings, McPhee was the only cop to step forward and give information about other suspicious activity by that officer, John Lambert. McPhee took a lot of heat from other NAGIS and patrol officers for ratting out a brother officer, but when the resulting federal investigation tied Lambert's deals with the gang to the murder of a cop five years earlier, people began to forget about McPhee breaking ranks.

As Flood and McPhee walked in to the Area Four detective division, Curtis Tally stood up and raised his arms. Looking about six-foot-three and 260 pounds, he wore a white dress shirt with a burgundy pattern tie. A badge and a black 9mm handgun were clipped to the belt on his tan dress pants.

Tally had been typing, but when he saw McPhee his voice thundered, "If it isn't Billy McPhee."

McPhee started to lean against the front counter like a visiting civilian, but Tally waved and said, "What the hell you doing? Come on in here, boy."

He wanted a hug instead of a handshake. Black detectives were scarce in the Chicago Police Department and McPhee had been a gem.

McPhee held the half-door for Flood as they stepped into the office area and made the introductions. "Tally, this is Augustine Flood, formerly of The G," McPhee said. "Flood, this is Curtis Tally, currently of the Area Four Violent Crimes dicks."

"A'right," Tally said, shaking Flood's hand and nodding. "You're the man took down Nicky Bepps and his brother."

"Something like that," Flood said. His head had stopped hurting from the morning's hangover, but his neck ached and he was tired. It showed, and part of him wished they'd just put this off until tomorrow. Tally saw all that in his face and felt like he'd made a mistake.

"I don't mean to make light of taking a man's life," he finally said.

Flood shrugged. "No offense taken. Shooting Aldo Beppo isn't what keeps me up nights."

"OK. Um, that whole thing was crazy. Obviously, it was the G's case, but we were a *little* bit in the loop on it."

McPhee dropped into a swivel chair and drifted a half turn before his short legs caught on the base of the chair.

"Indeed, Curtis, every now and again the beautiful lakefront of this fine city is visited with a taste of the mayhem that we know so well out here in the real world," McPhee said, grinning widely. "Which brings us to why we're here, Brother Tally."

"That's what the L.T. tells me. Gave me a heads up you were coming," he said, patting a thin folder file on his desk. "Pulled what I got, and I ain't got much. Afraid we haven't found a real good reason to call it a homicide at this stage, Billy."

"M.E. report in there?" McPhee asked. Flood had seen it but said nothing.

"And not much else. There's a supplemental in there with an interview of one of her boyfriends," Tally said, nodding at the file. "Let's see. BAC: .11. Tipsy more than truly drunk. She hit her head on a flat surface. Concussion, and she went in the water and drowned."

"But there are some unanswered questions?" Flood asked.

"Sure," Tally said. "Who was she with? Where'd she go in? Were there any witnesses to it? We don't know any of that."

"What are the theories on where she went in?"

"Well, the water's pretty warm right now. She come up Thursday night during the fireworks off Navy Pier. All them boats—big boats—churning the water off Chicago Yacht Club there. So maybe she'd gone in that morning or Wednesday night. Ain't sure, but most likely at night since nobody saw nothing. Allegedly. Could've been overnight sometime. Drinking all night, thinking dark thoughts about how terrible it is to be worth a couple hundred million bucks. She gets reckless, slips and falls and hits her head on something. Don't know if it was concrete of the sidewalk there along the lake or deck of a boat or what. If it's deck of a boat, then we've got the question of whose boat and where's that person and why didn't they report anything?"

It all sounded reasonable; they were asking the right questions, as far as Flood was concerned.

"Phone calls no help?"

"Well, here's where we got a couple of leads maybe, but where they get us I don't really know," Tally said, pulling out another two documents. They were a copy of the detective's supplemental report, a form with a large space for narrative description of progress in the case, and what appeared to be the itemization sheet from a phone bill. "Just got her cell phone logs a couple days ago. Guy named Warren Riordan called her cell phone Wednesday night about seven o'clock. Doesn't look like they actually talked on the phone. Girl's mother said Warren was sweet on her and she was not all that sweet on him. Anyway, young Warren's a bit of a player and got himself a 26-foot Sea Ray he keeps at Diversey Harbor."

"But you don't like it," McPhee added.

Tally shrugged. "We talked to him. Snot-nosed shithead, but I didn't see a temper, and he's got nothing in his past. I think he's a bullshitter who thinks he's a player but really had a crush on this girl.

"Let us search his boat. Suntan lotion and a few bottles of Heineken rolling around in a cooler. That was it. We talked to the guy whose boat's in the next slip. He sleeps there during the summer and said he never saw Riordan or any girl. Said he was up 'til about one and then slept with the windows open."

"Not much to go on," Flood said. "What about the heroin?"

"Yeah, I don't know," Tally said. "I mean, I guess, I don't really know how these rich folks live. Her blood was clean, as you saw, but she had a tidy little stash of smack in her bathroom drawer."

"Her prints on it?"

"Yep. Little zip-lock sandwich bag."

McPhee chimed in: "Shoot, snort or smoke?"

"Don't know. No kit or nothing. No syringes in the apartment."

"Odd," Flood said.

"I know. I don't know what to make of it. But it was there. And her prints were on it," Tally said. "And we ain't had time for anything since. Shit's really hitting the fan out here in the real world."

"Fools shooting each other day and night," McPhee added.

"Damn. Five murders in the last four days, in Eleventh District alone. That little girl got shot in the leg two nights ago. We're getting all kinds of pressure from 35th Street. And these ministers marching around like it's the police's fault, they're all over City Hall; the shit's coming down on us hard."

"What's it about?" McPhee asked.

"It's all internal Travelers," Tally said, talking about the Traveling Vice Lords, one of the numerous factions of the Vice Lords Nation street gang, which ruled most of the West Side. "Howard Purcell gets paroled in November, and all these young brothers on the street are afraid he's taking his corners back. They're trying to look bad now so he'll think twice about it come Thanksgiving. Bunch of fools shooting each other in the head on the sidewalk. Mexicans the only ones who do drive-bys anymore. Brothers out here just walking up on each other, *What you be about? Bam.* Just because. Anyway, it's a goddamn mess. Augusta and Hamlin been the worst of it."

"I don't miss it," McPhee said. "I do not miss it."

"I won't miss it either, my brother, but I got another five years before I'm gone. In the meantime, all this means is that you are more than welcome to dig in on Miss Ash because she ain't getting much of our time."

Flood was surprised. "You're not getting pressure because of who she was?"

Tally frowned and shook his head. "Nobody up here thinks it was a homicide, to begin with. And second, and more important, her father is the one listening and putting two and two together.

The mother thinks, or wants to think—I should say *prefers* to think—she got murdered. But the daddy's maybe got some common sense. He's afraid she just did something stupid and embarrassing and he don't want the family name dragged through whatever pile of shit might be out there. Mom's a nice rich lady, but he's the real bank. That motherfucker's got people who got people at the Hall, so nobody's pushing us."

From across the room, a man shouted, "Tally, your turn!"

The sergeant, heavy, balding and dressed in too many stripes and paisleys, stood up and started their way. The gun on his belt was an ancient, small revolver that looked better suited to start a race than stop a crime.

"Beat car's on scene on that cul-de-sac on Maypole just west of the park. DOA on the sidewalk. No legit ID yet, Scooby-something, according to a witness. Seventeen or eighteen. Most of his brains on the curb."

Tally sighed. His eyes met McPhee's. They all used the same callous language to talk about the dead—most of whom were offenders one day and victims the next. Black and white cops talked the same way. But for the black detectives and officers there was another layer. This chaotic, hopeless killing field was their community. These dead kids and their murderers were their people.

"Well, I got to track down young Fitzpatrick and get over there," Tally said.

"Yeah, I heard you got yourself a youngster to keep track of," McPhee said as they all stood up.

"Yeah, Ronny Pierczynski retired in March. I partnered with him six years, man. And so now I got this young man just start-ing out. He's all right. Looking to make his name and all that."

"Hope he knows what he's got in a partner."

"An old man who wants to retire. That's what," Tally said,

then stopped chuckling abruptly, like he forgot something. "Hold on."

He opened the file and pulled a set of paper-clipped copies. "Made one for you. Don't tell nobody."

He dropped the file on his desk and handed the copies to McPhee as they headed toward the stairs together. When they reached the main floor, Tally slapped them both on the shoulder and went out the back of the building to claim his partner and head to the murder scene. The young City News reporter watched them, torn between the homicide detective heading to the street, and the mysterious late-night visitors he was leaving behind. The kid chose the murder in hand, and asked Tally where he was headed as Flood and McPhee headed for the door.

"Low on their list," McPhee said.

"Just as well. Think they'll help us if we need things?"

"Oh, yeah. Tally's good police."

They were outside on Harrison, walking toward the corner across from the parking lot. A few young men and a girl, none of whom appeared to be together, loitered outside the police station. They were all probably waiting for somebody to be released.

A battered gray Crown Victoria passed them as its engine heaved in hard acceleration, squealing a little rubber as it took the corner onto Kedzie headed north. Flood recognized Tally's head in the passenger seat. A young white man with short, reddish-blonde hair and wearing a black dress shirt was driving. They sailed over the Eisenhower, released a couple of staccato blasts from the claxon horn at the red light and disappeared into the hazy yellow night.

"I can't help you tomorrow," McPhee said.

Flood nodded. "I've got plenty to do."

McPhee got behind the wheel of his Explorer and tooted the

horn as he followed the same path as the detectives, at a much slower pace. He was headed for his house in Galewood, a prim, racially mixed neighborhood tucked into a corner of the city where the Austin area butted up to Oak Park.

Flood got into his car and sat for a moment. He was deeply tired and had run out of things to do for this day. And he was sober. The last few nights, he'd have been well lubricated by now.

Jenny was on his mind, suddenly. Was it the violent end A.J. Ash had met that brought her back to his thoughts? How she had almost died a very unnatural death? Another day was gone without talking to her. Flood could feel the time passing and the gulf widening. There wasn't much for him to say. His feelings were divided, so he might as well feel nothing at all. Still, he could not accept that. He pulled out his phone and started to scroll for her number. Then he realized it was half past midnight. Half past one in D.C. He snapped the phone shut in frustration and dropped it on the seat, put the car in gear and started down Harrison to catch the Eisenhower ramp at Sacramento. The street was darkened by broken streetlights and young people drifted along the curbs like ghosts. At one in the morning, to an outsider like Flood, the West Side of Chicago always looked like a disaster area with the dazed and wounded wandering in the ruins, scavenging for survival. Many were half dressed, with the jeans and shirts they did wear hanging loose from their bodies.

They slid by his windows and he barely noticed, lost in his own funk. *Why do you do this?* The question throbbing in his head and chest, even his hands. He was tired but wanted to explode. *Why do you make a living like this?* He had quit the FBI because a very bad experience had made him feel helpless. Now he had too much control—all of the responsibility. Out here in the middle of the night stalking questions, the answers to which might lead absolutely nowhere. He wasn't fit to manage a business, but he had one, with people depending on it to pay their rent. Jenny left him over this chaos. What it had done to her and what it had taken from her, and kept from her. After the horror of what had happened at the hands of Nuccio Beppo, she had done her best. And Flood was simply not there for her.

Augustine Flood was about digging for what was lost, not holding what was found.

The present popped back into focus. Flood pulled to a full stop at Sacramento a little too late and almost hit a young man crossing the street. He stopped in the crosswalk, squared his body with the grill of Flood's car and spread his arms, as if to say *If you want to run me down, then do it.*

The young man's lips did not move, but Flood seemed to hear him say just that. He put the car in park and opened his door and stood up, leaning out of the driver's seat. In the middle of the night, a white man in a suit, driving a Taurus away from Harrison and Kedzie, was almost certainly some kind of cop, and the teenager braced himself for such an encounter.

But Flood said, "I'm sorry. I almost hit you."

The boy stared at Flood for a moment, trying to figure out whether Flood was mocking him or just crazy. He decided on the latter and dropped his arms, grinning.

"A'right, boss," he said, walking off into the darkness.

Flood got back behind the wheel and felt like he had just woken up from a bad dream. He took a breath and put the car back in drive.

CHAPTER 4

He woke up alone and sober the next morning. He had cleaned the place the night before while he wound down without pouring any whisky. Once the coffee was brewing he sat down at the table and opened the file he had started on A.J. Ash. Swain's secretary had faxed a list that included her apartment address, her phone number with its voicemail code, and her cell phone number. Curtis Tally had included her cell phone logs in the file he gave them. Her email address was there, but without a password. There was also no password to access her cell phone records online. He had forgotten to ask Tally about that, in case he wanted to go back further than the records the detective had given them the night before. Her email provider would have to reset her account and allow the detectives to choose a new password to gain access to her files. He doubted they had done that.

Swain also provided bank records, which included the five-thousand-dollar withdrawal from a money market account in October that left a remaining balance of seventy-three thousand. There had been another in August for the same amount. Flood flipped through the papers and found an invoice for a Volkswagen Golf TDI. She'd paid eighteen thousand in cash for the car the previous year. There were records of other accounts, as well. She wrote lots of big checks to charities, but in terms of personal spending, the records reflected exactly the frugal habits Swain had described: About seventy-five dollars a week at Fox

& Obel, an amount that wouldn't buy many groceries there. A monthly check for about a thousand to a condo association. There appeared to be no mortgage. There were daily three-dollar debits at Starbucks, a couple hundred dollars at Sam's Wine & Spirits on Marcy Street, a couple of decent dinner tabs, and not much else. He saw nothing at department stores or clothing boutiques. Perhaps she had taken out the cash to finally buy some clothes. She could clearly afford it. Scanning her investment accounts he totaled up about five million, and that was just the trusts in her name. It said nothing of her share of the Heidecke Family Trust, which was worth a little less than one billion, according to a three-year-old *Chicago Magazine* story he had found the day before.

Flood pulled out her 2004 tax return. On income of $575,000 she listed charitable donations of $423,000. She was giving away nearly everything she made. Then he realized he wasn't reading the return correctly and that her total income was more like six million, but nearly all of it appeared to be going into a complicated network of tax shelters. He leafed through documents and came up understanding vaguely that most of her wealth appeared to be managed by the family's own private equity firm in New York, and that her brother James, Jr. appeared to be in charge of her money.

Flood went back into his notes from the day before. James was twenty-eight, single, living in Manhattan, graduated from Dartmouth and Harvard Business School, and was a partner in HT Partners Inc., which managed a lot of family money and other investors' assets.

A.J.'s fortune might have been a motive for somebody to want her out of the picture, but everybody who could have laid a claim to it appeared to be rolling in the same kind of money, he thought.

Flood decided that he would try to reconstruct the last week of her life and talk to everyone with whom she had any contact. He opened a notebook and started to make a list. First he wanted to do a little research on the homelessness office where she worked. He wanted to know the names of as many coworkers and supervisors as possible before he went in. Then he started adding people to his list. All the security guards at her apartment building. Warren Riordan. Her brother James in New York. Her cousins. Roommates or friends from college and high school.

He put other questions on the list: Did she go to bars? Did she work out? If she was using drugs, where was she getting them? Who besides Riordan had a boat? What was her relationship with her family really like? Did the records shown to Flood account for all of her spending, or did she have accounts unknown to Swain? Maybe she had a secret credit card and the five thousand dollars was for that bill. It did not make a lot of sense, but he was just knocking ideas around. Was the five thousand dollars a one-time thing, or was it just the start of something?

Flood finished his list and looked at his watch. It was seven-thirty, and he decided to keep moving on his recovered sense of well-being. He would go for a run, stopping at DuSable Harbor along the way to see where A.J. Ash's body had floated to the surface and been discovered. He put on shorts and started down in the elevator. He lived on the twenty-fourth floor of a white condo tower on Wabash and Hubbard. The west side of his building had a circular drive that let out onto Wabash, and the east side fed into a small public plaza that cut through the two halves of the Wrigley Building. Flood walked through and onto Michigan Avenue, crossed and then descended a wide, curving flight of stairs at the corner of Pioneer Plaza that led to the river walk heading east toward the lake. He started to run, taking the path as far east as he could and then jogging north to Illinois Street, east under Lake Shore Drive and onto the lakefront path south of Navy Pier. DuSable Harbor was merely one of many jetty enclosures along the lakefront, thin-lined rectangles of concrete and rock that had been laid in the lake to calm the swells that would toss moored sailboats and create havoc along the seawall. The next enclosure south was Monroe Harbor and it stretched all the way to the point that jutted out into the lake, studded with Shedd Aquarium and Adler Planetarium.

The path was busy with other runners and cyclists sweating in the humid morning sunshine. The pavement was lined with shade trees on one side and curbed by Lake Shore Drive on the other side. On his way back, Flood crossed through the wide, steep promenades of the Museum Campus and caught the light at Roosevelt, crossed the Drive, and continued to run through the softball fields of Grant Park, and then gardens, and the expansive pink gravel plaza around Buckingham Fountain. There was a strong breeze off the lake and spray from the fountain's towering geyser misted him as he ran. He crossed Columbus Drive using the corpulent, silver Frank Gehry bridge at Millennium Park and finished his run coming up Michigan Avenue. He stopped on the bridge and looked down at the jade water of the Chicago River. The steel plate walkway shook under his feet as traffic rumbled across. People who didn't spend any time downtown liked to talk about how the city dyed the river green on St. Patrick's Day. It was true, but the river was usually green anyway. They just dyed it *kelly* green on March 17.

As Flood peered down at the water, a sleek cabin cruiser emerged from under the bridge. He saw its glistening white bow first, cutting the water silently, before the cockpit and then the stern came into view. The gasoline engines gurgled at a low throttle, churning a mild wake and spewing wisps of blue exhaust. A pair of men, muscular, tanned, and shirtless, lounged at the wheel. The locks they were about to pass through to enter the lake were just a few hundred yards from where A.J. Ash's body washed up against the DuSable Harbor jetty. The boat that deposited her there, if there was a boat at all, Flood pondered, could have come from anywhere. Lakeside harbors along twenty miles of shore, or one of the many river marinas up and down the North and South branches.

Whether or not there was anything sinister about her death, Flood had to answer the questions of when, why and how she actually went in the water. And who was the last person to see her alive?

Flood was showered and dressed in a suit by nine o'clock. He looked for a cab on Michigan but instead caught a convenient bus, which deposited him at Roosevelt Road in less than five minutes. The stretch of South Loop where A.J. Ash had worked was a still-gentrifying mix of old office buildings rehabbed into condos and new condo towers under construction. The area around the Chicago Initiative for the Homeless office was one of the shabbier stretches of downtown Chicago. There wasn't much litter anywhere in the central part of the city, but the sidewalks were cracked and uneven and most of the building facades were a bit forlorn.

When Flood found the address and tried the heavy wood and glass door, he found it was locked. He pressed the intercom button and waited a full minute before someone answered.

"I have an appointment with Ms. Schachter. This is Augustine Flood."

The door buzzed and Flood started up the creaky steps, which were covered in worn orange carpet. The plaster wall on his left had been replaced with drywall long enough ago that it was now gouged and worn in its own right, but still looking incongruously temporary opposite the solid, old plaster. Both walls were a pale pastel green, which, combined with the carpet, left Flood feeling glum by the time he reached the landing and the frosted glass door of the Initiative. Again, he had to be buzzed inside.

Helen Schachter had sounded reluctant to talk to him when he called her the afternoon before and asked for an appointment.

"Aren't the police investigating?"

"They are. However, Mrs. Ash hired me to independently investigate her daughter's death."

"Why?"

She sounded impatient, but at the same time she was trying to draw him out. Under the circumstances he found it a little more than annoying. It was none of her business, but if she cared about A.J. Ash she should want to help.

"Well, I can't really tell you about Mrs. Ash's reasons. Obviously, she loved her daughter and is deeply troubled by the circumstances of her death. Ms. Schachter, it's important that I talk to you if I'm going to do this correctly."

She was silent and then agreed without further complaint, telling him nine-thirty the next morning would be fine. When he arrived, he was greeted at the front desk by a young, plump Mexican woman who whispered into a phone when he handed over his card. She'd insisted on having the card, even though she had known who he was since he announced himself at the street intercom. She hung up and directed him to wait on a dirty couch that looked like it had been salvaged from a frat house on graduation day. Flood stood until Helen Schachter opened the inner door and waved him in, holding his business card in her hand.

"So you're the private detective," she said in a way that made him imagine she'd bagged him in with double-talking politicians, thug cops and tabloid reporters.

"Thank you for seeing me."

She smirked and started walking toward the back of the office through a maze of mismatched desks and clutter. "A.J. was very important to us," she said in a lower voice, once he'd caught up with her. "This is very disturbing to me. I would like to have found out that the police were devoting their best detectives and resources toward finding out what happened. Instead, I get a phone call from some detective who sounds like an arrogant football player, who asks a half-dozen questions and sounds like he's barely listening to my answers, and then a call from . . . you. A private detective."

Flood checked his annoyance as best he could. "Well, what can I tell you to make you feel better?"

She sounded like she'd been making a list: "For starters, what kind of experience do you have that makes you at all qualified to investigate a woman's death? You're really a lawyer, right?"

She said *lawyer* as though she was under the impression that what Jane Ash was probably up to had something to do with protecting herself, and her money, and not so much with an investigation of what happened to A.J.

"Before I became a lawyer I was an FBI agent for eight years. I investigated drug trafficking and money laundering, in the organized crime section, mostly."

That opened her eyes a little wider but didn't stop the scrutiny.

"Well, why did you leave?"

That was none of her business. He left because he discovered a dirty Chicago cop, turned him in, and was nearly crushed by political expediency in the wake of it. It had taken any remaining whiff of romance out of federal law enforcement for him. He had been headed toward a reassignment until the powers that be decided they couldn't massage the situation away for the sake of managing the Bureau's relationship with CPD, which had been in no hurry to mind its own store when it came to Officer John Lambert and his relationship with the Latin Kings. In the end, Flood had been commended, and he vowed to himself that the FBI would never give him anything again. He had already finished one year of night law school at DePaul—on the government's tab. He cashed in some of his inheritance from his parents' small estate, paid the Bureau back, quit, moved into a dingy studio apartment, took out loans and went to school more than full time. But he owed Helen Schachter none of that.

"I decided to pursue a career in the private sector. It's been a good decision, for the most part."

She seemed to be thinking of what she might throw at him next and he stopped her with a raised hand.

"Listen, maybe this is frustrating for you. I don't know, but I assure you I'm good at what I do. I'm ethical, respectful of people's privacy, and I intend to find out exactly how Miss Ash died. It would help me a great deal if you would answer my questions candidly."

Helen Schachter finally shrugged and sat back.

"Did you hire A.J. personally?"

She nodded, and he asked, "Why'd you give her a job?"

"Oh, God. She was great. She was smart, passionate. She seemed to get our clients, you know, despite the . . . difference. The privilege. I knew who she was when she came in for the interview and I was prepared to dislike her."

"Why?"

"I figured she was going to be some spoiled brat who thought she'd help poor people for ten minutes."

"Did anybody ask you to interview her? Anyone on the board, or something like that?"

"No. That was part of the reason I gave her a chance. I know there are people on our board she could have reached and she didn't do that. She wrote me a letter and called, and never mentioned her connections. Never even mentioned she was from the North Shore. That and the fact that she was coming from a really strong program in New York working with kids on the street. She actually had good experience for this and she didn't care about the salary, which was of course absolute shit."

At Flood's prompting Schachter began to lay out A.J.'s workload at the Initiative. "She was spearheading a new plan to serve homeless youth. Kids who are in and out of home, foster care, treatment centers, many of them end up in the sex trade, at least off and on.

"Lots of drug issues and really significant authority issues. It was a very tall order and A.J. was pretty much on her own. The rest of us have our hands full with our more traditional role, serving adult homeless."

"This was new?"

"Yes, there was some money. The Justice Department is trying to crack down on the child sex trade, so they say, and somebody told them it might be a good idea to fund services for homeless youth. It's totally half-assed, of course, and there's not nearly enough money to serve the population, but A.J. was making the most of it. She was also putting in her own money."

"How much?" Flood asked, trying to remember the figures for charitable giving he'd seen detailed in her papers.

Schachter hesitated, but then answered, "About seventy-five thousand dollars so far."

Flood nodded.

"I know," she said. "It's amazing. We really struck gold with A.J."

"How was the money being used?" It was an unusual arrangement. A.J. would technically have been a low-level staffer, but she was running a program and supplementing its budget

53

in a big way out of her own pocket.

"Mostly counseling for kids, and housing. She was trying to fund a group home for girls. But it's really complicated in these cases. The girls who are homeless, that she was trying to reach, are still minors, but the state doesn't want them because they'd broken out of the system over and over again. Their parents either don't want them, aren't fit to have them, or are the cause of their problems in the first place because of abuse. Usually the latter. So their legal status and guardianship is really confused. It's hard to create a safe haven for them, legally. And then there are all the behavioral issues."

"How many girls were involved in the program A.J. had created?"

"Probably a dozen girls, in and out. They came here once in a while, but mostly A.J. was working through a day shelter on the Northwest Side called Girls Refuge . . . there were a few I got to recognize. Tamika, that was her real name. She was from somewhere on the West Side. A girl named Britney, who was white, seemed to be close to her. I think that was a fake name. She used her street name here because she didn't trust anyone but A.J. At least that's what I think. Tamika and Britney seemed to have a bond, despite the cultural differences. I think Britney was from someplace rural. A few others: Erica, Jeanine, Paula." She pronounced it *Pow-la.*

"I'd like to talk to them."

She shrugged. "I don't know that A.J. talked to any of them about her own personal life. She had the right attitude toward them, but in terms of real-life experience, I don't think she would have felt she could relate to their circumstances. But I can ask them, if I see them. You may want to try Girls Refuge, they'd have more direct contact. Celeste Mayne is the director."

Schachter pulled a post-it note off a pad and scribbled the woman's name and the address of Girls Refuge on it in red pen.

He asked to see A.J.'s desk, and Schachter escorted him into a cubicle that was neat and orderly, with no personal effects anywhere in sight.

"I can't let you look at client files," she said. That was exactly what he had been about to ask for. He sighed and folded his arms.

"Listen, if I can't see them here, I'll tell the detectives they will want to look at them, and they'll come get them, and show them to me. That would be a big waste of everybody's time, if you ask me."

She folded her arms to mock him.

"I can't let you look at client files. HIPAA, for Christ's sake. I could lose my funding."

Flood let it go for the moment. It would go on his wish list for McPhee to take to the detectives.

"Was A.J. close to anyone on your staff?"

"Not really. I don't think she had a lot of close friends, actually. She was pretty reserved, and pretty focused on the kids and her work," she said, frowning. "She seemed to me to be sort of a sad woman, actually. They say rich families are usually pretty unhappy, and that seemed the case with her. I know her parents divorced when she was young. And also, I think she felt like she was sort of adrift. I don't think she really got much out of the wealthy set thing, but she didn't feel totally at home with people who worked for a living. I don't know."

She seemed to hesitate on a further thought. Flood caught her eye. She seemed to trust him a little now. Maybe it was the kinds of questions, or the number, at least.

"What is it?" he asked.

"Well, it's nothing. A few months ago—it was still cold—my husband and I went out for dinner. Kiki's, know it?"

He nodded. It was a nice French bistro on Franklin in River North.

"Anyway, we sat down and were eating—it was like a Wednesday night. When a table across the room got up to leave, I could see her there having dinner at the next table beyond them. Eating by herself. Reading a book and drinking a bottle of wine—this beautiful young, single girl—and she looked totally natural. Like she couldn't care less. I don't know, it just gave me the impression she ate dinner alone quite a bit."

CHAPTER 5

The image was sticking with Flood as he sat on the Green Line heading north back into the Loop. He got off the train at Adams and went into his office building to check in. Flood was very lucky to have found office space on the second floor because the elevators were old and slow. The building had been nearly emptied out after the landlord stopped renewing leases in a plan to sell the old building to the Art Institute for dormitories and classrooms. But that deal went south and Flood moved in when he left Cronin, Drew & Guzman after the Westlake case.

Jamie was in law school right down the street at DePaul and practically lived in the office. Veraneace he had acquired through Billy McPhee. She was a cousin's sister-in-law or something, and retired from the Department of Revenue, so she knew a few things about the way the city worked. She was fully pensioned and worked for little money because she liked being in charge of something and having a place to go.

The office was a converted jeweler's shop, so there was a front counter and a large open space where work benches had once been filled with jewelry-making tools. Now there were a couple of large rugs, sofas and a small conference table. Veraneace and Jamie had work stations along the front counter. Flood's office was a small space in the corner, which had been the safe room. When he rented the place, he had a contractor knock out the end wall and extend the office the length of the

57

short side of the room, so it was large enough to meet privately with clients. But he spent most of his time in the common area on the sofas.

He walked in at lunchtime to find Jamie back at his desk and Veraneace on the phone. She glanced at him for a second, noted that he looked sober and generally much improved from the days and weeks before, and went back to her quiet conversation. Jamie, on the other hand, leaned back and crossed his arms reproachfully.

"Back in business, I hear," Jamie said, sizing Flood up, conceding he was ready to move on.

Flood looked at his watch. It was twelve-thirty.

"Had lunch?"

They went down the street to Miller's Pub, got a booth, and ordered cheeseburgers and Diet Cokes.

"I behaved very badly, and I'm sorry," Flood said when the waiter was gone.

"You were a pig."

"Right."

Jamie shrugged then and pretended to watch the financial news on a TV over the bar.

"I screwed it all up," Flood said, shifting the topic back to Jenny.

"It was beyond your control. You just made it worse," he said, still watching the screen. Apparently he was going to have this conversation without making any eye contact. "She's still recovering from what happened. She needs to go back to the familiar things. Her childhood home, mommy."

Flood exhaled. The short take was that he was inadequate. And he had been damaged in the act of damaging her. After she was kidnapped, and thrown bound, gagged and freezing into the bloody endgame of the Westlake fiasco, she had emerged clinging to Flood. He had got her into trouble in the first place, but he had risked everything to get her back in one piece. When she had recovered from the physical injuries of a concussion and hypothermia, she went home from the hospital, slept a few days and then called Flood. And they cautiously began to spend time together again—quiet time in the wake of the crisis.

But somehow Flood, or maybe both of them, had mistaken relief for healing, and as the weeks and months went by, Jenny had problems that Flood did not see. She had suffered through a profound episode of terror.

There was also the fundamental problem that Flood did not feel bad. He really was relieved when it was all over. He had killed people, something he'd never done as an FBI agent, but they had tried to kill him first, and they had tried to kill Jenny. It made him harder, perhaps, stronger, and that was part of the problem. Jenny had nightmares and she did not tell him about them. She had fears of empty rooms and walking anywhere alone, and she kept it to herself. And because Jamie spent every day with Flood, she did not tell him either, and it ate away at her ability to function, while Flood got back to work.

They had planned a trip to Italy in September of that year, but Jenny took the vacation time in June, abruptly, and went home to Baltimore to stay with her mother for two weeks. When she came back she started sleeping in her own apartment most nights, and they did not talk about it. Alone, Flood went back to Keefer's bar for the nightly cocktail hours. He worked the cases that came his way after he left Cronin, Drew, but he didn't hump for new business, and the clients stopped coming in so easily.

Now a year had gone by since Jenny's trip home to Baltimore. Six months had gone by since she found a job at the Corcoran Gallery in Washington, and she had been gone four months. Flood had bottomed out.

"Yesterday morning I woke up with a girl in my bed and had

no idea how she'd gotten there."

"A *girl?*"

"Twenty-three."

"Oh, for Pete's sake."

"Yes."

Jamie was still facing CNBC, but he had closed his eyes. "Feel better telling me?"

"Not really."

Their burgers came and they ate in silence for a minute before Jamie asked about the new case. Flood laid out the basics, including the pay scale.

"You're not actually an alcoholic."

"I know."

Jamie took a bite of pickle and then wiped his hands with his napkin.

"So do you feel guilty taking that much money? It's probably what it looks like, right?"

"Maybe. But, no, I don't feel guilty. It was her first offer, which leads me to conclude she could have afforded a lot more. I looked into her and she walked away from that divorce with about sixty million."

Jamie pretended to drop his jaw and then nodded that Flood shouldn't feel guilty.

"Well, then you've hit the jackpot and saved your ass from certain failure."

"You mean my ass *has been* saved. I didn't do anything, it just fell in my lap."

"Well, they know who you are and decided you were the guy," Jamie said. "So, what are the chances she didn't die accidentally?"

"I won't know that until I know who the dangerous people in her life were."

Flood said he wasn't going back to the office after lunch and took out a sheet of paper he had printed up. It was a list of people he needed to schedule interviews with, including A.J.'s father and brother. The young suitor Warren Riordan, and two cousins she appeared to have some limited social contact with. Jamie said he'd take care of it, and folded the page into his pocket.

"I also need you to look through the Ash's divorce file, find anything weird. Or anything that might ruin her life, you know?"

"The suicide possibility?"

"I guess."

Flood paid the bill and they walked back up Wabash together until Jamie started to cross the street to return to the office. Flood patted him on the back and kept walking north up Wabash, past Marshall Fields, which had recently become Macy's. At the corner of Wabash and Lake, a large group of slacking junior college students, mostly black and Asian, milled around in clouds of cigarette smoke outside Harold Washington College. He caught an eastbound cab on Lake and asked to be taken to the corner of Scott and Stone.

His African driver started whispering into his cell phone earpiece. The conversation seemed to grow animated, and then abruptly ceased, and the driver turned his head to Flood and said, "Where is that?"

"About a block from Division and Astor, just aim for that."

They crawled from the Loop north into the Gold Coast by way of the touristy nightlife corridor along Division before tucking back into a shady, secluded enclave of stately apartment buildings and Gilded Age mansions that occupied several blocks just off the lake. A.J. Ash's building was a large limestone courtyard structure with lushly manicured formal landscaping trimming the foundation. Ivy crawled up the walls. The lobby was narrow with an immaculate marble tiled floor and a desk occupied by a fiftyish Hispanic man in a brown blazer, gray worsted pants and the sort of black patent leather shoes that bank security guards might wear.

"Good afternoon. Are you Humberto?" Flood said, handing over his business card to the man, who accepted it in his dry, calloused fingers.

"I am." He nodded. "You're the man coming about Miss Ash?"

"That's right. I'll be spending some time in her apartment today."

Humberto sighed and nodded, and held up Flood's card in a silent request to keep it. Flood nodded. The man picked up a very large ring of keys off the desk and stepped out toward the elevators. "I'll show you up."

Flood was glad to have a minute to question Humberto. "You knew her a little?"

"Of course," he said. "She was very kind. Very courteous to me. She remembered the names of my children. She would stop and talk to me."

Flood nodded. Humberto probably observed her more regularly than anyone, over a longer period of time, albeit for only seconds a day. "Did you notice any change in her lately?"

He nodded his head side to side, noncommittally.

"Oh, she was very busy lately. But maybe a few months. You know, she was still friendly, but seemed to have less time to stop and chat."

"Busy? Would you say she seemed preoccupied, or was it more like she was troubled?"

The elevator doors opened on the tenth floor and they stepped into a long corridor that looked like a floor in a fine old hotel. The brown and tan carpet was patterned to look elegant while hiding dirt and wear. Wall sconces were brass with frosted glass and the waiting area by the elevator was outfitted with two chairs, a side table and mirror all in matching Regency style.

"Her apartment is this way, down at the end," Humberto said, starting down the corridor. "I don't know what was on her mind. I think I know what you mean by troubled, but I don't think that. Some people have started a rumor that she killed herself, but I don't believe it."

"Why not?"

"Because she was not like that. She was a busy woman. She was not . . . lost."

He was emphatic, almost emotional. Flood listened and waited a moment, until they arrived at the last door and Humberto began to search through his keys. Flood pulled one from his pocket.

"I have it," he said. Humberto looked up, acknowledging it with some sadness. "Humberto, I need to ask you a couple of things that would be inappropriate under different circumstances. But I believe Miss Ash's family has told you they hope people will give me complete cooperation."

He nodded and folded his arms.

"Did she have visitors? Were there men in her life, maybe who spent the night?"

The question embarrassed him a little. "Uh, for the most part, no. I work in the mornings, you know, so I'm not here at night. But there was once maybe a month ago when she left in the morning and a man seemed to be with her. But that was it." Another shrug. "About your height, good-looking guy. Maybe skinnier, younger, I'd say in his late twenties. Curly dark hair."

"Any other visitors?"

"I don't think so."

"What about any young girls, like teenagers?"

Flood saw a flicker of recognition in his eyes.

"I, well, yes. Funny that you say that. A few days before she died, there was a girl here with her, they came in the middle of the day and stayed about an hour, and then left."

63

"Can you describe the girl?"

"Young, maybe sixteen or seventeen. Pretty girl. Blonde hair. I remember that she was wearing different clothes than when she left. She came in wearing a dress and when they left she was in blue jeans and a white t-shirt. It seemed to me that they were Miss Ash's clothes. The jeans were a little big on her. And she was carrying a bag that I believe was Miss Ash's, too."

"Can you describe the dress?"

"Oh, gosh. OK, red or, like, orange. Short, with thin straps. You know, maybe too revealing for a teenage girl to wear, in my mind."

Flood was writing in his notebook. "You recognized the bag she brought out?"

"Maybe I'd seen Miss Ash with it. Like an overnight bag with a shoulder strap. Black with a gray strap—I'd seen Miss Ash carry it before when she was traveling somewhere."

"Did they speak to you? Or did you hear Miss Ash call the girl by a name?"

"No, they were in and out of the lobby fast. Miss Ash waved and smiled and that was it."

"Anything else I should know about?"

Humberto shrugged that there was not. "Do you need me for this?" he asked, pointing at the door.

"No, thank you."

Humberto nodded and glanced at the door as Flood fitted the key into the lock. He padded off down the hall toward the elevators.

Flood opened the door to A.J. Ash's apartment and found it was surprisingly full of light. It was like walking into a different building. The short hall was highly polished oak, stained dark but gleaming in the sunlight that flooded the windows at the other end of the apartment. There was an antique side table just inside the door that held a brass bowl and a small art-glass lamp. There was a ring of two keys that looked to be for front doors to another apartment or house, along with some loose change and plastic hair clips. A short stack of mail next to the bowl contained nothing but advertisements and utility bills. Nothing personal. Flood picked up the phone bill and put it in his coat pocket.

The hall opened onto a spacious living room that faced the row of large, double casement windows with metal sashes. There were two long brown leather couches facing each other and upholstered pink club chairs between them at the ends. One chair was full of embroidered pillows; across the other chair a folded blue, purple and brown Native American blanket was laid. The coffee table was a heavy Prairie-style piece that looked like it might be authentic. There were other chairs against the walls that matched the dining set Flood could see through the rectangular archway that separated the living room from the dining room. There was no television in the living room, he noticed.

The wall opposite the windows was hung with a large abstract painting that was chosen without consideration for the rest of the décor of the room. From dating Jenny, Flood noticed this as a decision an artist would appreciate. Along the windows there was a long, ornate chest of drawers topped with a few photographs. There was a picture of a young boy and girl digging in the sand on a beach, which he guessed was A.J. and her brother James as children. There were some old people sitting in chairs on a plush lawn and looking very rich. There was a snapshot of Jane Ash, sitting at a table in a restaurant in daylight. It looked fairly recent. Finally, in back of the photo of the children on the beach, there was a faded picture of a man in a business suit walking up a large driveway away from a Mercedes coupe that looked to be a 1960s model. The man was grinning and pointing a finger at the photographer. Flood guessed it was James

Ash, A.J.'s father. It would have been taken before she was born, he figured.

Flood checked the drawers and cabinets of the bureau and found candles, playing cards, coasters and extra throw blankets. There was also a large plastic bin that contained more family photographs. He leafed through them for a moment but closed the top when he surmised they were all at least a few years old.

He found nothing of note in the dining room, and headed into the kitchen, which was appointed with professional equipment that Flood immediately envied. The array of Viking appliances included a well-stocked wine cooler and a large refrigerator that had been cleaned out. He checked drawers for notes or anything with her handwriting, but found nothing.

Next, he moved to her bedroom. The furnishings were expensive antiques, but there wasn't much personal there. There was a Barbara Vine novel and a book about the Iraq war on the nightstand next to a half-empty bottle of water. Judging from the bookmarks, she hadn't gotten very far into either of them. He remembered Humberto saying the teenage girl he'd seen with A.J. had left wearing different clothes, and he started to look in the closets and dresser for the little red or orange dress. He found nothing that fit the description. In fact, he found few clothes relative to the size of the closets. What was there looked like either expensive business and evening wear or very cheap casual wear, jeans and sweatshirts. It was mostly the latter.

He went back to the hall, where there was a long closet that contained a washer and dryer. Inside the dryer was a load of whites. The washer was empty. So much for the dress.

The second bedroom had been converted into a den and office. There was a day bed that could function as a sofa, a fancy leather recliner, and a wall of built-in bookshelves with a television in a large space in the middle. At the end of the room, next to more windows, was a large, L-shaped desk of Scandinavian design. Finally, he found papers, notes, files stacked and notes scribbled on numerous post-its. Flood sat down in the desk chair and set his briefcase on the floor. Finally, it dawned on him. No computer.

He thought for a moment that she didn't use one, but then saw under a stack of papers the glowing green lights of a wireless router. Somewhere, A.J. had a laptop.

The absence of a computer was jarring and he felt he was losing the rhythm of his search. Where next?

He was taking one last look at what was left on the desk when he noticed that the top sheet on the legal pad was separated slightly from the rest of the sheets, as if it had been turned previously. He lifted the page and found a small note scrawled at the top of the next page. "Class Pets?"

Flood had no idea what that meant, but decided to just take the whole pad with him after writing Class Pets down in his own notebook.

He decided to check the wastebaskets and found them empty in the bedrooms and bathrooms. In the kitchen, there was a tall stainless steel canister with a foot pedal that opened the lid. He opened the lid with his toe and peered into the folds of the white plastic liner. It seemed empty, but he caught a whiff of rotten fruit. He lifted the bag out and felt it was slightly weighted. In the bottom was half an apple, cleanly sliced.

Why would she throw away half an apple? Maybe it had sat out overnight, or gone bad in the fridge. But why was it the only thing in the garbage can? Flood dropped the rotten apple back into the trash and let the lid drop.

He locked the door and rode the elevator down to the lobby, where he found Humberto trying not to look like he was waiting for him. Humberto looked at him with searching, sad eyes.

"Did you find any information?"

Flood shrugged. "It's hard to say this early. Maybe something looks totally ordinary and meaningless, and then it means something down the road when you put it together with other information."

"I see," he said, nodding.

"Who's been in the apartment besides me?"

He thought a minute, puffing his cheeks out. "Mrs. Ash was here, and Mr. Ash separately. He came with another man, maybe his lawyer or an employee, I don't know. And then there was a police detective, a young man whose name I wrote down but can't remember. He came with Mr. Swain. I believe you must know Mr. Swain."

"I do."

Humberto shrugged again, indicating that was all.

Flood shook his hand and asked him to call if he thought of anything that might help. He was walking out when it dawned on him, and he felt stupid.

"Humberto, I forgot about Miss Ash's car. She parked it here?"

"Yes, there is a garage off the alley, and she had a space."

"May I see it?"

He looked puzzled.

"Oh, the car is not here. I thought you knew that."

"Where is it?"

"I don't know. I assumed the family had it."

CHAPTER 6

Flood walked around to the garage and examined the entrance, which required a keycard swipe. On his walk back to Division to catch a cab, he called Swain's office. The secretary put him through right away.

"Sorry to bother you, but I just left her apartment and I'm wondering, where is A.J.'s Volkswagen?"

There was a moment of silence. "Not at her building?"

"No, the manager said he assumed the family had it."

"They don't. Unless James took it. But I doubt that. Hardly seems like something he'd think about. Plus, it's my responsibility. To tell you the truth I'd forgotten about it."

"OK. Well, I need to find it. Can you check with Mrs. Ash, just to be certain. I'll see if it was towed."

They hung up and Flood called Veraneace as he stepped into a cab and gave the driver his home address.

"Who you talking to?" she demanded.

"You. Listen, I need you to see if a car's been towed."

"How'm I gonna do that?"

"You're going to call your girlfriends in Revenue."

"Now they're your friends, I guess," she said. "What's the plate?"

He read her the VW's license plate number from his sheet of notes and then hung up. The cab dropped him in the circle drive of his building and Flood gave him a ten and headed for the parking garage to get his car. It was three-fifteen in the afternoon.

There was already a lot of rush-hour traffic on the Kennedy Expressway, so he jumped off at Western and crawled north, turned west on Lawrence Avenue and drove another mile to the address of Girls Refuge. Lawrence was a busy thoroughfare of small businesses, many of their signs scripted in Spanish as well as English. He parked on the street and as he walked the last few yards to the door he noticed that this shelter for girls caught up in Chicago's underage sex trade was less than two blocks from the Commander Club, a strip joint. Probably not a co-incidence. The shelter appeared to be in an office suite on the second floor. It was not marked Girls Refuge, but rather the Chicago Project on Options for Women, *C-POW.*

The second floor was lined with worn white tile and solid wood doors. It looked like it had been a building full of doctors' offices in the sixties and seventies. Now it looked like a place for incompetent accountants and organizations that ran on donations. Flood tried the door and found it locked. He knocked and waited, heard footsteps and then felt the presence of a body on the other side looking at him through the peephole.

Finally, a teenager's voice: "Who is it?"

Flood held up a business card. "Augustine Flood, I'm a lawyer. I came to talk to Ms. Mayne."

"Hold on." Footsteps going away.

More footsteps, he felt the invisible eye on him, and then the door opened to reveal a woman of about thirty-five, a little heavy, with a pale complexion and an oval face that didn't match the suspicion he felt coming at him.

"I'm not expecting any lawyer visits," she said.

Flood smiled. She knew why he hadn't called first, and she wasn't happy about it. Maybe somebody he wanted to see was still in there.

"May I come in?"

"Why don't you tell me what you want first."

"Ah. OK," he sighed, handing over his card. "I think you knew A.J. Ash."

She looked up from the card and nodded at him. He could see from the momentary glimmer in her eye that her first thought was the will. But maybe the wording of his business card then caught up to her—it read "Attorney at Law, Licensed Private Investigator"—and a hint of guilt dropped the corners of her eyes.

Flood said, "Miss Ash's mother, Jane Ash, has hired me to look into her death. I'm conducting an investigation."

Celeste Mayne nodded slowly. "I see. How does that involve us?"

Flood looked up and down the empty hallway. "May I come in, please?"

She got his point, and let him in. The swinging door revealed two teenage girls standing behind her, listening intently. Both of them were giving Flood odd looks. Like they knew something about him, and it was halfway funny, halfway sickening. One of the girls was thin and African-American, the other was white and a little plump. Both wore embroidered blue jeans and tight white t-shirts.

He shut the door, and now they were standing in the foyer to the office. There was a countertop with no desk or chair behind it. On top there were two large clear plastic bowls of what looked like candy. Flood took a step closer and realized they weren't candy at all. One bowl was filled with flavored condoms and the other with single-use packets of lubricant. Rainbow colors, by the hundreds. They seemed absurd and Flood wanted to make a joke—*trick-or-treat*, perhaps—but found the strength to hold his tongue.

"You're inside now," Celeste Mayne said, sounding almost

out of patience.

"Right. I wanted to talk to you about A.J., and your last interactions with her," he said. "And I'd like to talk to the girls she dealt with through your organization."

He glanced at the two girls, having no idea whether they were among the girls Helen Schachter had named.

While Celeste Mayne was thinking, the black girl rolled her eyes and said, "I didn't even know her."

"Me either," said the other.

Mayne looked annoyed that these kids were even talking to Flood, a strange man who had just barged in off the street.

"Listen," she finally said, beginning to walk down the corridor. "I didn't notice anything strange. I talked to A.J. pretty much on the phone only. We talked business only. She was putting together plans to fund a larger space for us, and she was trying to create a housing situation for the youth. So, I'm devastated about what happened to her. She had access to money and power, and she knew how to use it.

"I don't know anything about her death," she went on, her voice rising and beginning to sound angry. "And, no, you may not speak to any of the youth who worked with A.J. They don't know anything that could help you, and they have been through more than enough trauma dealing with authorities who use them and don't give a flying fuck what happens to them. Wait there."

She pointed at the spot where he was standing, and disappeared around the corner. Bemused by her hostility, Flood put his hands up in surrender and waited. Both girls trailed down the hall after Mayne. When they were gone, he walked over closer to the countertop where the trick-or-treat bowls sat and peered over the top. On the floor there was a brown suitcase that looked full and a small, tattered old red duffel bag—the kind Flood used to tote to grade school basketball practice.

Hmm. Girls brought luggage here. Mayne and her *youth* were all still gone from view, and he looked down the corridor. There was a doorway open to a lighted room just a few steps away. He walked over and looked in. Children's artwork lined the wall, and there were tables with magazines for teenage girls, and all sorts of pamphlets on sexually transmitted diseases and substance abuse. At the far end of the room was a green metal coat rack. On top of it were a couple of umbrellas and a well-made black canvas overnight bag with a gray shoulder strap.

Flood muttered a profane word of triumph under his breath and walked into the room.

"Hey!" came the shout at his heels. Celeste Mayne was back, holding a slip of paper in her clenched fingers. Flood quickened his pace across the room to lay hands on the bag before she caught up with him.

"Get out of there, damn it! Get out of here right now. Don't touch that! I'm calling the police."

Flood reached for the bag, but the white girl had snuck up and snatched the strap, clutching it to her chest, and he made a clumsy reach for it. All he had was the ID tag in his hand as she started to pull it away.

Celeste Mayne rushed forward and gave him a shove. "Let go, you son of a bitch."

Flood peeled open the leather flap on the tag and read aloud, "A.J. Ash."

The girl pulled harder on the bag and he thought the leather strap on the tag was about to break. Instead of pulling back, he just moved with the girl, taking a step closer to her. Suddenly, everybody was screaming even louder. The girl looked at him defiantly, daring him to touch her. He wasn't about to, and after another thought, he let go. He'd made his point with the ID tag.

"Everybody calm down," he said, raising his voice. It gave

him a moment. "This bag clearly belonged to A.J. And a witness saw a blonde teenage girl leave A.J.'s apartment carrying this bag a few days before she died. That's who brought it here. What's her name?"

Celeste Mayne folded her arms. The girls remained silent.

"OK. Celeste, why should I leave the bag here?"

"It's not yours. It belongs to someone else. There are things in it that belong to someone else."

He thought a minute.

"If I'm going to leave this bag here, I'm going to call the Chicago police detectives handling A.J.'s death investigation and insist they come retrieve the bag as possible evidence. Since I used to be a federal agent, who had good relations with the cops, and my assistant on this case is a recently retired Chicago detective, they'll definitely do it. And they will then insist on finding and interviewing the girl who brought it here. How do you guys feel about Chicago cops?"

He assumed he knew the answer to the question, and he did.

"Please leave," Mayne said.

Bluff called.

Flood shook his head.

"I don't know what you think is going on here. But I'm serious about finding out what happened to A.J., whether you help me or not. If she died accidentally, I'll find out and that will be the end of it. If she was murdered, there's a possibility that the girl who had this bag, and maybe some of the other girls A.J. met through this place, know something that might be helpful. Maybe they're in danger. Maybe you don't want to be helpful. That's fine, I guess. I don't judge. But the contents of this bag could help me. You've got my card if you change your mind about being helpful. If not, the police will be around. I recommend you don't do anything stupid with the bag in the meantime."

Chapter 7

Flood sat down behind the wheel and rolled down the windows. The air in the street carried a little of the musty warmth of tortillas grilling. He was sweaty and angry, and felt childish at the same time. Did that really just happen? He looked in the rearview mirror.

"I have a bruise," he said to himself, astonished by the red mark on his chin that was already starting to turn a little bluish at the center.

His phone rang. A number he didn't recognize. The voice was young, female and black.

"You the man that just was at Girls Refuge?"

"I am. Who's this?"

"You want this bag, it's gonna cost you."

He was not completely surprised. There was too much desperation in everybody's eyes up there in that office.

"I want everything that's in it, you understand? Everything that was in it when I came up there."

"It's all in there."

"Which one are you?" he asked, knowing the answer would be that she was the black child who had stood behind Celeste Mayne during the tirade.

"Five hundred dollars," she said without addressing the question.

"Hold on," Flood said calmly. "First of all, I'm not negotiating if I don't even know your name."

"Tamika. Five hundred dollars."

"Tamika, that's way too high. How about seventy-five."

He figured he'd create the artificial threshold of a hundred and make it seem within reach, if she was lucky."

"Seventy-five, that's bullshit." She dragged out the u-sound for emphasis. "Boolshit."

"Well, I'm just trying to retrieve something that belonged to my client's daughter. If you can help me, I'd make a fair arrangement. But the kind of money you're talking about is unreasonable."

"What about four hundred?"

"More like ninety."

"Boolshit."

"Well?"

"Three hundred."

"Tamika," he said. "Hold on. Let me see a second."

He was pretending to check to see how much money he had available. He knew exactly how much money was in his wallet: one thousand dollars. He had figured this would be a day he might have to drop some cash here and there for information.

"Listen, I have a hundred and fifty bucks. That's more than fair for a bag that belonged to my client's daughter. It's one-fifty tonight, or zero tomorrow when the police come for the bag."

"You're lying. They ain't coming for this."

"If stuff is missing from the bag, they're going to ask, 'Where's Tamika?' You understand?"

"Bullshit."

"Let's get together, Tamika. What time you want to meet?"

"Nine. P'laski an' North. What kind of car you drive?"

Four hours later, she opened the door of Flood's Taurus and slid into the passenger seat holding the bag. "Go down that alley," she said, pointing to the lane shrouded in darkness just around the corner.

Flood saw no reason to do that, so he just took his hands off the wheel and sat back. "We can talk here. Let's see what's in the bag."

"Money," she said, showing no sign of opening the bag.

He pulled out his wallet and showed her three fifties. And then four more.

"There's the price of the bag, and maybe more if you can give me some decent information. Open the bag."

She huffed, clearly feeling pushed around when she was supposed to be in control, but unzipped the bag and pulled it open. Flood flipped on the dome light and looked in.

The first thing that caught his eye was the dress. It was more orange than red, but he was sure it was the garment Humberto had described. He took a pen from his shirt pocket and lifted the dress out by a spaghetti strap. It was cotton and skimpy, and its top was trimmed with a separate piece of white lacy fabric that was intended to look like lingerie poking through the top of the dress. He inspected the tags inside the fabric, looking for any markings that might have identified the owner, but found nothing. Disappointed, he started to lower the dress back into the bag, but as he did he noticed an unnatural crease across the seam between the orange cotton and the lace insert. With the pen, he nudged open the fold and found that a piece of paper had been tucked into a space where the seam between the two pieces of fabric was torn.

It was a business card, black and printed on one side and white and blank on the other. The black side was printed with white letters made to look like chalk on a blackboard.

"Class Pets," Flood said, reading the card. He remembered the note written on A.J.'s legal pad. The rest of the card read: "Private tutoring recommended . . . come visit our faculty lounge."

He looked at Tamika, but her expression was blank. "You know this place?"

She shook her head. "Some kinda place they party in the suburbs."

He gathered, from the address on the card, that Class Pets was a massage parlor in Roselle, a working-class suburb about thirty minutes west of the city. He flipped the card over and found a phone number scribbled in green ink. It was A.J.'s home number. The card was tucked into the bra of a dress belonging to a teenager who was the last person Humberto remembered seeing in A.J. Ash's apartment.

Flood officially had a lead.

"So what's her name?"

"Britney." She said it with exasperation.

"No, her real name."

She gave a bug-eyed shrug. "All's I know is Britney. She Britney."

The rest of the bag contained a clear plastic bag of cosmetics, two pairs of high-heeled shoes that were the sort strippers wore on stage, a cell phone charger, a snack-size bag of pretzels, a second dress the same style as the first but black and trimmed with turquoise lace, and finally a small brass pipe for smoking marijuana. He nearly missed the envelope. It was a plain white, empty, business letter envelope. Flood picked it up and saw the Harris Bank return address. All of A.J. Ash's accounts were with Harris Bank. The five thousand dollars, he thought.

"You and Britney stayed together when you were on the street?" he asked.

"Not together. Britney don't work out on Cicero, she up in them hotels downtown. They see a black girl in them, they know something up. Britney fit right in."

She looked pissed and embarrassed, like she was angry at Flood for listening as she spoke. She hadn't intended to say anything so revealing, he decided.

"You know about A.J.?"

"Not really."

"But you know Britney knew her?"

"I guess."

"What did Britney say about A.J.?"

"She jealous."

"Jealous because A.J. was rich?"

Tamika made a face. "No! Not Britney. That girl, A.J., she was jealous."

"Jealous of what?"

"Man Britney with. A.J. jealous. She wanted the same man. Britney told me that."

"You're saying A.J. was jealous over one of Britney's johns? That doesn't make any sense."

Wrong thing to say. She said, "This is bullshit," and fell silent, looking out the window.

"I just mean I don't understand," he said, trying to recover.

"I already told you shit. I want a hundred dollars."

"You've almost told me shit. Not quite."

Flood pulled out a fifty and kept it in his hand.

"Do you know why the thing with the man made her jealous?" he asked.

"Naw, I just know Britney said she was jealous and giving her the runaround."

"What about the guy? What'd you hear about him?"

"Rich, I guess. That's what Britney said."

He handed her the fifty but it didn't make her happy.

"This is bullshit. You shoulda give me a hundred by now. All the things I told you."

Flood's impulse was to say something sarcastically off-color. But he held his tongue at the last moment. She was fourteen.

"Where's Britney now?"

"I don't know. Gone. I ain't heard from her, and I'm out of

the life. My grandmother took me in."

"You were with your mother when you were in the life?"

"I wasn't with nobody. My mother use all my money to buy rock. I ain't with her at all."

"How often did Britney see this guy that A.J. was jealous about?"

"I don't know. Every week, about."

"Was that a hotel meeting?"

She shook her head. "No, they go right to his place. Britney and Zo."

"Who's Zo?"

The look of fear and surprise at herself was immediately obvious. She fell mute and turned her terrified eyes away from Flood. In fact, he felt her body leaning toward the door, like she was ready to bolt. The only thing keeping her in place was his wallet, he guessed. The fear told him Zo was a he and not a her.

"Who is he, Tamika?"

"Nobody."

She caught herself. Flood could not decide if Zo was a pimp or something else.

"She and who?"

"What?" she said, making a face like she hadn't held her tongue.

"Who'd she go with?"

Sour face. "Nobody. I 'on't know."

He made a show of starting to fold up his wallet and put it away.

"He'll kill me," she said in protest. This wasn't fair.

"Honey, when I find him he's going to have problems that will make him forget you ever existed."

A little silence. Finally, she looked at the wallet in his hand again.

"Zo. That's who we was with."

"I'm not supposed to call him a pimp?"

She scoffed. "Whatever."

"What's his real name?"

"I don't know."

"Where does he live?"

"I don't know. We stayed at a hotel out on Cicero sometimes."

"He have a car?"

"He drive a 300."

"Color?"

"Black."

"The car, I mean."

"I know what the fuck you mean. The car is black. Zo black too."

They were getting somewhere. He gave her a fifty.

"So, how did you hear that A.J. was dead?"

She shrugged. "Around, I guess."

A blue-and-white patrol car rolled past slowly, with the cop in the passenger seat glancing over her partner and eyeing Flood. At nine P.M., in this neighborhood, a forty-year-old white man and a fourteen-year-old black girl sitting in a car together was definitely probable cause to stop and start asking questions. In the instant that his eyes met the cop's eyes, however, Flood saw the hesitation. She knew she should stop, but they weren't going to. Too much work. Too much hassle. The car rolled on through a yellow light and kept going. Flood felt an odd combination of relief and disgust in his gut. Nobody was going to help this kid hustling on the street. Nobody knew how.

Tamika seemed oblivious to the police. She was used to being ignored, he figured. She was focused on the remaining three fifties in Flood's wallet.

"When's the last time you saw Britney?"

"Not since that happened. I said, she was gone."

"OK. And what about Zo?"

"I don't know what day it was, or nothing, but one night he just didn't come back. We were in a hotel out there. I don't know what it's called. He just didn't show. They kicked us out of the hotel. I was on the street out there about a day, and then I called Miss Mayne and she come got me and brought me back. That's when I went to my grandmother."

She claimed to have no further knowledge of where Britney or Zo were, or what their real names were. Flood gave her another fifty, said there could be more down the road if she provided more information. He argued to her the best he could that it made sense for her to call him if she heard from Britney. She shrugged and said nothing more and then got out of the car and crossed North Avenue, dodging between cars slowing for the red light at Pulaski. Without looking back, she walked off into the night and all the brutal potential that West Humboldt Park held for a child on the make.

CHAPTER 8

"I'm yours tomorrow if you need me," Billy McPhee said.

"I've got a lead on a girl who may have been with A.J. in the days before her death. And it's possible she got the five thousand dollars."

"All right," McPhee said, prompting more.

"I think the girl's a prostitute, and I found a bag A.J. gave her at a shelter for child prostitutes up on Lawrence. Got in an argument with the woman who runs the place. Anyway, I have the bag now. It had A.J.'s ID tag on it."

"Jesus, boy, you been busy today."

"It's a piece of luggage that A.J.'s building manager saw this girl carrying the last time he saw A.J. There's a dress in it that the girl was wearing, and a Harris Bank envelope. The five thousand was withdrawn from a Harris account."

"Hmm. I don't know. You think there's something going on with this?"

Flood sped through a yellow light and thought about what he thought.

"I might as well go hard at anything that comes up, you know? And this girl does seem to be somebody I need to talk to."

"Where is she?"

"Don't know. Probably on the street somewhere. But she had a card in the bag for a massage parlor in Roselle, so I'm headed out there."

"That'll be fun."

"I think the shelter people probably know where she is, too, but they really seem to hate my guts."

"Always burning your bridges."

"It just sort of got out of hand when·I spotted the bag."

"OK, enjoy your massage."

He clicked off. His phone beeped with a voicemail alert. He must have been in a bad cell area when the call came. It was from the office.

"Yes, the city has the car," the message from Veraneace said. "Central lot. Towed at three A.M. on Thursday, June third. One-hundred block of East Scott. That's all."

Why had A.J. Ash parked her car on the street in front of her apartment building when she had an off-street parking space? It didn't make sense. He called McPhee back.

"Can you reach out to Tally and tell them A.J.'s VW is in the central tow lot? I think they should look at it and print it."

"Why? She probably just left it someplace the night she died and it eventually got towed."

"It was towed from in front of her building. She had a private space right there. Why would she leave it on the street?"

"Is the lot secure?"

"Yes, you need a card."

"Hmm. I'll call him tonight."

It took Flood another thirty minutes to reach the address in Roselle. The purple awning on the building that matched the address didn't say "Class Pets," and it offered no schoolroom themes. It was a cinderblock two-story building, painted white. The front windows were curtained and rimmed in neon pink lights. One window framed a neon sign that said "SPA," and next to it a smaller neon sign: "OPEN."

A secluded parking lot down the side of the building away from Lake Street held four cars. He parked in front, and carted the black bag back to his trunk.

He figured this endeavor would take some money and a fair amount of silliness, but he needed to find the girl, Britney. He closed the trunk and walked in the front door, where he found a thin thirtyish man with a mustache and thinning hair sitting behind the chest-high counter, looking bored. The lighting was dim and tinted pinkish, and the walls were all mirrored. An old TV set on a cheap pressed-board stand was playing one of the crazy idiot talk shows, but the sound was down low. A man about Flood's age, wearing work boots and clothes that looked dusty from a construction site, sat in a chair reading *Sports Illustrated,* almost as if he was waiting for his turn in the barber's chair.

Flood wasn't sure what to do. He wanted to talk to one of the women but he wasn't going to question the man out front. When he hesitated, the man leaned forward on his stool.

"Half hour or full?"

"Uh, right. Half." Flood was already embarrassed and felt this was crazy.

"It's fifty."

He took out his wallet and handed the man a fifty-dollar bill. He was carrying about eight hundred after his negotiations with Tamika.

"Go ahead and sit down."

Flood was about to turn and do as he was told, out of mere bewilderment, but he needed to stay in control.

"How many women are available?"

The man raised an eyebrow. "You want more than one?"

"No, but, um, can I pick?"

"Well, they're all busy right now. So it's sort of whoever finishes up next. Unless you want to wait," he said, droning on as though bored stiff. "Janna, Crystal and Persephone are working today. Is there one of them you'd prefer?"

How would he know? He thought what he wanted was an

older woman who had perhaps been around the place longer. Then again, a younger woman, or actually a girl, might be more likely to know Britney. He decided it was pretty much a crap-shoot.

"Do you have pictures?" he asked.

The man squinted a moment. "No, we don't have pictures."

Flood shrugged and sat down. He studied the room without making eye contact with the other customer. There was a security camera high on the wall over the doorway that led back into the other rooms. The swinging saloon doors parted after a moment and a woman of about twenty-five stepped through wearing a short satin bathrobe. She was pretty, but her face looked a little gaunt and her skin was blotchy and pallid. There were tattoos curling down her forearms and bruises on her wrists. She smiled at Flood and the other man, who put down his magazine and stood up when the attendant nodded at him.

After they had disappeared through the doorway, the man told Flood, "You're next."

"Great."

Flood rested his head against the wall and closed his eyes. It was fascinating and revolting at the same time. He wondered what it would be like if he was drunk. He heard the saloon door swing again. This woman was taller than the first, and a bit older but healthier looking. Her tattoos were on her ankles and feet, which were fitted into high-heeled mules. Her bathrobe was red and short, her hair was reddish brown, and her eyes were blue. She gave Flood a comforting smile, and he stood up. She looked back at him as they passed through the door again and a wider smile revealed straight teeth. Flood realized there was a reason he felt so out of place. He was a decent-looking man in good shape and wearing a good suit. And he looked halfway sober. He looked like he didn't belong here.

They walked down a dimly lit hallway lined by walls that

seemed as though they'd been built in a hurry. She opened a flimsy white door and showed him into a room occupied by a massage table covered in a white fitted sheet with two folded white bath towels. There was a wire metal stand against the wall that held a small, cheap portable stereo, a short stack of CDs, a box of tissues and a bottle of hand lotion. The room smelled of bleach and coconuts.

"I'm Janna," she said, holding out her hand. "What's your name?"

Flood didn't want to start talking until the door was closed, but she had left it open.

"Flood," he said.

"Flood? Do you have a first name?"

"Yes."

She waited but got nothing. "You haven't been here before, have you?"

"No."

"You got a half hour, right?"

"Yes. Here's the—" He was about to whisper his need for the door to be shut, but she interrupted him and headed out of the room.

"OK, Flood. Go ahead and get undressed and lie down on the table and I'll be right back," she said, shutting the door on her way out.

He could feel his face flushing, and he muttered a string of profanities under his breath. Instead of undressing, he took out his wallet and extracted his business card and a hundred-dollar bill. He laid the card and the money on the table. Then he stood with his arms folded and waited.

When she came back in she saw the money first, and then noticed that he was still dressed. She tilted her head at him in suspicious questioning, and the gesture struck Flood for some reason. Perhaps the money on the cot like that was an insult, presuming something. And she was suddenly angry at him. The look she gave had for a moment broken through the barrier of prostitute and trick and they were a man and a woman who might be having a real disagreement. She seemed, he realized he was judging, not like a prostitute.

Walking into the sex trade was like landing on Mars, he thought—completely strange and different from regular, logical human interaction. But she had looked at him that way, letting her guard down.

"Whatever you think, it's not that," he said in as low a voice as he could. He motioned her into the room and she cautiously came in. He pointed at the door and she closed it.

She walked over to the table and picked up his card but left the money. She read it and then looked at him. He walked over to the portable stereo and turned the New Age whatever that was playing a little louder and then came back to her and whispered.

"I've been hired to look into the death of a woman. And I'm looking for a potential witness who may work here."

Janna's eyes narrowed.

"What do you want from me?" she said. Her casual, affectionate tone was gone.

"Information. I'll pay you for it, obviously."

"I don't know anything."

"Just hear me out."

"Are the police involved?"

"Not very actively."

"Who is it?" She now sounded downright jittery. And from her tone, Flood guessed she knew the answer to her question.

"I need to know about a girl named Britney."

Janna tilted her head again as she studied his card, and then looked up at him. He knew she knew.

"I don't know anybody named Britney."

"Then what's her real name? I know you know who I'm talking about. I can see it in your face."

With her finger she nervously stroked several strands of hair over her ear and then folded her arms defensively. She walked over to the door and put her ear to it. And then gave Flood a worried look. She didn't say anything.

"I need to talk to her."

She started shaking her head and came back to the massage table, where she reached out and slid the hundred-dollar bill back to him.

"You don't know what you're doing," she whispered. "These are dangerous people. I don't know anything, and can't tell you anything."

Flood didn't touch the money.

"I will keep you out of it," he said. "I just need her name and where I can find her."

"You don't get it," she said. "I think she's dead already. He probably killed her. I don't know why and I don't want to know. He would kill me in a heartbeat."

"Who?"

In her exasperation at his ignorance of the level of danger, she hissed out, "I don't know his name, I swear."

"Zo?"

She gritted her teeth and glared at him. So she did know.

"You know his real name?"

"I don't know anything about him except I think he killed that girl, and he threatened to kill me."

"He threatened to kill you?"

"All I did was ask about her."

"So, is Zo short for something?"

"No, XO, like the cognac, but they call him Zo."

XO, like the cognac. Of all the stupid shit.

"What do you mean, he killed her?"

89

"She's gone. I think XO killed her."

Flood took a deep breath, laid his hand on Janna's and squeezed gently. Something in her demeanor told him touching her like that would be OK, and she did not object.

"Janna, tell me her name."

She looked like she was on the verge of tears now.

"I don't get it," she said. "Who are you? Who are you working for?"

"I'm who the card says. A couple weeks ago a young woman was found in Lake Michigan. Nobody knows how she drowned or why, but she worked with girls on the street and she knew this girl I'm asking about. She was helping her, I think. The dead woman's name was A.J. Ash. Do you know that name?"

Janna shook her head.

"Her mother hired me to find out what happened to her."

She picked up Flood's card again. He looked at the clock on the wall. Twenty minutes of his half hour were gone.

"The name she used was Britney. She was cute and dressed like Britney Spears," Janna finally said, sounding like curiosity was melting some of her fear. "XO brought her here a couple months ago. He'd brought girls here from the city before. Younger, prettier girls. Kids. He seemed to have his own client base that came out here to see them. I think this one was only fifteen."

"Do you know her real name?"

"I don't know. She was pretty guarded. She was a nice kid, but all screwed up and XO was in complete control of her. He owned her. It was so creepy."

"Do you know where she was living?"

"Some motel out here, I think. He had other girls working tracks, like in Stone Park or maybe Cicero. I don't know those places, but some of the girls who come through here have done that. I think he kept them all in a motel."

"Was she local?"

"No. That I know. She said something stupid about Chicago once, and I asked where she was from and she said the name of some town and then said it was by Peoria. Reef Court, or Creek Fort, or something like that. I don't know. I said 'What?' and she just said, 'It's by Peoria.' "

"So why do you think she's dead?"

"She disappeared a couple weeks ago. She was here on a Monday and Tuesday night, and was supposed to be back on a Thursday night and wasn't. XO was here the next week with a new girl to replace her. A Mexican girl. I asked what happened to Britney and he grabbed my wrist, like this." She took Flood's hand and twisted it. "He almost broke it. And he told me to shut the fuck up and said if I ever mentioned her again I'd regret it. I don't know what happened but it was bad, and now you're here asking about it. Something's fucked up."

"Is the Mexican girl here?"

"No, I never even knew her name. She was here that one night, and then that was it. XO's gone, too. I asked sleazeball, out there at the desk, about him, and he said he'd vanished. Some of his clients showed up here on his nights for a while looking for his girls. The owners tried calling him and he doesn't call back. We heard that his girls have all either scattered or been picked up by other guys."

"Who owns this place?"

"I don't know. Nick runs it. I can't pronounce his last name. But I think he just runs it for somebody else. There are some scary people who come in here and act like they own the place, like they own us, a couple times a week."

"Nick's not the guy out front?"

"No, that's Kevin. He's just a junkie."

Flood now had his notebook out and was writing it all down.

"I should have known better," she said, watching him write.

91

"What?"

"I took one look at you out there and I thought this might actually be, you know, OK. But you totally didn't belong here. I just should have known."

Flood smiled. "You've been a big help. I'm sorry for the trouble."

He took out another hundred-dollar bill out of his pocket.

"Keep my card. If anybody asks any questions about me, and you feel threatened, give me a call on my mobile. I really don't want to cause you any grief."

"Please don't repeat to anyone that I told you anything."

"I promise."

CHAPTER 9

He left through a side door, like most of the customers, and felt nearly overwhelmed by the broad, open space. After the surreal pink light and pit-of-despair feel of the massage parlor, the parking lot seemed nearly infinite in its expansiveness. He regained his bearings stumbling across the chunky gravel to his car and turned on the air conditioning. It was almost midnight when he merged into traffic on I-290 and headed for the city. He thought about pulling off the Eisenhower at the Mannheim Road exit to take a look at the sleazy stretch of Stone Park that was populated by lingerie show bars, adult bookstores and streetwalkers, but he realized he would have no idea what he was looking for.

He called McPhee.

"I called them about the VW," McPhee said. "Tally said he'll schedule an evidence tech tonight. They'll go over to the tow lot tomorrow to print it."

"Thanks. I still don't get why she'd park it on the street."

"I'll admit that's a little odd, but there could be a few logical explanations."

"Where are you now?"

"Home. I've got to get some sleep if I'm going to be running for you tomorrow."

He told McPhee to come by the office in the morning, and they'd figure out who XO was. Flood didn't want to go home. He felt like he needed to keep moving. To keep the momentum and thoughts clicking and to keep at bay the thoughts of Jenny that kept trying to creep back into his head in the quiet moments. He hit a little traffic between First Avenue and Austin Boulevard, and the frustrating slowdown left him wallowing again in his loneliness and guilt. Here he went getting excited about a case. Had he put this much passion and commitment into saving his relationship with Jenny? He had stopped calling her. She had never picked up. Never called him back.

Before he met Jenny he was contented with a social life that consisted mostly of drinking with men, cooking and reading. He dated like a snake ate—gorging infrequently and moving on. It was a miserable life, but he had sort of liked being miserable because the only other life he had ever known was working for the government, and a brief engagement to a woman he did not love.

Jenny had changed all that. He had fallen in love, probably for the first time in his life. And now she was gone.

He thought about calling his friend Keith Reece, who was probably still at his desk at the *Tribune,* but then decided he wanted to be alone. He parked at his building and walked down Hubbard to Brasserie Jo and took a seat at the bar, ordered one bourbon and then another. The restaurant was popular with business people dining on modest expense accounts, and it struck Flood that there always seemed to be a party going on organized by grown children for an elderly parent's birthday or anniversary. Happy people in groups. He should have hated the place, but the food was good and it was a five-minute walk from his apartment.

He thought about rich A.J. Ash and the poor kid hooker Britney, or whatever her name was, while he drank his Wild Turkey.

Of the several girls A.J. seemed to be dealing with, why was she especially interested in this one? And what kind of trouble was the girl in? For some reason, he didn't believe she was dead. Janna's reasoning seemed stretched. Maybe just because there was no evidence, and if she was really a pretty little blonde who looked like Britney Spears, she was probably too valuable to kill without a very good reason. Maybe if she was twenty-eight and strung out on heroin, a pimp would kill her more readily. Maybe he would have killed Janna for some similar transgression, Flood thought. The thought triggered a memory. A very small amount of heroin found in A.J.'s apartment. Perhaps it had come from the girl. That wouldn't make things any easier if she was fifteen and already strung out. But the brass pipe in the bag smelled like weed, not vinegary traces of heroin.

He didn't know. But he needed to find the girl.

His cell phone rang and it was Helen Schachter from the Initiative on Homelessness. He glanced at his watch and saw that it was almost twelve-thirty in the morning.

"What did you do to Celeste?"

"I had a disagreement with her. I found a piece of luggage that belonged to A.J. there and I wanted it. She went nuts on me."

"Well, she's accusing you of assault and theft. The bag disappeared. And she's threatening me now, because I sent you to her."

"Huh," Flood said. "I left without it."

"Well, it's gone."

"Did she call the police?"

"She says she's going to."

Flood sighed. If she was going to call, she'd have done so already.

"Hey, while I've got you on the phone. The bag she's talking about belonged to this girl Britney you mentioned. I need her real name. Can you at least get me that? Maybe A.J. had some real records on her. I really need to find this girl."

"Like I said, I can't let you look at them. But I can maybe go through her files tomorrow and look for her. If I find anything, I might be able to help. We'll see."

Her response was more positive than he had expected, so he decided to let it go for the moment. He thanked her and said good night.

Flood nearly ordered a third whisky but thought better of it and put money on the bar and shook his head to the bartender. He rubbed his eyes as he built up the courage to walk home and then felt the shadow of a body sitting down next to him. He opened his eyes.

"Uh oh."

"I knew I'd run into you again," she said. Same black dress and strappy heels.

"You never told me your name."

"You can just call me the naked girl in your bed."

The bartender had arrived to take her order and his eyebrows arched.

"I'll have what he's having."

"I'm having nothing more tonight. How's that?"

She looked at his nearly empty glass and cocked her head at the bartender, who went away and came back with a Wild Turkey on the rocks.

"Tell me," he said.

"OK, fine. It's Molly."

He took her hand and shook it.

"You know," she said. "You were sort of a familiar face, so I Googled you."

"You shouldn't have."

"Oh. My. God," she said for effect. "I read all the stories. It was incredible. Is incredible."

"What else have you Googled?"

"You were, like, a hero."

"You should Google the '85 Bears. It was probably decades before you were born, but they're the real heroes."

"No, really."

He looked away. She read him and toned herself down a note.

"The woman who was kidnapped was your girlfriend, I guess."

Flood was about to tell her it was none of her business, but he had been the one to talk about Jenny in the first place, when he was drunk. Not that he remembered a bit of it, but he'd brought it up. In his mind, it would be hypocritical to shut her up now, so he just said, "What's it matter to you?"

She shrugged. "OK, it's none of my business. I just didn't understand the whole picture before."

"Now you've read the coverage."

"Were the stories true?"

"Pretty much."

"It must have been awful."

"It was worse six months later, I guess."

"Whattya mean?"

Maybe it was precisely because she was a stranger, but Flood found himself talking.

"When it happened, we were just happy to be alive. But later it was hard. It's hard to explain, but certain things just stick with you a while."

They had stuck with Jenny in ways that they had not stuck with Flood but he didn't say that, telling himself it was really none of her business.

Flood's law firm assigned him the case, which had little to do with lawyering. A client said he couldn't find his wife. She'd left him but the client didn't say that, exactly. He was desperate to withdraw money from an offshore account that she controlled. Flood started looking for Marcy Westlake and eventually figured out that her husband, Daniel Westlake, was lying. He and his wife were both crooks, though not together. They were tangled in a mobbed-up casino scheme, trying to compete with each other, neither one understanding how over their heads they were until it was way too late. Marcy Westlake was murdered by the Mob because she knew how they were rigging the bidding to build a casino in downtown Chicago. The husband was trying to use what she knew to help scam the Mob out of their own scam. When Flood caught up to everybody, the Mob kidnapped his girlfriend Jenny as a bargaining chip. Everybody had done the wrong thing, and Flood cleaned up the mess the hard way. He had been reckless, and in the end the Westlakes were dead, Flood had killed three mobsters and Jenny nearly died bound and gagged in the trunk of a car on one of the coldest nights of the year.

Flood had come out of the whole mess with something like maverick status. That was owed mostly to the fact that the three people he actually saved, the Westlakes' son Brandon and his girlfriend, and Jenny, were the only real innocents in the whole mess. His firm wanted nothing to do with him, but that was fine. He went out on his own and was a man to be reckoned with. Clients and money came in steadily for a while. But he was pretending to be getting on with his life, unscarred by the terror and bloodshed he had endured. Jenny wouldn't manage any such pretense. Soon they were in very different places. And then his life was out of control.

This girl Molly was where he had bottomed out. He was grateful to her for that. But it was really Jane Ash and Philip Swain who had saved him. There was no denying that.

They drank their whiskies and then he started to say good night. "I need to go home. I've got to start very early tomorrow."

"That apartment still a mess?"

"No. All cleaned up. The day I met you. You shamed me into it."

"Oh, really. Can I see?"

"Sorry, Miss Lyons. I'm not such a pushover tonight. I'm half sober."

CHAPTER 10

Flood couldn't sleep. He had drifted off at about one but woke and looked at the clock at three. An hour passed and he finally got out of bed. McPhee might be annoyed but Flood couldn't help himself. He called Area Four and asked for Tally.

"You ain't a cop no more, man. You get to sleep at night like regular people," Tally joked.

"I thought you might be lonely if nobody's killing anybody tonight."

"Somebody's always killing somebody out here. But I'm twiddling my thumbs at the moment. NAGIS thinks they've got three shitheads they picked up today who might know something about two murders from a week ago. They're bringing one of them over here for me to talk to."

Pressuring information out of gang members arrested in bigger drug cases was often how murders were solved. Still, fewer than half of the killings in Chicago were solved every year because most of them were gang and drug murders, and people with information tended to be criminals, their relatives, or people who feared or distrusted the police.

"Seems like a bad summer out there."

"It's been hellacious all over the West Side."

"You said some Vice Lord honcho's coming out?"

"Howard Purcell. Been in Menard six years for attempted murder. He's probably killed a half dozen people himself. Piece of shit. Anyway, you're calling about the girl. Billy McPhee

100

called earlier about the car."

Tally always said McPhee's whole name, like it was one four-beat word.

"Right. That's great, if you guys can get somebody to process it. I doubt there's anything there, but I think it's really odd the car was towed from in front of her building. She's got a parking spot."

"We'll check it out."

"I'm actually calling about another lead I want to run down. I'm looking for a guy with a street name. I think he's a pimp. Would you mind running him through CLEAR?"

The CLEAR system was an elaborate CPD database that contained, among many other things, intelligence on known criminals. The information went beyond arrest records, allowing officers to search for just about anybody the police had any significant contact with in the last several years.

"Pimp?"

"Yes, A.J. worked with child prostitutes a bit, and this guy's name came up today."

"Huh. I don't think I knew the prostitutes angle. Fitzie just said homeless folks after he talked to her boss."

"Well, there's some crossover, I guess."

"I suppose. What've you got?"

"Guy goes by XO, like the cognac."

"Like the cognac?"

"Right. It's a grading system. V.S. is crap, VSOP is a little smoother stuff, XO is a hundred bucks a bottle."

"I drink Old Style."

"Well, this guy's a connoisseur, apparently."

"Ha. I bet he is," Tally said, and then repeated it, amusing himself.

"Anyway, Capital *X*, Capital *O*. And I talked to somebody

who said he's called 'Zo,' for short, so maybe try it that way, too."

"Won't have to. XO comes up. Not a certain match, I guess. Melvin Runyon. DOB 1978. He apparently has 'XO' tattooed on his chest." Tally spoke haltingly, reading aloud as he saw the information for the first time. "One arrest for possession, three domestics—zero convictions. No busts in the last year, but a contact card on him in the one-thousand block of South Cicero in, let's see, March. Loitering. Possible involvement in prostitution at that location. Possible Four Corner Hustlers affiliation, but no known associates listed here. That your guy?"

"Probably. I really appreciate it."

CHAPTER 11

McPhee was an early riser, so Flood didn't hesitate to call him at six the next morning with the information. An Accurint search gave them the most likely address for Melvin Runyon, and they were easing down the block in Flood's black Taurus by seven-thirty. They rolled past a small frame house covered in dingy aluminum siding, with a concrete porch ringed by a black iron railing. The yard was minimal, just a square of hard dirt and thin grass, speckled with broken glass. The houses were all close-set on the block, with just a few feet between them, enough for concrete gangways and perhaps a chain-link fence.

The neighborhood was called Austin, far out on the West Side, nearly every inch of which was tightly controlled gang turf. This far west, and north of the Eisenhower, the gangs were all factions of the Vice Lords and their offshoot, the Four Corner Hustlers.

Runyon's information in the CLEAR system suggested he might be affiliated with the Four Corner Hustlers, but there was so little to go on that McPhee said he believed the notation was made merely because this address was on a block long controlled by the gang. If Runyon lived here, he would not be able to avoid some level of affiliation with them.

The sun was starting to cast long shadows from the rooftops and spill brilliant light on the trees. It was warm and muggy out already and Flood had the windows up and the air conditioning on. There was no one out in front of the house, but at the corner, a handful of boys and young men milled around on the sidewalk by a fence gate in front of a house where two older men, probably in their thirties, sat on a sofa looking at the black car as it rolled past.

McPhee noted a tree in the parkway in front of the house and pointed at it with the toothpick he slid out from between his lips. At the base of the tree, someone had arranged a tribute of two teddy bears, a stuffed white bunny and a large piece of poster board affixed to the trunk. The poster said something neither of them could make out.

"A fresh one," McPhee said. With the stuffed animals still there, the murder scene they marked must have been no more than a few days old.

Flood and McPhee stole glances at the older men on the porch as they passed by.

"Well, they're definitely looking at us, so we might as well stop here," McPhee said.

"Neither one's our guy, is it?" Flood asked.

"I don't think so. Those guys're in charge of these here young fellas. Old Melvin doesn't have enough of a record to be in charge of anybody on this block."

They parked the car at the curb and got out. The group of youngsters made a big show of staring them down as they passed and McPhee cajoled them with a few greetings that were completely unintelligible to Flood.

They walked two doors south to the little house that was supposed to be Melvin Runyon's last address. They had come out this early in the morning because people known by names like XO tended to be up all night, and in all day. In the seven o'clock hour, they might just catch him in transition. On the other hand, if this wasn't his address, they were about to annoy some poor soul who was likely still sleeping. It didn't bother McPhee and he punched the doorbell a couple of times without hesitation. As they waited, Flood watched the youths at the corner. Only one was eyeing them, almost as if it was his job to track them so the rest of the group didn't have to. He and Flood were staring at each other, but Flood averted his eyes when they heard stirring behind the front door of the house. Two deadbolt locks tumbled open heavily, and a chain clanked before the door opened slightly to reveal a woman of about sixty dressed in a housecoat, her thin feet shod in cheap drug store slippers.

"He ain't lived here in three years," she blurted out at them. "You fools ought to know that."

"Ma'am?" McPhee said.

"You looking for my grandson, Melvin. I said he ain't lived here in three years. I haven't seen him in a year. Ain't heard from him in six months. I kicked him out, and he ain't welcome to come back."

"You're right," Flood said. "We are looking for Melvin. I'm a lawyer and my colleague is a private investigator. Do you have any idea where we might find Melvin?"

She scowled at him. "Wherever young girls selling their flesh on the street, Melvin be there collecting the money," she said. And then gave them a defiant curl of her lower lip. "I don't care who knows how I feel about it. You come banging on my door before a decent hour, you're gonna hear what's on my mind. I don't appreciate it."

"We're sorry to disturb you, ma'am," Flood said. "But it's just very important that we find and speak to Melvin."

"I told you, I don't know."

"Do you have a phone number for him?" McPhee asked.

"No, I do not. Now, that's all I have to say."

With that, she closed the door and they heard all of the locks and chains tightening back up.

"Well, that went well," Flood said. It was never good to have the subject of questioning control the interview and end it before they were ready. But, from the sound of the old woman, it seemed that pestering her further would have done more harm than good. Flood took out a business card, scribbled a note on the back to have Melvin call and dropped it through the mail slot.

They left the porch and walked back up the sidewalk.

"I suppose it won't hurt to talk to the old boys up here on this porch," McPhee said.

As Flood held the gate open for McPhee, they saw a pickup truck coming around the corner. A white man who looked like a construction worker, probably on his way to work in some downtown skyscraper going up, was behind the wheel. He slowed in the street, and one of the boys from the group on the corner bounced out to the driver's side window, reaching into the pocket of his baggy jean shorts as he went. A lickety-split handoff was made and the pickup accelerated down the street.

McPhee and Flood climbed the creaky wooden steps together, getting a better look at the two seated men, who had clearly figured out they weren't cops. Otherwise, the drug deal that had just transpired would have been called off before it happened. Up close they looked to be in their late twenties, senior status in a world where half the men that age were either dead or in prison. Both were muscular, with extensively tattooed arms. One had a three-inch Afro and a beard. The other had shaved his head but had a thin mustache.

The bearded man spoke, "What's this, the CIA?"

"Publisher's Clearing House," McPhee said with a laugh. "Lady down the block didn't want the fifty million so we thought we'd try y'all."

"Every little bit helps, brother lawman."

Flood took out another card and handed it to the bearded man, who scanned it, scoffed and dropped it on the floor of the porch.

"Counselor, shouldn't I get locked up before you come handing out your card?"

Flood smiled.

"We're not looking for clients. We're trying to find—"

"Zo," said the other man. "We ain't idiots. Saw which house you went to."

"His grandmother said he hasn't been around," McPhee said.

"That's right," the man with the little mustache said.

"You know where we can find him?"

"Nope."

Flood could tell McPhee was about to get annoyed.

"He work any strolls besides Cicero?" McPhee asked.

"How the fuck I know? He don't come around here."

"Did he ever?" Flood asked.

The bearded one spoke up, like he wanted this to be over so he could go back to managing his drug corner. A middle-aged black man on a bicycle rode up on the sidewalk and bought from the kids, barely giving Flood and McPhee a glance. But the next customer, a few seconds later, was a white woman in a minivan who caught a glimpse of the white man in a suit and black man in golf shirt and pressed pants on the porch, and kept driving. It was the morning rush hour market. Drug corners like this one all over Chicago's all-black neighborhoods operated twenty-four hours a day, but they did most of their business with white suburbanites during the morning and evening commutes.

"He used to hang down here a little bit, five, six years ago. He turned his girlfriend out—little girl from around there over on Lamon. He started running girls he stopped coming around here. I don't know where he stay."

"That girl around?" Flood asked.

"Who?"

"The girlfriend from over on Lamon."

The one with the shaved head grunted a chuckle to himself but said nothing. The one with the beard shook his head. "No, she dead."

Flood and McPhee waited.

"OD," the bearded man finally obliged.

"Melvin's momma stay over here?" McPhee asked.

The bearded one shook his head. "She crazy. No idea where she at."

"Any other family?"

They bantered on futilely a minute longer and then they left. They had learned nothing other than where Melvin Runyon wasn't.

"I'm hungry," McPhee said.

"OK. What's out here?"

McPhee laughed. "Not much. Edna's, I guess, but let's go downtown."

"You want Manny's?"

"If you insist."

Manny's was McPhee's favorite place to eat any meal. It was only Flood's favorite breakfast joint. He typically had nothing but toast, orange juice and coffee for breakfast, but he would gladly break habit for corned beef hash, an egg and a poppy seed bagel. They took the Ike back downtown, split onto the Ryan Expressway for a moment and came off on Roosevelt and went east a few blocks to Jefferson. The neighborhood used to be called Jewtown, and was part of the Maxwell Street area. Flood had once been standing in line for what was called a Maxwell Street Polish, when a chatty black man got out of a broken-down old conversion van, got in line behind him and struck up a conversation. Actually, it wasn't much of a conversation. The man just kept saying, "Got to come down here and get me a Jewtown Polish. I live out south now, but I got to come down for the Jewtown Polish." He had never heard the expression before or since.

They got in line and both ordered the corned beef hash and eggs, bagels and coffee. It was about eight-fifteen when they sat down and started eating, and Flood's cell phone rang immediately.

"Hello, it's Donal Skiddy. I work for James Ash," the caller said. He had an Irish accent that had been twisted around a bit by living in the States, Flood imagined. "Mr. Ash is home if you still wish to come speak to him."

"Today?"

"This morning, if possible. Between you and me, I think he would like to get it over with. This is hard for him; I'm sure you understand."

"Sure."

"Very good. I'll tell him to expect you in about an hour."

Flood had thought it was strange James Ash went to Europe on a business trip so soon after his daughter had died, no matter what Jane Ash said. But now that he was back he seemed to be willing to deal with Flood promptly, so he would give him the benefit of the doubt. Flood and McPhee finished eating and Flood paid the bill on the way out while McPhee bought a pack of mints and a cigar at the counter.

After dropping McPhee in the Loop so he could catch a cab, Flood crossed Grant Park on Congress and headed north on Lake Shore Drive. The lakefront path, a wide ribbon of walks and trails, was sprinkled with people running and cycling in the late-morning heat. Traffic was light and he zoomed up the Drive, past Diversey, Belmont and Montrose harbors, past Lincoln Park, and the long string of lakefront apartment towers. The Drive ended at Hollywood, and Flood crept north in the narrow canyon of Sheridan Road, which always seemed so dim and claustrophobic after the wide-open spectacle of spinning along the lake.

The last stretch of Chicago lakefront was jammed with crowded, nondescript high-rises, liquor stores and other commercial chaos spread around Loyola University, which was hemmed between Sheridan and the water. Another mile, and a big curve along the lake, and he was in Evanston, winding his way past stately apartment houses, and then big lawns and enormous old Victorian and Georgian houses that loomed like hay barns across perfect lawns, with their soaring gables. He passed through the Northwestern University campus, and then Sheridan drifted back over to the lakeshore. On the left, inland, the neighborhood was grand, with blocks of big houses on leafy streets. On the right, the lakeside, it was opulent. Estate-size houses, mostly in gray stone, most of them shielded from the road by walls and gates, were nestled along the way in small clusters, seemingly on their own terms, taking up as much space as they liked. Without noticing, he was out of Evanston, and then out of Wilmette, and into Winnetka.

Flood slowed and started to search the street signs, looking for Sugar Maple Road. He found it, marked by a pedestrian crosswalk, and turned down into the wooded lane, catching glimpses of enormous homes recessed and screened by trees. The curving lane forked and Flood turned left into a drive where the gates were open, and a large, rectangular turnaround paved in red brick held a Land Rover and a big black Mercedes sedan. The house itself was still another hundred feet off. It was a red-brick full Georgian of three floors. Of course there were wings added on at either side of the house, and they appeared to turn corners and head for the lake, making the house a rambling—probably 20,000 square feet—horseshoe facing the water. There were hedges and flowerbeds everywhere, and to his right, through a screen of evergreens, Flood could hear a tennis ball being whacked back and forth on a court, apparently by people who knew how to play. The clap of his car door closing stopped the rhythm of the tennis ball. A moment later a tall, sweaty man in tennis whites emerged from a break in the hedges and waved as he approached. "Mr. Flood?" He stuck out his hand. "I'm Donal Skiddy. Good to meet you."

Flood shook his hand and pointed at the racquet. "Sorry to interrupt your game. Sounded like you were going at it pretty good."

Skiddy waved dismissively and pointed toward the house. "I'll get you pointed in the right direction and then head back and finish her off. My girlfriend. Mr. Ash is kind enough to let the help use the facilities."

"So you help manage the company?"

"Hardly management," he said with a laugh. "More of a glorified greens keeper, actually. I do work for Mr. Ash's resort development company. I met him in Ireland on a golf course project. I was head greens keeper of a little place they bought and redeveloped. Anyway, here I am still, and I occasionally help out with Mr. Ash's schedule."

"And keep the leaves off the tennis court."

He laughed again. "Precisely."

"So, where in Ireland?"

"Near Cork. Have you been to the homeland, Mr. Flood?"

"I'm afraid it's still on the to-do list. So, should I head up now?" They turned toward the house and started walking.

In fact, Flood wasn't much of an Irish-American. He never much went for the connections to the old country the way many in Chicago did. He hadn't grown up in one of the big Irish neighborhoods, and his spring didn't revolve around St. Patrick's Day. He'd been to the South Side Irish parade once, and vowed never to partake in that particular drunken mob again. No need to burden poor Skiddy with this. As a real Irishman, he had probably drawn his own conclusions about the ways in which Chicago Irish celebrated their shared heritage.

They climbed the wide path to the door together and ascended a terrace of flagstones. With everything on such a grand scale, the normal doorbell looked oddly miniature to him. Skiddy flipped up the cover on a security system keypad and was about to punch in a number when the heavy door opened.

A very plain-looking middle-aged woman wearing a very plain summer-weight dress stood before them. She said good morning with a slight Polish accent to Flood and ignored Skiddy.

"Right," he said. "Magda, this is of course Mr. Flood."

He turned to Flood and patted him on the shoulder and started back toward the tennis court.

Magda just said, "Come this way," and led him into a large receiving hall that was well lit and cool. The floor was marble and the woodwork on the balustrade of the stairs was polished walnut. The walls were painted pale blue with white crown molding. He had taken in everything there was to take in by the time the Polish housekeeper excused herself to go alert James Ash. But she came back alone after a couple of minutes and asked him to follow. They turned down a side hall and past a dining room that was about the size of his apartment, maybe a little bigger, and then past a very large kitchen with a view of the lake on the other side. They went through a living room, and another room that Flood thought might be called a gallery, and down a narrower and darker hall lined with closed doors until they arrived at a dim study where the shades were drawn. Two leather sofas faced each other, some matching club chairs were scattered about and a carved wood game table was by the window under a hanging lamp, with a deck of cards on its polished top. The light hit the playing cards in such a way that a layer of dust on them was immediately evident.

"Mr. Ash will be with you in a few minutes," she said, closing the heavy door with a hard click. She hadn't offered him anything to drink or waited around to see if he had a question. It was dimmer than the rest of the house because the shades were all drawn, and warmer, as well. Paintings hung on the walls, but as Flood noticed them it seemed they might be rejects from other rooms and other generations, speculative purchases that hadn't panned out, pieces shuffled away from the main rooms until they reached the end of the house, this strange room that reeked of disuse.

Flood stood in there alone for another fifteen minutes and started to become truly annoyed before the door finally swung open slowly, as if of its own volition, and revealed a tall man of about fifty, as dark as Jane Ash was blonde. His hair looked jet black, artificially so, but full and very well kept. He was dressed for a summer afternoon in a ten-million-dollar house, wearing a lightweight blue blazer, a black linen shirt with two buttons open and crisp gray slacks. Black suede loafers and no socks on his feet. From the light tan on his forehead and hands, Flood guessed the European trip had been to the Mediterranean. When he finally entered, he only glanced at Flood, in a way that made him feel there must be other people in the room. But it was just a very well-practiced manner of making others feel unimportant.

"So, what does Jane think you're going to do for her?"

It was a rhetorical question phrased in such a way that Flood almost decided to ignore it.

"Mr. Ash, there are circumstances surrounding your daughter's death that have not been explained yet. Your ex-wife would like to know exactly what happened."

Ash was finally looking at Flood, but as if he pitied him. His mouth twisted around a little as he figured out how to respond. The room now smelled slightly of gin, Flood decided.

"I don't think she's going to like the answers she gets, if you're any good. Not saying you are."

"Well, I came here to hear your thoughts."

"Hmmf. My thoughts." Ash smiled, as if repeating Flood was a witty thing to do. "My thoughts are that my daughter was an unhappy girl who did not take care of herself. I blame myself, and Jane. We made her unhappy by being very unhappy ourselves in a failed marriage that ended in divorce. A.J. might have bounced back, gotten over it, like her brother did, and moved on. But she didn't. She was at a very impressionable age when the divorce happened."

"What do you think happened?"

"I think she was drinking. Well, I know she was drinking. It's what the autopsy says. I think she was despondent, reckless and had an accident. If she was with somebody, that person is the sort of person who does not take responsibility for whatever he did, and . . ."

His words were flowing loosely enough that Flood decided he definitely had been drinking. He still wondered if the man was confused by grief and trying to put on a show of toughness, or just a callous prick whose nerve endings had long ago been cauterized by his family's wealth.

Ash had left the sentence hanging, so Flood tried to finish it. "Someone who is afraid of the consequences of questions about what happened?"

Ash shrugged. "I really don't think it matters. Maybe she was with somebody she knew, maybe it was somebody she'd just met. Maybe she was alone. I don't know. But I know in my heart, she put herself in that position. She was, as I said, very unhappy."

He seemed sure of himself on this point. It wouldn't have surprised Flood if she were very unhappy when she was around her father, if he was like this all the time. But Ash's take on things was at least plausible.

"Well, just the same, I'd like to ask you a few questions."

He threw up his hands gently and slumped down on one of the sofas. "Ask away," he said without inviting Flood to sit.

"A.J. grew up in this house?"

He nodded. "This house was a wedding present to my father and mother, from my mother's parents."

"Did she keep a room here?"

"Hell, no. She hadn't been here in two years. Whenever I saw her, which was rare, it was either at my office or the club."

"And those places are where?"

"Club's right down the road. And our offices are in the Hancock."

Flood had passed a country club on Sheridan that looked exclusive enough for James Ash.

"When was the last time you talked to her?"

"I don't know. Couple of weeks. She didn't have much to say to me, I'm sure you have gathered," he said. "So what do you think happened that's worth investigating? Or are you just taking my ex-wife's money, which, of course, is actually my money. Or was."

"I'm just getting started. There are several people I'd like to talk to."

"Who, the kid with the boat?"

"I'll talk to him, but the police checked him out thoroughly and I doubt he saw A.J. the night she died."

"Then who?"

"A couple of young girls your daughter worked with. They may have been involved in prostitution. A man who may have been involved with that. I don't know."

"Prostitution? What are you talking about? For God's sake . . ." Ash grunted.

"Some of the young girls whose cases your daughter handled—they were prostitutes."

"Underage?"

115

"That's right."

He made an aggrieved face and grunted, as if it was too much to bear hearing how the other ninety-nine percent lived, like animals. "Well, that's terrible. But I still don't see what it might have to do with A.J. hitting her head and drowning."

"Perhaps it doesn't. Perhaps the explanation of what happened is as simple as you suspect."

"Perhaps, indeed, Mr. Flood. Tell me, you still get to keep . . . oh, never mind. How long's this going to go on?"

"I don't know." He wanted to take control of the questioning again. "Did A.J. grow up around boats?"

Ash frowned a little to answer in the negative. "Not really. I have a boat I keep in the Mediterranean, at Portofino, but A.J. has been on it just a few times, and not since college. My brother sailed Lake Michigan years ago, but he's kept that boat in Santa Barbara since the late eighties. He hasn't been here in three or four years."

"Who maintains your boat?"

"Crew. They change every season. I couldn't tell you their names at the moment. Captain is a Frenchman who's been with us five years. Never been here."

"Sailboat?"

"Of course it's a sailboat. Do I look like I'd have a motor yacht?" There was derision in his voice.

At that moment, Flood noticed there was a woman standing in the doorway to the room. She was listening to them, with her arms folded over a large chest. She wore a blue v-neck sweater and silky white shorts that did not make it quite to mid-thigh. She was slender, but something about her was unpleasant. It might have been the mottled skin, or just her bloodshot eyes. She'd had a pretty face, but the skin sagged a bit here and there. Her green eyes were watery and her auburn hair was unnaturally stiff. Another drunk, he surmised. And he learned he was right when she opened her mouth.

"This is the guy?" she slurred a little to Ash.

Ash's back was turned to her and he didn't need to turn around.

Slowly, drawing out each word, he said, "This . . . is . . . the guy."

Flood figured Ash was mocking both him and this woman, who must be his new wife.

"Mr. Flood, this is my wife."

He didn't put a name to her but she sauntered into the room and the scent of gin in the air grew a little stronger. Flood shook her hand and introduced himself. She gave his hand a squeeze and said, "I'm Belinda Ash."

She sat down on the sofa next to her husband and crossed her legs. Somehow she looked better seated.

"What'd he say?" she said, and Flood wasn't certain whether she was talking to him or her husband.

"He hasn't said anything," Ash said impatiently.

Flood was starting to feel like he was in a strange dream.

Ash sighed and asked, "What's Jane paying you to pour salt in family wounds?"

Flood just looked at him now, knowing he knew better.

"Well, give me a number and I'll double it for you to drop the whole thing."

"Pardon me?"

"You heard me. Jane's acting like a fool. We both know how and why A.J. died. She didn't kill herself and she wasn't murdered, for Christ's sake. Honestly," he said. "Fifty thousand? Christ, I hope she's not stupid enough to pay you that much."

Flood was embarrassed, for them, he guessed. He didn't know whether there was anything further to learn here, but he didn't really care. He wanted to leave. He thought about saying something polite, but then just softly said, "No."

James Ash looked up abruptly, not so much disappointed as startled to hear somebody refuse him.

"I'll leave you alone," Flood said. "I guess you're concerned that something about A.J.'s death may embarrass your family publicly. I'm not an amateur, Mr. Ash. If a crime was committed, the police will handle that. If not, whatever I find will be sealed in an envelope and given to your ex-wife. I think I can find my way out."

Ash stood up, finally.

"Wait a minute, Mr. Flood. Don't get so excited."

Flood stopped and looked at him, waiting for an explanation.

"I take my family's reputation very seriously." He gave Flood a look.

"Ah. This was a test?"

Ash paused a moment.

"Well, Mr. Flood, you neither passed nor failed. But if you're asking whether I learned something about you, yes, I did."

He looked like he thought he'd been clever, and now Flood should feel flattered that he'd found his way into the great man's good graces.

"So?" was all Flood said.

"So," Ash said, sounding disappointed. "Whatever you need from me, just ask. But ask Mr. Skiddy, please. He has access to pretty much everything, and has the authority to act on my behalf. And I'd appreciate it if you'd keep me informed of what progress you do or don't make."

The new wife looked like she wasn't really understanding what was going on.

"I'm afraid I can only make reports to Jane Ash," Flood said. "She's my client. Maybe you can work something out with her or Mr. Swain."

Ash frowned, but then smiled. That wasn't what he wanted to hear, but given the last ten minutes of conversation it was

Flood's only possible response. Ash managed a shrug.

Flood nodded and said goodbye again. Nobody tried to stop him this time.

The Polish housekeeper was lingering in the kitchen, waiting to be summoned. She looked startled when he appeared in the hall unaccompanied. Quickly coming to his side, she peered back down the hall looking for her employers, and instructions.

"I'm leaving," he said.

"Ah," she said, hesitating. But when he continued toward the main hall, she caught up to him and paced ahead so that she could open the front door. When he reached the parking turnaround, the Land Rover was gone, and he noticed that the sound of the tennis ball had ceased. In his car, he opened the windows and drove too quickly down the lane, back to Sheridan Road. The miles of slow, winding asphalt through rich neighborhood after rich neighborhood was infuriating. He wished he was lying on some nameless expressway littered with plastic bags and beer cans, anywhere but here.

CHAPTER 12

"First of all, not one single, goddamned print," McPhee said.

"Anywhere?"

"Not anywhere that matters. Hers on the radio, the glove compartment and the hatchback. But the wheel, the ignition, the door handles and the console lid—all of 'em wiped clean. Try that shit on for size."

"That's not right," Flood said, very surprised.

"No, it is not. It is wrong."

The waiter approached and bent forward slightly, somehow knowing not to say anything just now.

McPhee gave him an appreciative glance out of the corner of his eye. "Bone-in ribeye, medium. Those potatoes you do?"

"Cottage fries, sir. They come with the steak."

"That's right. And the house salad."

"Very good, sir."

Flood said, "Same thing, but medium rare," and handed over his menu.

They were in the front room at Gene & Georgetti, drinking martinis and watching the entertainment of the bar, which was crowded with young women showing cleavage, their questionable dates, and old men drinking clear booze on the rocks and grimacing at each other, hoping the youngsters would take a hint and scram. One or two of them might have been connected Flood thought. Perhaps he'd seen them on a chart somewhere in the past. He was watching the old men dying up there at the bar, but he was thinking about A.J. Ash's Volkswagen Golf Tur-bodiesel.

"Somebody wiped the car down," Flood said.

"Mmm hmm." McPhee took another sip and bit into a skinny breadstick.

"Was there anything else in the car to explain that? Like a spilled Coke and a bunch of napkins on the seat, or anything?"

McPhee looked at him to let him know that if there had been any such indication he would have told him upfront.

It was still possible that she had wiped the car herself, either as a part of a routine cleaning or because she had spilled something. But coupled with the odd fact that the car had been left on the street, it seemed too strange.

"What do you think of that?" Flood asked.

McPhee grunted. "I think it bears further investigation," he said. "Tally was tied up and I talked to this kid, Fitzpatrick."

"What'd he think?"

"Said they'd look into it," McPhee said, shrugging.

"Look into what? What's that mean?"

"I don't think the kid knew what he meant. Dickens said he's bright, but I don't see it."

"Can you talk to Tally about it tomorrow?"

"Sure, but it doesn't really get them anywhere. Tells us there's something funny going on. Maybe they go over the car again and look harder, but I bet they don't find nothing."

The waiter appeared with salads. The restaurant was crowded, with a pair of couples waiting to be seated at the front by the door. Of all the great steakhouses in town, Gene & Georgetti was probably the most authentic, feeling as if this was how things had been done here for seventy years. Some of the other places felt like a bunch of sales and marketing guys got in a room and decided they were going to go overboard putting on a show about a steakhouse. G & G was basically an old tavern that had taken over rooms in adjacent buildings. The exterior and interior both felt a bit rickety, as if they wouldn't withstand a legitimate fire inspection. Not that there would ever be one.

The place to sit here was this front room, where the bar crowd and the diners waiting for a table would look at you and wonder who you were. The maitre d' knew exactly who Flood was, from the Westlake case, which put Nicky Bepps in prison for the duration. Some people said there was no downtown casino and never would be one because of Augustine Flood. Flood thought that was an exaggeration, and was glad the number of people who thought that, and who knew his name at all, was relatively small. Nonetheless, he had a good table at Gene & Georgetti whenever he called.

They ate the salads and ordered Chianti. Flood's phone vibrated in his shirt pocket and he fished it out and answered.

"It's Jane Ash," she said.

Flood was surprised. He had been led to believe all of their contact would be funneled through Philip Swain.

"Where are you?"

"Gene & Georgetti. Where are you?"

"I'm at home. Can you meet me tonight? I would like to hear what progress you're making."

It was eight-thirty and the steaks had not arrived yet.

"Is ten o'clock too late?"

"No. Meet me at the Peninsula bar. I live next door."

She hung up, and Flood folded his phone back into his pocket.

"The boss," he said.

"What's that about? Ten o'clock?"

He held up his hands. "I'll do what I'm told. She sounded like she had a point."

It was nine-fifteen when Flood and McPhee emerged from the

restaurant. They talked a moment about the next morning's plan.

"What are we gonna do about old Melvin?" McPhee asked.

"I'll run him through the databases in the morning and see if we can't come up with some other relatives and addresses. Somebody will know where the hell he is."

It could be a wild goose chase, Flood knew. Databases that searched for information about people tended to scrounge official public records to build their profiles. For a fairly transient criminal like Melvin Runyon, the information that it popped up could very well turn out to be bum leads. But there would almost certainly be leads on relatives.

The valet brought McPhee's Explorer around and Flood caught a cab and took it east on Illinois, up Rush a few blocks and onto Michigan. It was a clear, warm night and the Magnificent Mile was still crowded with people strolling and window-shopping under the glitter and glow of store lights. The cab dropped him on Superior at the Peninsula Hotel's front door just west of Michigan. Flood had never been to the hotel before, and was directed to an elevator that carried him up to the bar, which was all burnished wood and tawny leather upholstery. It was a fashionable crowd. The cocktail waitress was gorgeous.

Jane Ash was alone at a table sipping a highball that looked like gin and tonic. She did not see him immediately and he studied her a moment. She was wearing a black skirt and black satin pumps that accented good, tanned legs. She looked very different from the other day in Swain's office. Under a short suede jacket she wore a tight tank top that hugged her body. Her hair was sculpted away from her face with gel or something, and overall she just looked sleek and sexy. Finally, she looked up and met his eye. She raised her drink and smiled a bit as he started over and took the seat opposite her.

"What can I get you?" she asked as the beautiful waitress appeared at the table.

He ordered a bourbon and Jane Ash asked him if he'd enjoyed his dinner. Apparently she would not start talking business while he didn't have a drink in his hand. When he'd taken a few sips, he told her about Helen Schachter, the girl Humberto had seen leave with A.J.'s overnight bag, and then his recovery of the bag at Girls Refuge.

"My God," she said, as he took her on a tour of the Class Pets massage parlor in Roselle, and then his early morning visit to Austin.

"Did A.J. ever mention any of these girls? A black girl named Tamika, or a white girl named Britney. Especially the white girl."

"No."

"Child prostitutes at all?"

"Well, yes. She said that's how these kids survived, but nothing specific."

"What about this guy XO, Melvin Runyon? Did she ever mention him?"

She shook her head. "No. Do you think," she stammered a little. "Uh, do you . . . did he have something to do with A.J.?"

When the notion of a threat to her daughter had been no more than a theory Jane Ash had been fully, coolly composed about it. But now that Flood was putting together pieces of a puzzle that involved real people, she was clearly shaken.

"I don't know," Flood said. "I'm looking for leads and this is what's coming up. It seems that this girl Britney may have dropped out of sight at about the same time A.J. drowned."

"How do you know that?"

Flood was about to tell her but then caught himself, remembering how terrified the massage girl, Janna, had been. Divulging her identity, even to his client, would have been a betrayal of the promise he'd made to protect her anonymity.

"You'll have to trust me for a bit. I spoke to a person who did not want to be identified to anyone."

That alarmed Jane Ash further. What did his mystery source fear?

"Sometimes people are overly cautious," he said. "But I gave my word I'd keep the confidence."

She drained her drink and ordered another. This had not been exactly what she'd planned, Flood realized. Her reason for inviting him out for a nightcap finally dawned on him, and she had not bargained on hearing about disturbing progress. She had wanted to hear only what one person had said. Her ex-husband. Flood could see it in her eyes when he'd sat down. But now, he'd dropped some strange and troubling developments on her and she needed a minute to settle down.

Nothing happened until the waitress brought them fresh drinks, and then Jane Ash's expression changed enough to see that she was both upset and satisfied. Flood knew he was earning his keep, as far as she was concerned.

"Did you tell any of that to my husband today?"

"Vaguely."

"And what did he say?"

"He offered me double what you're paying to walk away from it."

She took that in and nodded slowly.

"Were you tempted?"

"No."

"It's a lot of money."

He smiled and took a drink. It was a lot of money to him, she must be thinking. It was money to play around with for them.

"But then I'd have no work to do."

She liked that.

"Even so," she said, a twinkle in her eye. She wanted a few more nuggets of this, and he guessed it was because she knew how her ex-husband must have been surprised. Maybe she also suspected it was merely a first effort from James Ash, and there might be more lucrative attempts.

"You're paying me a lot of money to get through obstacles in finding out what happened to your daughter. I wasn't all that surprised that your ex-husband was an obstacle."

She sat up, agitated. Flood had an investigator's skill—and habit—of studying the people around him without looking at them, and he could tell a few of the men in the room were more than aware of Jane Ash's presence and their attention was on her as she reacted to what he'd just said. She might be twenty years older and less physically stunning than most of the women in the room, but she was one of those women whose appeal was probably greater at fifty than it had been at thirty. And she was also carrying around the aura of freedom and confidence of being divorced and crazy rich. She flaunted nothing, but she was definitely something to look at.

"How could you expect that," she said, in an explosive whisper. "A.J. was his daughter. He wants to pretend it didn't happen."

Flood took another sip. "He's not pretending it didn't happen, he's just made up his mind that nothing good will come of finding out the details."

"He's afraid of the gossip."

"More or less. He thinks she got drunk or stoned and hit her head and drowned. He seems to be willing to accept the idea of never knowing whether someone might have been with her and failed to save her, and failed to report it."

He nodded his head to the side, noncommittally, and went on.

"It is what it is. I noted it and left," he said. "He seemed to be drinking in the morning, and the second wife is definitely an alcoholic."

"Is she?" She arched her eyebrows, seeming genuinely surprised.

"In my opinion."

"Interesting. She didn't seem to be when I met her, but that's a couple years ago. A.J.'s graduation." She took a drink and mulled Flood's report, then made eye contact again. "Maybe James is drinking just to get along with her. So, who else did you meet?"

"Donal Skiddy and the housekeeper, Magda."

She smiled fondly. "Magda's the only person I miss from that life. She's been there thirty years. Her mother before that."

"She seemed sort of anxious about my presence."

"Yes, I imagine. She's probably very distraught about A.J.'s death. I guess she came to the funeral and was a mess, though I wasn't in any condition to notice."

"Does she have any family of her own?"

Jane Ash took a drink and made a sad face. "Her husband left her years ago. She had a daughter A.J.'s age, actually. But the last I heard they weren't in touch often. The girl left home right after high school. James paid for her tuition at Lake Forest College, but that didn't work out. Anyway, she joined the military and then got married. I think she lives in Colorado, or someplace out west."

"Were she and A.J. friends?"

"They played together when they were little. But then when A.J. went off to boarding school, you know, they didn't really keep in touch. At that age, the whole bit with employer-employee stuff gets more awkward, I think. Anyway, Katja went to Regina Dominican, and when A.J. dropped out of Exeter and came back to New Trier, they just had different friends."

Flood didn't see how this history would help him much. A.J.

appeared to have little contact with her father's world, by choice. He wanted to move on.

"So, this guy Skiddy works for the company?"

"The Irish greens keeper," she said, a little derisively. "James found him in Ireland when he was developing a golf resort over there," she said, and then registered that she was getting ahead of herself. "You know how the companies are set up?"

"Not really."

"OK, well, Heidecke Tool is no longer in the family."

"I knew that. Sold to a German company."

"Right. That created all this cash. A billion dollars, roughly. James and his brother, Edgar, started this company that develops resorts. Neither of them really plays golf very well, but they've built courses all over the world. James and Edgar bought a little course in Ireland, along the southern coast, and were developing it into a big place about ten years ago and he found this guy Skiddy working as the greens keeper. Some kind of screw-up from a well-off family, or something. Anyway, they hit it off, and Skiddy came back and he's been James' right-hand man ever since. Pays him a fortune. He practically lives at the house."

"Does he bother you?"

"Oh, I was just joking. It's just that everywhere James goes, Skiddy's a half step behind. Makes all his travel arrangements. Keeps him entertained. James hasn't got any real friends anymore."

"I wonder if his wife is jealous?" Flood said. He almost told Jane Ash she sounded jealous, but decided that would be out of line.

"Maybe it's why she started drinking."

They finished their second round.

"It's late," she said. "What are you going to do now?"

He wasn't sure if she meant the rest of the night, or with this investigation. She seemed lonely and a little tipsy.

"McPhee, the man helping me, and I will continue tracking down this guy Runyon tomorrow morning."

"Ah," she said in a way that didn't clear things up about what she had meant. "Well, if you need anything at all, don't hesitate to ask Philip. You've made more progress in a day than the detectives had in two weeks. And another thing. I'd like to make these progress reports a regular thing. Philip's a dear friend and I've known him all my life, but he makes me a little nervous. And I hate to take up his time."

"That fine. What's today, Wednesday? I can check in Monday."

"Let's meet back here Friday. Same time?"

She was standing now, and she looked taller than she had the other day when he met her. The shoes, he figured, and maybe the difference between dark clothes and light clothes. They walked out together. The lights of the canopy over the hotel's front door blinded Flood a bit as he stepped out of the soothing, elegant lobby. The sidewalks along Superior and Michigan were less crowded as midnight neared but there were still many young people milling around.

"I'm just in here," she said, waving at the Park Hyatt next door. Many of the upper floors of the needle-thin tower were condominiums.

"OK. I'm walking the other way."

She nodded and he turned and left her there and started walking south, slightly uphill, down the Magnificent Mile toward his apartment.

CHAPTER 13

"What did the old lady want?"

"Not an old lady," Flood responded into the phone in his office.

McPhee said, "Ooh, I see. Well, what did the damsel in distress want?"

"Mainly, wanted to hear what her ex-husband said about her."

"What'd you say?"

"That he said she was a fool."

McPhee grunted and dropped it. He was home in Galewood. "Well, I'm about to start running some paper on Melvin Runyon, unless you want to do it."

"No, just email me what you get and we'll divide up the names and addresses. I'm going to try Pialetti out in DuPage. The girl at the massage parlor said this guy was running girls through that place for a while and keeping them in motels. Maybe they've heard of him."

"All right. Call you back in an hour."

Flood maintained plenty of law-enforcement contacts after he left the FBI, and one of the friendliest was with Jake Pialetti, a smart, connected investigator with the DuPage County State's Attorney.

Most of Chicago's far western suburbs were in DuPage County, from the cozy affluence of Hinsdale to sprawling Naperville. Most of DuPage was white and middle class, and it was home to the power base of the Republican Party in Illinois. After Cook County, DuPage had the largest population—about one million—of the six counties that made up the Chicago metropolitan area.

Flood tried to check in with Pialetti, preferably over lunch or beers, every six months or so. But it had been more than a year since their last conversation.

"The last time I saw you I thought you were going to have a heart attack," Pialetti said when Flood reached him on his cell phone.

The meeting had been over lunch, when Flood sought information in the Westlake case. Pialetti had stunned him with the news that the police were investigating the murder of a Jane Doe who fit the description of Marcy Westlake, whose husband had hired him to find her. The Jane Doe turned out to be a prostitute murdered by a john, unrelated to Flood's case. But in the end Marcy Westlake had met a similar fate.

"Don't remind me," Flood said. "As a matter of fact, though, I'm calling about a prostitution-related situation."

Pialetti chuckled. "C'mon. You're going to give my county a bad reputation. What is it this time?"

"I'm trying to get a line on a pimp from the city who runs underage girls out of a massage parlor in Roselle."

"Jesus. You get into the weirdest shit, Flood. Which place? There are three—all valued contributors to the county tax coffers."

"Class Pets."

"Oh, yeah. Pedophilia themes are always popular."

"Well, this guy apparently specializes in juveniles."

"And you're asking do we know him?"

"Right."

"I doubt it, but give it to me. I'll tell you we've prosecuted exactly zero pimps in the last five years."

"Really?"

"Nobody complains. The girls don't. The customers certainly don't. Anybody and everybody involved makes a miserable witness. There's never any evidence," he said. "We run stings from time to time, but they accomplish nothing. Handful of misdemeanor charges, couple grand in revenue from towing cars. Maybe a divorce lawyer makes a few bucks when wives read about their hubbies in the paper."

"You're not likely to have much intelligence on a pimp who's never been busted, then."

Pialetti asked for the name, and Flood spelled out Melvin Runyon and gave him his date of birth.

"Lemme look." Flood could hear Pialetti tapping at a keyboard. "Well, here's a CPD hit in I-CLEAR, but you probably already know that. Goes by 'XO'?"

"Yes, I started with the street name, and that's how I got his ID."

"Let me check the clerk's records. Here he is. Two hits. Moving violation, it looks like."

There was a pause as he scanned down through an electronic file. "Blew stoplight on Lake Street in April of last year. That's close to your massage parlor. Second case is older. Speeding in Bloomingdale on Army-Trail Road."

"An address listed?"

Pialetti read back to him the address on the West Side that McPhee and he had visited the day before. None of it told Flood anything new and he was frustrated.

"I'll talk to some vice people in the area and see if anybody knows this nitwit."

"That would be great, Jake. I'd appreciate it."

They talked a few more minutes before the other line started ringing and then Veraneace appeared in his door and whispered, "Billy."

He nodded and said goodbye to Pialetti and then tapped the other line.

"Hey."

"I sent it," McPhee said.

Flood wheeled around in his desk and checked his email. He opened the message from McPhee. "I see it."

"OK. Looks like he drives a black Chrysler 300 that's registered to the address where grandma said she don't see him ever. I got one address around Garfield Park that looks like it might be his sister, and that's really it in Chicago. But lots of addresses down in Mississippi."

"The old country," Flood said.

"Looks like they're all still down there," McPhee said. "Clarksdale, Tutwiler, Webb. All those are places close to each other in the Delta, about an hour south of Memphis."

"You have family down there?"

"Helena, Arkansas. Across the river."

"Let's look at the spot in Garfield Park."

"Gimme a half hour and I'll pick you up in front of the office."

Flood hung up and walked out into the main room of the office. Veraneace was paying utility bills now that there was money in the firm account.

"Where's Jamie?" he asked to her back.

"School. He left you a file of stuff he said you wanted. On his desk."

Flood walked over to Jamie's desk. There had always been a snapshot of Jenny on it. She was Jamie's best friend from their Art Institute days, and he had been the one who insisted Flood meet her. As Flood sat down, he didn't see the photo immediately. The file Jamie had prepared was front and center on the desk. Once he had the file in his hands he spotted the photo, moved to the back of the desk, partially hidden by a stack of books. Flood figured Jamie had moved it in deference to him. It was the right thing to do. Her smiling face and the carefree, loving look in her eyes seemed like a different woman who no longer existed for Flood. It was as if he had not gotten there in time after all and Jenny, at least his Jenny, had perished that freezing night. Flood carried the file and walked over to one of the sofas and sat down.

Jamie had typed pages of contact information for the names of A.J. Ash's acquaintances and relatives that Flood had given him at lunch the day before. There were five names, including some cousins and Warren Riordan, the young investment banker who was romantically interested in A.J. Detective Tally said they had talked to him and dismissed him as a possible person of interest. Suspect was too strong a word for the circumstances.

A.J.'s brother James was also listed in Jamie's file, although Swain had already given Flood his contact information. Little good it had done. The guy wasn't thirty yet, but he had a secretary who ran interference and shielded him from people like he was CEO of a Fortune 500 company. Multiple calls had gone unreturned.

Jamie had managed to get cell phone numbers for the others and with the minutes remaining before McPhee arrived, Flood started calling.

Two of the cousins, sisters, he reached together in New Hampshire where they spent their summers. They'd been there since a week before A.J.'s death. They flew home for the funeral and that had been the first time they'd seen her in three or four months. Neither of them seemed to have enough guile to lie about something like this.

"Did A.J. have any friends she sailed with on the lake?" Flood asked Evelyne Ash, the daughter of James Ash's brother, Edgar.

"Not any more. Not since my father moved to California. We all used to sail with him as kids," she said. "There was this guy who A.J. was sort of seeing. She told me once in, like April, that he wanted to take her out on his motorboat, when it would have been way too cold. She thought it was funny."

"That's Warren Riordan?"

"He works for Richmond Merriam?"

"Yes. They were actually dating?"

"Oh." She laughed, a humorless chuckle. "Probably too strong a word. I don't know if he really liked her or just knew what he had on the line."

"A very rich girl."

"Yes."

"Did you ever meet him?"

"No. I travel a lot for work and I don't have a lot of free time in Chicago. A.J. and I rarely saw each other, which is so sad now."

She didn't sound that sad, he couldn't help but think.

"You work for the resort company?"

"No, I work with Scott."

"Who's Scott?"

"A.J.'s brother. Sorry, nobody calls him James. Scott is one of his middle names, and he's always been Scott or Scotty. Um, we do private equity. I'm in the Chicago office, Scott's in New York."

"I see," Flood said. "Tell me, Evelyne, what does your heart tell you happened to A.J.?"

"Oh, I don't know. I don't want to believe she committed suicide, and I don't blame Jane for hiring you. But I'm afraid it's something like that. Otherwise someone would have been there. There'd be a witness, you know? I don't believe she would have been alone unless she was in a really bad frame of mind. It makes me so sad. None of us really saw it coming."

He thanked her again and was about to hang up when he thought of something.

"I need a favor. I've actually been trying to reach A.J.'s brother and can't get through to him. If you work with him, could you perhaps ask him to call me?"

When Flood stepped outside, it was hot and muggy out. The sky was quilted gray and silver, making Wabash as dim as mineshaft under the L tracks. Flood stepped off the curb and came around McPhee's black Explorer to get in the passenger side. Inside, the air conditioner was humming.

"Where we going?" Flood asked as he settled in.

"Flournoy and Springfield, roughly," McPhee said as he wheeled the truck back into traffic on Wabash and headed for the Congress Expressway, which would turn into the Eisenhower and deliver them to the West Side. Traffic was light and it took him fewer than five minutes to reach the Independence Boulevard off-ramp at the south end of Garfield Park.

"Her name is Virginia Jackson, she's thirty-five, which makes her six years older than Melvin," McPhee said. From the records McPhee had gathered, it appeared she was the only person living at the address, which was the first-floor apartment of a three-flat.

They were coming down Central Park past a liquor store with men and boys scattered on the steps when Flood's cell phone rang.

Flood had tried twice to get A.J.'s brother on the phone. And then he'd talked to Evelyne Ash and twenty minutes later Scott Ash was calling him.

"I'm grateful that you're helping my mother with this," he said.

"I'll do my best to find out what happened," Flood said.

Scott Ash said thanks again and Flood asked if there was anything out of the ordinary about his recent contact with his sister.

"Not really. The normal course of things was that I'd call her

whenever there was a decision being made about her money—
which was every couple of weeks, usually. She'd have absolutely
no interest, and then we'd talk for twenty minutes about family
stuff or whatever, you know."

"Did she talk about men at all?"

"No, I don't think she was dating much. She was fairly merci-
less about turning guys down, actually."

"Do you know why, why she wasn't interested much in dating?"

"Not really. My armchair psychology would be that she was
pretty reckless when she was younger, and she'd kind of done a
one-eighty. And I think she's got more, um, relationship issues
than I do because of our parents' divorce."

"Why did your parents break up?"

"I don't know. The usual reasons, I guess."

Scott Ash was reluctant to go there, so Flood decided to
push a bit.

"Most marriages break up over one of two things: money or
affairs. I doubt your mother and father had money problems."

"I don't really want to talk about it," he said.

"Fair enough, I don't mean to pick at personal things. I'm
just trying to get at A.J.'s frame of mind, to see what matters
and what doesn't."

"Yeah, I don't really know. I wasn't really asking for details
back then, you know?"

"OK. Can we talk a little more about friends or boyfriends? I
don't really have a handle on who she was spending time with
here in Chicago, other than maybe this Warren Riordan guy."

"I don't think she went out much. She was really into that
job working with homeless people. Do you, like, have her phone
records to see who she called?"

"Yes, that's why it bugs me. She didn't call anybody. It's
almost all work, some calls to your parents."

"My mom?"

"Both. Is that out of the ordinary?"

"No," he said. "They're her parents."

"What about kids you grew up with?"

"Uh, probably not. Most of them would have more in common with me than A.J.," he said. "Investment banking and trading and stuff. And a lot of those kids still party pretty hard. That would definitely not have been A.J.'s thing these days. And, you know, screw them. Very few of them even could be bothered to come to my sister's funeral."

"Oh, that's too bad. Who did come?"

Scott provided a couple of names but was iffy on spellings and had no other information. The interview ground to a halt, and Scott Ash returned to his gratitude theme.

"Again, thanks so much. This is very important to my mother."

"No need to thank me. It's my job."

"Sure," he said, and then hesitated. "Um, please don't put that stuff I said about A.J. being screwed up over the divorce in a report or anything. I'm just talking and I don't really know."

"I won't. But I need to know this sort of thing. Like whether she was depressed, or suicide was a possibility. It's an avenue I can't ignore."

"I know. I don't know what to think. A.J. really kept to herself with emotional stuff, at least with me. All I really know is that it makes no sense to me that someone would hurt her."

"What about one of those men she was blowing off?"

"Maybe."

"You know this guy, Warren Riordan?"

"No."

"She saw him a few times recently."

"Never mentioned him. Who is he?"

"An investment banker, about your age, but I think not really in your league."

"Who's he work for?"

"Richmond Merriam."

"Oh, wait. I think Evelyne may have mentioned that guy. Sorry. But A.J. never said a word about him. You're suspicious of him?"

"I don't know. He has a boat and A.J. had been out with him on it at least once. I'm just trying to size him up at the moment."

"Maybe I should call him."

"I'd rather you didn't. Let me figure him out, if you don't mind."

Scott Ash agreed and then seemed to do his best to answer the rest of Flood's questions. But it was a struggle to get details. It was clear brother and sister weren't terribly close. He was better acquainted with her money than he was with her personal life.

Flood snapped his phone shut and McPhee put the Explorer back in gear and eased back into the street.

"What did you learn?"

"Very little. I don't think A.J. shared much."

Virginia Jackson's West Side neighborhood was among the worst spots in the city for drug dealing and regular violence, but her block was trying to live it down. None of the houses was boarded up, though a few looked truly dilapidated, with handfuls of young men camped out on their porches. Her three-flat was fairly tidy. The front stoop even sported a potted plant with plump green leaves. McPhee and Flood climbed the steps and rang the bell. A girl of about fifteen answered, keeping the aluminum screen door locked as she opened the front door a few inches. In the shade and dimness of the interior, Flood could barely make out the features of her face. She didn't say anything audible but just stood there.

"Ms. Jackson home?" McPhee asked.

The girl shook her head.

"She at work?"

"Yes."

"My name's McPhee. This man's Augustine Flood. We need to speak to Ms. Jackson. You got a number where we can reach her during the day?"

"No, she's at work."

McPhee sighed.

"Where's she work?"

"County."

"County-what, miss? What office?"

"I 'on't know."

"For real?" McPhee curled up the words at the end.

The girl merely repeated her ignorance.

"OK. What time's she get home, then."

" 'Bout six."

Flood held out a business card and stuck it between the door and the frame. "Please, ask her to call us when she gets home, OK? Thanks."

The girl looked back at McPhee and he gave her a disapproving look before she shut the door.

Going down the steps, McPhee was annoyed while Flood fished his cell phone out of his pocket.

"We didn't try very hard," he said.

"It's OK," Flood said, the phone now at his ear. "Hey, it's me." He was talking to Keith Reece at the *Tribune*.

"You sound lucid," Reece said.

"I've got work. Do me a favor?"

He gave Reece Virginia Jackson's name while the reporter ran it through his database of the Cook County payroll.

"Assessor's office. Hired in '93; making forty-five. Just says clerical."

"That's got to be downtown, right?"

"Could be a suburban courthouse. Where's she live?"

"North Lawndale."

"Probably down here."

They got back in the truck and left Virginia Jackson's block by the west end of the street, and as they came north on Springfield, Flood saw another fresh shrine of teddy bears and balloons tied to a tree. McPhee saw it, as well.

"Another fallen soldier," McPhee said.

"I guess things aren't cooling off out here."

"Things never cool off in 11. Never-ever."

McPhee hit the gas as they roared down the ramp back onto the Eisenhower. They parked in a deck on Lake Street where the PA system on each floor played a different city-themed song to help parkers remember where they had left their cars. Flood and McPhee parked on "By the Time I Get to Phoenix."

"Think you can remember Glen Campbell, Billy?"

"I hope I can forget."

They crossed Lake and walked past the James R. Thompson Center, which was once called the State of Illinois Building before somebody decided Big Jim—one of the few former governors in recent memory not to end up in federal prison—had earned a fifteen-story glass and steel bubble. Across Randolph was the County Building and City Hall, one hulking neoclassical fortress that housed chunks of both governments. The city occupied the west side of the building and the county had the east. The county also had the Daley Plaza, a Mies van der Rohe skyscraper across Clark Street, and another high-rise at the south end of the plaza, 69 West Washington. But the assessor's office was in the old building. McPhee and Flood took the elevators to the third floor and waited in a short line.

McPhee had the touch, so Flood let him ask to see Virginia Jackson. In no time he had the middle-aged black woman at the counter walking back into the rear rooms of the office, asking, "Where's Ginny? Y'all see Ginny?" They heard the question grow fainter with each repetition until it ceased. Five minutes passed and the woman reemerged, accompanied by a younger, fairly slender woman with short-cropped hair wearing a crimson smock that bore the emblem of the office.

She whispered, "I don't know them," to the woman who had gotten her, but kept walking up to the desk and gave them a puzzled hello.

Flood apologized for bothering her at work, and then explained that he was a lawyer conducting a private inquiry for the family of a deceased woman. He said it this way to make it sound as devoid of suspicion as he could. He didn't want to call it an investigation, certainly not a death investigation. If he could give the vague impression that her brother might be named in a will he would have succeeded. But she wasn't really buying it.

"We're looking for your brother, Melvin."

"Don't you mean XO?" she said, rolling her eyes.

Flood and McPhee played dumb, figuring it might help to seem ignorant of his street identity.

"I don't know where he is," she said. "I hear about him through our grandmother, but he knows not to come around my house anymore. I've got young girls I'm raising."

"Is there someplace he might stay in Chicago, other than your grandmother's?"

"He's not in Chicago," she said. "Best thing you can do if you really need to talk to him is leave a message with my grandmother. She might seem like she wants nothing to do with you, but she'd give him the message."

"How do you know he's not in Chicago?"

"Because he comes around her house when he's in town, and he hasn't been around in two weeks. I talk to her every day," she said as she started to roll her eyes. "He's probably on one of his business trips."

"What kind of business?" McPhee asked.

She gave him a look that said it was one thing for a white man to play her for a fool, but McPhee was another matter. She looked back at Flood.

"You know as well as I do what business my brother is in. Now, leave me alone. I got nothing to do with Melvin."

She walked back through the doorway and vanished without another word. The woman who had gone to get her looked up at them from her desk and arched her eyebrows a little but said nothing as they walked out. In the long marble lobby of the building they could see that it was pouring rain outside now. They decided to wait it out at a diner across LaSalle Street on Randolph.

"What's she mean?" McPhee asked.

"I don't know, recruiting trip. Working the girls out of town. I really don't have a handle on the sex trade."

"What about Mississippi?" McPhee asked.

"What about it?"

"I don't know," McPhee said. "Something that woman wasn't telling us. I believe she doesn't know anything about his pimpin' business. But I don't believe she knows nothing about where he is now. That makes me think family."

"Mississippi?"

He shrugged.

"Well," Flood said. "Those towns are pretty small down there, aren't they?"

"Clarksdale's about fifteen thousand. Rest of them mostly in the hundreds. Real small."

Flood nodded and said, "Maybe the locals pay attention when

shitheads from Chicago show up for R&R."

McPhee nodded that it wasn't a terrible idea as their food arrived. Flood put a fork in his omelet with one hand while dialing information with his other. He asked for the non-emergency number for the Clarksdale, Mississippi police department.

"Hello, ma'am," he said, putting the fork down. "My name is Augustine Flood. I'm a lawyer up in Chicago and I'm looking for some help. . . . That's right. Well, thank you. Do you have an investigations or detective unit? . . . You do. Captain Fry. I see. Is he available? . . . I see. Well, I'd sure like to talk to him . . ."

He gave her his number and said thank you another dozen times and then hung up and finished his omelet. They were drinking coffee and watching the rain pound the pavement outside when his phone buzzed and the caller ID showed a 662 area code.

Captain Fry was more than agreeable when Flood explained who he was, who he had been and what he wanted. He had not heard of Melvin Runyon, but the county was chock full of Runyons and their close cousins, the McDades. Captain Fry seemed to view the fact that Flood was interested in Melvin Runyon as a matter of immediate concern to Clarksdale's public safety. Either that, or he didn't have much to do. Anyway, he took down the plate number for Runyon's car and said he would put all the family addresses on his afternoon rounds and call him back later in the day if he saw anything. Flood thanked him over and over again, and set the phone on the table. The rain had stopped finally.

"Captain Fry is on it," he said, smiling. McPhee had heard most of the conversation because of the volume at which Captain Fry spoke when he was excited.

"It sounds like it," he said. "Let's get the hell out of here. I'm starting to smell like onion rings."

Chapter 14

Flood was at the office trying to track down Warren Riordan when the phone rang at six.

"It's Cap'n Fry in Clarksdale, Mr. Flood. Your boy Runyon's down here."

Flood was astonished. "He is? Where?"

"Out on Sharkey Road. There's a little town out there, about ten miles southeast of here. I seen the car parked in front of a trailer where Marlon McDade lives. Must be his cousin. You want me to pick him up? Marlon sells dope and I'm sure they got something they shouldn't have sitting around there."

"Um, hold on. Let me figure a couple things out and I'll call you right back. Thanks a million, Captain."

Flood hung up and took a breath. Melvin Runyon was not directly connected to A.J. Ash. He was connected to a teenage prostitute who was connected to A.J. He was pursuing all leads, but now he had to decide whether this was a waste of time. He made up his mind, and called Philip Swain's cell phone.

"I think I need to go to Mississippi for this."

"Explain," Swain said. He sounded slightly impatient.

"A.J. was working with a teenage prostitute who has been missing since about the same time A.J. died. This girl's pimp also abruptly abandoned Chicago at the same time. I've found him in Mississippi."

"Do you think the girl is with him?"

"I don't know."

"Well, what do you think?"

"I think that it may be more than a coincidence that these people left town immediately after A.J.'s death."

"Then go to Mississippi."

He called McPhee.

"Pack a bag."

"Clarksdale?"

"Captain Fry found him in some cotton-field trailer park or something."

"I'll be damned."

"I'll get us on a flight to Memphis in the morning," Flood said. "You should probably at least leave a message for Tally, right?"

"I'll call him."

Flood called Captain Fry back and told him that he and a retired Chicago homicide detective would be coming down.

"Well, all right," Fry said loud and clear.

Fry volunteered to show them around when they got to town, and even gave him the number of the motel. Flood booked two tickets to Memphis, rented an SUV and a pair of rooms.

He called Jane Ash. She had the same stunned reaction as the night before. Flood was taking an abstract feeling, an aspect of her grieving, and turning it into a living, breathing villain. There was a man out there named Melvin Runyon, aka XO, and the man investigating her daughter's death was hunting him down.

"What do the police say?"

"My associate, McPhee, is telling them."

"So what do you think he did?"

"I don't know. But I have to talk to him. And the girl—he probably knows where the girl is."

Flood hung up the phone in his private office and walked out into the main room. As he crossed through the doorway, a moving figure outside in the hallway caught his eye. His front windows were fitted with top-down shades, and he could just make out a crown of curly dark hair, and a silhouetted figure abruptly moving out of sight. Startled, he walked slowly over to the door, which was old and closed loosely. He supposed he was talking on the phone loudly enough that someone could have been listening. Flood opened the door and saw no one in the corridor, but then heard footsteps clattering down the marble steps. He closed the door hard and ran down the corridor after the footsteps, which seemed to quicken as Flood began to make his own racket in pursuit. The building was mostly deserted at this hour and the corridors were empty. It was two flights down and when Flood reached the lobby he found nobody. He ran to the front door and onto the sidewalk and looked up and down Wabash in the fading light. There were people everywhere, but he did not see the curly dark hair. The man was gone.

Flood went back into the building, checked the men's room on the first floor but found it empty. He went back up the steps, briefly looked around on the second floor and then climbed back to the third floor. He went into his office, marked the spot where he'd seen the top of the man's curly hair and judged it against his own height. About six-foot-two, he figured. He did not have much more he could do about it, so he locked the office and started for home.

On the walk back to his apartment, he checked in with McPhee again.

"Tally said good luck."

"Did he say anything more about her car being wiped down?"

"Naw. They got another child shot out there. Twelve-year-old boy this afternoon."

"Jesus."

"He wasn't lying. It's a real war out there. I haven't seen it like this since crack."

"Well, I don't know what to do about that car, but it bugs me."

"I know, it doesn't fit."

"Somebody was snooping around the office tonight."

"Like how?"

"I was on the phone and came out of my office. There was a guy standing outside in the hall. Up close to the glass. I couldn't see his face because of the shades, and he ran. I chased him out of the building but didn't see him."

"You get any kind of look at him?"

"Not really. All I can tell you is at least six-one and curly dark hair."

"Huh. Tally said that kid Riordan has curly hair. His interview in your file?"

Flood stopped walking. He opened his briefcase and took out the folder he was keeping on the investigation. The detectives' supplemental reports, which were used to record subsequent developments in the case after the initial death report, were clipped together. He found the interview with Warren Riordan on his boat at Diversey Harbor. Tally had noted curly brown hair, and the information recorded from his driver's license said six-foot-two, 190 pounds.

"Goddamn," Flood said. "I think it's time I paid him a visit."

"I'll come with you."

"No, stay put and get ready for tomorrow. The flight's at eight-thirty. I'll take care of him and call you after, OK?"

"Hmm. If he's stalking you, it might not be a bad idea to take me along."

"It'll be fine. I think I can handle Mr. Riordan."

"Call if you change your mind."

CHAPTER 15

Diversey Harbor was shaped like a chili pepper and was part of a larger lagoon that stretched south of Fullerton Avenue, lying along the west side of Lake Shore Drive. It was part of Lincoln Park, the center of North Side affluence. All of the vessels in the harbor were motorboats, because access to the lake was under Lake Shore Drive, a clearance far too low for a mast. In fact, most of the boats were similar to Warren Riordan's 25-foot Sea Ray, cabin cruisers that were large enough to hold their own on a lake that routinely produced four-foot swells when the weather kicked up, but small enough for the average yuppie to afford. Most of the grander yachts were moored at Belmont Harbor a half mile north, or at the yacht clubs downtown.

Flood parked near the boat launch and then walked down in the darkness to the tree-lined concrete path that met the docks. In Detective Tally's supplemental report, the man who lived on the boat next to Riordan had said he spent most of his nights on his vessel. He remembered the night A.J. Ash died because nobody was on the boat. Riordan lived a short jog away in an apartment building that towered over the park, and usually stopped by the slip at least briefly. Flood could see Riordan's building from where he stood, just on the other side of St. Joseph's Hospital. The condo tower was a secure building and if Flood was going to surprise Riordan, he'd have to find him here at the boat.

As he scanned the hundreds of boats that floated before him

he thought for an instant that he had made a mistake not ac-
cepting McPhee's offer of back-up. But he pressed on. Tally had
noted the slip number in the report, for which Flood was thank-
ful. He never would have found the boat on his own. Lights
flickered on the dark water and voices carried to him from near
and far. But the first thing he realized was that the docks were
gated, with steel mesh doors and wings that extended over the
water to keep people from grappling around them. The locks
were controlled by a keypad. He located Riordan's dock, found
the gate was indeed secure, and then retreated to a park bench
on the concrete path and waited.

Ten minutes passed before a man came along, laden with
shopping bags from different stores—food, liquor and marine
parts—and Flood saw his opportunity. He came out of the
shadows holding his cell phone, as if he'd been standing there
on a business call and let the man pass. He said goodnight to
his imaginary caller and then caught up with the man with the
packages, just as he struggled to reach the keypad with all the
bags.

"Can I help you?"

The man, fiftyish, heavy and sweating, looked back and nodded. "Just grab the gate, maybe."

Flood watched him punch in a five-digit number, memoriz-
ing it, and then pulled on the gate when the lock clicked.

"Thanks, buddy. Go ahead of me, if you want."

Flood offered to carry some of the bags, but the man refused
so he went on ahead, the coated metal planks under his feet
swaying a little on their floats. As he made his way down the
dock counting slips, he realized that Riordan's boat was occupied by several people sitting on the back deck drinking beer
by candlelight. A girl was laughing as a young man told a story
but they all fell quiet abruptly and looked at Flood as he stopped
at the boat's stern. There were three women and two men, but

neither male was Riordan. One had dark hair, but it was cropped close and he was short. The other could have been Riordan's height but his hair was blond and straight.

Flood smiled.

"Hey, sorry to interrupt. Is Warren around?"

The short man spoke up. "He's on his way. You wanna hang and have a beer?"

"Oh, no. Thanks. I'll just catch him later. He work late?"

"Yeah, and said he had an errand to run. We all work with him. Are you a buddy of his?"

"Sort of." Flood decided it was time to tell a lie in order to forestall a cell phone call from one of the friends that might spook Riordan and keep him from showing up. "I was visiting a friend two docks down and I was just going to stop by and say hey. I'll catch him later. Enjoy your night."

They all said you too, and Flood turned and ambled nonchalantly down the dock. The man with the bags had turned into a slip and boarded a larger cruiser. He didn't notice Flood passing, heading back to wait for Riordan at the end.

Flood sat on the park bench again and fixed his gaze on the walk leading north. Riordan could come from either direction, but his apartment building was about two blocks north, so Flood figured he'd be on foot coming from that direction. Another five minutes passed and then a man came jogging down the walk from the north, dressed in baggy khaki shorts and an unbuttoned and untucked dress shirt. From the curly brown hair, Flood recognized the head that had been spying on his office. He waited until Riordan was even with him before standing up, startling the young man.

"Warren."

Riordan spun to the side to face Flood, slowly backing away and then freezing. He said nothing.

"You came to see me but didn't stick around to talk."

"Uh, what are you talking about?"

"An hour ago you were outside my office, eavesdropping. I came out to see you and you ran away. Don't tell me it wasn't you. I got a good enough look at you."

He offered another denial that didn't even register in Flood's ears. He just kept staring Riordan down until he cracked.

"Why are you after me?" Riordan said, like a boy whining.

"I'm not after you. I want to talk to you about your friend A.J.'s death. You haven't returned my call and then I find you sneaking around outside my office and running away."

"I wasn't running. I left. I didn't even see you."

"OK, Warren. Let's say you didn't see me. You're just a really fast walker. As long as I'm here, why don't we talk about A.J.?"

He put his hands on his hips and nodded his head back a little bit. "She was a really great girl. It's really awful what happened." His tone carried just a hint of that frat-boy chauvinism that Flood liked so much.

"I see," Flood said. "She was a great girl. Who wasn't in a huge hurry to be involved with you."

He shrugged after a moment's thought. "It was casual."

"When was the last time you talked to her?"

"Couple days before she died. We were talking about going out that weekend."

"Not the day she died?"

"I left a message but we didn't talk."

This was true, as far as Flood could tell from the phone records he'd seen.

"Did you ever take her out on your boat?"

"Sure, bunch of times."

"When was the last time?"

"I don't know, maybe a month ago."

"Late May. So you took her out a bunch of times before June first? Pretty chilly on the lake."

Riordan looked annoyed. Flood was teasing him over the exaggeration.

"Maybe just once or twice. I don't know."

"Once, or twice?"

"Once, maybe."

"Maybe," Flood said, not asking. "Here's the thing, Warren. You're a good-looking kid, with a good job and a nice resumé. But I looked into you. You're from Glen Ellyn. That's not exactly the east side of Sheridan Road, is it?"

"Screw you, man," he said in response to the slight. He started to walk away.

"Warren," Flood said calmly, a little frighteningly. It stopped him. "A.J. was a beautiful woman who came from a shitload of money and a world that people like you and I know nothing about. You caught her eye for ten minutes, and you got a peek at that life, and it looked pretty damn good. But she kept you at arm's length. And that must have been a bit frustrating, especially since it wasn't like she was burning through three guys a week. And, Warren, you've got a boat. This is why you're a person for me to be interested in."

Flood studied his face as he took in the logic of it. His eyes finally narrowed.

"You're accusing me of doing something to her?"

"I'm looking for answers, and I look at you and see nothing but intriguing questions that you don't seem to want to explain."

"I didn't do anything. I told you, I didn't even see her that day."

"OK. Where were you the night she died?"

"The cops already asked me that. I was home watching TV."

"What time did you leave work?"

"I guess around seven-thirty."

"What time did you get to your apartment?"

"About eight."

"You work late much?"

"Yeah, of course."

"Take the bus home?"

"No, I usually cab it."

"Anybody with you?"

"No."

"Was A.J. the only woman you were seeing?"

He made a sour face. "I'm done talking to you. You're not a cop. This is bullshit."

"Was she the only woman you were seeing?"

"Yes."

"Did you tell her you wanted to see her more?"

"No."

"Warren?"

"You don't know. She just had a lot going on right then. It was cool. We were going to see more of each other when things calmed down at work. For both of us."

"Did you argue about wanting to spend more time with her?"

"No."

"Why did you feel the need to come to my office tonight?"

Warren was flustered and seemed out of lies. "I don't trust you. You're not a cop. Why should I have to talk to you?" He sounded like a kid.

"OK, Warren," Flood finally said. "Next time you come to my office, just come on in and say hello. The door is usually open."

Flood walked away, back up the concrete walk toward the south end of the parking lot. He listened for the sound of the steel gate opening but heard nothing. He didn't need to look back to know Riordan was still standing there watching him.

Chapter 16

The Memphis Airport was small, old and hot. It was, however, not crowded and Flood and McPhee were grateful for that. Their rental car was a blue Nissan SUV and Flood let McPhee drive because he knew how to get to Highway 61. They crossed into Mississippi and drove about ten miles through sparse suburbs before the hills relaxed and rolled out into long stretches of flat farmland drying in the sun. It was ten forty-five in the morning and about ten degrees hotter than it had been in Chicago.

"You told Fry you wanted barbecue?" McPhee asked.

"I told him I wanted to buy him lunch. He presumed I wanted barbecue because I'm from the North."

"You sound like you don't want barbecue."

"Barbecue's fine, even though I just had it with you the other day."

"Oh, well, eating barbecue in Chicago, even at Lem's, isn't the same as getting it down here. The wood's different or something."

"I'm looking forward to it."

"Abe's is well-known. You should be full of anticipation and excitement."

"I am delighted. Didn't I mention that I'm delighted to be eating Abe's barbecue today?"

"What, are you hung over again?"

"No, I am a moderate drinker once more. I promise."

"Veraneace said you patched things up with Jamie."

"It's fine. I wasn't mad at him."

"You're mad you let her go?"

Flood shrugged. He didn't want to talk about it.

"She didn't ask. She needed to make a change and she made it. That's it."

"You're sure that's it?" McPhee pressed on.

"It's not one of those things where you win her back by doing something crazy."

"It's about what happened."

"Yes. It doesn't matter whether it's my fault or not. What happened, happened."

"It's too bad."

"Yes, it is," Flood said. "Anyway, Jamie's earning his paycheck again. I told him to go through the Ashs' divorce file. I still can't rule out suicide for this girl. Maybe there's some indication in there that the mother's not telling me about."

McPhee nodded, understanding that there would be no more talk of Jenny.

There were cotton fields and old pole barns, irrigation systems spread across fields like pipelines of swing sets, blasting water into the southern heat. They went through Tunica and south of town ran past a line of casino marquees. Another twenty miles and they hit Clarksdale. The town looked rusty and weedy, baking in the Delta sun. Abe's was tucked back behind a laundry and a pawnshop at the intersection of Highways 61 and 49. The spot was marked by two big blue guitars crossed against each other, mounted on a pole with a sign that said *The Crossroads*.

"Here we are, on hallowed ground," Flood said, noting the Church's Fried Chicken, a gas station and a lot of other strip mall clutter that littered the famous intersection.

McPhee pulled into the parking lot. Captain Fry was stand-

ing in the middle of it waiting for them. He was a fat little hair-
less man with dark glasses and dark gaps in his smile that made
him look like a pale jack-o-lantern. He was hatless in the sun,
wearing a t-shirt stretched thin over his belly and tucked into
blue Dickies—the black semiautomatic velcroed to his belt the
only thing giving him away.

When McPhee parked, Flood noticed he had plenty of spots
to pick but chose the one next to two women who sat chatting
in a gleaming white Escalade with a stars-and-bars Ole Miss
decal in the back window.

The thing to eat at lunch was pulled pork sandwiches on
plain white bread and iced tea. Fry didn't bother with barbecue
sauce, but Flood and McPhee squirted it on from plastic bottles
on the table.

"Sharkey Road on down past Webb," Fry said, his mouth
full. "I'll run you down there after we're done. You might not
find it on your own."

"Does Melvin Runyon have any kind of record down here?"
Flood asked.

Fry shook his head. "Your Chicago gang members come
down here to lay low. They do what they do up there, but they're
usually quiet as church mice down here. Maybe they go to the
casinos in Tunica when they get antsy, but that's about it." He
couldn't contain his curiosity any longer. "What'd he do?
Somebody sent two private detectives down here, like y'all—ex-
FBI, ex–Chicago police detective—something's going on."

"A girl drowned in Lake Michigan," Flood said. "Nobody
knows how it happened, but she was doing social work with
young prostitutes. Runyon's a pimp to some of the girls. A few
things don't add up and we need to talk to him."

Fry grunted his approval. "Somebody's got deep pockets."

Flood nodded and changed the subject. "We're looking for
one of the girls, too. Fifteen or sixteen, blonde."

"White? I don't think so. That'd stick out down here if she was running around with the McDades."

Fry glanced at McPhee—a sheepish, southern white man's look at a northern black man, who was more than his equal, to see if he'd offended. He hadn't and McPhee let him know.

"I would think it would."

"She the one you really after?" Fry asked.

"Probably," Flood said.

When they finished eating Flood paid the bill and they followed Fry, who drove his unmarked Crown Victoria out to the intersection. It put a little smile on both of their faces as they turned east onto 49 and headed out of town. The Crossroads. Flood looked at the strip mall clutter in one direction and the warehouses and feed stores in the other, and wondered exactly where it was that Robert Johnson allegedly sold his soul to the devil. They drove southeast on Route 49, and after miles of country, and a few blink-and-miss towns, they passed through a place called Webb. They turned off on a real country road that started to wander haphazardly along the flat, bottomland cotton fields, with a line of trees that edged a bayou in the distance. After ten minutes of this, Fry pulled to the gravel shoulder and got out.

"Half a mile up is Sharkey. Ain't much but a little store and about ten houses. There's a green house just the other side of that store, long gravel driveway by it that goes back to a double-wide trailer. That trailer is McDade's place. You should see your fella's car parked back there."

He made sure they had his cell phone number, told them not to shoot anybody without calling first, and then wished them luck and turned around and headed back toward Clarksdale.

They stood there on the pavement until the sound of tires on hot asphalt faded out.

Flood said, "I'll be good cop. You're crazy, unbalanced bad cop."

"Sounds about right. But I guess we'll play it by ear. See what the situation calls for."

The Chrysler 300 with Illinois plates was parked under a tree beside the trailer, just like Fry promised. McPhee drove in fast and slid to a stop on the gravel behind the car, blocking it in. In Flood's experience, nobody in the world drove like big-city cops. The vehicle was always a weapon and most cops handled it much better than they did a gun.

The trailer was a mess. Its seams were badly rusted and mold stained. A small, uncovered porch was built onto the entrance, rotting from lack of paint, and missing a few floor boards. One window was slid open but another was still covered in plastic sheeting and duct tape to stop the damp drafts of last winter. Through the open window they could hear a television playing too loudly. While Flood stepped up and knocked on the front door, McPhee jogged around back to make sure there was no back door. A sleepy woman in a long t-shirt decorated with a faded Tweety Bird finally came to the door. She looked about twenty and was followed by the smell of stale, unwashed clothes. Flood handed her his business card and then told her what was printed on it.

"Tell Melvin to come out, please. We need to speak to him."

She squinted back at him. "Who?"

"XO," he said and then turned around and pointed at the Chrysler. "The guy who drove that car down here from Chicago."

"He ain't here."

McPhee came up the steps. "Oh, he's here, all right. Bring his ass out or we'll invite ourselves in."

"We'll call the police."

"Police?" McPhee said. "How you think two boys from

Chicago found your asses out here."

The woman looked scared, and Flood felt bad about it. She hadn't done anything wrong. But she was harboring Melvin Runyon, or XO, or whatever he was called down here, and they weren't here to ask pretty please for her help. They were here to lean on people, or worse. He was a pimp of children and if they needed justification to push people around a bit, that was plenty.

"How long are you going to stand here arguing?" Flood said coldly.

She tried to stare him down but her eyes seemed to retreat into her head. In the midst of an awkward moment, they heard a dull thump come from inside the trailer. McPhee instinctively jumped down and trotted back around to the side of the trailer. He threw up his hands. "Fuck! There he goes."

"Window, shit," Flood said to himself. He gave the woman one last look and saw that she was really scared now, fearing repercussions. McPhee was already running to jump in the Nissan. They piled in and he wheeled it around and into the pasture behind the trailer. A muscular, shirtless man in knee-length jean shorts was sprinting away, his braids flopping wildly as he ran. He was making good time toward the banks of the bayou and tree cover about three hundred yards off. McPhee hit the grass and then rumbled on, gaining on him quickly as the interior of the Nissan bumped and shook violently. The runner tried to shift direction but it was no use, there appeared to be nowhere in sight the Nissan couldn't go. They were now thirty feet behind him but he showed no sign of giving up. Flood sized up the space left before they reached the trees and water.

"Let him run out of gas. If he's still going up by the trees we'll cut him off."

As they got farther into the pasture the turf became chunkier, and Flood and McPhee both put a hand against the ceiling to keep them from bumping their heads as they bounced around.

160

The grade rose slightly and they came over a little hill, dipping suddenly and unexpectedly.

They saw the rusty hunk of metal an instant too late. The Nissan lunged over the rise and came down hard on a jagged, twisted old piece of car chassis. The impact sounded deadly, like two cars crashing, though the impact was all on the underside of the vehicle. The right front tire blew out like a rifle shot with an echo. Obscenities flew. The Nissan careened. But McPhee wrested the steering wheel back and hit the gas.

"Sonofabitch!" Flood shouted.

The view through the windshield blurred with the shaking, but the Nissan surged ahead. They could probably keep this up for about ten seconds. Runyon had stumbled as he dodged the junk metal and McPhee was able to pull even with him. Flood flung the door open and leaped out, hitting the ground in stride, stumbling but regaining his feet and running hard at Runyon. Runyon cut to his right, but Flood was close enough and dove, tackling him around the knees. They both went sprawling. Flood rolled on top of him, pinned him down, resting his weight on Runyon's sweaty, slick back. McPhee was out of the truck and added his knee to Runyon's neck. Chest heaving and sweat pouring, Runyon was hysterical. "Can't breathe! Fuck, man. Fuck! I didn't do nothin'!"

"Calm down," Flood said.

"Damn, boy," McPhee said to Flood. "That was some serious Urlacher shit."

Runyon couldn't catch his breath, and now Flood noticed his chin was bleeding from hitting the ground.

"I'm filing charges on your asses," he shouted at them when he finally hauled in a breath, then started coughing.

McPhee was still in Bears play-by-play mode: "*Special* Agent Brian Urlacher makes a spectacular, come-from-behind, game-saving tackle."

Flood ignored him and shouted at Runyon. "Sit up and shut up for a minute. We just want to talk to you."

"About what?" Runyon exclaimed, now alert enough to be truly frightened. "This is crazy."

Flood laughed. "What do you mean, about what? If you're running from us, you know damn well what it's about—A.J. Ash drowning in the lake and a teenage hooker you run named Britney. That's what, jackass."

Runyon made a crazy face and hunched his shoulders. "I don't know nothing about no woman drowning."

"How'd you know A.J.'s a woman?"

"What?" His face twisted again, like it was *them* making no sense. He had on a pair of wraparound gold-tinted sunglasses that now had a plug of grass lodged in the bridge of the nose, making him look utterly ridiculous.

"We have no patience for lies, Melvin. You understand?" Flood said.

They stood there for a moment letting Runyon catch his breath, letting the facts sink in. He was alone in a field in the middle of nowhere with two men who appeared ready to harm him if he didn't tell them what they wanted to know. His chest still heaved, and Flood wondered if he had asthma or just hay fever. The field was covered in long, scrubby grass that crunched underfoot a bit, but the only sign of the livestock that it fed was a slight smell of manure in the air that mingled with the funk of river muck breezing off the bayou banks fifty yards off.

Flood hadn't run very far but the adrenaline and the bumpy ride had brought the smoky taste of barbecued pork bubbling back to his mouth, making him wish they had come straight out here without stopping for lunch.

"Let's take a look here," McPhee said, bending down to examine the blown tire and the undercarriage of the Nissan. "Melvin, you going to help me change this tire?"

Runyon looked at the flat, bewildered by the shifting tone and focus of the two men. He turned back to Flood. "Who are you?"

Flood took yet another business card out of his pocket and flung it at him.

"I'm working for A.J. Ash's mother," he said. "Time to talk. Why'd you pick now to come down here for a visit?"

"I'm seeing cousins. Don't you ever visit family?"

"Is that right?" Flood said. "Hmm. Well, everybody I've talked to who knows you described you as such a dependable business-man. And then one day you and your top girl just vanish. Poof. No forwarding address. Here you're saying you bugged out to Mississippi for a family visit while all your customers back home are wondering what happened to you. And so much money to be made letting pedophiles fuck a fifteen-year-old girl. What's the going rate for that?"

Flood could see the wheels turning slowly as Runyon tried to decide who had talked to Flood. "I don't know what you're talking about."

"You'll figure it out in a minute. I guarantee."

Runyon looked back at McPhee, who was pretending to pay him no attention while he continued looking at the wheel.

"I go where I want, when I want," he finally offered.

"Did you bring Britney with you?"

"I don't know what you're talking about."

McPhee turned around from his inspection of the flat and smacked Runyon across the back of the head with his open hand. "Quit fucking around, Melvin."

Runyon winced and rolled over on his side, making a face. "You must be the *real* police, Sambo. You Burge's monkey or somethin'?"

Jon Burge had been a notorious white Chicago detective com-mander in the 1980s who oversaw the torture of black suspects.

McPhee did not appreciate the reference. He took hold of Runyon's ear and twisted until the man was on his feet, howling in pain. McPhee shoved him against the Nissan. Flood watched, waiting for Runyon to crack.

"Listen to me, motherfucker," McPhee said, stilling hanging on to his ear. "You selling little girls' bodies to perverts. Don't talk to me about Burge. You won't walk out of this mother-fuckin' field. Now, we're in Bumblefuck, Mississippi. Them dumbasses on the porch got no idea who me and him are, and I guarantee nobody with a badge down here would break a sweat figuring out who beat your black ass to death. I will hurt you, motherfucker. So you better look at that man over there and start answering his goddamn questions."

Runyon started to grunt something that McPhee took as defiance but he didn't get it out. The heel of McPhee's hand hit him full in the mouth and bounced his head off the roof of the Nissan. Runyon cursed and sounded teary.

"Look up at that man," McPhee said into his ear. At last, Runyon, holding his bleeding lip, timidly looked up at Flood.

"What's her real name?"

"Britney?"

"Yes."

"Her name's Kelly. With two Es. Kellee. I don't know where she is, man. She split. I split."

"Why? And don't tell me about your cousins. I know you left town after A.J. Ash died."

"I don't know, man. Kellee knew her, not me. She was freaked out after that chick got killed. Drowned or whatever. She split, I figured she had something to do with it. When I heard who she was—rich, North Shore shit—I split, too. Figured they'd come after me because of Kellee. I didn't expect 'em to send no fucking assassins after me."

McPhee and Flood both laughed.

"What's her last name?"

"I don't know. She ain't got a driver's license or nothing."

"Because she was fifteen," Flood said, letting his blood rise again. "Probably fourteen when you met her and started pimping her. Where'd you meet her?"

Runyon didn't answer. He was thinking.

"Come on," Flood said. "Don't make my friend smash your head into the car again."

"Mall."

"OK, which mall?"

"I don't remember."

Flood cleared his throat and McPhee took a hard step at Runyon, raising his hand.

"OK," he cried, shrinking away and trying to cover his head. "Downstate. Peoria."

"Oh, you have cousins in Peoria too?"

"That's where I met her."

"Recruiting trip?"

"I had business."

"So her name is Kellee and you met her at the mall in Peoria. You know nothing else about her, except you think she had something to do with A.J. Ash drowning. Is that your story?"

"It's the truth."

"Give me your cell phone."

Runyon made another one of his grimaces.

"The one sticking out of your pocket, genius."

"You can't just take someone's property."

McPhee reached down and roughly snatched the phone out of his pocket and tossed it to Flood. He scrolled through the numbers and found a Britney entry with a Chicago area code. He called the number but got a disconnected message. He kept clicking, looking for a Kellee entry, but there was none.

Perhaps there were other girls in the phone who would have

had contact with Kellee. He went back to the beginning of the phone list and started scrolling. Nothing stood out.

"Where are your other girls? I'm not seeing names here, Melvin."

"My other girls don't have no phones. I take care of them."

"Who takes care of them when you're down here visiting cousins?"

"They on their own."

"So you don't really take care of them."

"They know I'll be back."

"Where were you that night?"

"What night?"

Flood just looked at him.

"I was with my girls. Out on Cicero."

"Kellee didn't work the street. Where was she?"

"I don't know, man. You have to ask her."

McPhee had him by the ear again.

"Aww. She was with some trick, man. Hotel downtown. I don't know. I don't keep an *itinery.*" He subtracted an unnecessary syllable.

"She told you A.J. was dead?"

"No. I ain't seen her."

"Since when?"

"That night. That hotel trick. She split."

"So how'd you find out?"

Runyon started to raise his arms, "You know, I just heard it on the street. Girls talking about it. Britney gone. That bitch rich. I figured she knew something about it and there'd be trouble. I come down here to chill. That's it!"

It was the raising of his arms that told Flood he was lying. Most of what he said seemed to be plausible, but this was the first time he'd gestured and it just screamed *I'm full of shit.* McPhee saw. He'd seen it thousands of times more than Flood, this kind of gesture.

McPhee bent down by his ear.

"You're lying." He said it softly.

"That's the truth."

Flood said, "Woman's dead. You've got nothing to do with it, you hear it secondhand, you've got girls making money on the street, and yet you pack up and come on down to see Cousin Pookie. That's not what happened and you're not leaving this field until you tell me what the fuck did happen. In ten seconds we're both going to start hurting you."

Flood was pointing at McPhee. The whole thing was getting more unpleasant by the second and Flood knew he was approaching the line where he'd lose his nerve. McPhee looked like he had about had it with this routine, as well.

"This is bullshit," Runyon said.

"You ain't got but a few seconds left, dipshit," McPhee said, mocking Runyon's speech.

Runyon recoiled a little and looked like he might brace for the worst, but then he seemed to relent, unable to bear it.

"A'right. Kellee saw the bitch that night. Wasn't no hotel trick. That's all I know. Kellee split. Then I found out bitch is dead. I knew they be coming after me."

"Why was she seeing her?" Flood asked. The scenario sounded true, and that was a relief.

"I don't know. Probably talking about how they was gonna cut my mo'fuckin' throat or something."

"Which brings us to you. A.J. was trying to help your star girl get out of the life. You don't like that. Makes you a prime suspect."

He shook his head.

"I got plenty of girls want to work for me. That one splits, I got five more behind her, you understand?"

"Bullshit," Flood said. "You had one white girl who looked

like an escort you could work in the hotels downtown and a bunch of 'hood rats you were grinding into the pavement on Cicero. Kellee was your franchise."

Runyon just shrugged.

Flood thought about it. He certainly didn't believe Runyon would let go of his girl so easily. Even if he could replace the income with some hustling, his pride would be at stake. On the other hand, why the lake? Runyon was a West Sider. Perhaps it was the aftermath of some trick Kellee turned downtown. Still, it wouldn't make much sense for him to kill A.J. Ash by the lake, where he would be out of his element. The question compelled him to let it go. So far this wasn't very satisfying. They'd beaten the crap out of a pimp who may or may not have known anything of any use. Either way, they had gotten little of value out of him other than half a name and a probable hometown of Peoria.

"So when are you going back?" Flood asked.

"Soon as I can."

"What's keeping you?"

"I ain't gonna be scapegoated."

Flood raised his eyebrows. "For this? I doubt it. You've got a rock-solid alibi. You were pimping your hos out on Cicero, right?"

"Whatever."

"And what about Kellee? Maybe you can persuade her to come back home where she belongs, with you."

"She won't pick up the damn phone. Man, I'm out money. That girl brought it in," Runyon said, getting animated. "If I knew where she was I'd be right there with her."

McPhee was rummaging in the back of the Nissan and came out with a tire iron in his hands. He twirled it in his hand in view of Runyon's worried eyes.

"I'm serious, man. I don't know where that bitch is."

Flood and McPhee just looked at him. Runyon looked at the tire iron and slowly shook his head.

"Maybe I heard she might try L.A. or Vegas. That's all. Bitch don't answer her phone. I got no idea she even really there. She always talking about L.A. How she was going there."

"You base this on what? Somebody told you she went, or she just talked about it back in the good old days?"

Runyon looked up like it was an unfair question. "That what she said."

McPhee shrugged. He moved on and started in with the jack to lift the Nissan.

Flood and Runyon watched in silence as he used the tire iron on the lug nuts and pulled off the flat. He dumped it in the back of the Nissan and then bounced out the spare. When he was finished he got in the truck and drove it in a wide circle, to see if the damage was more than just the tire. He pulled around to Flood and rolled down the window.

"Guess it's OK."

Flood turned back to Runyon, who was standing and awaiting their next move.

"What made her such a moneymaker?"

"What you think? She's a freak. Doing that little school girl thing. You know, Britney. Britney Spears. Rich mo'fuckers eat that shit up."

"You put her picture on the Web?"

"Hell, no. She ain't but fifteen. Looked fourteen. I keep that shit under wrap. Don't need no task force and shit coming down on my enterprise."

"Who's got a photograph of her? A current one."

He gave another evasive shrug, saying nothing. But his hand nudged his empty pocket, seemingly involuntarily. The pocket that had held his phone.

169

"Ah," Flood said, looking at the screen in his hand. He found the menu and then the photo selection. They were numerous.

"You're an idiot, Melvin. Anybody ever tell you that?" he said as he scrolled through. Black girls, white girls, Hispanic girls, skinny, fat, naked, clothed—most of them in various poses—some performing sex acts on a man who would logically have been Runyon, documenting the encounters with his cell phone camera. Creating evidence. Among them was a pretty brown-eyed blonde wearing a white blouse, black necktie, red plaid skirt and white knee socks. He found a photo that was not obscene and showed it to Runyon.

He nodded. Flood sent the photo to his own phone. He then scrolled through his own contacts and found the cell number for Special Agent David Mulaney, an old colleague who worked on the FBI's sex trafficking unit. He started sending him all the photos.

"What are you doin'?" Runyon said. It was taking a while.

McPhee, who was slouched behind the wheel of the idling Nissan, pulled a chewed toothpick from his mouth and threw it at Runyon, hitting him on the side of the face.

"Don't make me get out," McPhee said. "Sit there and shut up."

When Flood was finished he called Mulaney's number and got voicemail.

"It's Flood. I just sent you a bunch of photos from a pimp's cell phone. Don't dump them. I'll explain."

He threw the phone back at Runyon, who wasn't ready for it and flinched. He gathered that Flood had just sent evidence of child pornography and sexual assault to the Federal Bureau of Investigation. He made a sour face.

Flood asked, "How much did Britney make for you in a day?"

It seemed a serious question to Runyon so he answered.

"A grand."

"OK. We're coming back tomorrow morning. You'll be here," Flood said, leaving no room for debate on the issue. "If you can put me in touch with Britney, or Kellee, or whatever her name is, I'll pay you half a day's profit from selling her fifteen-year-old body to God knows who."

"Five hundred for her phone number?"

"Not quite. I want her on the line talking to me. Not some number that she's not going to pick up."

"When I get my money?"

"It's not your fucking money yet."

Flood got in the Nissan and leaned across McPhee so he could look at Runyon through the driver's side window.

"You make it happen and we'll drive you to the bank."

McPhee smiled at Runyon when Flood sat back.

"You be out here," McPhee said. "I have to come find your ass, it's gonna be unpleasant."

He eased on the gas and the Nissan rolled through the grass, leaving Melvin Runyon standing alone in the field.

Chapter 17

The motel was everything Flood had hoped it would be. Deserted. Some walls not covered in mildew. They sat in Flood's room with a view of a ditch and nothing to drink, and called Captain Fry.

"We've got a night to kill," Flood said.

"You probably want to go on over to Ground Zero. You know, Morgan's in town."

"Morgan?"

"Freeman. The movie star. He owns Ground Zero."

"It's a bar?"

"A blues club. Across the street from the blues museum. You know where you are, right?"

"Right. The crossroads."

"Uh huh."

"Morgan Freeman is from here?"

"Charleston—about thirty miles east."

"Cool." Flood didn't know what else to say. "Can we buy you a drink?"

"Thanks, but I got a boy to look after. So how'd it go out there?"

"OK. We talked to him. We made him an offer for some information and he's thinking about it. We'll go back out in the morning to see him."

"Give you any trouble?"

"A little. He ran. We caught him."

"Yeah, OK. Anything I need to hear about?"

"I don't think so."

"All right, then. You have a good one. Tell Jeannie behind the bar over there I sent you and she won't bite."

McPhee said he was going to take a nap. When Flood went back to his own room, he called Swain's office. The secretary said he was tied up and would call. While he waited he took the Nissan down the road, which was cluttered with shabby stores and strip malls building up to the climax of a new Wal-Mart at the very end of town. Among the clutter was a liquor store that was the product of some odd tradition or regulation: All the booze was shelved behind the counter and you pointed and the clerk—a stooped old bald man in short white sleeves—would fetch. Flood bought a bottle of Jack Daniel's and was paying when Swain called him back.

"You're in Mississippi?" the lawyer asked.

"We found the pimp. He claims the girl saw A.J. the night she died. Also claims he has no idea where she is."

"You believe the former but not the latter?"

"That's right."

"Whatever it takes."

"I offered him five hundred dollars to remember where to find the girl. He's sleeping on it."

"Is that enough?"

"We're pushing the limits of decency as it is. He's a child pimp. If it can be bought, that will do it. He's terrified McPhee will accidentally kill him on purpose."

"Use your discretion. I'm not worried about five hundred dollars."

"I figured."

They were about to hang up but Swain said, "Jane is pleased, so far."

Flood wondered if he had figured out that she was meeting

with Flood and was bent out of shape about it. He didn't bring it up.

"Well, we haven't answered any questions yet. We've only found some of the right people to ask."

Flood took a shower and then filled a plastic motel cup with ice and whisky. McPhee knocked on his door at five o'clock and they sat sipping drinks and watching CNN, feeling like it was bringing dispatches from another planet. The Mississippi Delta, Flood thought. Strange place.

McPhee's phone rang. It was Detective Tally. To their surprise, he wanted an update. The lack of fingerprints in A.J.'s car had caught Lieutenant Dickens's attention. The case wasn't front burner yet but it was on the stove, apparently.

Tally asked about Melvin Runyon.

"We're in process," McPhee said. "He knows something. Flood thinks there's a girl we need to find—little teenage hooker. All we got's two different first names. One's a street name."

While McPhee listened to the phone, Flood sat up and snapped his fingers.

Into the phone, McPhee said, "Hold on, Curtis, the *special* agent has an idea."

"Ask him to go back to Helen Schachter," Flood said. "The woman who runs the homeless program, and get the ID on our girl. Kellee—with two Es. It'll be in A.J.'s client files. I know she's got it."

"You catch that?" McPhee said into the phone. He listened and relayed the response. "He'll have Fitzpatrick call her. Might need a subpoena, though."

Flood thought a little more and wondered if he'd spoken too quickly. "Ask him to hold off until tomorrow."

Tally heard and told McPhee he wouldn't get to it until the next day anyway.

McPhee asked how things were in Area Four. Bad. Three murders overnight and a radio car responding to shots fired in Garfield Park got into a chase and hit a light pole. The officer driving was in serious at Stroger. Vice Lords on edge. Police on edge. Very bad.

"I haven't seen it this bad in fifteen years," Tally told him.

"Get home safe," McPhee told him.

They bantered a bit more.

"It's all turned around down here, man," McPhee said before hanging up. "Negroes living in the country and all the Escalades driven by white ladies in khaki pants."

When McPhee hung up he drained his cup and poured a fresh whisky.

Flood called Helen Schachter and got her voicemail. He begged for Kellee's name and date and place of birth. He said they'd found the pimp. Flood feared Kellee was in danger, and if she didn't give him the information the police would be asking for it, and he wasn't sure how they would treat her. He left his number.

Flood drained his own cup and stood up.

"Let's go find Morgan," he said.

"Huh?"

CHAPTER 18

"Are you Jeannie?" Flood asked.

"Yes, I am." She was pleasantly plump, stuffed into jeans that looked like they would pop if dinner time rolled around. Frizzy hair, no makeup and a Ground Zero t-shirt.

"Captain Fry sent us over to make sure you weren't watering down the liquor."

"I bet he did. Where y'all from?"

"Chicago."

This brought a two-minute refresher on the Blues Highway. When she took a breath they ordered Budweiser.

"You see Morgan?" she asked.

"We heard he's afoot," Flood said.

"You just missed him."

"Maybe we'll get another chance."

"You should eat at his restaurant tonight."

"I thought this was his place."

"It is, but he and Bill have a gourmet restaurant, too. Madidi."

"What the hell," McPhee said.

"It's wonderful."

"Who's Bill?" Flood asked.

"Morgan's partner."

McPhee raised an eyebrow.

"Business partner. Bill's a lawyer in town."

Clarksdale was a small town by any standard and everybody

176

knew each other's comings and goings. The addition of genuine celebrity to the mix was disorienting.

"Where's Madidi?"

"Couple blocks. It's not cheap, but it's worth it. Y'all should have a few beers, go on over and eat dinner and then come back for the band."

Nobody had a better idea. It was a quiet walk through the deserted streets of the small downtown. Madidi was on a forlorn main street corner next to an appliance store with an empty showroom save for a single dusty dishwasher that looked used. But the restaurant was slick, polished wood and exposed brick, big canvases on the walls. A cheerful hostess seated them in the empty dining room and sent out an equally cheerful young waitress who said her name was Joy.

"Where y'all from?"

"Chicago."

"Have you seen Morgan?"

Flood ordered a bottle of very good pinot noir. The menu said things like roasted duck breast with red pepper corn cakes, black-eyed peas and truffle cranberry reduction. Eventually a second bottle was ordered and they continued to enjoy the undivided attention of Joy. McPhee finished the lemon cheesecake and drained his coffee cup.

"Joy, what time you get off?"

She was handing Flood the credit card slip to sign. She had been flirting with him and, when she took their first empty bottle away, McPhee had said it wasn't just boredom.

"An hour," she said. "You guys got a big night in Clarksdale planned?"

"We're gonna find Morgan," Flood said.

"You just missed him here."

"I'm not surprised."

"Well, we're going back over to the other place to hear some band," McPhee said. "Augustine Flood, here, wants to buy you a drink."

Flood penned in a twenty-five percent tip and said nothing until she asked, "You named after Saint Augustine?"

"More or less."

"He had a wayward youth."

Flood smiled. "So I've read."

"I might see you over there. Slade Family is good."

"They're the band?"

"Yeah. From Oxford. Real good."

They walked back and got lost, wandering around a couple of blocks until they found the railroad tracks and followed them back to the bar. By this time they were more than half drunk and in a quandary about what to drink next. They'd gone from whisky to beer to wine. They weren't the sort of men who ordered glasses of merlot in a bar, so a fork in the road lay ahead.

"Back to beer, I guess," McPhee said. "Don't touch the whisky again. Hell to pay."

Flood ordered Jack Daniel's and McPhee looked up at the ceiling and said make it two.

"Where the hell is Morgan?" Flood asked Jeannie the bartender.

"You just missed him."

The bar was a cavernous old warehouse with a twenty-five foot ceiling, decorated in junk, road signs and old blues posters. The Slade Family played electric Beale Street blues under colored lights. The acoustics of the place were a bit loose and boomy, but none of the college kids or goofy blues tourists seemed to mind. Flood and McPhee left the bar and sat back in mismatched folding chairs at a table in the middle of the room.

And then came Joy. The starched white shirt and snug apron had given way to a tank top and low-rider jeans. A belly ring.

Fit as a fiddle. And her blonde pony tail had been set free, in a shoulder-length flip that had a habit of drifting partly over her face when she laughed. She came to the table loaded up with a gin and tonic and two more whiskies on the rocks. McPhee cursed.

"Find Morgan yet?" she said.

"We think he's from Alabama," Flood said.

"He'll show," she said, nibbling on the stir straw. "So you're a lawyer and you're a detective?"

"Retired," McPhee said.

She nodded, no longer their server. "Y'all are downright mysterious."

"Speaking of mysteries," McPhee said. "Small town. Pretty girl. No ring."

"You saying I'm too old to be single?" she said, laughing. "Four years in the Army. Three years at Mississippi State. Now I'm in law school in Oxford."

She looked at Flood. They had something in common, didn't they?

"What kind of law you do?" she asked.

"I specialize in gray areas," Flood said.

"Clarksdale is a gray area, all right."

"We came down to take a sort of deposition."

"Huh. Maybe we'll learn about *sorta depositions* in third year."

She smiled like she knew somebody was up to something.

"I don't think we're gonna see Morgan tonight," Flood said.

CHAPTER 19

The banging on the door would not have awakened Flood. Joy had to nudge him.

He sat up, expecting the room to spin, but it wasn't so bad. Good wine, he thought. Thank God they hadn't gone back to beer He put on pants and a shirt, peeking through the hole in the door. It was Captain Fry and some others. The man looked terrified. Flood opened the door.

Fry gave him a searching, pleading look, his mouth bending into an anxious, unhappy grin.

"You got to put on your shoes and come with us."

His *shoes.*

Fry looked past Flood into the room.

"Joy, get dressed. I'll have Larry run you home, girl."

"Wait a minute," Flood said. "What the hell's going on?"

Fry studied him a minute.

"Melvin Runyon's dead. His cousin found him in his car out there in Webb with his brains blowed out. Said you and your friend come out there today and beat hell out of him. We both know that's at least partly true."

They separated Flood and McPhee. Flood was interviewed by a Mississippi State Police detective named Wilmer. He seemed to have been given the impression that Flood was a sleazy private investigator and it was just a matter of time to get a murder confession out of him.

"Do you have the 9?" Flood asked.

"You know damn well it wasn't a 9, it was a .45." He slapped his hand on the table for effect.

"Oh, for Pete's sake," Flood said. "Go get a real cop. I'm not talking to you."

The idiocy of the interrogation, until dawn, helped distract Flood from the queasy despair he felt about what had happened. They had roughed Runyon up a bit. They certainly had threatened worse. But the bottom line was that they weren't finished with him. They had made an offer for information and had reasonable hopes of a deal to find out where the girl, Kellee, was. Flood told the state cop none of this. Finally, as the fluorescent light was giving way to the cool gray dawn filtering into the room, Fry came in and the trooper left.

His shortness and weight hung hard on him, like humiliation. He looked at Flood with betrayed eyes that said, *you gave me your word.*

"You better tell me *something.*"

"I'll tell you everything, Captain. I would have told you three hours ago if you hadn't sent that idiot in."

"Murder happened in their jurisdiction, technically."

"That doesn't bode well for solving it if they're all like him."

"Start from the beginning."

He did. Dead girl. Rich family. Child prostitutes. XO.

"What did you do to him?"

"Slapped him around a little. But I told you we offered him money and were going back out there this morning. I need to contact the girl. He was my access to her. Now he's dead."

"Two of you are pretty much alibied," Fry admitted.

"What time did he die?"

"Between nine and eleven, probably."

Flood shrugged. "Joy was with us the whole time."

"And you longer," Fry said, not being funny. Flood sensed

181

resentment for the carpetbagger from the North. "Joy's my second cousin."

Flood nodded. "Sorry to involve her."

Fry didn't nod back. That was that.

"So, who do you think killed him?" Fry asked. "I don't know what all he was up to up there in Chicago. But your gangbangers come down here all the time to hide out with cousins and aunts and uncles when they get in trouble."

"We don't think he was heavily involved in the drug trade. Doubt it was that."

Flood was realizing what this meant—that the murder of Melvin Runyon and the death of A.J. Ash were probably connected. That meant she was probably murdered, too. He probably owed this to Fry, but it was just a theory, and he didn't want to talk about it yet. He'd have the Mississippi State Police dogging him at every turn if they thought his case was their case.

He just shrugged.

CHAPTER 20

Tally seemed genuinely frightened by the news. He was looking at it two ways. First, his friend, a black man, was being questioned in a murder investigation deep in the heart of Mississippi, and who knows what the locals would do. Then there was the trouble of himself helping McPhee and Flood with active investigative files, and it had turned into a real mess.

Tally's boss, Lieutenant Dickens, called McPhee.

"What the fuck, Billy."

"Ain't what it looks like, L. T."

"Really? That's good, because it looked to me like you and Lagoff were making me look like an asshole for helping you. Tell me how getting witnesses killed isn't making me look like an asshole."

McPhee was already pissed off by the whole thing, and Dickens didn't help. He wasn't feeling remorseful.

"It looks like we got into a homicide investigation that you all were intent on calling a suicide by stupidity. That's what it *looks* like. We're in the middle of a goddamn mess because we're the only ones looking seriously at it."

"Well, don't call us for help anymore. Consider yourselves cut off."

Runyon had been shot as he sat behind the wheel of his car, parked at an abandoned gas station in Webb, the little town about ten minutes outside of Clarksdale and a few miles from the trailer where he had been staying. The only thing Fry would tell Flood was that there was a forty-five-second phone call to Runyon's cell phone from a pay phone in town, three hours before his body was found. Flood and McPhee had been seated at Madidi's when the call was made. Fry finally released them, and they discovered the location of the pay phone when they went to Abe's for lunch, after showering and checking out of the motel. There was a state police evidence crew set up around the pay phone outside the pawnshop next door to the barbecue joint. There wasn't much else to learn from the scene so they drove past into the barbecue's parking lot.

They were starving and ordered sandwiches, rib tips and beans.

"Now what?" McPhee asked.

"I have to call Swain," Flood said, pulling out his phone. He saw that he had a message. It was Helen Schachter saying call her.

"I have deep reservations about this," she said when he got her on the line.

"Nobody else is going to know you gave it to me. And nobody is going to look for her unless they want to hurt her."

"What will you do when you find her?"

"I'll call you if you want. I can offer her some money," he said, thinking he'd give her at least the five hundred earmarked for her pimp. "But she knows something and I need to know what it is."

There was a pause.

"If I give you this information, I could lose my license."

"Like I said, nobody will know."

"Kellee is spelled with two Es. Middle initial M., and it's L-E-O-N-A-R-D. Born 2-23-90 in Peoria. Mother is a Janice Merrian, Creve Coeur, Illinois. Do not screw me over, Mr Flood."

184

CHAPTER 21

Veraneace put them on a Memphis to St. Louis flight, with a puddle jumper to Peoria. They landed at midnight, rented a Buick and asked directions to Creve Coeur. Not far, it turned out. It was just down the road on 4-74, the Peoria bypass. The road wound though the darkness in wide sweeps, rolling through the last hills of the river valley. They crossed the Illinois River over narrows south of town on a double bridge set aglow by the beacon of a river barge coming north. Veraneace had put them in a motel in East Peoria. It seemed Creve Coeur was a poor suburb of East Peoria, which was a working-class suburb of Peoria. There was a packet from the fax machine waiting when they checked in. An Accurint database run on Janice Merrian, with mapped directions from the motel to her trailer court. She was forty-one, the registered owner of a 1992 red Lumina. An ex-husband named David T. Leonard, and another, perhaps current, mate named Brian Merrian. But he had a different address, in Pekin, Illinois.

McPhee was reclining on the other bed with his shoes off and a Jack and Diet Coke in a plastic cup.

"Where's David Leonard live? That'd be her daddy."

Flood flipped a couple pages. "Hmm. Maybe Germantown, Tennessee."

"Oh, fuck that," McPhee groaned. "I ain't going back down there."

"We'll try the mom. And it looks here like there's a David

Leonard, Jr., who lives in Peoria. Age twenty-one. Kellee's brother, I guess."

"Maybe the brother's a better shot than the mom."

Flood stood up, stretched and glanced at the mirror. He looked like garbage. Planes did that to him, especially when they were surrounded by hours of driving and fast food. He had unpacked the bottle of Jack Daniel's but took none for himself. He was thinking about Kellee Leonard. This was the first place she had disappeared from—the fringes of a slightly shabby rust-belt town. Why had she run out, and not run back when her flight turned out to be an adolescence of prostitution? Things were bad here, he guessed. Mom was in a trailer park, with two husbands who looked estranged. A brother was twenty-one. Maybe there were beatings. Maybe there was sexual abuse, or worse. Talking to any of these people could be touching a live wire.

"Let's split them up," Flood said. "I'll go to one, you go to the other. We won't talk to either until we've both found them. We'll hit them at the same time."

"Mom and brother?"

"Yes."

"Keep one from shutting the other up after we visit?"

"They all seem like bad apples to me."

"I hear you. Who you want?"

"The brother."

"I figured. You think he's the key."

"It's mom's job to protect the kid. This girl's less than 150 miles away servicing the paying customers of Melvin-fucking-Runyon, and she doesn't come home. There's a reason for that. If she's in touch with either, it's him and not her."

"Unless he's the one mom didn't protect her from."

"Then we're probably wasting our time."

"We'll need another car."

The Accurint gave an address but nothing further for David
Leonard Jr. Flood left McPhee with his nightcap and went down
to the front desk, tipped the desk clerk twenty dollars to open
the "business center," a closet with an Internet connection and
a laser printer, and sat down at the computer. He used Nexis to
find that David Leonard was the registered owner of a green
Dodge Ram pickup truck. He wrote down the plate number in
his notebook. The address appeared to be a single-family house
near a dead end on Tripp Avenue, across the river in Peoria.

The desk clerk told him there was a rental car agency just
down the road and gave him the number. Flood was a little
worried about losing sight of the brother if he worked early. He
went back to McPhee's room, where he was dozing off a bit.

"I want to go stake out the kid. There's a rental place down
the road. I want you to take a cab down there in the morning,
get a car and go to the mom's. Call me when you get there."

McPhee went to bed, and Flood went to his own room,
started coffee in the little pot in the bathroom, took a shower
and shaved. He dressed in blue jeans, a golf shirt, sneakers and
the hooded windbreaker he'd packed for rain and then headed
out. He crossed the river on another double bridge—Interstate
74—into downtown, which surprisingly looked like a real city.
There were a lot of lights, and a cluster of buildings taller than
twenty stories, including a pair of black and white twin towers,
wide streets and some handsome old architecture. He followed
a map and headed north on Adams Street. Downtown gave way
to a dilapidated industrial area, some beat-up neighborhoods
and then a bit of greenery. He made a turn and headed up a
long winding hill on a four-lane road and found Prospect
Avenue and then Tripp. It was three o'clock when he found the
house, with the green pickup parked in the driveway. He set the
alarm on his phone for four forty-five at full volume and then
reclined the seat a bit and closed his eyes.

He woke in a panic when the alarm went off, but then the green pickup came into focus through the darkness. The house was still dark as well. He needed coffee and thought he remembered an all-night gas station or two that he'd passed. But he didn't dare leave. He turned on the radio instead. There was a bit of crackle in the WGN signal, but soon he was listening to Spike O'Dell.

At six the kitchen light came on. At six-thirty, a smallish, thin young man in a ball cap, matching yellow t-shirt, jeans and work boots came out. It was too early for the coordinated ambushes with McPhee, so Flood let him pass and then followed. Flood waited along the road while David Leonard Jr. went through the McDonald's drive-through, and then followed him downtown by a different road than Flood had taken. Just south of the tall buildings they turned onto a side street and the pickup parked outside a paint store. Leonard got out and went in through a back door. He did not come back out. At eight forty-five Flood's phone rang.

"I'm here. You didn't tell me I was checking into a Klan compound. Gravel road back here. Trailer next door flying the stars and bars on a pole. Black man could get lynched back here and nobody'd know for weeks."

"Sorry, man. I never would have guessed you'd run into that sort of thing down here."

"Yeah, right."

"She's there?"

"One red Lumina here. Can't tell if anybody's in there."

"OK, let's go."

The bell jangled on the glass front door of the store as Flood entered. The place smelled not unpleasantly of turpentine and wood. The floors were dusty and dulled his footsteps. It was the sort of store used more by contractors than retail shoppers. Leonard was with a customer in white pants and an undershirt lugging a cardboard box loaded with a half-dozen gallon cans. Flood stepped up when the customer left and gave Leonard his card.

"I'm trying to locate your sister."

He studied the card. "Somebody die?"

"Why do you ask that?"

"You're a lawyer. I don't know. She in somebody's will?"

"Well, somebody did die. But I don't know about the will," Flood said. "The woman was a friend of Kellee."

"Who?"

"Alice Jane Ash. People called her A.J."

"Never heard of her."

He was still looking at the card but now looked up.

"I haven't seen Kellee. You come all the way down here from Chicago to ask me this? You could have called."

"She's left Chicago."

He didn't say anything to that. Acknowledging Kellee was in Chicago might be the same as acknowledging his kid sister was a prostitute.

He was fairly clean cut. One of those little soul patch tufts of beard under his lower lip, but short hair and otherwise shaved. He was fit, clear-eyed, and had no visible tattoos. The orderliness of the paint store rubbed off on him a bit, Flood figured.

"Do you know how I can contact her?"

He shook his head.

"She don't come home. I haven't seen her in a year. Heck, two years."

"When's the last time you talked to her?"

"I don't know." He lied, but with a purpose. "So, why do you want to talk to Kellee? I don't get it."

Flood leaned in a little and lowered his voice. There were a couple of people behind him in a loft-level office that might hear.

"The woman who died was murdered. Kellee may have been the last person to see her. And now Kellee has disappeared. She ever tell you about a man she lived with sometimes? A guy named Melvin Runyon, people called him XO?"

"Uh, maybe."

"He's been murdered as well."

Leonard squinted back at Flood.

"What about the police?"

"They're a little behind. Miss Ash was killed in Chicago. Runyon was murdered in Mississippi."

"Why do you know all of it?"

"Because A.J.'s family hired me to do just this. And I'm a trained investigator. I used to be an FBI agent."

"In Chicago?"

"Yes. Now I'm a lawyer."

The cell phone on Leonard's belt rang. At the same time, the phone in Flood's pocket vibrated. He pulled it out and looked at it. Text message from McPhee: "Freaked. Slammed door."

Leonard was reaching for his cell phone.

"That's your mother calling to tell you a private detective just came to see her."

Leonard looked at the number and then back at Flood. He put the phone back on his belt. He looked scared.

"Somebody come down with you?"

"Yes."

"Wait here a minute."

He walked off toward the office. Flood noted that he didn't bother answering the call from his mother. Flood guessed she wasn't much of a parent. In a minute Leonard came back with a man a few years older than Flood. He looked like the owner.

"I'm Carl Strack," he said. Flood noticed that his golf shirt, and Leonard's t-shirt and cap, all said *Strack Paint Co. Since 1937.* "Dave asked me to listen to this, can you explain it again?"

Flood did, sensing he was talking to the father figure in David Leonard's life.

"You know his sister, Kellee?" Strack asked.

"I have never met her. But I have spoken to several people about her. Social workers, other runaways she knows."

He left out that the other girls had attacked him.

"Listen, David," Flood said. "You're trying to decide what to do. So, that tells me you know how to reach her. I'll give you any information you want. The names of the Chicago detectives assigned to the case. The name and number of my client, and her family attorney who hired me. You can call my office. You can call my old boss at the FBI. But I'm telling you, your sister is in more trouble than usual. I think she's at real risk of harm. And I'm the only person who cares. Chicago police don't really care about her. They barely care about A.J. Ash's death, and she was rich."

Leonard sighed. Strack studied Flood. Looked at the card. Back at Flood.

"Can I get the old boss's number?" Strack asked.

Flood took out his phone and scrolled through to John Ridgeway's office number.

"You'll get his secretary on this. If you want I can call his cell and put you on."

Strack hit speakerphone on the counter extension and dialed the phone number Flood gave him.

"FBI."

"My name is Carl Strack. I'm calling from Peoria, Illinois. May I speak to John Ridgeway?"

"May I ask what it's about, sir?"

"Um, a man named Augustine Flood."

"Ah," she said. "He no longer works here, sir."

Strack looked at Flood. Maybe he read her tone as negative. Good riddance to bad agents.

"I know. But I have a question about him."

"Hold a minute."

There was a pause. Strack decided to pick up the phone and turn off the speaker.

In a minute, he said, "Thanks for taking the call and I'm sorry to bother you. . . . You know him. . . . I run a paint store in Peoria. . . . He's looking for a family member of an employee of mine."

A longer pause. Then Strack looked at Flood.

"Yes, he's here . . . Thank you very much, Mr. Ridgeway."

Strack covered the phone and said to Flood, "He wants to talk to you."

Flood took the phone. "Hello, John."

"What the fuck?"

"I'll tell you later, but it's important."

Ridgeway made a disgusted grunt and hung up.

"I think it's OK, David," Strack said after a moment. His blood was going, having just spoken to a real-life FBI agent, and he was now a little eager to be involved, Flood thought.

David Leonard waited a second and then finally made eye contact with Flood.

"She called me from Las Vegas three days ago. She wouldn't tell me what was going on. When I tried to call the number back later, it was a hotel."

"Do you know which one?"

"New York, New York."

"What did she say?"

"She asked if I was OK. Asked if my son was OK. My girlfriend had a baby six months ago."

"Was she alone?"

"I don't think so. She was whispering on the phone. She said she was fine. Said she was going to be a dancer in one of the shows." He sounded frustrated, like he might cry. "She's fifteen."

Flood nodded. "She won't come back here?"

He smiled a cynical smile and shook his head. "She won't go near my mother. Or her husband."

Flood noted that he didn't use *stepfather.* He didn't need a roadmap to figure out what had driven Kellee Leonard from home.

Anyway, Las Vegas was the place.

CHAPTER 22

They drove like hell in the Buick.

"I'm going to Vegas," Flood said.

"What am I doing?"

"Fixing things with the dicks."

"And getting up to speed. Jesus, this is a mess."

McPhee fell silent for a bit. Then said, "You know, we went all the way down there to Mississippi. Got that motherfucker killed, and in the end it was this lady back in Chicago that gave you the name."

"She could have saved us a lot of trouble."

"Yes, she could have."

"Maybe she wouldn't have told us if Runyon wasn't dead."

"Well, I don't really care about Melvin Runyon so I'm not gonna lose much sleep over it."

Jane Ash called Flood just as they hit Joliet. "Philip said you killed a man in Mississippi."

"Jesus Christ, he did not."

"Who was he?"

"A pimp. And somebody else killed him."

"Who?"

Well, that was the question. Did it have something to do with A.J. Ash's drowning? Did the same person kill both people? He would have asked himself whether Kellee had been killed yet, but three days ago she'd talked to her brother. There was hope.

"Meet me for a drink tonight." She didn't ask. She told.

"Can't. I'll be in Vegas."

"Why?"

"To find this girl."

"I can't keep up."

"I'll call you when I have something real."

Veraneace had booked another flight, and put him in a room at New York, New York. Flood dumped one bag, packed another and caught a cab to Midway. He left a long message for Special Agent David Mulaney, the same agent to whom he had forwarded Runyon's child porn photos. When the flight attendant ordered his phone turned off, he finally had to sit there with nothing to do. He would have liked a seat in first class so he could have a drink. But he had nothing but the smell of a Quarter Pounder in the hands of the big woman sitting next to him. He rarely rested on planes but the loss of his phone was like hitting a brick wall. They taxied out onto the runway and waited. He closed his eyes and nodded off. He slept though the delayed takeoff, turbulence over the Rockies, and the landing. Last one off the plane.

It was midnight again. The desert air was cool but the earth smelled hot. The rental car was a Mazda that he left with valet parkers at New York, New York. As he was telling the valet he'd need the car within an hour, a roller coaster zoomed overhead. He would have preferred to stay someplace else, but the hotel was his only lead. Standing in line to check in, his phone rang. It was Mulaney.

"Flood, you shouldn't send child pornography from one cell phone to another. Even if you think you're sharing evidence and helping out. What the hell is going on with you?"

"Sorry about that. The circumstances were extremely extenuated."

"Do you have the guy's phone?"

"I don't. Um, he died anyway."

"He what?"

"Yeah, he was murdered right after that thing with his phone. It's a pretty weird story. Listen, about the other thing?"

"What other thing? Uh, who killed this guy?"

"Don't know. But, um, I'm in Vegas."

"So what about these girls in the photos?"

"I don't know."

"You don't know?"

"Mulaney, I'm in Vegas."

"Oh, right. Call this guy, Ray Garza, in their vice unit. He knows the skin trade better than anybody. Talks at conventions and shit."

"Skin trade conventions?"

"For vice cops. Not pervs."

"OK."

"Oh, and he works midnights, I guess. So you need to call him right about now."

Flood called Garza, who agreed to meet him at an In-N-Out Burger parking lot behind the Strip on Dean Martin Drive, which had been called Industrial Road the last time Flood had been in Vegas. It was a long bland commercial thoroughfare, except for the outcrops here and there of strip clubs and massage parlors. Flood was looking for an olive-skinned Hispanic who looked like a cop. He was lingering around an unmarked Impala when a tall, thin man in jeans, running shoes and a fleece jacket came up behind him. He had a shaved head, fair skin, blue eyes and an angular, hawkish face and was built like a long-distance runner. He was slurping from the straw of a soda cup and it took Flood a moment to notice the bulge of a weapon under the fleece jacket, the badge in a leather case hanging around his neck and tucked into it.

"I'm Jay Garza, get in," he said, smiling and pointing at the Impala.

They pulled into traffic on Dean Martin and headed north, paralleling I-15.

"How do you know Dave Mulaney?"

"Used to work with him."

"In the Bureau? Huh," he said. "Why'd you leave?"

"I became disillusioned."

"You like this?" Meaning whatever he was doing, which Garza was apparently unable to define.

"I wouldn't go back."

"The only guys I know who want to go *back* to being a cop are the ones who can't go back."

They passed through a stoplight. The road curved a bit and then straightened again as they started to pass a line of sex businesses.

"Tell me what you need," Garza said.

Flood told him what he knew about Kellee Leonard, and showed him the photo of her on his phone.

"Would she have come by bus?" Flood asked.

"Maybe. She could have hitched with a trucker. Gotten to a truck stop around Chicago and worked her way out here."

"Where do I start?"

"We'll try a couple older girls I know who work New York, New York, and then we'll check in with hotel security. When did she make the call from the room?"

"Four days ago at ten-thirty P.M."

"Oh. Couple of those security guys might be around tonight. They hang out at a bar back on the Strip we can try. They watch the pimps fairly closely. If she's new, pretty and too young, they're probably already working on it."

Garza sent a text message to somebody and checked his phone when it jingled back. They drove through another two lights and pulled into a two-story strip mall and parked. Garza pointed three doors down to a storefront with black windows and a green neon sign that advertised "Relaxation Spa." In a minute a young woman emerged from the shop wearing a strapless black dress that barely covered her bottom and a pair of Uggs boots. She bounced off the sidewalk and slid into the back seat of the Impala.

"Hey," she said as the car filled with the vanilla scent of her perfume. "Who's your partner?"

"Ginger, this is Mr. Flood. Flood, this is Ginger."

Flood stuck his hand back and took hers. She squeezed.

"Show her the picture on the phone," Garza said.

He did, and she leaned over the seats to look closely, the perfume coming with her, along with her soft breath smelling of spearmint gum.

"Sorry. But I don't hang out in the hotels. Not anymore. Jay, you know I'm strictly massage."

"Right," Garza said skeptically. "Thought maybe you'd seen her around. You still in touch with Pearl? If she was hanging around New York, New York she'd be dealing with him one way or another, right?"

"I don't know. I stay the hell away from him. I really haven't heard from him or seen her."

"Flood says she worked massage in Chicago. You're sure you haven't heard any word about her?"

"If she's in a spa, she's not with Pearl. He doesn't do that."

Ginger sat back in the car and sighed. Flood wondered what she got out of talking to Garza. Protection from what, arrest? She seemed frustrated with all this boring business talk.

"Mr. Flood, do you have a first name?"

"I do. Augustine."

"Sort of an old man's name."

"It's good to be prepared."

"You know this girl?" she asked.

"No. Looking for her," he replied.

"Why, you a cop?"

"No."

"Then what are you?"

Sometimes it was convenient to be a lawyer. It meant anything and nothing. She said *hmmph,* and gave up on him.

Garza said, "Ginger, who besides Pearl would be running girls at New York?"

She shrugged. "Maybe Eugene, but probably just Pearl. You know that."

"Anybody new?"

"I said I'm not working over there."

Edge in his voice: "Anybody new?"

"No, that's it," she said like a scolded child.

"What's Pearl's deal lately? I haven't seen him a lot."

Now she was the bored girl. "He's in L.A. a lot. Goes back and forth."

Garza leaned back and tugged at the zipper of his fleece. "Where can I find him tonight?"

She waited a moment, considering her options, but then relented. "I'm sure he's at Meter. That's the only place I see him."

"All right, sweetie. Thanks. Give me a call if you hear anything. About Pearl or this girl we showed you."

She sighed and reached for the door handle. "Used and abused again. See ya."

They drove over to the Strip and pulled into the parking lot of a no-name casino. It was part motel, part tourist trap gift shop, and part dive bar with slots and a couple tables. It was a big rectangular bar, with Bob Seger and slot-machine bells making noise together. Two men sat on bar stools in suits, drinking Bud Light in bottles, watching Garza and Flood make their way toward them.

Flood wanted a beer but he respected Garza's on-duty rules

and ordered a Coke. Nobody really introduced anybody, but the two men in suits were security from New York, New York. Garza pointed at Flood's phone and he showed them the photo of Kellee. One of the men, with thinning blond hair, nodded right away.

"Couple of nights ago, with that shithead, Pearl. Got in an argument while she was eating a grilled cheese with him and she poured a Coke on him. Still have the video if you want to see it tomorrow. What's her deal?"

"Witness to a crime, I think."

"In Chicago?"

"Yes."

"But you're private?"

"Yes. Victim's family hired me."

"How long you been looking?"

"About a week."

"You tracked a fifteen-year-old hooker out here in a week? That's not bad."

"What'd the pimp do when she threw the Coke on him?"

"Nothing, he knows we're watching. I'm sure he beat the shit out of her later."

Flood lost track of where they drove next. But they ended up at a big casino he had never heard of. They parked in a side lot and a security guard let them in a service entrance. They passed through a laundry room, a sprawling kitchen and then a series of corridors and onto the casino floor. On the open mezzanine level they came across a line of young people waiting to be let into the club that Garza had been talking about. The architecture of the entrance was black granite and brushed stainless steel. A bouncer nodded at Garza, despite his jeans and fleece, and they bypassed the line and plunged into the darkness and deafening beat of the place.

Flood followed Garza around like a puppy dog. All of it was overwhelming—the flight in, dumping his bags, back in the car and out here into the depths of Vegas nightlife in all of its sordid glory. The thumping music was as disorienting as the strobe-cut darkness. They wove their way back through people and tables and around bars to a row of booths that lined a back wall under dim blue lights. Finally, Garza faded to the side of the room and took up a spot facing back toward the front of the club. He leaned against the wall and motioned Flood to lend his ear.

"That middle booth," Garza shouted into his ear.

Flood did not look at the booth; he looked at one a few over, close enough to see what he needed with peripheral vision. He saw a white man of about his own age, maybe a little younger. Lean, angry look, stubble, collar-length oiled hair, velvet jacket, tattoo on his neck. Some kind of snake. Bluetooth on his ear. There were two girls in the booth with him. Neither looked happy. Both looked like candidates for prostitution, though neither was Kellee Leonard.

Flood looked away and back to Garza.

"What do you want to do?" Garza asked.

"I don't like the idea of confronting him here, but I'm not going to waste a lot of time sitting on him when I'm not sure he's even running her," Flood said.

"It's too damn noisy in here. Let's take him outside. Go ahead and I'll bring him out."

Flood nodded. "OK. Don't bring up the video if he says he doesn't know her. If he'll lead me to her, I want to do it that way. If I don't have her by six in the morning, I'll light him up."

Garza nodded and Flood started back toward the front. As he rounded the bar and was about to lose sight of the back wall, he turned around and saw Garza sitting at Pearl's table. The girls were gone.

Outside the club on the mezzanine level of the casino, the

cacophony of slot machine bells resumed. Flood was exhausted, and he wondered whether he would sleep at all in the next twenty-four hours. He might have just gone to bed and started fresh in the morning, but the murder of Melvin Runyon had charged this case with a frightening urgency. All he could do now was push through until he found the girl. If they came away from this interrogation of Pearl thinking he knew Kellee, then Flood would tail him until he led him to her.

A minute passed before Garza and Pearl emerged. The pimp had clearly been annoyed with Garza, and Flood's appearance suddenly put a little worry in his eyes. Who knew what he had done in the course of pimping women, but he looked suddenly frightened that he'd gotten himself in over his head. Because what was Flood? He looked like a cop, but not ordinary. It was three in the morning and they were pulling him out of a nightclub. It gave Flood a little burst of adrenaline. He opened his phone, pulled up the photo of Kellee and held it up for Pearl to see. Flood said nothing.

"I don't know her," Pearl said. In that instant, Flood could tell he was lying. The fear in his eyes had shifted. The trouble wasn't what he expected, apparently, but clearly there was something about Kellee that made this seem plausible.

"Who are you, anyway?" Pearl said.

Garza picked up on it and stepped into Pearl's face a little. "What the fuck do you care who he is if you don't know her?"

"I don't know her."

Garza stayed in his face a little, staring him down.

"How much of your night am I going to take having this conversation?" Garza asked. "We need to talk to her."

"I said," he was being obnoxiously emphatic now. "I don't know her."

Flood put the phone in his pocket and looked at his watch. It was three-fifteen A.M.

"I know she's not sleeping," he said. "Bring her to the restaurant of this casino at six A.M. If you don't, you'll deal with me alone. Not this police officer."

Flood made it clear what he meant by the idea that a police officer would not be present if he had to deal with Pearl. He turned and walked away. Garza slapped Pearl on the shoulder and left him there.

They took the stairs down.

"Scared me," Garza said. "Just don't kill the guy."

"That's what the last cop who helped me out said. Anyway, I expect to find her before six o'clock."

"Yeah, he's a lying sack of shit."

"If you run me back to my car I'll come back and sit on him."

When they got back in the Impala, Garza got on the radio and ran a motor vehicle check on Pearl. Real name: Jon S. Perlstine. He was registered to a silver Jaguar XKE. Garza drove around the parking lot until he found it. He started to dial his cell phone.

"I'll ask a couple patrol guys to keep an eye on this Jag until you get back."

Garza spoke to the officer on the other end for a minute, thanked him and then tucked the phone back in his pocket and hit the gas hard to get Flood back to his car at the In-N-Out Burger as fast as possible. Flood was back at the casino and staking out Pearl's car in twenty minutes. When he pulled up, an LVPD patrol car rolled past and the cop in the passenger seat gave him a friendly wave as they departed.

At four-thirty Pearl emerged from the building without either girl. He headed south on the Strip at a rapid pace and Flood had to run a red light to keep up. Blowing the light, and the horns honking at him, made him nervous that he'd blown the tail, but he kept at it, winding into a more suburban part of town and an apartment complex that looked fairly new. Pearl parked in a covered space opposite one of the buildings. For a guy driving a high-end Jaguar, the apartment complex was pretty modest. All the lights in the building were off except one apartment, the upstairs right. Flood parked in an empty space in the next building's garage and walked up. He watched for movement in the windows and saw a shape pass once behind the thin curtains. The front door was locked. He went back to the rental car and opened the trunk. He had packed his lock picks in the bag he checked and now dug out the kit. It took about thirty seconds to open the front door. He went to the top of the stairs and listened. No voices. But the walls and door were thin and he could hear something inside. Then an interior door opened, and he could hear the muffled drumming of a shower. Flood went back outside and put away the picks. He had parked the car facing out and he sat in the driver's seat and watched. At five Pearl came back out, in different clothes, and got back in the car. Flood let him pass out of sight before following. It was light enough now to drive without his headlights on, so he left them off to draw less attention.

Flood knew Las Vegas only slightly. He had spent a week there once during an organized crime investigation of Chicago Outfit control of a pair of strip clubs where money was being laundered. But all this residential terrain was unfamiliar, so he followed a little more closely than he wanted to, fearing that he would lose the car at a light and not be able to catch up. They were back near the casinos, in a second-rate-looking area between the Strip and the airport. Pearl took a right and headed down another street lined with dingy motels. The Jaguar pulled into one, an old motor court where all of the rooms opened onto the central courtyard and parking lot. Flood curbed the car and watched. Pearl went upstairs and down the walkway to a room near the corner and entered with a key. Almost immediately a young woman in miniskirt and tank top exited, carrying her shoes in one hand and looking scared and hurried. She had long black hair and looked Asian or mixed race. Flood pulled his car in and quickly headed to the steps. The girl looked like there was trouble brewing in the room. He met her on the stairs and she glanced at him as she hustled past. He stopped her with a hand on her arm.

"Not now!" she said, annoyed and thinking he was looking for a date.

"That's not what I want. Hold on," he said. He pulled out his phone and pulled up the photo of Kellee Leonard again. "She in there with him?"

The girl looked even more frightened.

"I don't know anything. Just let me go."

"You have a key?"

"No. Just her and him."

Flood still had hold of her arm. He considered whether to take her up there to use her to get into the room. He decided against it and let her go. Pearl hadn't been armed at the nightclub, but in this part of town things might be different.

"Does he carry a gun?"

She looked at him with eyes that betrayed fear for him. She nodded slowly.

"OK, get out of here."

CHAPTER 23

Flood ran up the stairs and looked for Garza's number on his phone as he walked down the mezzanine. But as he got closer he could hear the screaming from the room. Pearl's voice, shrill and crazy. A girl's crying in fear. He put the phone in his pocket and ran down to the door and pounded on it. The screaming stopped. The crying did not. Flood put his thumb over the peephole.

"Open up."

"Everything's fine," Pearl, sounding harried and furious.

"Open up or I'm calling the police."

"I can't see you."

"It's smashed."

"Bullshit," Pearl shouted back.

"I'm calling the police."

"Fuck you. Wait a minute."

The deadbolt turned over and the door started to open. The chain on.

Flood took a step back and kicked. The chain snapped and the door caught Pearl in the face. He screamed and reeled back. Flood kicked the door again and swung it open. The revolver was in his hand. Short barrel, nickel-plated .38. Holding his nose with one hand, he started to bring the gun up with the other, but Flood was on him and twisted the weapon out of his hand with his fingers still in. He howled in pain. Using both hands, Flood released the cylinder and spilled the cartridges on the floor and then palmed the gun and brought it down on Pearl's forehead, not hard enough to fracture his skull, but it broke the skin. The pimp dropped to the floor.

The girl was cowering in the corner, her face bloodied, mascara run all over the place. Despite the mess he knew immediately that it was Kellee Leonard. She looked at him through her fingers.

"Kellee, my name is Augustine Flood, and I came here from Chicago to find you. A.J.'s mother hired me to find out what happened, and I want you to come with me." He pointed down at Pearl. "You can't stay with him."

She was in shock or close to it. She looked like she was as terrified of Flood as she was of Pearl. He thought about pulling out a business card to show her he was legitimate, but that seemed absurd. There was no badge to flash anymore. He stepped back over Pearl and shut the door. Pearl was trying to scramble up, but Flood grabbed his oily hair and shoved him back down, putting his shoe on the back of his neck.

"Stay down. It won't take much more pissing me off to really hurt you."

He looked around the room and eyed the clock radio.

"Kellee, I need you to get up and help me."

She complied, her whole body shaking as she crawled over the bed. He told her to unplug the clock radio and hand it to him. He used the cord to bind Pearl's hands behind his back. She sat on the bed and watched, looking like she was unable to move.

"Come on, honey, get your stuff together."

Pearl was ranting, threatening death to all. Flood kicked him in the ribs and shut him up for a second. He went to the bathroom. There were no clean washcloths, so he rinsed out a damp one and soaked it in cold water, and then went back and knelt down in front of the girl.

207

David Heinzmann

"Let me see," he said, gently moving her hands away from her face. The cut looked worse than it was. He wiped the blood away and found that it had already stopped bleeding. He rinsed the cloth out again and then helped her clean off the rest of her face.

"Do you understand what I'm saying?"

She nodded, now studying his face.

"Are your things all here?"

She nodded. Still saying nothing, they moved through the room and gathered things into a backpack. She nodded again when she had it all. While Pearl was looking the other way, unable to turn his head and see, Flood put the gun between the mattress and box springs of the bed closest to the door.

Pearl rolled over, moaning and cussing. He was pathetic to Flood, but Pearl caught Kellee's eye and she stopped. She couldn't take another step. Pearl just stared her down.

"I'm not going," she said to Flood.

"You want to stay for the police?"

"No."

"OK. So you want to untie him or should I? We'll pretend this is all just a misunderstanding."

No answer to that. Beyond all the horror and squalor, she was still a fifteen-year-old girl. She was afraid to say anything. Flood stepped over Pearl, gently took her hand and said, "It's OK. Come on."

When they were outside he called Garza's cell phone.

"I have the girl. Pearl's tied up in a room at this shitty motel." He gave him the name and told him where to find the gun. "I can't stick around."

"So I'm cleaning up your mess?"

"Leave him if you want, but there's a gun. His prints will still be on it. Mine will, too, of course. I bet he doesn't have any paper on it. You wouldn't get him for much else anyway. He hi

208

her, but she'd run before you made your case."

"Fine. You owe me something."

"Come to Chicago. I'll put ten pounds on you in a weekend."

Garza was annoyed, but Flood couldn't help it. A runaway fifteen-year-old prostitute was not likely to be cooperative with anybody for very long. He needed to talk to her right now and get what he could.

He drove.

She looked a little worse for wear than the girl in the photo. At this rate, she'd be a ruined woman by nineteen, he figured. She just looked terrified right now.

In the car, he said, "He beat you because of me. I'm sorry."

She laughed. Finally, something verbal. "Don't flatter yourself. He found something to throw a punch over every day."

"How long you been here?"

"I don't know. Two weeks. Time flies when you're having fun."

"How'd he find you?"

She shrugged. "I thought I'd go independent. I was on his turf, I guess. He didn't like it."

There was silence for a bit. Then she finally started to stare at him.

"What?"

"You knew A.J.?"

"No," he said. "Her mother, Mrs. Ash, hired me last week to find out how and why A.J. drowned. She doesn't believe it was an accident."

"What do you think?"

"I'm leaning toward agreeing with her."

The girl said nothing but he could see the wheels turning.

"I think you were the last person to have contact with her," he said.

"Maybe it was an accident, but I don't really know what all happened."

Flood thought about when he should tell her that Melvin Runyon was dead. He decided to wait. They pulled up to the casino and got out. He took her hand and she allowed him to lead the way up to his room. It was undisturbed. He'd spent a total of about four minutes in it, so far. He decided there would be no sleep in Vegas because there was no way he was letting this girl out of his sight.

Kellee asked to use the bathroom and while she was gone Flood had an idea. He pulled his digital recorder out of his bag, turned it on and looked for a place to hide it. Finally, he decided on the lampshade. He unscrewed the bulb and rested the recorder in the well of the socket. When she came out he was sitting in a chair by the window. She sat on the bed.

"I need to know what you know about A.J.'s death."

"I told you, nothing."

"Why'd you run?"

"I didn't. I had been planning to come out here."

"I don't think so. Melvin Runyon told me you vanished on him."

The mention of his name registered alarm. "How do you know about him?"

"I'm an investigator. I ask questions and find things out."

"Is he here?" she said, the alarm increasing.

"No. I found him in Mississippi. He said he went there to hide after you ran away because he figured you knew something about A.J.'s death. He was afraid of getting tangled up in it."

She looked at him like he'd just said the sky was green. Then recovered, and asked, "Is he still there?"

"He's dead."

The reaction was about what he'd expected. She was too broken down to put on a show. Her eyes went wide. "What do you mean?"

"Someone murdered him in Mississippi. After I talked to him. I think it was someone from Chicago, and I think they had something to do with A.J.'s death."

"Did he follow you here?"

"Who's he?"

"I don't know. Whoever did it."

"Nobody followed me here."

"I have to get out of here. They'll kill me too." She was starting to panic.

"Listen, you're going to be OK. Stick with me and I'll protect you."

"They'll find us," she said with a shakier voice. Her eyes were starting to well up.

"It's going to be OK," Flood said as firmly as possible. "I have help. And the police will help."

She shook her head. "I can't talk to the cops. No way."

"Kellee, who are *they?*"

"I don't know, I don't know."

"Listen, I need to ask you a bunch of questions."

She shook her head, like even that was too dangerous.

"Listen, if you want, I'll call the Chicago police and they'll get a warrant to pick you up, and then you'll spend a couple days in lockup here with the Vegas cops. Or, you could sit here with me and talk about what happened. I'm not a cop, and I don't want to make things more miserable for you. Understand?"

"I don't know anything."

"You know, too many people have told me you were in the middle of this mess. Sorry, but I just don't believe you don't know anything."

She sat back.

"I want to know about you, for starters," he said.

She laughed. "Not much to know, dude. What you see is what you get. You want me to blow you, it's a hundred and fifty. You want to fuck me, it's two hundred. How's that?"

"You left home at thirteen?"

"Fuck you."

"What about your brother? He's an adult."

"What about him? Leave my brother out of this."

"Your mom lost custody of you?"

"She didn't want custody of me. So she didn't really lose anything. You want to hear all about me and her boyfriend, Rick. He had a lot of free time on his hands at night when my mom was tending bar and snorting meth. He helped me with my homework."

"How many foster homes you been through?"

"I forget."

"Done with that?"

"Yeah."

Maybe she was warming up a little. Give her some room, don't try to pin her down, and don't say anything that could be construed as judgmental.

"When do you turn sixteen?"

"September."

"And here you are in fabulous Las Vegas, Nevada."

She got the sarcasm. "Living the dream."

"You want to stay here?"

"You ruined that."

"I want you to come back to Chicago."

"No. Way."

He didn't push.

"Who would want to kill Melvin?"

He could tell the topic frightened her. But she was quick-witted. "Probably some gangbangers, who else? And, dude, nobody called him Melvin."

"He wasn't really affiliated, I thought."

"You think you know how stuff works, but you don't," she said. "XO brought girls to their parties. The gang did what they wanted with them and then gave XO coke."

She said it like *Zo*.

"He sell, or use, or both?"

"Mostly sold it. He smoked some weed, but the coke he sold to johns."

"He ever take you to gang parties like that?"

"No way," she said, making a face. "Girls I know, though. From the West Side."

"I don't think gangbangers killed him."

"How do you know?"

"Because he wasn't really in their game. He wasn't dealing drugs on a corner on Austin, so there really wasn't any competition. And whatever drugs he did get from them sound like they were payment for sex from his girls. Even if he pissed somebody off, I can't imagine it being a big enough deal for some Four Corner Hustler to get sent down to Mississippi to carry out a hit. That's just not how things work," he said, mocking her know-it-all tone. She seemed to like that.

He was trying to gauge her fear. Mainly, she looked like she wasn't surprised.

"Kellee, who are you thinking of?"

"Nobody."

"OK." He backed off and let it go for a moment. "Tell me about you and A.J."

"What's to tell? She's dead. And here I am."

"She had planned to help you."

"She said she would help me. But that's not how it worked out. And she's still dead, right? So what's it fucking matter?"

"But it seems like you were special."

"Yeah, real special."

She didn't know quite what to do with her anger. Flood waited for it to come flying at him. But she asked a question instead. "What's her mom's deal?"

"She doesn't believe it was an accident."

She gave a little nod but said, "You already said that. What's her *deal?*"

"The mother? Um, strong. Refined."

"Refined. That sounds nice." Her tone wasn't completely mocking. "Does she know anything?"

Flood smiled. "If she did, I wouldn't have had to come out here and disrupt your career development."

She smiled. Flood went on. "She has a hunch. She also has resources. I think she can help you if you help her."

"I don't need any help."

Flood nodded, said nothing, letting her chew on the aftertaste of such a ridiculous statement.

"She doesn't want to help me," Kellee finally said. "Everybody wants a little something from me, and once they got it they can't throw me away fast enough."

"Well, she doesn't know you and you don't know her."

"Whatever."

He thought that was it, but then she had more to say, in a rush. "I know me. People like her don't like to think about girls like me. Nobody does unless you're some guy with a stiff dick who gets off on fucking teenagers. That's probably what you want."

He shrugged. "Can I ask another question?"

She just looked at him.

"When did you first meet A.J.?"

Kellee rolled her eyes, not so much at the question as at the idea that this conversation really wasn't over.

"At Girls Refuge. She knew Tamika."

"When, though?"

"I don't know. Like a year ago. Maybe a little longer."

Flood played dumb and said, "And Tamika is a friend of yours?"

"She's out of the life now."

"Are you still in touch?"

"She's with her grandmother. On the West Side. That's how XO found her."

"Did you see her over there before you left town?"

Kellee shook her head. "I kinda stick out over there. And Tamika's grandmother is pretty strict. She didn't want her running with any of the girls she knew."

"Did A.J. help her?"

"I guess."

It went on like this a bit. Flood ordered breakfast delivered to the room. Just talking. Nothing concrete. She looked sleepy after half a Belgian waffle. Flood asked, "Tell me what you know about when A.J. died."

She hesitated a bit, thinking, before saying, "She gave me some money."

"Five thousand dollars."

Her eyes went wide. "Did XO tell you?"

"We already knew about it when we got to him." He didn't want to correct her if she was impressed by the idea that Melvin Runyon had told Flood that. So he fudged it a bit.

"Who's we?"

"Guy who works for me. He's back in Chicago."

"Did XO tell you he fucking took it?"

"No. He left that part out."

"Fucker," she said, and then added, "God, I can't believe he's really dead."

"So he found the money and took it. A.J. found out and confronted him?"

She didn't answer. She glanced at Flood and then just stared

215

off into space a moment. She seemed still lost in the idea of Runyon being dead.

"Kellee?"

"What?"

"Did A.J. confront Runyon about him taking the money she gave you?"

"Sort of."

"Where did that happen?"

"I don't remember. It was a long time ago."

"Hey," he said, not taking her bullshit. "I bought you breakfast."

She dropped her fork. "I don't really remember. Might have been some guy's boat, or something."

Flood felt his pulse quicken.

"Warren Riordan?"

"Maybe. I don't know. Who's that?"

"A guy A.J. knew. Late twenties, tall, curly dark hair. Good looking."

She shrugged. "I don't think so."

"What was going on?"

"It was a date."

"Arranged by Runyon, on some guy's boat?"

"Yeah."

"Can you tell me about the boat? Which harbor?"

"I don't know. You know, on the lake. It was a big boat. Really fancy. Like a houseboat. It had a living room and stuff."

That burst Flood's bubble a bit. Warren Riordan's boat was not so grand. He could show Kellee all the harbors—Montrose, Belmont, Diversey, Monroe and on down—to figure it out.

"Was the guy a regular?"

"Yeah," she said, rolling her eyes. "I was there a few times."

"So, A.J. followed you and Runyon there to confront him?"

"I don't know. I was down below in the bedroom with a guy.

216

"Another guy?"

She nodded. "Listen, sometimes there's more than one guy."

"So you didn't see this happen?"

She shook her head.

"But you think she got in a fight with Runyon and ended up in the water?"

"I guess. I really don't know," she said. "I'm tired."

And then she broke into a sob. Flood tried to read it for clues to what she really knew, the motivation of her tears. Nothing was coming. Maybe she was so damaged by experience that she didn't know what she felt. The tears came harder now and obscured everything anyway.

"I don't know what happened, but then she was dead," she sobbed. "She was my friend, and she cared about me, and then suddenly everything was all mixed up, and she was dead. I saw her in the water. And they made me go below. XO came down and started hitting me because I was crying. And then they took the boat out to dump her in the water. I knew they were going to kill me too, so I got off and swam."

"You swam?"

"I'm a good swimmer," she said, sobbing and nodding.

"How'd you get off the boat?"

She was trying to calm down, and she wiped at her runny nose with the palm of her hand even though there was a napkin in her lap.

"XO went back up on top and there's a hatch on the front of the boat. They were in the back steering the boat, and it was dark by then. They didn't even see me get in."

"How far did you swim?" Flood was still astonished by that.

"I don't know. Pretty far."

"Then what?"

"I hid in the park until my dress dried out. It was freezing. Then I made some money and took the bus to Girls Refuge the next day. I changed my clothes. I kept a bag there."

By this time, he knew better than to ask about the making of money.

"You got rid of the wet orange dress?"

"How did you know?"

"I picked up the bag. It was A.J.'s, right?"

"Yeah."

"She gave it to you when she gave you the money?"

She nodded. "XO let me keep the bag."

"Why'd you leave the bag there?"

"I had to leave fast. XO went to Girls Refuge looking for me the next day. I couldn't go back, so I just left."

"Your friends at Girls Refuge didn't mention all that."

"They probably thought you were with XO."

"Maybe. Listen, I really need to know whose boat that was."

"It was just this gross guy."

"What was gross about him?"

She made a face.

He added: "Other than the fact he was paying Melvin to have sex with you."

"It's hard to explain."

"Was he friendly or mean?"

"He could be friendly. He had a big smile but it was fake. He was pretty nasty. He was gross when we were together."

"Violent?"

"A little. But like he was funny. Like it was hilarious to scare me while he was on top of me."

This is so awful, was all Flood could think. *Welcome to adolescence.*

"You were with him more than once?"

"Yeah. XO set it up," she said. "Are you getting off on this or what?"

He just looked at her.

"Not going to dignify that?" The joke seemed to help her stop crying. She smiled at him, telling him she knew she had a grown-up wit.

Flood sighed heavily and said, "You're a kid and they should have left you alone. Your mother and father shouldn't have been trash. Your brother should have stepped up, and none of these people should have been having sex with you."

She barely waited for him to finish. "You gonna cry about it?"

"No. You want me to shut up?"

"I don't care what you do."

"OK. Tell me more about the guy."

"He had dark hair. I don't remember his eyes at all. He was pretty checked out most of the time. So was I."

"Stoned?"

"Me? Yeah. Him? Maybe."

"Clothes, jewelry?"

"I don't remember. Dress shirts and pants, I guess," she said and then laughed. "He didn't wear underwear."

"Weeknights? Weekends?"

"Mostly weeknights."

"So did it seem like he worked in an office?"

She just shrugged. "How should I know?"

"OK. How about the boat? What color was it? How big?"

"White. Really big. Maybe the biggest one there."

"If I showed it to you, would you recognize it?"

"You're not going to show it to me."

"I'll protect you."

"Bullshit."

"You hang around on your own and eventually you'll get the Melvin Runyon treatment. The only way out for you is to fix his."

"Fix what?"

"Somebody killed A.J. I didn't know that for sure until Melvin was murdered in Mississippi. Now I know. And I don't think Melvin was being punished for killing A.J. So who killed her? I think you know. If it wasn't the guy on the boat, it was somebody close to him. Was he married?"

"I'm not fixing anything with you."

"We'll see. I need to find out how A.J. died. You were there. You can solve this. I'd like your help. That's all I'm saying."

The big risk of talking to her like this was that it gave her power she did not know how to exercise. The benefit was that she might listen to him for a few minutes.

"By the way," Flood said, partly to give the impression he didn't care. "The cops found a little bag of heroin in A.J.'s apartment. Did she use?"

She made a face. "No way. She drank wine. And it's not mine, if that's what you're really asking. I smoke some weed but that's it."

His phone rang. It was Captain Fry in Clarksdale.

"I don't know what's comin' next. It's all messed up," Fry said.

Whatever anger and resentment Fry had felt had withered away. They were conspirators again.

"What happened?"

"Prints on that pay phone. FBI in D.C. went berserk when we ran 'em. They come back to a feller from Boston supposed to be dead. Some kinda mobster, they say. Name's Burke. Finn Burke."

"What the hell?"

"And he was reported dead ten years ago. In *Ireland*. Lost at sea. *What in the hell?* is right."

"Lost at sea?"

"Sailboat in a storm."

"Really."

"That matter?"

"Probably not. Just, we're, you know . . ."

Either Flood hadn't told Fry about A.J. drowning, or he'd forgotten, or Fry didn't get the possible connection.

"It's real weird. They won't tell us nothing else."

"I'll try and find out what I can."

Flood asked again for the name, and then hung up. He turned his attention back to Kellee.

"You know what a Boston accent sounds like?"

She shrugged. "I don't know."

"The guy who owned the boat, he talk funny at all?"

"Maybe a little. Kinda faggy. Kinda foreign. But not really."

"He ever say his name?"

"I told you I didn't know," she said, yawning. "I don't want to talk about it anymore. Who called you?"

"Cop I know."

"What was it? He freaked you out."

"The fingerprints found in Mississippi, where Melvin was killed, matched a guy who shouldn't really have anything to do with this."

Wheels turning in her head. "Who is he?"

"Some guy named Finn Burke. Ring a bell?"

She shook her head, looking confused and lost. She still wanted to change the subject.

"So, how are you and A.J.'s mom going to help me?"

Progress, he thought, probably motivated by fear of the piece of this she was withholding.

Flood told her to get some rest. She gave him the look of sexual suspicion again. Her most frequent expression and response seemed to be just this—accusing whoever of trying to defile her, whether by trickery or plain demand. He knew it came from experience rather than insecurity—it was a learned defense. He tried to ignore it because it shouldn't apply to him.

But that wasn't the way she saw it.

Eventually she sat on the bed and let her legs stretch out a bit. In five minutes she was sound asleep. Flood left the room and walked to the end of the hallway by a window that looked west, out the back of the hotel over a sprawling complex of low, flat roofs peppered with air conditioners. His first call was to McPhee.

"Found her."

"Damn, boy. What'd she say?"

"A.J. gave the last five grand to the girl. Melvin took it, and A.J. confronted him. Happened on a boat of one of the girl's customers, and she was down below with the guy, or one of the guys. She's not sure what happened but suddenly they were motoring out onto the lake to dump the body. She sneaks off and swims back to the harbor."

"Swims!"

"So she says."

"Which harbor?"

"She doesn't know. Doesn't know names, etcetera."

"You believe that?"

"Don't know."

"Now what?"

"I want to bring her back to Chicago to see if she can show us the boat. It's probably Diversey."

"You think she'll come?"

"I'll talk her into it."

"I should update Tally?"

"Yes. Are we on speaking terms with them again?"

"It's all right. But it'll be a while before they get to this. He's in a real bind out there. Working a quad—New Breed went into a house on Homan yesterday morning and executed two brothers, a girl and one of their grandmothers."

"Jesus," Flood said. "What the hell is going on out there?"

"Summertime on the West Side, son. I told you them Vice Lords are at war . . . with everybody."

"Well, if we're still on our own, that's fine," Flood said. "Where are you?"

"Your office."

"Can I talk to Jamie?"

McPhee put him on the phone.

"I need you to come out to Vegas," Flood said.

"I'm studying."

"Next flight you can get. Take a cab to my hotel. Call me when you land."

He was about to hang up, but Jamie protested.

"Wait a minute, what am I doing?"

"Chaperoning a fifteen-year-old girl."

"You found her?"

"She thinks everybody's trying to fuck her."

"So you need a fag."

"Yes."

"All right."

"What hotel?"

"New York, New York."

"Ick."

"I'm serious. I want you in a cab to the airport in a half hour."

"Oh, hey, before you hang up on me, ever so rudely, the Ash divorce file . . ."

"What about it?"

"The settlement is under a protective order. Sealed."

"Well, that's not unusual, especially at their level."

"But when I looked at the docket, there were two separate hearings on the motion to put the protective order thingy on, so I decided to order the transcript."

"Aren't you enterprising; spending money without approval."

"Shrewd, too. Something very fucked up was going on. Listen to this, at the start of the hearing, one of daddy's lawyers, Wendy Becker, says to the judge that there's been a conference and counsel on both sides has decided it won't be necessary to—get this—contact the state's attorney's office. What the fuck?"

"Huh. I wonder what that's about?" Flood said. He'd never heard anything quite like that in court.

"Wife beater?"

"Maybe. But at that stage, bringing it up seems like a stunt," Flood said. "What happened next?"

"Oh, the other lawyer for daddy, Peter Littlewood—I shit you not, that's his real name. He interjects right away, and asks for that to be stricken from the record. Littlewood's a partner, by the way. I looked Wendy Becker up and she was, like, twenty-eight at the time. U. of C., law review, very nice resumé, but a youngster. Anyway, the judge agrees, but the court reporter goofed, maybe, because it's still in the transcript. Littlewood gets a recess, and that's the last we hear from Ms. Becker. She's not in the transcript again, and I looked at all the motions in the rest of the case and her name's not on any. She'd signed every piece of paper filed until that hearing. So, he definitely gave her the boot after that comment. Isn't that just weird as shit?"

"She still at Burke and Leigh?"

"Nope. I've been dying to answer that question," he said. "She's an assistant U.S. attorney in L.A."

"No shit."

"Want her number?"

Flood wrote it down and reminded Jamie that he should be on the way to the airport already. "One more thing."

"What now?" Jamie was whining.

"Put Veraneace on."

She came on.

"Don't tell Jamie this yet. But when you book him a flight out, can you get him on a flight back late tonight? And buy a ticket for this girl. Kellee Leonard. And make sure they get seats together."

"I'll take care of it."

"Send me a text message with the return flight time."

Even if it was just to know who he was dealing with, Flood needed to know what Wendy Becker's comment was about. It was intriguing. In the middle of an acrimonious divorce case involving tens of millions of dollars, a lawyer stands up and says they've decided not to go to prosecutors with some piece of information. He couldn't wait, and called the number Jamie had given him. He got the switchboard for the U.S. attorney in L.A., and she said Ms. Becker was unavailable. He got voicemail and left a message including that he was investigating a death that brushed into work she'd done in private practice, but he didn't mention the name Ash.

Next call was to Swain, who couldn't take his call either. Left a message with the secretary. So he called Jane Ash. He wasn't about to tell her that he was now digging into her divorce. Luckily, there was plenty else to talk about.

"A lot has happened."

"A.J. was murdered," she said. "I can tell by your tone."

"Well, it could have been an accident, but I found someone I believe is a witness who told me A.J. was with people when she died and they at least covered it up."

"Who?"

"I don't know yet, but I found the girl A.J. was helping. Jane, she was there when it happened."

"Oh, God."

He could hear the gasp. He was going to overstep badly here, but he couldn't help himself. "I would like you to help her."

"Help her what?"

"Take care of her. She's fifteen, a prostitute and can't really go home to her family. She'll need financial support, counseling, a place to live, money for school."

"Uh, but what does she know about my daughter? What happened?"

"A.J. gave her some money—the five thousand dollars—but her pimp stole it. A.J. went to confront him."

Horror in her voice: "A pimp killed my daughter over five thousand dollars?"

"Maybe. The girl didn't see exactly what happened."

"What's going on, then? If the girl doesn't know anything . . ."

"We can work with her. She knows things she doesn't know she knows. Anyway, I need to bring her back to Chicago and if she's going to help us, we need to help her. You need to help her. Are you understanding me?"

"OK, I guess."

"I'm sorry to bring it up like this, but I need to be able to give her a guarantee of some kind that we'll take care of her. She doesn't really trust people, you know?"

There was an awkward silence and Flood took a breath as his brain caught up to his words. He sounded idiotic. Chalk it up to the lack of sleep, maybe, but Jane Ash didn't know that. His assignment was not to go find a teenage prostitute to save. It was to find out how her daughter died.

"You think she's critical to finding out what happened?"

"I do."

"Well, do whatever. Talk to Philip about it."

"Right. Thanks." He paused awkwardly. The other thing he was leaving unsaid, this question about her divorce, left heavy dead air hanging on the line. She could sense it. Flood was getting more addled by the minute and desperately needed to lie down for a few hours.

"Is there something else?"

"No," he said, embarrassed. "I'll talk to you when I get back."

CHAPTER 24

Flood was headed back down the hall toward the room when his phone rang. Caller ID said "Private Number."

"Flood."

"Hello, this is Wendy Becker. You called me."

Flood told her who he was again and said, "I'm working on a case that led me to look at James and Jane Ash's divorce file."

"Really." She was immediately annoyed, as though he had intentionally misled her by leaving out the names in his message. "I thought you were investigating a death."

"Their daughter drowned in the lake. It's not clear whether it was murder, or suicide, or an accident."

"A.J. Ash is dead?"

"Yes."

There was a long pause.

"That's awful. But I'm afraid I can't help you, Mr. Flood. I'm sure you're a fine lawyer, so you'll already understand that I'm still bound by the protective order on the settlement."

Her condescension was intentional. Flood didn't take it personally.

"Oh, of course," he said warmly. "No, this is something that caught my eye from the public record. The transcript. You said in open court that there had been a discussion between counsel and it was decided there was no need to contact the state's attorney's office. I was just curious what that was about?"

He created a fib because all the other lawyers who had been

involved were still attached to either Jane or James Ash. "I can't find anybody else who knows."

Silence, and then a confused, "No."

"No?"

"Uh."

"What was that about?" he said, still sounding amiable but letting her know he had her.

"Uh, I don't believe that was in the record, was it?"

"Yeah, I just read it from the transcript. That's why I'm calling."

She couldn't resist, even though she would be admitting it had happened.

"I thought that was stricken."

"I guess not. I didn't know anything about it until I read it in the transcript," Flood said. "What were you talking about?"

Her voice hardened a little. She was figuring out a little too late that Flood wasn't bumbling.

"OK, what's this about? What's this have to do with anything?"

"I'm the only one looking at this woman's death. CPD's not really working it because they think it was an accident, maybe even suicide. And James Ash is helping them along in that belief, trying to tamp things down in order to save the family any embarrassment. Jane Ash hired me to find out what happened to A.J. I'm sure it's nothing, but the way I operate, this is a loose end that I can't have. It looks like something very out of the ordinary went on behind the scenes in this case, and it involved a possible criminal investigation. Maybe James Ash was abusive, but I don't know why you said that in open court. You clearly got in trouble for it."

She made some noise, too guttural to express mere annoyance, but then hardened again. "I can't talk to you."

"Listen, I'm crossing things off my list. This is a tangent but I need to know."

"Well, I can't tell you."

"I need to know whether it's possibly relevant to A.J. Ash's death."

"Sorry, I can't help you. I've got to go."

"You're not putting my mind at ease."

"Sorry," she said, and then paused and asked, "So do you think she could have killed herself? The daughter, I mean."

"I think she was murdered."

"Murdered? Over what?"

She was at least interested, Flood thought from her responses. But the only way he was going to get anything out of her was to keep trickling things out, hoping some detail would click for her and change her mind.

"Don't know, but she was trying to get a fifteen-year-old prostitute off the street, and the girl's pimp didn't like it. A.J. worked for a homeless program and befriended the girl there."

Silence on the line.

"Wendy, you there?"

"Uh, I really have to go. Good luck."

She hung up. He cursed under his breath and felt like throwing the phone. At the door of his room, he took a deep breath and exhaled, and then slid the key in and entered as silently as possible. Hotel room doors were so damn clunky, it was a feat to enter without waking Kellee up, but she was sleeping hard and barely stirred. He sat down in an uncomfortable chair and stared out the window, over the endless flat tan rooftops and air conditioners, and into the white desert heat.

He started thinking about James Ash again. Wendy Becker had voiced the point about the state's attorney, so maybe the issue had to do with Jane Ash, but that struck Flood as unlikely. Jane Ash was a lawyer and he didn't imagine her acting like a fool. He didn't believe that Wendy Becker had spoken up by mistake. He thought she meant to do it. And if that was the case, she must have been angry about something. She was paid to be on James Ash's side. Flood thought about him sitting there in his lushly furnished den in Winnetka—a room that was large, but seemed small because all of the other rooms in that enormous house were so much bigger. He thought of his drunken wife wandering in, and how they seemed to be talking past each other but were really communicating on a different level. And he thought about how Ash had offered to double his ex-wife's payments in order to make Flood go away. He was used to getting his way. Given Jane Ash's seeming independence, it's unlikely she would have tolerated much physical abuse. Perhaps this was what happened and Jane was just toying with him, threatening to press charges in the midst of the divorce case and getting the other side flummoxed to the point that Wendy Becker goofed and made an idiotic statement in open court.

He was considering asking Jane Ash about it, as well. But for some reason he knew it was the wrong move. If he'd doubted that, the tone of her response to his request about helping Kellee had affirmed his thoughts. Even exhausted and not thinking straight, he still heard the note of self-preservation in her voice. He didn't know enough about these rich people and their loyalties and strange alliances to speak up freely about where his questions led.

The cell phone buzzing in his shirt pocket woke him up. He was still sitting upright in the chair by the window, and his back ached. After three vibrations the phone rang before he could pick it up, and Kellee woke up. The sun was low and a deep orange over the distant crusty line of the Sierra Nevadas. Kellee squinted and sat up defensively, wrapping her arms tightly around her knees as she studied Flood and analyzed the distance between them. She'd slept hard, whereas Flood had barely nodded into a fog. He opened the phone.

"I'm in a cab. Are we having dinner, or what? I'm starving."

Flood cleared his throat. Nearly five hours had gone by, but it seemed so much less.

"There's a restaurant on the casino floor called Gallagher's. Meet you there in ten minutes." He looked at the girl. "Kellee, you have an ID?"

"Nope."

"Who's got your birth certificate?"

"My mom."

Flood thought a minute.

He scrolled on his phone again until he found her brother David's number. Before he dialed, he saw the text message from Veraneace. Jamie and Kellee's return flight: "12:05 A.M. 21D&E."

Flood called David Leonard, and got an answer on the third ring.

"David, it's Flood, the guy looking for Kellee."

"Oh, hey."

"I'm in Las Vegas with her, and I need to buy her a plane ticket to Chicago, but I need a favor from you."

"What?" Kellee interjected. She was on her feet now, angry someone was making plans without consulting her, but anxious about talking to her brother at the same time.

"OK, sure," David said. "Is that her?"

"Yes. You think your mother has a copy of her birth certificate? I need it faxed to me. And I need it tonight."

"I've got it. I took all that stuff."

"Perfect."

"Um, OK. Can I talk to her?"

"Hold on."

Flood stood up and handed her the phone. She gave him an

angry look but then cradled the phone close to her ear and turned away.

"Hey, Dave . . . yeah, it's me. Yeah . . ."

Flood couldn't hear the rest because he'd picked up the room phone and called the desk for a fax number. He wrote it down and waited for Kellee to finish with her brother. When she said goodbye, he gave David the number and told him the faster the better, and then hung up.

It was six-fifteen.

"You hungry?"

She nodded, but said, "I'm not going to Chicago. I'm not going back."

"We'll figure something out."

Flood washed his face and she did the same. They rode the elevators down to the casino floor and waited for Jamie.

They went into the steakhouse off the casino floor, where it was very dark, and Flood wanted a martini in the worst way but ordered coffee instead. If he had a drink he'd start running his mouth, thinking he was entertaining everybody in the room, and then get sloppy and mean and have to curl up somewhere and sleep about ten hours. Kellee maybe sensed it in him and decided it was time for her to act up a little, too. She ordered a steak that was too big for her to eat, a porterhouse, and made eyes at the waiter when she ordered it. He had no idea what to think. Forty-year-old man about ready to keel over drinking coffee and a fifteen-year-old tart, who was not likely his daughter, ordering a pound of red meat. When the waiter returned with a basket of bread, he found a younger gay man sitting at the table, who immediately looked at him and said, "I'll have a Cosmo with a twist, and please draw me a hot bath."

Flood shook his head. "No booze, you're going back tonight with her."

Kellee and Jamie in unison: "What?!"

"You heard me."

"I'm not going anywhere tonight," Jamie said. "Tomorrow, *maybe.*"

"I want you out of Vegas and back in Chicago," he said to Kellee.

She just looked at him. He realized that when push came to shove, Kellee was tired of being on her own, and the lure of being taken care of, even momentarily, by adults who weren't case workers, saps, pimps or pedophiles apparently had some appeal.

"You're serious?" Jamie whined.

"The tickets have been purchased. Waiting on her birth certificate to be faxed so she can travel."

"You're killing me here," Jamie said.

CHAPTER 25

Jamie started calling Kellee *Little Sister*, and she appeared to buy it. They started making fun of Flood, always among Jamie's favorite ice-breakers. It gave Flood some confidence, but not enough to let Jamie drink that cosmopolitan. David Leonard came through with the birth certificate and Flood drove them to the airport, dumped his car and then bought a ticket to L.A.

He couldn't shake the oddness in Wendy Becker's voice.

The flight was at six A.M. and would put him at LAX an hour later. This side trip would not go on his expense reports. He didn't want Jane Ash to know he was going, in fact. He'd be back in Chicago by the end of the night. Maybe he would sleep in his own bed.

Flood wondered if he could get a car and be on Wendy Becker's doorstep before eight A.M. Anything later, he figured, and he'd miss her and have to wait until the end of the day. Flood thought about just driving to L.A., but it was out of the question. He'd be asleep at the wheel, without a doubt. Ticket purchased, he found his way to the gate and spread out across the seats in the waiting area, setting the alarm on his phone to go off at five-thirty at full volume.

The blaring ring jolted him upright. He felt like he'd been asleep for ten minutes, but it had been about four hours. He did not feel great. The terminal was percolating with early signs of life, travel and commerce as he shuffled down to the bookshop and bought a disposable razor. He'd lost his to the security search. The bathroom smelled like a bathroom smells when there is no ventilation, and there were menacing puddles of water on the floor. He used the soap dispenser to lather his face, and shaved and brushed his teeth. He decided to wait on coffee and boarded the plane, buckled up and was asleep again in minutes as they taxied toward the runway. There were no dreams.

CHAPTER 26

Wendy Becker lived in Glendale, a suburb north of downtown L.A., and a long stretch of freeway from the airport. Flood of course missed her in the morning. He'd rented a car and been on the road by seven forty-five, but it took him another forty-five minutes to get across the city with Veraneace on the phone feeding him Mapquest directions as he sat sipping coffee and looking at car bumpers. L.A. was extremely unfamiliar terrain and his dislocation was only deepened by the aching fatigue corrupting his body and mind. He rolled down the window, letting the still, warm air of a hazy morning surround him.

"What are you going to do now?" Veraneace said.

"I guess I'll go downtown and find the federal building and just call her."

"You could have done that from Las Vegas. Or here."

"No, I need to get to her in person."

"Whatever."

"Have you heard from Jamie?"

"Yes, he claims he's on special assignment and is staying home with this girl."

"That's absolutely right."

Flood looked at his watch. It was ten-thirty in Chicago. He called Jamie.

"Is she still there?"

"Hold on, let me check. I put her in my room so she'd have to come past me to sneak out," he said. Flood could hear a

236

door creak slightly, open and then shut again. "Yes, she's in there. Sleeping like a baby. What do I do the rest of the day?"

"I don't know. Take her shopping for clothes or something. McPhee will be over at some point to help babysit."

Jamie whispered, "What about the c-o-p-s?"

"Not yet. She'll run immediately if we try that."

"Fine by me."

Flood staked out Wendy Becker's house for a few minutes to take the place in—a well-kept white stucco that Flood guessed was fashioned to look like a French farmhouse. There was a small courtyard enclosed by a stucco wall and the gables were steep. Flood drove around the block a few times. Getting the feel for a neighborhood was an old habit. Then he returned to I-5 and drove downtown, past the federal building at Temple and Los Angeles streets, and then found a Denny's and parked. He left her another message. He went into the diner, bought the *LA Times,* ordered an omelet and toast, and started drinking coffee and reading the national and foreign news. The idea that anyone had ever thought the war would go well puzzled him. But Flood got none of his news from TV, so he really didn't know what most of the country had been led to believe.

He'd left the FBI before 9/11, a matter of happenstance for which he would be eternally grateful. If he had been an agent at the time, it would have been harder to leave, he thought. And he really did not want to be a part of this Justice Department. He could feel the anxiety and disappointment in his old colleagues.

After the eggs were gone he had another cup of coffee and then ordered an orange juice, hoping it would pick him up.

His phone rang.

"It's Wendy Becker. I told you I couldn't help you."

"I'm down the street."

"What?"

"Let me buy you lunch. If you don't want to tell me anything, fine. But hear me out."

"I'm not having lunch with you."

"Why'd you call me back?"

"I looked you up. You're an interesting character. Why didn't you tell me you'd been with the Bureau?"

"Does that make a difference?"

"A little. Why are you in L.A.?"

"I came to see you."

"You've wasted your time and money."

"But you think I should know something."

"I didn't say that."

"OK, let's meet and you can explain why I should go home empty-handed."

"Jesus. Where are you now?"

"At a Denny's."

"For real?"

"I wasn't suggesting we eat lunch here. I'll meet you wherever."

"No, Denny's is appropriate. On Ramirez?"

"I guess."

"I'll be there at noon. What am I looking for?"

"Gray suit, white shirt, haven't slept in a bed in three days."

"You'll look like every other guy there. I'll find you."

CHAPTER 27

Thirteen years had passed since the Ashs' divorce. A.J. would have been twelve at the time. Her sixteen-year-old brother probably would have been away at prep school most of the time, so A.J. might have been on her own for a few years as the family splintered apart. Divorce would be wrenching for children of any age, but Flood suspected it was worse for an adolescent daughter. James Ash had mistresses, no doubt, and spent a great deal of time traveling for his resort developments. But none of that had been in the divorce court file Jamie dug up. In fact, the court papers had been almost completely devoid of detail—except for the little items that didn't add up. Two days of hearings for a protective order. Jamie had not ordered the transcript of the complete court proceedings because it would have been a prohibitively expensive waste of time. Wendy Becker would have to fill in the blanks.

As it turned out, Flood was the only sleepless man in a gray suit at the Denny's and he was easy to pick out of the crowd. From his booth, he could see the parking lot, and a woman crossing the lot from a parked Subaru wagon. She was tall and slender, with dark hair and dressed in a gray suit a shade darker than Flood's. He rose to meet her when she spotted him and smirked. They shook hands and she sat down.

"You must be on a fat expense account," she said, making a wave at the Denny's dining room.

"This is what happens when you don't know your way around town."

"Well, there's an In-N-Out Burger close by if you're around for dinner."

"I usually splurge on Applebee's."

She ordered a BLT and iced tea. Flood just had the iced tea. She didn't question it.

"So, you're on a fishing expedition for something that you think will tell you what?"

He shrugged.

"I think somebody committed a crime in A.J.'s death," he said. "If somebody in this family committed a crime ten years ago, I need to know what it is."

"What did Jane Ash say?"

"I haven't asked her."

"And my former client?"

"I haven't asked him."

"You ask his assistant?"

"His assistant?"

"Irish guy, Donal Skiddy. Works for Ash."

"Oh, yeah. Him. Haven't asked him."

She nodded and nibbled her sandwich.

Flood could see it in her face.

"OK," he said. "I'm getting warmer. What about Skiddy?"

She shook her head, but meekly.

"C'mon. He's part of whatever it is, isn't he?"

She just looked at him.

"Did you guys find some kind of real estate deal that wasn't kosher? I mean, I can't imagine Ash would embezzle money from anybody. But if somebody had a piece of land he wanted somewhere, and they didn't want to give it up, then I can see maybe they—"

"It wasn't a land deal," she said flatly, like he was talking gibberish and giving her a headache. Then, slower, "It wasn't a land deal."

Flood slid the sweaty glass of tea away from himself, as if he was making space for what she needed to tell him.

"Then what was it?"

She'd eaten half the BLT and dropped the napkin on top of the sandwich. She was finished. "I am still bound by a protective order."

"We're not having this meeting. I haven't told anyone that I've spoken to you."

"I will deny speaking to you," she said. "And before you get all worked up, you won't find any evidence."

"What was it?"

"Girls," she said, eyes wide. "It was young girls."

"And it was illegal, how?"

"*Young* girls. Fourteen, fifteen. Girls who rode at the stable where Ash and Skiddy kept their horses."

Flood felt like his heart was stopping. Girls. Like Kellee. Flood's ability to think it through stopped there for the moment.

"Uh, how did you know about it?"

She scoffed.

"The wife had found out about it. She threw it on the table as a bargaining chip. Littlewood acted like he was ready for it. I was dumbfounded. Jane Ash's lawyer, the big shot, Swain, sat there with this smug look on his face. Skiddy reeled the girls in, apparently. Sort of a fast crowd at these stables, but not in James Ash's league. Sometimes Skiddy used GHB, the date rape drug. Or so we suspected. I don't know. But the allegation wasn't just James Ash having sex with girls, it was James Ash having sex with girls that Skiddy had procured for him. All I could think was that they were alleging sexual assault, of children, and nobody cared about anything but how it would affect the settlement. I asked what the girls' parents were planning to do, and Swain said they didn't know about it—yet. Leverage. I told Littlewood later that we had an obligation to report it. He told me to shut up. They ended up settling for sixty million instead of forty million, and everybody was happy."

"You don't know any details of who the girls were, or how many?"

She threw up her hands faintly, in disgust. "No idea," she said, and then added, almost as if exhausted by the thought, "But, here's the thing. A.J. rode at that stable. I came across the bills for her horse and lessons when we were sorting through Jane Ash's expenses."

He sat thinking, and his thoughts started to catch up. Jane Ash knew all of this. Swain knew. Flood felt sick.

"What do you know about Skiddy?" she asked.

"Nothing, why?"

"I don't know. I met him when they deposed him. Something was off about him. He said he was from Ireland, but I grew up in Connecticut, and I would have sworn he sounded like he was from New England. I never believed he was what he said he was. And then the pedophilia stuff . . ."

The words hit Flood like a ton of bricks. New England. Boston.

"Oh, God," he said. "Wendy, I have to go."

"What?"

CHAPTER 28

The midday traffic was light enough for Flood to speed back to LAX. Once he had his bearings and was on the I-110 he called McPhee.

"It's her dad and that guy, Skiddy."

"Whattya mean?"

"The big secret they didn't take to the state's attorney from the divorce case. Skiddy was arranging young girls for A.J.'s dad. I think Skiddy is a bogus identity. I bet he's Bobby Finn Burke, the Boston guy who left his prints in Clarksdale."

"The guy who's supposed to be dead? Oh, lord."

"I need you to bring Jamie and the girl in, and sit on her. And call Tally."

"I'm on it. When you back?"

"Not soon enough. There's a two o'clock I can maybe make."

Flood dumped his rental car and boarded a shuttle to the terminal.

Thoughts raced through his head. He thought of Jane Ash and his blood began to boil. He called her number and she picked up, sounding like she was still annoyed from their last conversation.

"Tough shit," Flood said. "I don't know what you really know, but you should have told me. For Christ's sake, A.J. chose to work with child prostitutes, kids sexually exploited by men! Ring a bell, Jane?"

"What are you saying?"

"I'm saying A.J.'s father was fucking Kellee Leonard, the fifteen-year-old girl your daughter was helping. A.J. found out."

"Oh, my God."

"Does Skiddy have a sailboat?"

"Uh, yes. You think . . ."

"Yes, Jane. I think."

"Did the girl tell you that? I think I'm going to be sick," she said, and then added, "James knows?"

"Jane, shut up and listen. I want you to stay home, and don't talk to anybody until I get there. I'm getting on a plane. Call Swain, if you want. But do not call your ex-husband. Understand?"

"God." She was teetering on hysterical.

"Call Swain."

His plane was boarding.

He called McPhee back. "You get Tally?"

"Paged him. Nothing yet. I'm on my way to Jamie's place. He said they'd sit tight."

He was still jostling for position in the aisle of the plane when he hung up and dialed Jamie.

"She behaving herself?" he asked when Jamie answered and sounded not quite completely self-possessed.

"Sort of. Getting nervous."

"Don't tell her what's going on."

"Um, she's sort of figuring it out. I think she knows more than she's let on."

"I know she does."

"McPhee was loud on the phone," Jamie said. "I think she heard a few words."

"OK, put her on," he said as the flight attendant announced that they were leaving the gate and cell phones must be turned off.

"Hold on, she's in the kitchen."

Flood listened to Jamie's breath on the phone as he covered the few steps to his kitchen. "Kellee?"

Flood could hear the surprise in Jamie's voice. "What?" he demanded.

"Oh, fuck. Kellee?"

"Jamie!" Flood shouted, turning heads in the seats next to him.

"Fuck me. She must have gone out the back door."

Jamie ripped open the back door, which was unlocked. Flood didn't know what he said back to him, but the flight attendant was now tapping hard on his shoulder, demanding he turn off the phone.

"Call McPhee, Jamie. Call McPhee."

"I gotta go," Jamie said. The line went dead.

CHAPTER 29

Philip Swain was more than a little embarrassed. When Flood landed at Midway, there were three messages waiting: One from a panicking Jamie saying he had not found Kellee, a subsequent message from McPhee saying he had not found Kellee, and finally a message from Swain saying he would be waiting for him in the limo lane at passenger pickup. As he hustled down the corridors he scrolled through the contact numbers in his phone, looking for the one guy he knew in the FBI's Boston field office.

Special Agent Dale Wittington answered on the first ring.

"Let me guess, Flood, you're calling about Bobby Finn Burke?"

"My name came up, I guess."

"We have three agents on a plane to Clarksdale, Mississippi right now."

"Witt, who the hell was this guy?"

Flood thanked Wittington and snapped the phone shut as Swain's driver opened the back door of a black Town Car. Flood slid in next to Swain, who had a manila folder marked "Skiddy" resting on his lap. It was a dossier his firm had put together while representing Jane Ash in the divorce case.

"I'm sorry," Swain said. "We had no idea any of this was relevant. How could we have?"

"You might have given me a hint," Flood said as he slammed

the door shut.

"There is a protective order, remember," he said lamely. "We're prohibited by court order from disclosing any of this."

"Oh, so if you'd told me about it, Jane might have lost the sixty million she got by agreeing to have everything sealed?" Flood said. "Fuck your protective order."

He was not going to answer the question directly. Instead, he just plopped the file on the leather seat.

"Take a look," he said. "And where do you want to go?"

"Lawrence and Pulaski."

"What's there?"

"Shelter. The only people the girl trusts."

They lurched away from the curb and headed toward the inbound Stevenson to take them back north. Heading downtown at the tail end of rush hour, they might luck out with the traffic and be there in thirty minutes.

The file on Skiddy contained photographs of his cars—a Land Rover and a Jaguar XKE—his townhouse in Lincoln Park, which looked like at least a million and a half, and the boat. It was a white 70-foot ketch called the *Ballylickey*, kept in a slip at Belmont Harbor. A paperclip held together several photographs on printer paper of what looked like surveillance work—grainy long-lens shots of Skiddy sitting on the aft deck of the boat, a very young woman standing before him in a bikini.

"Who's the girl?"

"Unclear, but she at least appeared to be of age."

Under the photos there were several public records—information about the title and mortgage on his house. Vehicle registration. In a separate manila envelope Flood found the real news. It was a death certificate for one Donal Skiddy, recorded in County Cork, Ireland, twelve years before.

"Oh," Flood said. "From my conversation with him, I had

247

mistaken Mr. Skiddy for a live person. How did he die?"

"Car accident. Age thirty-one. No survivors to speak of. No great loss. He had been prosecuted for petty fraud numerous times. Check kiting, I believe. Drug addict."

"Why not keep him alive, then," Flood laughed. "Am I going to find documents proving who he really is in here?"

"No. We didn't get that far. Once we got into the sex stuff in the divorce, the negotiations bent sufficiently in Jane's direction. We closed the Skiddy file. He's a bit of a mystery still."

"Of course. What do you care?"

"You have an idea who he is?" Swain asked.

"Yes. A Boston gangster named Bobby Finn Burke, supposed to have been lost at sea off Cork, Ireland, at about the same time that Mr. Donal Skiddy left the grave and met James Ash."

"What was Bobby Finn Burke up to?"

"From what I was told five minutes ago, he was a financial whiz for the Irish Mob in Boston. Went to prison for a real estate fraud scam, did his time and moved to Ireland when he got out. Then he died. Then he was raised from the dead with the name Donal Skiddy, became James Ash's best friend and came to Chicago."

"A killer?"

"I think he is now," Flood said. "What in the world would James Ash find attractive about this guy?"

"Oh, Mr. Skiddy is not without charm," Swain said. "He's also very effective in some situations, I presume. James and his brother, Edgar, were going into these places all over the place and building golf resorts. Spain, Ireland, the Caribbean. They didn't know anybody. Skiddy became the advance man, would go in, figure out how the locals did things, who had influence, spread a little money around, etcetera. He was a sort of fixer, I guess."

"He undersold his position to me in our conversations, I guess."

"I'm sure James and Edgar don't like to acknowledge they use such a person."

"I think he fixed a few things here in Chicago, too."

CHAPTER 30

Celeste Mayne dispensed with the formalities.

"Where's the fucking bag?" she said, facing them in the threshold of the Girls Refuge office.

Flood shrugged. "You'll remember that I left here without it."

"Somebody took it."

He thought she might throw a punch.

"I haven't been back until now," he said, checking his temper. "Listen, forget the fucking bag. Kellee's in trouble. She could be murdered over what she knows. Tonight. I need to find her."

"This is a shelter, not a police interrogation room."

"You're not listening to me," Flood shouted.

That at least shut her up. She seemed to at least be listening now, going back over what he'd said.

"Who wants to hurt her?"

"The same people she was running from when she left that bag here. The same people who killed A.J. Ash, which is where come in. Remember, I have a job."

"What are you going to do about it?"

"I'm going to find the people who killed A.J. Ash, tie them up in knots and take them to the police. I'd like to do that before they put a bullet in Kellee Leonard. I'd like for you to help me."

She looked at him like he had already failed. She didn't necessarily doubt his intentions, but she doubted he was up to th job. Resignation covered her face. Like he was the best she could hope for, and there was no way he would be enough.

"With Tamika. They're both on the street," she said, showing her own frustration, running a hand through her hair. "Kellee's never really worked the street, but I gather they need money, and I'm worried about them."

"Where?"

"I don't know. Maybe the Cicero track. Try the Prestige."

"Motel?"

She nodded.

Flood said thanks and ran back out to Lawrence Avenue. McPhee had arrived in his Explorer and was idling at the curb when he emerged from the door. Flood left Swain on the Lawrence Avenue curb looking lost, and jumped in McPhee's truck. They took off westward toward Cicero Avenue.

"You tell Tally?"

"Got him on his cell. But they got something big going on. Where'd you say this Tamika's grandmother lived?"

"Somewhere in Austin, according to Celeste Mayne, who I don't really trust for a straight answer."

"Well, shit."

"Why?"

"Tally said things are outta control. Three shootings since noon. Whole West Side—most of Eleven and Fifteen—going up in flames. They got everybody in there tonight: TRU, SOS, pulled in Tac from Twelfth and Thirteenth districts."

"Well, we'll try to stay out of their hair. But I've got to find her."

"I know, I'm with you. I'm just saying it's really the old wild, wild West Side tonight."

"Maybe the girls will be out on Cicero and we won't have to step into this Vice Lords mess tonight."

251

CHAPTER 31

After the Great Fire of 1871 Chicago was rebuilt from scratch, planned on a simple grid system of streets. All the presidential streets of the Loop—Van Buren, Jackson, Adams, Monroe, Madison and Washington—stretched all the way from Michigan Avenue across seven miles of city and into the suburbs. The landscape was as flat as the lake. The shallows of the West Side began at Halsted in Greektown and the UIC campus. Then came the meatpacking district, which still packed meat but was beginning to give way to chic restaurants and yuppies. At Ashland Avenue the expensive condos thinned out, and at Damen Avenue the United Center was the last outpost of first-world commerce. Over the next four miles of real estate a shadow economy run on narcotics defined the lives of three hundred thousand people living in poverty and the constant danger of gunfire—both stray and aimed. It was rough territory mostly carved up by factions of the Vice Lords Nation. It was the world that produced Melvin Runyon and Tamika Moten.

It was a hard place where people made bad choices from a poor list of options.

Most young men chose to have some affiliation with a gang both for protection and to have some shot at an income. It was a guaranteed descent. Starting out in a gang meant you were on the street, handling the dope, the most vulnerable to arrest. Most kids had been arrested by age eighteen, and had been to a penitentiary by twenty-one. With a felony record and little education, that was pretty much that. Chances of making a legitimate living outside the gang were slim. So back they went.

The Prestige Motor Lodge was on Cicero Avenue just south of Roosevelt Road. It was actually in the town of Cicero, but the Chicago city limits were across the street. The motel didn't offer hourly rates, but at sixty-five dollars a night for a room, two or three girls turning five to six tricks apiece made it a lucrative choice. For their pimp. It wasn't like the girls were making any money. That wasn't how the system worked. Pimps controlled all of the activity at places like the Prestige—probably kicking back a portion of their income to the Outfit or whoever actually controlled the place. Anyway, if Kellee and Tamika were out there working, some man would have to be "taking care of them."

It seemed like an insane place for her to run, but from her perspective Flood and Jamie were all from the same world as Skiddy and James Ash. If she was going to be protected from Skiddy, it made more sense to return to the vicious streets controlled by well-armed gangs. Donal Skiddy wouldn't understand the geography, the rules of engagement, or, for that matter, the language.

McPhee had a cold look in his eyes. Nobody was going to hide from him on the West Side of Chicago. He knew the language and the rules.

"I'm tired of these piece-of-shit pimps," he said.

Flood had nothing to add to or detract from that statement, except to say, "Yet another situation arises where I wouldn't mind having a gun."

McPhee gave him a hopeful glance, but Flood said, "Nope. Don't even think about it."

They dropped down Cicero Avenue, over the Ike and into Cicero.

"I got a Louisville Slugger in the back," McPhee finally said, as if reading Flood's mind.

Flood smiled and said, "You have a permit for it?"

CHAPTER 32

Kellee had never seen McPhee so he started walking around the L-shaped courtyard of the motel, up and down, looking for an open door or window or a girl who fit the bill to emerge from any one of the three dozen rooms. He left the Louisville Slugger in the Explorer.

Flood was in the office holding up his business card and showing the picture of Kellee on his cell phone to the desk clerk, a stout and muscular woman of about sixty who looked like trouble.

"This isn't a bordello," she said, like he must have got lost along the way from the lakefront playground he came from.

"Technically, you're right," he said back. "Listen, this isn't a sting operation to close you down the rest of the week. This girl is in trouble that has nothing to do with this place. She's in danger and I need to find her. If she's here or she's been here, I need you to tell me what you know."

She had his business card and let it drop on the counter. "You're not a cop."

"Not anymore. But this is an open police investigation. It just happens that the family of the victim in the case hired me. So you can deal with me quietly now, or I can tell Detective Tally at Area Four Violent Crimes that I didn't get anywhere with this part of the investigation and they'll have to come out with flashing lights, probably a courtesy escort of two or three Cicero PD squads, and they can all park in the middle of your motel for a couple hours and talk to you and all your guests properly."

The muscular old woman shrugged and didn't bother to say, *that all you got?*

Instead, it was just, "You want a room? If not, leave."

Called his bluff, and the best he could do was delay a bit, suggesting she'd just signed on for a world of trouble.

"OK, we'll do it your way." He stepped out the door onto the concrete walk that smelled of piss and spilled gasoline and summer heat. Flood raised the phone to his ear, showing he was about to summon the badges and search warrants. Actually, he dialed his own voicemail and turned his back to her so he wouldn't have to stoop to a pretend phone conversation with the police.

McPhee was strolling the open second level of the motel when a girl finally came out of one of the rooms. Wrong girl but right trade, and she was followed by a young man who reminded him of Melvin Runyon. Taller, dressed in a stiff new St. Louis Cardinals cap with the price tag dangling off the back. He wore a matching red Cardinals jersey over a black t-shirt and baggy jeans and polished chocolate-brown Timberland boots. All his clothes looked off-the-rack, stiff and new.

McPhee stopped walking and stood there taking up most of the walkway. The man in red noticed what he was doing right away.

"I help you, gramps?"

"Oh, I'm almost certain you can. The both of you. Looking for a white girl about fifteen in your line a' work. Call her Britney. She put money in your pocket, young man?"

The girl looked scared. The pimp was playing the game, staring back at McPhee like there was going to be trouble if gramps didn't hobble on home.

"Naw, man. I don't know what the hell you talking about."

He started forward, but McPhee wasn't moving. The girl hesitated and stopped, making the pimp stumble a bit as he tripped over her foot. His face screwed up like a spoiled boy who'd just been humiliated in front of the older kids. He brought the flat of his hand up quickly against the back of her head. She yelped as her head snapped forward, but as he was scowling and spewing, "Watch your ass, bitch," McPhee had him by the wrist, twisting, and then buckled his legs with a swift kick to the back of his knee. In an instant he had the pimp bent over the rusty metal railing staring down at the asphalt and the hood of a Chrysler fifteen feet below. Flood was standing down there looking up. He folded his arms and watched in admiration. These nitwits never suspected McPhee could drop them on their heads in an instant.

"What the fuck you think you're doing, slapping a little girl in front of me?"

"Who the hell are you? You're breaking my arm."

"I'm *gonna* break your fucking arm, you don't tell me where the girl is. Don't say you don't know unless you want me to drop your ass next to that man down there on the pavement."

"*God*-damn," he said. "She ain't here, gramps. Crazy old man. She up and left a hour ago. With that little sister ho."

"Where'd they go?" He twisted a little harder and brought a "Yow" out of the man.

"Back where they come from. I don't fucking know. They walked up the road. Pro'ly took the L back home."

McPhee said, "I'm thinking about sending your ass over just to do everybody a favor."

"That's all I know, man."

Flood looked over to the motel office and saw the muscular woman standing there watching. Making up her mind whether to call the Cicero cops. Maybe not. Flood thought she had the dullest, meanest face he'd ever seen.

"You about finished with him?" he yelled up.

"I think so." He turned and looked to the girl who had inched away down the balcony. "You know where they went?"

She shook her head silently, trying to figure out just how her pimp was going to end up blaming her for causing these two minutes of terror. A beating lay in store for her almost immediately, it seemed. She shook her head more vigorously.

"Like he said," she mumbled. "Back that way." She raised her hand, pointing vaguely east.

McPhee hoisted the pimp back up a bit and then spun and tripped him, sending him sprawling on the concrete floor of the balcony. He headed down the steps without looking over his shoulder.

Chapter 33

As soon as they were on the Ike headed east McPhee got Tally on the phone and asked, "We're looking for this little girl lives over by Garfield Park somewhere. Can you look and see if maybe you got a contact card on her or something?"

There was a lot of background noise and Tally said, "I'm tied up on the street. But call over to the area and get Fitzpatrick. He's doing reports until I get back."

"All right. Thanks, man. Listen, shit's happening with this. Me and Flood about got it figured out. Might need the cavalry tonight."

Tally made a noise that sounded like impatience. "Bad night, Billy. Can't you sit on it for a couple days?"

"Ain't gonna wait, I'm afraid. You got a minute, I'll bring you up to speed."

"I really don't. I'm out here at Sacramento and Monroe. Gun Team got three knuckleheads lined up on a wall. They all know who the shooter was on this double this morning, and one of these motherfuckers is gonna give me a name. Tonight."

McPhee could sense the excitement and stress in Tally's voice, so he decided to let it go. He said thank you, hung up and called the Area Four violent crimes desk.

"Why ain't you out there on the street helping a brother out?" he said, seeing how Fitzpatrick would respond.

"I'm just waiting for him to bring them in so we can split them up. I'm bad cop, you know."

"I bet. He told me to call. I need a favor."

"Name it."

"Need an address for a juvie. Don't know if she ever got picked up, but maybe you got a contact card, at least."

Fitzpatrick wrote it down and then typed Tamika Moten into the CLEAR system. "2700 block of Gladys."

"2700! That's over by Rockwell."

"What used to be Rockwell, old man. You know they're torn down. Nothing but a seniors' building over there now."

"I know. Just that we heard she stayed in Austin."

"Well, let me run the address." He tapped some more. "This place belongs to a Geraldine McKinney, age fifty-six. But I got a handful of names popping on the address. Here you go: Ronald Moten, nineteen," Fitzpatrick said, pausing a moment before getting excited. "Hey, I know this shithead. Actually, we're looking for him. He's a Traveler."

"Gotta be our girl's brother. What you looking for him for?"

"He's part of a crew that slings dope on Maypole. The cul-de-sac over there west of the park. It's ground zero for this war going on right now. Three murders right there since the end of April. Witness puts Ronald at the scene for the last one. We want to talk to him. What do you want with him?"

"The white floater, Ash," McPhee said.

"No, I know that, but what's that got to do with Ronald Moten?"

McPhee was losing his patience. "Got nothing to do with him. His little sister, Tamika, been tricking, and she's friends with a girl we looking for, witness to *our* case."

"Huh," Fitzpatrick said. "No shit. So you guys coming over that way to look for her?"

"Yes, we are. I tried to tell Tally, but he was busy."

"I'll tell him. Keep your heads down if you go in there tonight. It's Loony Tunes out there and Ronald's house might be hot before it's over."

"Well, we'll try not to step on our dicks. I owe you one for the info. Thanks."

CHAPTER 34

"I want to go find Skiddy," Flood said.

Their blind side was Skiddy. Where was he? Was he looking for Kellee? Had he already found her?

"The girl would run from me," McPhee said. "Skiddy I can handle."

That made some sense. Flood called Jamie.

"Did you find her?" Jamie said, breathless.

"Not yet. But it's going to be OK. I need you to come get Billy. And he needs your car."

"How do I get there?"

There were simpler tasks than explaining to Jamie how to drive to a short street in East Garfield Park, but Flood eventually launched him on the mission. They were just getting to the address themselves. When he hung up, Flood noticed his cell phone battery was almost dead. He dug the charger out of his suitcase in the back of McPhee's Explorer and plugged it in as McPhee pulled to the curb at Gladys and Rockwell. The block was mostly vacant lots; so much of the brick and mortar of the neighborhood had been pared away that the remaining few houses looked like lonely wanderers lost on a snapshot of prairie.

"The white one," Flood said. It was a typical two-flat, steps up to the first floor, with a separate outside door to the basement unit tucked under the stairs.

While they sat and watched for activity in the house, McPhee filled Flood in on Detective Fitzpatrick's information about Tamika Moten's brother, Ronald, being wanted for questioning in a murder.

"How big a deal is he?" Flood asked.

"Sounds like not too big. Slings dope on the corner."

The windows of the house were dark, and the street quiet, a streetlight casting a bluish glow over the faded white brick of the house. Sitting there in the quiet was driving Flood crazy. He needed to act, but he had no option except to wait. This house was the only likely lead they had. When his nerves began to settle, another thought began to trouble him.

"How did I lose her? Christ, I almost got killed and charged with murder tracking her down," he said.

"No time to get mad about it."

"I'm still missing so many pieces. She knows it's Skiddy. She knows I know it's Skiddy. Why is she trying to get away from me?"

"This girl doesn't trust anybody," McPhee said. "And all the men your age she knows were renting her ass from a sleazy Negro. The whole thing makes me want to vomit, over and over again."

Flood nodded. But still, the logic of Kellee's actions seemed to not fit.

"I dangled Jane Ash's money in front of her. You'd think that alone would keep her hanging around."

"You think there's an angle we don't know about?"

"Several—but specifically, one that makes her feel like we're not her best bet for help."

A blue Mini Cooper zoomed through the intersection in front of them.

"Well, there he goes," Flood said. It was Jamie, missing the turn, getting lost. Several minutes passed in silence before the Mini came back up the street, timidly turning the corner and crawling toward them. McPhee got out and stood by the open door.

"All right, she's all yours," he said, pointing at the steering wheel.

Jamie looked worried. He peered out the window of his little car at Flood.

"I totally fucked up, I know."

Flood waved it off. "If she wanted to sneak out, she was going to find a way. Not much you could do about it."

McPhee asked to drive and Jamie climbed into the passenger seat.

"I'll be in touch," McPhee said, shifting into first and zipping down the street.

CHAPTER 35

As he sat, Flood wondered about the fact that he had watched Kellee for a day and then she decided she needed to get away. It would be nice to get a straight answer from somebody. If Skiddy hadn't killed Melvin Runyon, they'd have gotten it out of him.

Flood heard a lot of sirens in the blocks around him with the occasional flicker of blue strobes in the night air. But the sounds and lights came and went, giving the impression of routine mayhem in one of the most dangerous neighborhoods in America. He was mainly watching the house and the intersection in front of him, though he was aware of the rearview mirror, alert for flashes of light. But he only caught a glimpse of the headlight darting past in the intersection behind him. He turned just in time to register the lines of a big red pickup truck, tricked out with rims, passing out of view. He heard the motor revving, accelerating out of the intersection after slowly rolling through. He wondered if it was one of the gangbangers involved with Ronald Moten, and whether it was a friend or foe. The sound of the police sirens came back to him, and the warning of Tally and Fitzpatrick that this was not a good night to be bumbling around on the West Side.

Another ten minutes of listening to the ebb and flow of distant battles passed and then a car slowed in the intersection. An old gray Buick Century with some rust idled to the curb in front of the Moten house. The rear passenger side door opened and out stepped Tamika Moten and Kellee Leonard.

"Hallelujah," Flood said under his breath. He waited to see what the rest of the people in the car would do. The motor was still running. Tamika shut her door and leaned in the open window of the front door for a moment. While she talked to whoever was in there, Kellee looked around, taking in the neighborhood, yet more unfamiliar terrain for a homeless girl with nowhere to go. Flood slouched to be less visible, but the Explorer was on the far side of a streetlight, and would be difficult to see clearly from where she was standing. As she stood there unaware of being watched, she looked frightened. Flood thought of all the things he was about to say to her to lure her back into his car, but what he really felt was dread. Her problems were beyond this drama, were far beyond anything he could fix. In the end, he was really just using her to get what he needed—an explanation of who killed A.J. Ash, how it happened exactly, and why. What was he going to do for Kellee once those questions were answered? What could anybody do for a girl like this—a fifteen-year-old girl who lived pimp to pimp because there wasn't much of an option for her elsewhere?

Tamika stood up and the car drove off. They started to walk toward the house. Flood reached for the ignition, planning to roll up close before getting out. But somebody beat him to it. The red pickup he'd seen minutes before came rolling around the corner and pulled in diagonally toward the curb between the girls and the house.

It was too dark for Flood to see the driver in detail; just a dark form shifting quickly. The door opened. Then he came into view. The mask looked absurd until Flood's eye registered more of the scene and realized the front license plate on the truck had been removed. Tamika, who was standing between the man and Kellee, attempted a few brave obscenities. Kellee saw the situation for what it was and was torn between bolting and staying close to her friend. Maybe it made sense for her to run.

After all, it was her Skiddy wanted to kill. The gun came up, in his left hand. All this in about three seconds: the time it took Flood to turn the ignition key, drop into drive, and floor the gas pedal. Bright lights, barking rubber and a roaring engine coming out of the shadows made Skiddy turn and look. Seeing the chance, the girls turned and started to run up the sidewalk, losing sandals and screaming. Skiddy whirled back and fired a hasty shot in their direction as Flood flew at him, not quite sure what he was going to do when he got there and the bullets started flying at him. Run him over? Crash into his vehicle? He had no gun. The steering wheel felt loose in his hands as the Explorer accelerated. His vision blurred, with the distance shrinking from a hundred feet, to fifty, to twenty.

After the muzzle flash, Flood saw a spark off the concrete sidewalk and watched Tamika tumble to the ground. Kellee was standing there screaming as Tamika lay on the ground rolling in pain. Skiddy could have finished her with another bullet, but he turned to Flood and aimed. Three bursts from the gun as Flood ducked, bending over into the passenger seat, unable to see where he was going. The first two shots thudded on the windshield, making thin spider webs that obscured the entire expanse of glass. The third came through, piercing the headrest.

His foot had come off the gas but he found the pedal again and buried it, praying he'd hit Skiddy. Instead, he went over the curb and plowed into a light pole. The force tossed him forward into the dash, wrenching his body at the hip. His face and nose hit hard against an air conditioner vent. The truck came to a stop and rolled back a bit. The engine had died and Flood reached for the key and turned. Nothing but electrical clicks. A gunshot shattered the driver's side window and revived his senses. He lunged over toward the passenger door, opened it and somersaulted onto the grass of the parkway. He kept rolling, over a rusty iron rail and down the garden steps in front of the Moten house into the darkness of the gangway. Skiddy fired again and the bullet ricocheted off the concrete behind him and found the brick wall in front of him to his left. Flood scurried deeper into the gangway between the house and a solid wooden fence that had once ringed a vacant lot next door. He felt the burning in his abdomen from the crash. He'd torn something. The lights were on in the house now and he heard the front door open and a woman start hollering Tamika's and the Lord's name over and over again.

He listened helplessly for the kill shot from Skiddy's gun. He expected him to be standing over Tamika by now, killing her and then probably wasting the grandmother as she came down the front steps. Flood had failed to stop anything.

No sound came but the slamming of a car door and the whir of gears in reverse. Skiddy didn't care about Tamika. He was after Kellee. Flood finally came back out to the street, avoiding the hysteria at the corner, and went back to McPhee's Explorer. The grill was smashed and the windshield was opaque with the effect of the gunfire. He was about to try anyway when he noticed the front passenger side tire had gone flat. He weighed his options and wiped blood that had trickled from a small gash in his forehead. The grandmother started screaming at him to do something, but he looked back her and said nothing. She was also screaming into her cell phone. Tamika was holding her hip with a bloody hand and screaming. She looked like she would live. An ambulance was surely on the way.

The approaching rattle and whoosh of the elevated train two blocks away joined the cacophony of screams and distant sirens. That's where she would go, he decided. She'd be lost in this neighborhood without Tamika. He turned and ran. The sore muscles in his belly seared with pain but he kept going, trying to run through the ache. Back through the gangway and across the alley, diagonally across a vacant lot on the next corner and into the street. He loped up California toward Lake Street and the Green Line station. She might be there by now, but she couldn't have caught the train that just passed. As he ran in and out of the glow of streetlights, drawing a few heckles from youngsters on porches wondering out loud what a white man was doing out here when the shooting had started, the same Buick that had dropped the girls off minutes before flew past. He heard the tires squeal as the driver hit the brakes and the car came to a halt in the middle of the street. He kept running without looking back as he heard the doors open and a few shouted obscenities flew his way. A door slammed and the car launched onward. He finally looked back and saw that a young man was following him, keeping his distance. He was surrounded. An armed killer lay ahead of him, and a gangbanger was closing in from behind. As he ran, he suddenly realized in a panic that he had no phone. It was still in the Explorer.

There was no turning back to get it. The elevated train station was suspended over Lake Street ahead of him and looked deserted. Sirens continued to blare in the distance. It felt like the night was teetering on something apocalyptic, but only because he was not used to the chaos of the West Side.

As Flood came closer to the station, he saw the pickup pulled into a vacant lot. Twin staircases straddled Lake Street: one for the outbound side of the tracks, one for the inbound side. He considered which stairwell Kellee would have used and decided she'd try inbound, to the Loop. He hoped she'd figured out which was which. He went up, hearing nothing. The kid tailing him was short and hefty, and Flood could hear him huffing into his Nextel that they'd come to the Green Line. Flood trusted the kid was just an observer and did not have authorization to shoot anybody.

At the top of the steps the small concourse was separated from the platform by a row of turnstiles and a station office kiosk, which appeared to be vacant. Flood stopped and listened. At first he heard nothing and then stepped closer to the turnstiles. He used the small office kiosk as cover—though he was a sitting duck if Skiddy came after him. No gun, no place to hide. If he could get close to Skiddy before he had a chance to fire, he might take him. Otherwise, he'd be out of luck.

Through the thick tinted glass of the office, which had plate windows on all four sides, he finally saw Skiddy step into view. Flood thought he had not been seen yet and waited and watched.

Skiddy spoke. "Kellee, I'm not leaving without you, dear. Come on out. You're not in any trouble, but we need to come to terms. You hear me?"

Nothing. Skiddy walked a few more steps out onto the platform, his back still to Flood. When he started to talk to the unseen girl again, Flood eased himself over the turnstiles silently and made his way a few steps onto the platform. If he could creep up slowly while Skiddy was distracted by the sound of his own voice and the search for the girl, he would have a chance. They were separated by about fifteen feet of concrete. Skiddy's hands were at his sides, one of them holding a large-caliber semiautomatic.

Flood heard a vehicle come to a stop down below on California. One door opened and closed, but he heard no voices. Skiddy heard it too, but didn't turn toward the railing to look over. He was preoccupied with the edge of the platform and stepped out to the blue rubber caution strip and stood looking down. Flood was about to rush at him, but something in Skiddy's posture made him hesitate. He waited. And Skiddy turned around and smiled at him. He had known he was there all along.

"Thought you might try," Skiddy said, his grin growing wider. Flood took a step back toward the turnstiles.

"Glad you're here, Mr. Flood," Skiddy went on. "Let's talk about this. It's been one misunderstanding after another, hasn't it?"

Flood desperately needed to buy time. He said, "Oh, I think I understand."

"You think you understand," Skiddy went on. "You think I'm the bad guy. Pains me to feel that. Maybe you dislike my employer and you're holding it against me."

Flood stood there feeling naked.

"I try not to get personally involved in the cases I take," he said. "It's unprofessional."

"Well, here I am trying to uphold a sense of right and wrong," Skiddy went on.

"That's a fine idea," Flood said. "Let's let the police sort this out."

Skiddy grinned again and bent his long body straight down into a sudden crouch, reaching over the side of the platform. He yanked at something. Kellee was hiding down there and he now had her by the hair. She screamed and flailed, but Skiddy wrenched her up onto the platform.

"Here we are," he said. She had been trying to hide down on the tracks, tucked against the platform, but there was really nowhere to hide, no way to get far enough underneath. He now had her half up, her legs dangling over but her head face down on the concrete. He was still holding onto her hair but he'd stood up a bit, placing his foot on her neck. It looked like he might snap her spine if he shifted his weight. She sobbed and begged. The noise and helplessness of the moment throbbed though Flood's body. He wanted to scream.

Skiddy said to Flood, "Why don't you come on out here? We'll have a chat and sort all of this out."

"Let her go."

Skiddy smiled. "Out here, please."

Flood stepped away from the turnstiles. He took three steps. He might as well get too close for comfort. If he was going to disarm Skiddy, it would be the only way.

"Good enough, Flood. Rather not feel your breath."

"Pretty exciting night for a guy who's just a glorified greens keeper."

"You're so right. I should be home mowing the lawn."

"Let me give you a list of reasons you don't want to shoot us."

"Ha. If you make it quick. Time's short, I'm afraid."

Kellee sounded like a puppy being stepped on. "Please," she wailed. "I won't say nothing. I promise. I didn't tell him nothing."

"Let's start there," Skiddy said. "What would you tell if you wanted to spill some beans?"

"It was all my fault. I'll . . ."

Kellee's face was pinned against the platform, looking past Flood. She stopped talking, as if recognizing it was no longer her turn to speak. Skiddy looked, too. Flood only sensed the presence but knew who it would be. He heard the voice behind him, moving past him.

"You the one shot my little sister," said a young black man in a long white t-shirt. He had come over the turnstiles at some point and stepped out from behind the wall of the kiosk. He held a gun, leveled at Skiddy.

There wasn't much to argue about. Skiddy raised his gun and fired three times, the bullets whizzing past Flood. He dove back to the turnstiles as the return fire came back.

The noise turned the moment upside down. Flood was on the floor, rolling across the smooth concrete of the platform, assuming he'd been shot. The blasts still ringing in his ears, he rolled into the refuge of the turnstile and crouched, rubbing his head and neck looking for blood, opening his coat, doing the same. Nothing.

Skiddy spilled backward, letting go of Kellee, stood up straight, fell down, got up and stumbled backwards, crimson spreading through his khaki shirt. He fell again, looking confused as he slumped out of Flood's sight. Kellee slipped back down onto the tracks and vanished.

Ronald Moten was flat on his back, a pool of blood forming around his neck. His foot twitched and then he didn't move again.

Skiddy said nothing more. Flood's ears rang and the smell of gunsmoke hung in the air. Assuming the amount of blood meant Ronald Moten had been shot through a major artery and was dead, Flood looked the other way, down the length of the platform. Skiddy's shirt was drenched from the sternum down.

For the moment, Flood was staying put. "Skiddy, you don't look so hot," he said.

"What of it?" Skiddy said, sounding merely winded.

"There's nothing left to protect. Why don't you tell me the story?"

There was a cough and a laugh. "You're not going to call me an ambulance, Mr. Flood?"

"I don't think it will do much good."

"I didn't think so, either. So maybe, I'd like a little peace and quiet here, if you don't mind."

"Plenty of that later. You might as well tell me all about it. Taking secrets to the grave won't help you any."

"Oh, of course. Recollections might fatten your paycheck a bit, though, won't they? Or don't you care about the money? Just out for the truth? It's all about closure for Janey Ash, is that it, Mr. Flood? Like I give a fuck about Jane Ash."

"All of it," Flood said. "Come on. You don't have a beef with me anyway, do you, Mr. Burke?"

"Ah, very good," Skiddy said, weakening. "You figure out

who I was on your own?"

"Half of it. The actual name came from the FBI."

He tried to laugh at that, but it brought a coughing fit. Gradually, he recovered.

"I didn't do it, you know," Skiddy said.

"Do what?"

"Kill A.J."

"This isn't going to help anybody."

He laughed hard enough to moisten his lips with blood. Time running out.

"No, it should have been me. You're right. That's the laugh in it."

Flood wasn't sure if he believed him, but he played along. "Melvin Runyon?"

"That idiot."

It wasn't an answer or an accusation. It only seemed that the name was unpleasant to Skiddy, and he needed to curse it just to clean his palate.

"We were all fools for A.J., Mr. Flood. Even you, I suspect, as you went through her lovely things, and looked at the photos of how fucking lovely she was, and people told you how humble and troubled the poor girl was. You didn't know her. Fuck, I didn't know her."

Flood stood up and walked down the platform a bit, still careful to have someplace to his right where he could duck if Skiddy raised the gun that still lay in his limp hand.

"A.J. . . . she was so appalled by the girls we had, but she wasn't much more than a girl first time I . . ." He coughed up more blood and whatever remained in the thought was lost. He finally added, ". . . Whole family, sadists."

"How did she die, Skiddy?" Flood drew it out. This was the question, damn it. *Answer it before you die.*

Skiddy had no smiles left. "Give it a rest, Flood. What does it matter now?"

"It matters a lot. It matters to a mother to know how her daughter died."

"You're so fucking naive. But good for you."

"Did the girl really jump off the boat and swim to shore?"

Skiddy looked like he was going to laugh at that, but he coughed harder than he could afford. Blood and bubbles this time. He looked at Flood again and all the humor had gone from his eyes. Flood didn't lift a finger to help him. He just sat there watching the life run out of him.

He wanted to be funny, but didn't have the breath for it. He just said, "No, she didn't swim. Would have taken care of her right there, but the pimp fell in the water. He couldn't swim."

He paused, teetering on the abyss. "Got him. She ran. Got away."

"You put a bag of heroin in A.J.'s apartment?"

"Yeah, what the hell. Muddy the water a bit. Everybody knew she was a lush. Make her a junkie and . . ."

One last rally from Skiddy.

"Oh God, I've had it. But my conscience is clean, Mr. Flood. Clean. I didn't kill the boss's daughter. You understand me?" he said, and then went on. "Boom, down she went. Hit her head just so . . . Was it. Just chance. Anyway, wasn't me."

"OK," Flood said, "You're just a pedophile."

Skiddy spit out a laugh with a bubble of blood. Seconds left.

"Just whores," he said. "Ain't been children in a long time."

"Thanks to you."

"Gimme a fucking break."

"And Runyon, don't forget him. I do think you put a bullet through his head."

"The pimp? Jesus, I did the world a favor on that one. Shoulda left him in the water."

"Because he pimps these whores who aren't worth being saved from you? OK, I guess the world's been done a favor tonight, too."

But Skiddy didn't hear it. He was thinking his last thought.

"The girl shoulda stuck with me, Flood. I was her only friend. If she stuck with me I could have handled every . . ."

And that was it. He had his peace and quiet. And it was quiet there on the L platform. For one moment, there were no sirens in the distance. No voices screaming outrage from stoops, no crack of small arms fire. For a fleeting moment, there was nearly perfect silence in the hot, heavy summer air on the West Side of Chicago.

Flood called out, "Kellee, it's OK. He's dead. You can come out."

No response. She'd heard Skiddy ramble. It made little sense but these people were all crazy.

He walked along the edge of the platform looking down into the darkness of the tracks. He saw nothing but wooden ties and brown steel.

He called out one more time, "Kellee. It's OK. It's just me, Flood."

Nothing.

After a moment he walked over to the body of Donal Skiddy, or Bobby Finn Burke. Take your pick. For a moment he stood over the body deciding whether it made sense to go through his pockets looking for a phone. By the time he made up his mind it would be fine, he heard the rattle of an inbound Green Line train. The bright green placard and twin yellow lights marking the top of the train brought him to his senses. There was a call box by the station office. He pushed it and turned around, seeing the driver in the train go wide-eyed as he caught a glimpse of the carnage. The train pulled through the station and stopped a safe distance on.

He had wanted the phone so he could call McPhee and get him looking for Kellee. But that didn't happen. The police handcuffed Flood for their convenience and put him in the back of an unmarked car, where he sat for the better part of an hour. Finally, he was driven to Area Four by a middle-aged white detective with steel gray hair, wire-rimmed glasses, no smile and teeth that never stopped kneading a wad of gum.

As he jammed the Crown Vic into gear, he said, "I'm Symberski. They said you used to be on the job with the Bureau. That right?"

"I quit four years ago. I'm a lawyer now."

"All right. Save the rest 'til we get to the area."

Symberski did not say he was doing Flood any favors but he took the cuffs off when they parked behind the building. They walked in side by side and headed up the stairs to the detective room. On the drive over, Flood had been preoccupied with two tasks—assessing Symberski's attitude toward him, and organizing his account of what happened so that he didn't dig a hole with inconsistencies once they started talking on the record. But as they passed the detectives' bullpen on their way to an interview room, Flood scanned the desks and the faces looking at him, and there was Fitzpatrick with a phone stuck to his ear. His eyes glued on Flood. He stopped, knowing in that instant that his gut was right. He walked over to the railing and took a deep breath.

"You fucking idiot," Flood shouted.

Symberski grabbed him by the collar. "Goddammit. Shut up," he barked, confused about why Flood was suddenly ranting, but angry nonetheless. Anybody who didn't behave got the same treatment. It didn't matter whether you used to carry a badge.

Flood didn't budge. Fitzpatrick was mute.

"He was the bad guy, you moron," Flood said. "You were

feeding information to the fucking killer."

Now he had everybody's attention. Symberski said goddam-mit again and yanked.

The hefty sergeant who had been there the night Flood met Tally with McPhee stood up, showing no sign that he had ever seen Flood before, and shouted at Symberski, "Shut that fucking jagoff up and get him out of here!"

Symberski yanked on Flood's collar again. "Shut the fuck up and keep moving."

Flood wanted to dump Symberski over the railing, but that would be serious trouble, so he kept his mouth shut and started walking. He looked back at Fitzpatrick, who was turning pink.

Symberski slammed the door and cursed again. He looked like he might choke on his gum.

Flood slumped into a chair. "It reeks of piss in here."

Symberski regained his composure, sat down and said coolly "I'm going to rip your head off and piss down your throat if you don't tell me what that was about."

"I'll tell you exactly what's going on. Go take Fitzpatrick's cell phone away from him. I bet he's got half a dozen phone calls over the last two days to the DOA on the Green Line platform."

Symberski raised his eyebrows and leaned forward. "Excuse me?"

"That's right," Flood said, and commenced to explain the identity of Donal Skiddy, AKA Bobby Finn Burke. When he got to the part about the fingerprints on the pay phone in Clarksdale, Mississippi, coming back to the late Mr. Burke, Symberski said, "Stop."

He got up and left the room. In ten minutes the door opened abruptly and another angry white man with a badge on his belt walked in with Symberski.

"You know who I am?" the new guy barked at Flood.

"Probably Lt. Dickens."

They started over, and eventually came around to the train platform.

"What was the conflict between Donal Skiddy and Ronald Moten?" Symberski asked.

"Skiddy shot and wounded Moten's little sister about an hour before this happened."

"So Donal Skiddy goes on a rampage across Garfield Park over a little black hooker named Tamika, who happens to be the sister of Ronald Moten?"

"Not just her. There was another girl he was after. I don't know what happened to her."

"Who is she?" Dickens asked.

"White girl who used Britney as a street name. She was one of Melvin's girls, and we went to Mississippi looking for her."

"You and McPhee?"

"That's right."

"And you didn't find her?"

Flood shrugged. "We weren't done talking to Melvin and then he went and got his brains blown out."

"So Skiddy wanted to wipe out Melvin's operation?" Dickens asked.

"So it would seem."

"Where's your client's dead daughter figure in?"

"She worked with the girls. She also was the daughter of Skiddy's employer, James Ash."

"We get that. This is all real fucking cozy," Symberski interjected. "But what was going on?"

Flood nodded. "If you're going to ask me the chicken-or-egg question, I really don't know."

Dickens rubbed his face like he was trying to wipe away the fatigue. "But what's your gut, Flood?"

Flood wanted to tell them that he'd slept about four of the

last seventy-two hours and no longer felt that he had a gut, but it wouldn't get him anywhere.

"A.J. Ash was working with these girls. She stumbled across Donal Skiddy using them. She confronted him and he of course saw the consequences—that he'd be permanently separated from the platinum tit of the Ash family fortune."

"So he killed your woman, the pimp and tried to wipe out the girls, too?"

"It'd be far-fetched if Skiddy wasn't a ghost from the Irish Mob in Boston. He can't afford any trouble. He can't afford to ever get fingerprinted."

"So, he killed your woman," Dickens repeated.

"I thought maybe Melvin helped him, but who knows. It's all guesswork, at this point."

Truth be told, nobody at Area Four was too broken up about the death of Ronald Moten.

"He was one of the up and coming knuckleheads trying to stake his claim before Howard Purcell gets out of Menard," McPhee said when he picked Flood up at three in the morning, still driving Jamie's Mini. The Explorer was totaled. "Tally thinks things might actually calm down a bit out here with him gone."

"They're going to give Skiddy a posthumous good-citizen award?"

"What they're gonna do is forget any of this shit happened because of the Fitzpatrick fiasco."

"They're not going to chase down Kellee?"

"Nope. They'll let the FBI do whatever on Skiddy. Deal with James Ash's wall of lawyers about harboring a fugitive, etcetera."

Flood threw up his hands. The whole thing was absurd. "There was no fugitive. Bobby Finn Burke was officially—though incorrectly—dead."

"Well, now it's super official."

"I guess." Flood sighed.

"You satisfied?"

"Not exactly."

McPhee handed him a slip of paper with a phone number on it.

"What's this?" Flood asked.

"A lead off Skiddy's cell phone that nobody's gonna follow up."

McPhee said this was what would happen to Fitzpatrick: Dickens would initiate a complaint register against the detective. He would conduct an "investigation," at the end of which he would recommend a two-day suspension for Fitzpatrick's behavior. Improper communication with a witness or something. The command channel review would knock it down to one day. Fitzpatrick would protest and they'd probably do away with the suspension altogether.

"Whatever," McPhee said as he drove Flood home. "As long as Brother Tally can get away from him. I would not tolerate that motherfucker as a partner for one goddamn minute."

CHAPTER 36

It was close to four o'clock when Flood crawled into bed. Twenty minutes later he was still lying awake in the darkness as his cell phone rang. The Caller ID register said "private number," but he had a feeling.

"Is he dead?" Kellee Leonard asked.

"He is."

"Do you believe what he said?"

"I don't really understand what he said."

"What are you going to do now?"

"I'd like to talk to you about getting you some help."

"That's not going to happen."

"Let me try."

"I'm fine," she said. Every bit as convincing as when she'd said it the day before in Las Vegas. "Are the cops coming after me?"

"It didn't come up," he said. "I don't think they will. And my understanding is that James Ash was not a witness. Is that true— that he wouldn't have seen what happened?"

"Why's that matter?"

"Because the others, besides you, are all dead."

Silence.

"I don't think he saw."

She sounded genuine. If the answer did not quite ring with certainty, Flood thought it was because she could not be completely sure of what James Ash witnessed. He wanted to draw Kellee in.

"Will you let me help you?" Flood asked, returning to the topic.

"You can't help me."

"Well, maybe, maybe not. You can at least just take what's given."

"Ha. Right. What's being given?"

"The Ashes can afford to come up with something for you. Money and help to start a life. If they don't, I will."

"I don't want their money."

"Kellee, you should take it. It could help."

"Don't tell me what I should do," she said in disgust. "I'll see ya."

And she was gone.

He exhaled and dropped the phone at his side, nestled in the rumpled sheets like a visitor in his bed. As he lay there looking out at the city, checkerboards of light glowed from the tall buildings across the river.

CHAPTER 37

The next afternoon he was back in Philip Swain's office. The old gray man looked a little softer than he had at their first meeting, but Jane Ash was just as cool and maybe even a little tougher than he'd first found her to be. She had not fully expected the consequences of what she'd asked Flood to do, the ugliness that might be revealed, but the result had not crushed her. It had sharpened her edge.

It was gray and muggy on the street and the view from the top of the Sears Tower was whitish and vague, making this feel even more unpleasant than it was and giving him the urge just to have his feet back on the ground. Swain fidgeted and looked at Jane Ash for direction. What a changed man he seemed. She didn't acknowledge him.

"Just tell me," she said.

"Your husband was there. With Skiddy."

"On Skiddy's boat?"

"Might have helped if you'd told me what you really figured from the beginning."

"I didn't figure *this*. For God's sake."

"If I'd known who everybody was and what they'd done from the start, some people might still be alive."

"On the boat?" she asked again.

"Yes. In the slip at Belmont Harbor. The pimp, Melvin Runyon, would bring girls to them there. Mainly Kellee Leon ard, age fifteen, formerly of unsafe home in Creve Coeur, Illinois."

"A.J. knew her?"

"Yes, Jane. A.J. knew her. What the hell was she doing?"

"I don't know. I really don't."

"Why don't you tell me what you want me to find out and I'll give it a whirl. Because I'm not confident you want the truth anymore."

Jane Ash's eyes got hot and her cheeks reddened.

"Watch it," she snapped. "I'm not paying you for lectures."

"And I'm not in business to make an ass of myself."

"Spare me."

Flood stood up. It was time to cut this off before it got ugly in a terminal way. The fact was, he wasn't finished and he didn't really care what her marching orders, or even her explanations, were at this point. Whatever she said was unreliable, so he might as well not hear it. He was better off just digging on his own.

"Where are you going?" Swain asked, looking befuddled. He had adjourned nothing.

"Back to work. I'm spinning my wheels here."

He was in the hallway by the time Swain managed to sputter, "Well, wait . . ."

CHAPTER 38

Flood took a cab back to his apartment building and brought his car out of the garage. He took the Kennedy to Lawrence and headed toward Girls Refuge. He had seen too much of the life of the girls Celeste Mayne served since his last, incendiary visit. From his distance, their plight seemed hopeless. But for her, he realized, being with these girls every day, it was just life. Pain, struggle, damage, poverty, the hustle: that was their reality and it went on every day whether you stuck with them or walked away. Most people walked away, eventually, but Celeste Mayne stayed.

Flood felt tired, and angry, and guilty. He also had that false fervor that he knew was the result of all these emotions, a fantasy he conjured to combat how ineffective he felt.

She answered the door and started to shake her head and laugh. "You've got to be kidding."

Flood raised his hands in surrender. "I came to apologize, and to ask for help."

She put a hand on her hip. "Well. You've apologized. Good for you. Now, please go away and don't ever come back. I really am not interested in whatever you're begging for."

"Please, let me in for a minute."

"No. I mean it."

She wasn't looking over her shoulder this time. Perhaps there were no girls there at the moment.

"I want to help Kellee," he said. "I think she can be helped."

"You have no clue what can or can't be done for her. Really. And by now, you ought to understand you are a threat to her. You'll get her killed."

"That's over. Skiddy is dead. Melvin Runyon is dead."

"Yeah, I know," she said, cutting in. "I read about it. And I saw that you kept yourself and your clients out of the news. So, there's no real accountability, is there? Even though you saw Tamika get shot and just left her there."

She shouted the last part.

"Skiddy was after Kellee. That's where I went. I'm telling you, I accept responsibility for Kellee. And I can help her."

"And what about James Ash?" she said, pausing to enjoy the effect of saying his name. Making it understood that, yes, she knew that part of the story. "He's alive. And no one seems to be asking questions about him. Oh, right, I forgot. He's a gazillionaire."

"He wasn't there."

"Wasn't where?"

"He wasn't there when A.J. Ash was killed. You want to prosecute him for raping Kellee? Will she come forward, give a statement?"

He was crossing Celeste Mayne's temper again, which was not what he had intended to do. It just seemed inevitable. She was such an angry person. Whatever he said seemed to set her off. Maybe she would stop hating him if he stopped breathing. But he doubted it. Not that she didn't have a point. He came here hat in hand because he knew her rage was justified. The more abuse suffered by girls like Kellee and Tamika, the more debased they became, and the more disposable they were to everybody else. And what could be done about it? There weren't really any answers.

"Listen," he said. "I believe James Ash has committed crimes against Kellee Leonard, and crimes against humanity, for that matter. But I'm also a realist. And a lawyer. The witnesses against him are either dead or teenage prostitutes who will never let themselves be reliable witnesses. Even if Kellee was willing, would that be good for her?"

The notion of Kellee cooperating with a criminal investigation was so far-fetched that Celeste Mayne seemed struck mute by the thought of it. And maybe she was running out of fuel for punishing Flood. She just shook her head. They had reached some uncomfortable, momentary truce.

Flood let a moment pass and then asked, as plainly as he could, "Do you know how to help her?"

Celeste's sigh was benign. They were still in that clearing of understanding.

"Help her what?" It was partly a rhetorical question. Where to start?

"I don't know. Live a life. Have friends. Got to school. Trust somebody."

"Love somebody?" She said it almost as if Flood was no longer standing there.

"I guess."

"I don't know. Some are beyond that kind of recovery. They'll struggle with self-hating, self-destructive behavior all their lives. Or they won't make it at all. Drugs, STDs."

Celeste Mayne didn't have the answers either. All she could offer these girls was herself. And her rage, he guessed. Anger could be worth a lot. He finally nodded to her and handed her his business card.

"If you hear from her . . . for what it's worth, Jane Ash would give her money."

He half expected an onslaught, but it did not come. She just took the card and smiled, and then gently shut the door. He was left alone in the dingy old corridor. He started for the stairs, comforted by the sound of his own footsteps.

CHAPTER 39

When Flood got back to the office he sat down at a computer and took out the phone number McPhee had passed on from Tally's perusal of Skiddy's phone. He signed into Accurint and found the phone search engine. It was a mobile phone listed to a woman named Ana Maria Mirabelli. Her address was listed in the Rush Street area of the Gold Coast. The search of her identity showed a possible criminal record, so Flood signed off and went for a walk. It was Tuesday and the farmer's market was doing a brisk business in Daley Plaza. Inside the county building, a black Mies van der Rohe cage of a skyscraper, he ambled through the metal detectors with everybody else, and took an elevator to the seventh floor. Any of the elegance that may originally have been conveyed by the spare design of Mies's building had long since succumbed to the harried clutter of Cook County's bottomless bureaucracy.

Flood tapped into a public access computer, did a name search on the old-fashioned green-on-black screen and found two case records for Ms. Mirabelli. She had a retail theft case. Location appeared to be North Michigan Avenue. He scrolled through the screens of the court docket and found that she had pleaded guilty to a misdemeanor charge and received probation.

Then she'd been arrested for solicitation of prostitution. An address on Mannheim Road in Rosemont. Must be an airport hotel, Flood thought. He could see where this was going. Skiddy, a crook hiding his true identity in Chicago would have been unlikely to form a steady relationship with any woman. He was unsentimental, ruthless and able to spend cash freely. Ana Maria Mirabelli was probably not the only escort in his Rolodex.

The prostitution case was less than two years old, so Flood asked for it at the counter and it was quickly brought to him by a clerk. He was lucky. Such was the volume of cases in Cook County that anything older than a couple years would likely be archived in a warehouse and take several days to retrieve. The file was mostly flimsy, wrinkled sheets of procedural court actions. But there was a stapled copy of her arrest report, which included a mug shot of an unremarkably pretty brunette, looking bitter, defiant and a bit puffy-eyed.

Flood scanned the narrative section of the report, which had been filed by the Cook County Sheriff's office. As he suspected, she'd been arrested at a hotel. It was a sting operation run by the Sheriff's vice squad. Mirabelli had placed an ad on Craigslist offering a "girl-friend experience" at a rate of two hundred-fifty dollars an hour. An undercover officer had contacted her by email, and they arranged to meet at the hotel. When she arrived, she offered to "perform certain sex acts—including fellatio and intercourse," according to the report.

Flood flipped through the rest of the file, landing on a motion to dismiss the charges filed by her attorney, who appeared to have an address within a block of the suburban courthouse in Rolling Meadows. Each courthouse had its own cadre of defense lawyers who focused their practices on that particular courthouse. They were rarely stellar litigators, but on run of the mill cases, their familiarity with the judges and prosecutors was often the path to the best possible deal. In this case, Mirabelli's lawyer argued that there was no proof of any negotiation for sex, and that the undercover officer merely inferred such an illegal offer from the unusual circumstances of the meeting. The sheriff's deputy must have screwed up, because the state's attorneys had dropped the charges before the judge issued a ruling on the motion. Lucky for Ana Maria, too, because with her shoplifting conviction she might have spent a couple of weeks in Cook County Jail if she had been convicted of soliciting.

Flood made a copy of the arrest report and turned the file back in.

He rode the elevator down and caught a cab on Dearborn, shooting straight up the street about a mile to Ana Maria Mirabelli's address. It was a slender high-rise of about twenty stories, white-stucco and dark glass in cubed spaces that made the building look dated. The neighborhood was posh, nonetheless, in a way that was not trendy, not classic, but somehow fashionable.

Flood was always struck by the Rush Street area as a place where the tourists and diners were having a grand time in the steakhouses and expense-account bars. But the residents, small-apartment dwellers, looked joyless and overdressed.

It was mid-afternoon and it was a long shot, just sitting there on a park bench looking for a woman resembling the distraught girl in the photocopied mug shot. But Flood didn't really care. He had the time. He wasn't sure exactly what he was doing, but it felt like this woman might be able to explain a few things. She was a different kind of prostitute from Kellee Leonard, but she served the same clientele. Skiddy was the key and every person who might have had something to do with A.J. Ash's death was somehow linked to the business of money for sex.

It was a fine day and Flood felt comfortable in his suit sitting in the shade, a very slight breeze on his face. The street was a puzzle of yellow and maroon cabs, luxury cars and shiny black SUVs. No matter where you went, the streets were full of huge SUVs, it seemed. They loomed over all other vehicles, haughty and indulgent. Three of them were idling in front of Tavern on

Rush, a scene-to-be-seen joint that Flood loosely associated with organized crime wannabes and divorce. Ms. Mirabelli wasn't fooling around. She was practically living at the office in this intersection, so aptly called the Viagra Triangle in the local parlance.

His mind wandered back to Skiddy, imagining him prowling this neighborhood at night in his Land Rover, handing the keys to some valet parker and then ordering drinks until he spotted some girl working the bar for dates. Flood was looking without seeing for a moment and then his faculties kicked in and he realized that his eyes had been tracking a girl on the sidewalk from the front door of Mirabelli's building heading east. Dressed in tight white pants and a matching clingy halter top, big sunglasses and her chestnut hair gathered loosely over her shoulder, she paused and smiled as a middle-aged man opened the door of the coffee shop for her, attempting a line. She smiled wider and tilted her head but then walked in without another glance at the man. He let go of the door finally and sauntered down the street.

When he walked in and was met with the cool, slightly damp air scented with darkly roasted coffee beans, Flood took off his own sunglasses and let his eyes adjust to the light. She was at a little window table for two, sipping an iced latte and thumbing her BlackBerry.

Flood slid the chair out and sat down without a word, startling her.

"Ms. Mirabelli, I need to talk to you."

Her head snapped up at the sound of her name.

"How do you know my name?" she demanded.

"I just do," he said, trying not to sound too menacing.

"Mirabelle."

"What?"

"My name. It's Ashley Mirabelle."

"Not according to the Illinois Secretary of State's office. But if you want me to call you that, I will."

"I don't know you," she said, the alarm in her voice belying the cool facade presented by her big sunglasses.

"That's right. But you have some information that several people need, including me," Flood said, sticking his own folded sunglasses into the breast pocket of his jacket. "The others are unpleasant people. Badges, attitudes, handcuffs that aren't fuzzy. If you help me, maybe they won't need you."

She didn't know what to say, so she said nothing.

"A client of yours," he added, by way of explaining what this was about. "Don't say no, because I have his phone records."

He slid her Skiddy's photo. She started to say no, but Flood cut her off.

"Wait, there's more. He's dead. Somebody shot him on the West Side last night. Want me to tell you his name?"

"Donny's dead? How?" She removed her sunglasses, revealing pretty, nervous eyes.

"Somebody with good reason. Nothing to do with you. But you're not out of the woods yet. He was a big deal, so I need to know everything that happened between the two of you."

"Like what?" She rolled her eyes, clearly thinking, *You idiot— I'm an escort, he's a john.*

"Humor me. How did he find you? What was out of the ordinary about your business with him? And I'm not talking about how he liked it, necessarily. I mean about other interactions. Other people."

"Who *are* you?" she said, not totally faking her bewilderment.

"I'm a lawyer. A woman was murdered. Donal Skiddy, your *Donny*, was involved. The woman's family hired me."

Silence. Flood took out a photograph of A.J. Ash and showed it to her. Ana Maria's eyes gave her away.

"OK, come on," he said. "Your face keeps telling me you've

got plenty to say, but I haven't heard a word yet."

She tried to shrug.

"Sorry," Flood said. "That's not going to cut it. You know this woman."

He tapped the photo on the table.

"What does it matter," she said, "if they're dead?"

There was only one way to talk to this woman, who made her living illegally and most likely lived a lie for her family.

"Stop thinking, and talk," Flood said.

She glared at him when it was clear she was out of ideas and had given up the impulse to make a run for the door. Perhaps she feared what Flood would do to her if he caught up with her outside the view of the café crowd.

"She came up to me in a bar one night."

"Which bar?"

Ana Maria nodded out the window and down the street. "Over there."

"You were working?"

Her eyebrows twitched in assent.

"So then what?"

"She just walked up and said she had an offer for me. I said I didn't do girls, but I knew that wasn't what she meant. She laughed and said she'd give me ten grand to give something to one of my regulars. Just like that. Ten grand."

"Donal Skiddy."

She nodded. "She gave me a business card for some sleazy massage parlor in the 'burbs."

"Huh?" Flood wasn't following.

"A massage parlor."

"The name?"

His skin was starting to prickle.

"It was so cheesy." She squinted. "Oh, God, what was it?"

"Maybe it had a theme," Flood said, and now his stomach

was turning cold and tight. "Something to do with school."

Her face lit up. "That's it. Class Pets. You know, the whole schoolgirl thing."

"Ten thousand dollars for that?" he asked, saying it slowly, trying to get his own head around it.

"Well, five to give him the card, and tell him they had some awesome younger girls there. And another five if I could get him to actually go."

"She wanted Skiddy to go to this place and use the girls there?"

"Exactly."

"And you weren't to tell Skiddy what was going on . . ."

"Who? Oh, right."

"And you did it?"

"Yeah, I did it. I didn't care about Donny. I didn't owe him anything, that's for sure. And, in a way, she was scarier than he was."

Now she was covering too much ground at once. His head was spinning and he needed to slow down.

"Donny was scary?"

"Creepy, I guess. Like he was hiding something. More than usual, you know. Not like a wife. Like something serious."

"But she was scarier than that?"

"Yeah."

"Did she threaten you?"

"No, but she was, I don't know—real direct. Maybe it was that she was willing to pay so much money for something that seemed so, like, little. I could tell the money meant nothing to her."

"Did she pay you?"

She paused, regretting that she had just said the task wasn't that big of a deal.

"It's OK," Flood said. "I'm not a thief and I don't work for the IRS."

After a moment, she said, "Yes, she paid me."

"How did you make the transaction?"

She glared again. "Listen, who the fuck are you? You're not a cop. You come in here and threaten me, like you're going to *do* something. Hurt me or something. And now it's an interrogation. What gives you the right?"

Flood stuck out his hand. She didn't take it.

"Augustine Flood. I'm an attorney, as I said before. The family of A.J. Ash hired me to conduct an investigation of why and how she died. That investigation led me to Donal Skiddy, who is now dead. Skiddy's connections led me to you, and you're still alive and able to talk. And now it turns out you were in fact involved in . . . something . . . between Ms. Ash and Skiddy. I don't know if I have a *right* to anything, but that's why I'm not going to leave you alone until I know everything you can tell me. I don't mean you any harm, I really don't. I doubt this is about you in any way. But I have to have answers."

"Oh, God, what did I get myself into?" she said, mostly to herself. "OK, both times we met in Millenium Park, by the fountains with the faces. Where the little kids splash around. She'd show up, say hello, and hand me an envelope with the money. Twenties in those paper-band bundles. Straight from the bank. The second time she just said thanks and that was it. I never saw her again."

"When was that?"

"Early last fall, I guess. Kids were still playing in the water, but not as many."

Flood asked about her and Skiddy.

She laughed. "We were done when I turned him onto that place. They must have really had young girls because he never called me again. And this girl was right about that—it was totally his thing."

She made a face and went on, "I was totally ready to be out of that. He never did anything really weird but he was kind of creepy, like I said, edgy, and not a guy I wanted as a long-term regular, you know?"

"I can totally relate," Flood said, not meaning to be so flippantly insulting, but he was having trouble keeping his thoughts together as her story about A.J. Ash's scheme spun in his head.

"Fuck you," she said, but then laughed and smiled at him. She looked as though his reaction had shaken her. It was hard to tell what was really going on.

"And he never suspected A.J. Ash was involved in this?"

"That's her?" she said, pointing at the photo. When he nodded, she shrugged. "Not that I knew of."

Flood pulled up the photo of Kellee Leonard on his phone and showed it to Ana Maria Mirabelli. She looked a long time.

"I don't think so. Who is she?"

"Ever hear of a girl in the life named Britney?"

"I get it. This is the kid Donny was seeing? Britney Spears schoolgirl get-up. What's that video?"

"I don't know. But, yes. You're sure you don't know her?"

"Yes," she said, huffing. "She was at that Class Pets place in the 'burbs? I've never been there. This is where I work, down here. I charge an extra hundred and fifty just to go to O'Hare hotels and it's not worth it."

"Not if you get busted by the sheriff's vice clowns every time you set foot in a Ramada."

Her mouth dropped open a little and she stared at him.

"I know," he said. "The charges were dropped."

"You're freaking me out."

"So you were never at Class Pets?" he asked, trying to get things back on track.

297

"No. I sure as hell don't go to massage parlors to jerk off construction workers."

Right. He just nodded.

"So, did Skiddy ask how you knew about Class Pets? How were you sure he wouldn't get suspicious?"

"I told him I had a friend who used to work there. I used to tease him about the little girl thing, you know."

Flood sighed deeply. "You know, in my line of work we have a word for the *little girl thing*. It's called pedophilia."

"Right, whatever—so you're Saint-friggin-Francis. Anyway, he always told me to dress young. I'm telling you, this woman had him nailed. He totally jumped on the idea."

"And that was when?"

"Last fall."

"And you're sure you didn't have any contact with Skiddy recently."

"I didn't."

"None at all?"

She knew that he knew. Her shoulders drooped a bit.

"OK. Fuck. He called me a few days ago and left a message to call back. But I didn't. I swear."

That was that. Flood felt scattered and overwhelmed, like he was being bombarded from all sides with questions and information he couldn't process. But it was just him and Miss Mirabelli and her untouched cup of coffee in a quiet coffee shop.

He fought the impulse to ask if he could help her. Instead, he gave her a hundred dollars and thanked her for her time. She took the money with a smile and said, "You're all right, I guess. So, how big a deal is this?"

"Sort of big. You'll probably get an FBI visit."

Her mouth dropped open and she leaned into the table a bit. She had truly lovely brown eyes with long lashes. She was beautiful when she was terror-stricken.

"Don't panic," he said. "I can help manage it."

"How?"

"I used to be one of them. If I figure this out fast enough, they'll realize you're not a bad guy."

"You were a fed?"

"Yes, but not anymore."

He was on his feet and handed her his card.

"Call me if anybody tries to make things difficult for you."

He left feeling a little disoriented. What in the world was A.J. Ash doing?

There was really only one way to see this, he finally admitted. She was blackmailing Skiddy. Or she planned to. But at the moment, that seemed almost beside the point. She was manipulating Skiddy by steering him, at great expense and effort, toward the fifteen-year-old girl she had pledged to protect, Kellee Leonard.

He was on a roll talking to prostitutes, so he dialed Jana, the redhead from Class Pets. To his surprise, she picked up.

"Augustine Flood," she said.

"Wow, you put my number in your phone."

"I did."

"You were pretty sure there was going to be trouble?"

"But I haven't seen XO anymore."

"That's because he's dead."

"Oh my God, what happened?"

"I'll buy you lunch and tell you all about it. I need to show you a couple photos of people."

She lived out in Lombard with her nine-year-old son and a severely diabetic aunt, an arrangement she described when Flood arrived at the restaurant she had recommended. It was a cavernous, slick sports bar franchise near the Yorktown mall.

She pecked at some kind of salad that filled a platter twice the size of the average human stomach. Flood ate a bacon cheese-burger and coleslaw.

He put the photo of Donal Skiddy on the table and said, "This guy was the source of your peril. He's dead now, so there's not much to worry about."

"He's dead too?" She said oh-my-God again, and went on. "This guy came a couple times and XO was falling all over himself kissing his ass. So weird. Now they're both dead."

"Why was Melvin, I mean XO, so worked up over him?"

"Oh, he dressed like a rich guy. I don't know, it just seemed like he had a lot of money and they were making some kind of arrangement or something."

"He came out there twice?"

"At least. It was all about that girl, Britney, who you were asking about. And I think she went to him after that. I'm sorry I didn't tell you all this the first time, but I was really scared. XO had threatened us."

"It's OK."

Jana picked up Flood's phone and looked at the picture of Kellee Leonard again.

"She was a really pretty girl, and not . . . I don't know, um, this life, it sort of takes it out of you pretty fast," she said, holding Flood's eyes.

He was sorry they'd found this topic, because he could see the shame on her face. Whether it was because of Flood, or her little boy at home, or just her own broken expectations, he didn't know. It hardly mattered. She put her fork down.

"You know, after a while you give up on doing anything else. Anything legit, anyway."

"How long have you worked at that place?"

"Seven years. I dance too, at a club. That's how I got, you know, started."

"That's supposed to be good money."

"Not if they give you the weekday shifts."

"They don't like you?"

She smiled. "Let's just say they're on friendlier terms with some of the other girls."

"That sounds difficult. I'm sorry."

She smiled and picked up her fork again, but didn't eat.

"Anyway, the girl you were looking for," she said, trying to be a good sport and change the subject. "None of that had happened to her yet, or at least not much of it. So she was pretty valuable, I'm sure."

Flood nodded.

"So you found her?" she asked.

"I did."

"And she's OK?"

He was finished eating now, too. He pushed the plate away.

"No, she's not really OK. Since you last saw her, some more of *that* has happened to her."

As Flood drove back downtown on the Ike, he tried to play as much of his conversation with Kellee back in his head as he could. He feared that it all made sense to him now. It would be better if he was wrong and still wandering in the dark. The tape, he thought to himself. The little Olympus digital recorder he had hidden in the lampshade of his room in Vegas was at home in his overnight bag.

The conversation with Kellee in his room lasted a little under two hours, but the recording was more than three hours long because of the nap she took. He hadn't bothered to risk shutting it off and having her wake up and catch him. When he was back in his apartment, he placed the device on his dining room table and started pushing the tiny buttons, listening to the beginning of their discussion for several minutes. Then, getting a sense for what he wanted to hear, he fast-forwarded through several minutes until he found what he was looking for:

Flood: *"OK. Tell me about you and A.J."*

Kellee: *"What's to tell? She's dead. And here I am."*

Flood: *"She had planned to help you."*

Kellee: *"She said she would help me. But that's not how it worked out. And she's still dead, right? So what's it fucking matter?"*

Flood: *"But it seems like you were special."*

Kellee: *"Yeah, real special."*

Flood clicked off the recorder and called McPhee.

"You figured it out?" McPhee said.

"Maybe. Can Tally get me into Skiddy's house? I think he took A.J.'s computer, and I think there might be something on it."

"Like what?"

"Not sure. But I think she was up to something."

Donal Skiddy's townhouse in Lincoln Park was just off of Webster and Halsted, and would probably fetch close to two million whenever it was sold by whoever really owned it. If Skiddy had bought instead of renting, untangling the assets of a dead man with a false identity would be a real treat.

But it was a nice place, the sort built just after the Great Fire, with a formal layout and lots of heavy white crown molding. An interior decorator had been turned loose, plunking lots of expensive old furniture in every room but the kitchen, which was recently refinished in state-of-the-art appliances and granite that roughly resembled Carrera marble. As Flood put on latex gloves and washed his hands in the kitchen sink to eliminate traces of talc, he considered that the kitchen was not unlike A.J.'s new kitchen. Maybe they'd shared a contractor, he thought as he opened closets and drawers without finding anything on the first floor.

A.J.'s laptop was sitting in plain view in a small study on the second floor in the rear of the home. Next to it was an expensive Nikon camera with a three hundred millimeter lens attached. Flood started the computer and turned on the camera. The screen on the back beamed to life and showed him there were only about fifty images saved on the memory card. While the computer booted up he scrolled through the photographs and soon understood. There were a few shots of a man he did not recognize getting out of a silver SUV, but then he saw photos taken from a distance showing Kellee Leonard boarding Skiddy's boat in Belmont Harbor. The harbor was shaped like a violin, with the mouth of the harbor in the middle of the body of the instrument. Rows of docks lined the east bank just north of the inlet from the lake, with the first dock closest to the opening filled with the biggest boats, which all appeared to be sixty-footers or better. The view of Skiddy's boat in the photo was unobstructed only because the slip next to the seventy-five foot ketch was empty. The photos appeared to have been taken from the lakefront path across the harbor, from a vantage high enough to see into the parking lot. There were multiple images of Melvin Runyon sitting in his car alone.

Kellee was telling A.J. where the tricks were taking place and A.J. was staking them out with a camera. Flood kept clicking and found several images of A.J.'s father leaving the boat, getting in his black Mercedes and heading back toward Lake Shore Drive.

The laptop was ready now and he moved through the programs to archived photos. All the images he'd seen on the camera were saved on the hard drive.

Flood wondered why she hadn't just staked out the boat. Why did she need to control the bait—Kellee? He finally figured there were a couple of reasons. First, there was no particular reason to use the yacht. It could have been Skiddy's house, a hotel room, or several other places. And without Kellee, A.J. would not have had proof of what was going on behind closed doors. She would have had no details.

It turned his stomach. And then it made him angry. As he sat there in Skiddy's bedroom thinking about it, his rage started to quicken his pulse and he found himself balling his fists to control the tension.

How could she?

Such calculation and manipulation was beyond reprehensible. And for what? To shame her father? To ruin or merely humiliate him?

And Kellee Leonard had thought A.J. was finally the one who had come along and truly wanted to help. Then it hit him: the thread he had blocked out of his mind. He could not deny it any longer.

Flood took a deep breath and collected his thoughts. He took the flash drive off his key ring and plugged it into the laptop.

The photo files were large and copying went slowly. Flood felt impatient. He was onto something very troubling and needed to close the remaining holes before doubts about it made him crazy. His cell phone started to vibrate as he was thinking about where to go next. Even though the house was empty he did not want to make noise. He answered the call just before the ringtone kicked in.

"You're not still at Skiddy's house, are you?" McPhee asked.

"I am. For a couple more—"

"Get the hell out. Tally's rolling your way right now with two carloads of Fibs from Boston."

"Now?"

"Right now. He just called me. Said he was on his way there from Harrison and Kedzie when he figured he'd better just make sure. He's got the key and gonna let them in."

Flood raced down the hallway to the front bedroom that

overlooked the street. The blinds were drawn and he gingerly inched them aside to peek down. The hair on his neck stood up. Two black Tahoes were double parked outside. Three agents in suits were standing on the sidewalk talking to a pair of agents dressed in khakis and blue golf shirts that labeled them FBI evidence technicians. Flood looked down the street and saw a battered gray Crown Vic turning into the street. Tally was arriving with the key.

He had seconds to find his way out the back. Flood raced back down to the study and yanked the flash drive from the laptop without even checking to see whether the files had finished copying. He slammed the computer shut and ran down the stairs, which faced the front door in the foyer. He could hear the key starting to scratch at the lock. He thought he'd had it. The lock turned and clicked. But the door didn't open. Flood kept running back toward the kitchen. The key started scratching again. The second lock, the deadbolt that Flood had not bothered to relock, was making a rattling sound. Tally was fumbling around on purpose, stalling for his sake. Flood unlocked and opened the back door and closed it quietly. Skiddy had installed tall wooden privacy fencing to enclose his backyard, which was surprisingly large for the heart of the city. He opened the latched gate at the back and stepped into the alley, turned and came face to face with an elderly woman dressed in elaborate gardening clothes. She glanced at his latex gloves and drew a quick breath.

"Who are you?"

Flood smiled.

"Federal agents are searching the property, ma'am," he said. "You're aware of the interest in your late neighbor?"

He got a blank stare in return.

"It's OK," he said. "You may hear from an agent after today. There may be a few questions."

She nodded and looked around as Flood smiled again and walked down the alley, stripping off his gloves and heading for Webster to catch a cab.

Flood had all of the photos except for the last image, of James Ash's car leaving the Belmont Harbor parking lot. The images were all date-stamped the Wednesday a week before A.J. Ash's body was found. It seemed she had collected her evidence and then come back a week later to confront her father in person. If Kellee didn't know who James Ash was, her advocate's father, then why had A.J. done this? To catch him in the act. He could only guess she was mentally unhinged by this time, crazy with rage and her own deranged morality.

He was about to close out of the photos he'd saved when he remembered the few shots of an unfamiliar man. It was a series of five shots snapped in a different location, a motel parking lot in the suburbs. Flood still did not recognize the man emerging from a silver SUV. He appeared to be about fifty, with sandy hair going gray and not much of a gut. Flood enlarged a photo that included the SUV's license plate in the background. The image blurred badly as it grew, but he could still make out the letters and numbers. He wrote them down, switched screens and started a database search for the identity of the vehicle's owner. When he had a name and a Google search to further identify the man, he called McPhee.

"I've got an idea on how to bring Kellee in. We're going to Park Ridge."

In an hour he picked McPhee up at home and headed up Harlem Avenue toward a belt of comfortable older suburbs that bordered the Northwest Side of the city.

"Randolph M. Kern, age fifty-one. Married to Ann Marie, nee Doyle; twin boys Sean and Michael appear to be juniors at Niles Notre Dame. Mr. Kern is vice president of Sheridan

Cleaning Supply Company, which sells most of its inventory to various agencies and departments of the city of Chicago."

McPhee leafed through the file Flood had handed him, which included A.J. Ash's surveillance photos. "And he likes doing teenage girls while Mrs. Kern ain't around."

"Yes, he does."

"We're going to the home or office?"

"Actually, we'll try the office first. It's in Niles."

Sheridan Cleaning Supply was housed in a yellow brick one-story building in an aging office park near the Kennedy Expressway. Flood drove in and circled through the parking lot. In back, near the truck loading bays, he found Kern's SUV in a marked spot reserved for him. Flood parked opposite the vehicle and got out, leaving McPhee at the wheel to watch the back door. Flood walked around to the front door and entered the lobby, where he found a woman seated behind a reception desk.

"My name is Augustine Flood. Could you tell Mr. Kern that I'm here to see him?" Flood said, placing a business card on the desk.

"He doesn't have any scheduled appointments," the woman said. "Is he expecting you?"

"He's not," Flood said, turning the card over to reveal notations he'd made on the back. "But you can tell him I'm following up on his June eighth meeting at the Inn-n-Suites on Mannheim Road in Rosemont."

The woman gave him a puzzled look but then inspected the card and picked up the phone and called Randolph Kern's extension. She whispered and Flood could not make out everything she said. But he did hear part of his own phone number being recited in response to something said on the other end. When she hung up, she said, "Mr. Flood, he asked that you take a seat and he'll be with you in a few minutes."

Flood didn't bother sitting. He knew McPhee would see Kern before he did. He waited ten seconds and then told the receptionist he was going to step out front for a cigarette. He walked around the corner and saw his car had been pulled up to the rear bumper of Kern's SUV, blocking his attempted exit. McPhee was standing by the SUV's driver side door. As Flood jogged over he saw that Kern's face was red and sweaty.

"What the hell's going on? Let me the hell out of here. I'll call the police."

"Relax, Mr. Kern," Flood said.

"How much, asshole?" Kern said. "How much do you want . . . Fuck that fucking . . ."

He stopped himself from saying it but couldn't stop a furtive glance at McPhee.

"Shine pimp?" McPhee offered. "Yeah, XO's a real piece of work, ain't he?"

"Just listen a minute," Flood said.

Over the next five minutes, he gave Randolph Kern a heavily abridged summary of the situation. Another two minutes after that, a sweaty Kern had his phone out. Kellee's number was filed under the name Virginia McCaskey, which everyone agreed was amusingly clever. Then Flood told Kern to call Mrs. McCaskey and arrange a meeting for that evening. Kern made the call and punched in his callback number. Eight minutes later the phone rang, showing a blocked number.

"Hey there," Kern said. Flood and McPhee stood there marveling at the tone of voice a grown man used on the phone when arranging a sexual encounter with a fifteen-year-old girl. Eventually, Kern said, "You bet. Tonight, I hope."

More listening.

"Ha. Yeah, rough day. Usual place? . . . Okay, sweetheart. See you at ten."

Kern snapped the phone shut and then dropped his head,

looking like he might vomit.

"This is good," Flood said. "You get to go home tonight without Mrs. Kern knowing what you've been up to, and Mr. McPhee and I will help you extricate yourself from an unhealthy and, indeed, criminal, relationship with this girl who is the same age as your twin sons."

Kern's head snapped back up at Flood. "You leave my boys out of this."

Flood took the phone from Kern's hand.

"You'll get the phone back later tonight. And maybe think about those boys the next time you go looking for a teenage prostitute."

The hotel was a standard chunk of gray stucco near the airport. The lobby was wide and felt under-furnished. The dark carpet smelled of mildew. Flood checked into a room and then used Kern's phone to text Kellee the room number, as was their standard procedure. McPhee took a seat in the lobby and waited. They were early and had to wait forty-five minutes before Kellee appeared on the sidewalk outside the lobby. McPhee peered over his newspaper looking for a vehicle that might have been her ride, but saw none. This troubled him. He wanted to know how she got there and whether she was alone. But he needed to follow her up so she didn't flee when Flood opened the door instead of Randolph Kern. Kellee was wearing jeans, a tight-fitting white t-shirt and lime green sneakers. She carried an oversized shoulder bag of crumpled-looking yellow leather. McPhee had never laid eyes on her before and she didn't give him a second look as she headed for the elevator. After she got on he dropped his paper and pushed send on a text message to Flood as he headed for the stairs, giving the parking lot outside once last glance in search of her ride. He saw nothing of note.

The room was on the fourth floor and McPhee wanted to be in position by the time Kellee knocked on the door.

Flood was inside the room when his phone pinged with McPhee's message that she was on the elevator. A few seconds later there was a knock on the door and he took a deep breath and opened it.

"Oh, fuck," she said.

"Come on in, Kellee. We need to talk."

She took a step back instead and caught a glimpse of McPhee stepping out of the stairwell.

"He's with me," Flood said.

"No fucking way," she said, sidestepping away from McPhee. "I'm outta here."

The elevator doors opened again and out stepped the young black man in the St. Louis Cardinals jersey. The same young pimp McPhee had dangled over the railing at the Prestige Motel. As soon as he saw McPhee, his eyes bugged.

"Oh, I know you, motherfucker," he said, starting to raise the jersey with one hand while the other hand disappeared under the shirttail.

Flood and McPhee knew instantly that he had a gun.

McPhee made a quick sidestep at the man but there was too much ground to cover and suddenly the gun was out and pointed at his face. He stopped and put his hands up.

"Whoa there, young man. Let's stay cool."

The man shook the gun a little.

"I'm cool, old man. I'm real cool. How you like this?" He stepped closer to McPhee so that the barrel of the gun was just inches from the bridge of his nose. "You ain't so cool."

Flood figured it was his turn to try to diffuse the situation.

"Let's calm down," he said. "This is a public place and there's no quick way out of here. Think for a minute, man."

Kellee was scared stiff and kept quiet. She wanted to run but it looked like she wasn't sure her new pimp wouldn't put a bullet in her. So she just stood there in the middle of the three men.

"In," the pimp finally said, jabbing his gun at the open doorway. Flood slowly backtracked into the room, followed by Kellee, McPhee and the man with the gun.

"You two motherfuckers, up against that wall," he said, jabbing his gun again in the air. "Bitch, sit your ass down on the bed."

Kellee sat on the first bed. Flood and McPhee did as they were told and retreated to the outside wall, standing in front of the window, which had curtains drawn.

"This bitch belongs to me now. You mess with her, you messing with me."

The gun was a cheap little .380, probably the most common gun on the street. Half the potato chip bags and drain pipes in Chicago had .380s stashed in them by gangbangers. They were largely throwaways used for gang security that nobody would miss if they had to be tossed in a dumpster. To Flood it meant this pimp—whose name he still did not know—probably carried a gun for protection but was not in the habit of using one. If they pushed him too far he would probably pull the trigger, but they probably had a little room to push.

"If she wants to stay with you, she's going to stay with you," Flood said. "We're not cops and we're not DCFS. If we take her it's kidnapping, I guess."

"Just leave me alone," Kellee said.

Flood looked at her. She was waiting for the pimp to backhand her, but apparently she'd said the right thing. Flood figured this was his only chance to say what he came to say.

"Listen, Kellee. I figured out what happened. I know what A.J. was up to."

Her eyes focused on him a little more tightly but she said nothing.

"I'm not going to talk about it here, but I know what happened. I know how you must have felt standing on that boat when she showed up. I can only imagine the anger you felt when she and Skiddy started talking and you realized they knew each other. And that the creep in the stateroom downstairs was her father. I can't imagine how that made you feel. I am very sorry that happened. That she used you that way."

She was crying.

"You don't know anything. Fuck you. You don't know anything."

Now the nameless pimp did swing a backhand and caught her across the mouth. She went reeling across the bed.

McPhee took a step forward, but the gun turned toward his face again. They'd pushed about as far as they could, Flood figured. He raised his hands again.

"We're done with her, man," he said. "If she wants to stay with you she can stay with you. We don't need any trouble."

The pimp cooled off a bit.

"Yeah, we're done here," he said. "Empty your motherfucking pockets. On the bed. All of it. All your money. All your cards. Your phones. Gimme all it."

When they had complied, the pimp ordered them to face the wall and kneel. The command sent a peal of panic through Flood's gut. This couldn't be happening. Not like this.

"Now," the pimp commanded when nobody moved. Slowly, Flood and McPhee turned toward each other, and to the wall, and knelt.

"You don't want to fuck with me, old man," the pimp said as he stepped closer. The butt of the gun came down hard on the back of McPhee's head and he crumpled forward. It was revenge for the treatment at the Prestige. On the follow through, the man raised the gun to Flood's ear, stifling any thought he had of making a move.

"I don't think so," he said and tapped the barrel against Flood's temple. McPhee was hunched forward, his hand smeared with blood as he covered the spot where he had been struck. The room was silent. Flood kept his eyes on McPhee until Kellee whimpered as the pimp seized her arm and dragged her toward the door. At last the door slammed and Flood and McPhee were alone.

"You okay?"

"Fuck no, I'm not okay. My fucking head is bleeding."

"You need an ambulance?"

"No. I need a gun, is what I need. Fuck me, this hurts."

"I'm going after them," Flood said, springing to his feet and heading to the door.

"Wait. You'll get your ass shot. We'll find him later. And I'll take him apart piece by fucking piece. I swear to God."

In the moment of hesitation, Flood knew the chance to take him was lost. He looked down at the bed. All their stuff was gone. Flood went to the phone and dialed Jamie's number.

Flood cleaned up his friend's head and neck with a washcloth and a helpful desk clerk was able to locate a large adhesive bandage. The bartender provided ice in a clean towel and two scotches while they waited for Jamie to find Rosemont.

"Well, we're pretty much done," Flood said.

"That's it?"

"I'm not getting you or I shot over this. This is the second time somebody's pointed a gun at my face in the last couple days. I don't like the odds if it happens again," he said. "Besides, I know what happened. I'm going to tell Mrs. Ash what her daughter was up to, and I guarantee she won't want to know any more."

"She's still going to want to know who killed her."

"Skiddy killed her."

McPhee gave him a look.

"Melvin Runyon killed her."

"Okay."

"I'm not putting this on Kellee Leonard."

"I understand."

"I don't have any proof."

Flood drained the whisky and tipped the glass to get the bartender's attention.

"If she asks you point blank, you gonna say Skiddy or Runyon did it? Actually pushed A.J. Ash?"

"I don't know."

The idea of filing a police report in which they had to explain how they'd set up a date with a teenage prostitute only to be robbed by her pimp appealed to neither of them. So they canceled their credit cards and phones. Neither of them liked the idea of having all their contacts in the hands of Kellee's new pimp, but they figured the phones had already been tossed. The only thing they'd lost was a couple hundred dollars in cash.

They went to the Thompson Center in the morning and procured new driver's licenses, and then McPhee did go see his doctor for proper stitches in the back of his head. All was relatively right with the world by the cocktail hour, and McPhee and Jamie dropped by Flood's apartment for steaks.

They drank the whiskies and then sat down and ate salad while the meat rested. Flood opened a bottle of wine and then served the rest of the meal. McPhee nodded more approval and said, "This is a nice way to end what I would call a troublesome and fucked-up job."

"It was an education," Flood said. He was eating and drinking at the same time. Hungry. Planning to have too much of everything.

Jamie wasn't saying anything. He had been silent about the whole thing for a week. Flood and McPhee knew it was because he had let Kellee slip away. There wasn't much to say about it. Flood didn't blame him, but it was what it was. But Kellee Leonard weighed on Flood's mind. Not because he had promised to keep her safe. Just because she was out there. Because she was fifteen and knew only one way to survive.

McPhee was still mulling his desire to track down the pimp and put him in Mt. Sinai for a week, but better judgment was prevailing at the moment. And, in any case, roughing up the pimp wasn't going to save Kellee from anything. If she didn't want to be rescued, there wasn't much they could do about it.

She was profoundly messed up and Flood couldn't think of a way to fix things for her. If the likes of Celeste Mayne and Helen Schachter, professionals at this, could only nibble at the edges of Kellee's problems, then what were a couple of ex-copper private investigators going to do for her?

He had not even told her about his conversation with Jane Ash. That if she wanted out of that life, the resources would now be there. The support, or whatever support money could buy. But Flood knew it probably wouldn't work. It wasn't about money, it was about the girl she was, the way she saw the world and the way she saw people. The way her experience had shaped her. You don't just turn around one day and say people are different. People love you and you can trust them. People won't fuck you.

"Jamie, I don't think there's much you could have done to stop her. I sort of think she was meant to run," he said. "I can't explain it, and I'm getting drunk, but we weren't going to be able to help her, no matter what. That was her problem, but it was her decision."

Jamie looked at McPhee, who shrugged and made a face.

"I don't know what you're trying to say," Jamie said.

"I'm just saying let it go. Don't feel bad."

"But I do feel bad."

"I know."

"Are you saying things happen for a reason? She ran off and almost got you killed, and that's all part of some cosmic plan?"

"Not really. But if it had not happened just that way, we might not have gotten a straight answer out of anybody. If I had gotten close enough to Skiddy and James Ash, they were just going to lawyer up. There wasn't any real evidence other than what Kellee was going to tell us, and she was going to lie, either way."

"So, this was a good thing?"

"Well, I almost got my head blown off. But Skiddy is dead, which I think is probably the right outcome there. And that led us to the answers. I just don't see us finding out another way."

They were sprawled on the living room furniture drinking the end of the wine when the phone rang. Jamie picked it up and looked at the caller ID. He made a face and said, "You'd better take this, boss man. Maybe in the office."

He handed the phone to Flood. The area code was 202. Washington, DC. Flood looked at Jamie.

"You knew she was calling."

"I never know anything for sure," Jamie said.

McPhee took a sip of the wine and smiled. Flood got up and answered the call as he walked toward the second bedroom, which was his office.

"Hi," she said.

"I think Jamie had an inkling that you were calling."

"You were set up."

"Fine by me."

"You've been trying to call me."

"For a while."

"I wasn't picking up."

"So I gathered." His tone setting her at ease, allowing her to laugh like everything was going to be all right. It sounded lovely, but he had felt this before and knew it might not last. But maybe it was just all right in this moment, and that was all there was. He hated not being sure of this. He hated being afraid.

"So," she said with a pause. "Were you calling to tell me you love me?"

He could feel her cringing as she said it. The wrong words, but he didn't mind. "No. I was going to tell you I felt like I'm losing a friend and I'm afraid."

"I don't want you to be afraid," she said.

"Well, it's very good to hear your voice."

"Yours too."

"So just talk to me," he said.

"Hmm. I guess you're back on your feet."

"More or less."

"Now what?"

"I'll try to not let the business fall apart again. People are depending on me, you know. I've never really had that before. I'll try to start paying attention."

"You're more dependable than you think."

"Remains to be seen."

"In your mind."

"So, how do you like it? Washington."

"It's fine. The museum is wonderful. But it's DC, you know?"

"Not really."

"It's a funny town. Not really a home."

"I've never really spent any time there. Other than training in Virginia."

"You should come see."

"Really?"

"Really."

317

"I'd like that."

Just like that. He had not expected her to want that, or at least to offer it. His heart began to race, and his mind started to rebuild its images of Jenny, head to toe, freshening up his recollections and blurring them a bit in the excitement.

"You've been through something—again," she said, bringing him back to sobriety.

"Yes."

"You need to find normal work if you're going to have room for me in your life."

"I know."

"I can't relate."

"I know. It's not fair."

"What happened?"

"We don't have to talk about it."

"No, tell me."

CHAPTER 40

When they parted in Swain's office Flood had declared himself finished with Jane Ash. But he couldn't let go of James Ash. The man and his casual depravity weighed on Flood's mind. It was really Celeste Mayne's accusations that had hold of him. The desire to protect the privacy of all these rich people would shield James Ash from the punishment he deserved. What he deserved was humiliation, and Flood wanted to give it to him. Whatever Jane Ash planned to do to him would be carried out privately. She didn't want A.J.'s story hashed out in the media. That was fine. But Skiddy was another matter. That was a story for public consumption. And Skiddy was the way to touch James Ash, Flood thought.

So he called her from his apartment.

"Oh," she said, sounding surprised to be hearing from him. But not put out. "I'm tied up at the moment. Why don't you come by for a drink. Like before."

"The Peninsula at ten?"

Flood arrived first and sat down in the same leather club chair that he'd occupied during their first meeting. He was sipping a very nice bourbon on the rocks when she walked in—every bit as sleek and attractive as at their last meeting. She said she would have what he was having, and Flood started to talk about putting the Skiddy story in the newspaper. She was immediately against it.

319

"It will raise questions about A.J."

"I'm the only one who can answer those questions and I won't. If the cops were going to leak it, they would have done so by now. They're embarrassed by that idiot Fitzpatrick who was keeping Skiddy apprised of every move we made. Plus, they never did anything. They don't even know Kellee's name. She's not in any of their reports. Skiddy's not even in any of their reports on A.J. I don't think they really have anything they could feed a reporter who's going to want documents, or at least hard statements from cop sources. They don't have any of that. What the media could say is Donal Skiddy, James Ash's right-hand man, was really an Irish mobster from Boston who faked his own death and was helped back into this country by your ex-husband, who helped him live well until he lost a gun battle with crack-dealing gangbangers on the West Side."

He took a drink and she took a drink, studying him over the rim of her glass.

"I'll admit," he went on. "This is vengeance for me. I really need to hang Bobby Finn Burke on your husband."

"Vengeance?" She was surprised.

"I saw things you didn't see."

"Not quite what I hired you to do. But I like your . . . verve."

"I did what you hired me to do, and more. You owe me."

"I paid you handsomely."

"Money can't cover this."

"Mr. Flood, are you no longer trustworthy?" She said it and smiled. That was it. Somehow he had won.

His glass was empty and the gorgeous waitress appeared Jane Ash said, "Why don't we have another?"

He smiled and said, "I'd love to, but I have a plane to catch tomorrow."

He decided to walk home again. He left Michigan Avenue and

walked over to the relative calm of Rush Street, south of the cluster of big-shot steakhouses and bars where Ana Maria Mirabelli was likely out plying her trade. He walked in darkness past the Bentley dealership and pulled his phone out and called Reece, the *Tribune* reporter.

"You up?"

"Yeah. I'm watching Dempster blow a three-run lead in San Diego."

"Um, I might have a story for you."

The conversation became difficult, as Flood had expected, when Reece kept asking what this had to do with the Heidecke heiress.

"Listen, the story of the girl is a long road that will end up being a dead end. It would help me if you left me out of it. The story is that this bad guy wasn't dead. He was here in Chicago working for James Ash."

"Flood, you know what I do when lawyers tell me what the story is?"

"I know, you jump up and down and shake your fists."

"You're asking a big favor."

"Keith, I know how you work. If the story of the girl was there, and gettable, and worth the effort, I wouldn't have called you."

"You're turning into a real shit, you know that?"

CHAPTER 41

It was a fine summer morning with a cooler breeze blowing along the beach on the North Shore, rustling the leaves of the tall oaks and maples. None of the other mansions were visible through the foliage. Flood imagined what it must look like in the bare months of winter with the hulking stone edifices looming through the sticks in all directions. For most of the people the winter brought isolation, huddling indoors. Up on the east side of Sheridan Road it was the opposite. The lush summer foliage gave the rich the feel of seclusion, and only in the barren winter would they feel their numbers, a nodding line of fortresses up here along the beach, somehow astonishing in their frequency.

The Polish housekeeper came to the door and immediately looked alarmed. It was barely eight in the morning.

"I need to see Mr. Ash."

"Is this an emergency? You would need to phone first."

"It's about his daughter and it can't wait."

"You don't just come to see Mr. Ash without an appointment."

"Magda, go get him. Now."

She glared but shut the door and walked off. When she came back she said nothing, just held the door for him to pass. The main hall of the house had grown grander in his mind, he realized, and now it felt slightly cozier than he remembered. They headed in a different direction this time, down the opposite cor ridor of polished cherry and into James Ash's study. The place was straight out of Agatha Christie—Persian rugs, oxblood leather wingback chairs, built-in floor to ceiling cabinets and bookshelves of very old reddish-brown wood. Cut crystal bar service. A couple of well-disguised doors hidden in the walnut paneling. James Ash seated at a sprawling desk. Blazer, ascot, the whole deal.

"Aren't you finished making a mess yet?" Ash said without looking up from the paper on his desk.

"Almost."

"Well, what do you want? This is an unwelcome intrusion."

"I found some interesting clues in Mr. Skiddy's personal effects after he died."

Ash didn't look up, but he stopped looking down.

"You go to hell, Mr. Flood. I'm not talking to you about Donal."

"Without a lawyer present?"

"I mean it. We were all deceived by Donal. I wouldn't believe anything he said."

"Tell that to the reporters when they call."

Ash looked up finally, glowering at Flood. There was a drawer open in his desk and at least half his attention was there. Flood fought the impulse to go over and look. He said, "By the end, Skiddy may have been the only person telling the truth."

"That tells me well enough what kind of investigator you are. I can see that my money would have been well spent if you'd taken it."

"Well, from what you've just said about Skiddy you're not much of a judge of character, are you?"

"I don't see much point in this. I'm busy and you seem to have nothing very relevant to say. I certainly hope you're not going to embarrass yourself further by asking me for money for something at this stage."

"No, I really just came here to tell you one thing, and then I'll leave your house." He was careful not to say he would leave him alone.

"And what's that?" Ash shut the drawer a little and sat back. Whatever was in there didn't strike him as relevant, either. He held up his hand to show his impatience.

"I came here to tell you that no matter who pushed who, and no matter what A.J. was up to, I blame you for your daughter's death. The things you have done—the crimes you have committed—ruined your daughter. She died because of the horrible things she learned about her father, and you let your accomplices dump her body in the lake. Whether you take it or not, it's your burden."

Flood felt sweaty and tingly. For him the words had power. Ash responded with a laugh that was more of a cough that caught in his throat.

"You would make a better priest than you are a detective, Mr. Flood—making your moral pronouncements on matters you know nothing about. Perfect."

Flood turned his back and started for the door, ignoring the rest.

"Get back here, you piece of shit," Ash suddenly exclaimed, real anger in his voice now. Flood heard the drawer slide back open and the clunk of metal against wood. It was a heavy, too-familiar sound that made him turn around. Ash was drawing out a long-barreled revolver, his face nearly purple with rage. The third time somebody had pointed a gun at him. Not good. The heavy gun lolled in Ash's hand, as if its heft was too much for him. It appeared to be an antique Colt, the sort a Civil War officer would have worn as a sidearm, its steel a mottled blue and gray. Probably a collector's item worth a small fortune that hadn't been fired in fifty years.

Finally, he had it leveled at Flood, his hand shaking. If he fired and hit Flood it would be almost completely by chance. Flood stood there until Ash made actual eye contact with him. The crazy man's face was unreadable. Fear, anger, he couldn't really tell which way Ash was really tilted.

"Was your daughter's love really that unbearable?" Flood asked.

That seemed to send him reeling.

"My daughter didn't know anything about love," he said after a beat, spitting it out.

James Ash's own incapacity for love seemed to be implicit in the remark, so Flood let it go. He said no more, turned and walked out. As he headed down the hallway he half-expected the report of a single shot putting an end to this family's madness. But Flood had only the sound of his own footsteps to mark the seconds as he passed over the dark polished wood. Ash didn't have the will for anything further.

CHAPTER 42

It felt good to be packing a bag to get away from the Ashes and Kellee Leonard. The excitement of suddenly being back in Jenny's life, and being on his way to see her, was dizzying. As he stuffed socks in the duffel bag he felt free of the cold, coarse corruption of the city. It had a way of sneaking up on him in times like these and making him wish he was someplace else, someplace new and sterile where he could be free of the knowledge of how things worked. Money and politics, cops and gangs, everybody on the make, the wrong kind of people winning again and again, and always too many losers.

He called Jenny to check in about his flight.

"You're still coming?" she said. "I thought you might chicken out."

"I just want to know where you're taking me to lunch."

Flood carried his small overnight bag the three blocks to State and Lake to catch the Orange Line to Midway. The train crawled south over Wabash, split from the Loop tracks and rattled across Chinatown and Bridgeport to the airport in the corner pocket of the southwest side. He was through security by one in the afternoon and waiting for his one forty-five flight to board. He was hungry but his stomach was jumpy, so he passed on the sandwiches at the Manny's counter. He bought a pack of mints and a paperback instead and tried to clear his mind and relax. He thought about how he would kiss her. Just to hold her would be enough, but he didn't know what to expect. For some reason the idea of a kiss started to trouble his mind. What if he reached for her and kissed her and then sensed her reserve? What if it told him what he didn't want to know, and what she felt she must find a way to say in person? That didn't make any sense, though. If she had planned a brush-off like that, she would have come to Chicago to say it, not invited him to Washington.

Nonetheless, his anxiety crept on. What would they talk about? Would they have to cover the details of how things went wrong right away or could that come later? Later, he hoped.

A crowd had gathered at the adjacent gate for a flight to Philadelphia. Flood studied the people. Mostly business travelers pulling black cases on rollers and shouldering black laptop bags. Some kids—college students on summer break. They were mostly white and mostly well dressed. Flood had never felt at home on the East Coast. Sticking around Boston after college never occurred to him. He always believed he belonged back in Chicago. But at the moment it felt good heading east. His Chicago fatigue, combined with the desire and hope conjured by thoughts of Jenny, overcame all of his anxiety about the unknown. He didn't care if he didn't know what he was doing.

The Philly flight boarded and the gate area felt empty again. People were just starting to muster for his flight. Perhaps it was undersold.

His phone started to vibrate in his pocket. A blocked number. He ran through all the cops and FBI agents this might be, and he didn't want to talk to any of them. Flood was inclined to let it go to voicemail. When it stopped ringing, he sat there holding the phone, waiting for it to jingle that he had a new message. It didn't. It started ringing again. Blocked number. The effect of this was another aspect of the caller ID phenomenon. A second call with no message suggested urgency, almost panic. It wasn't good enough to leave a message. They had to try again right now, to persuade you to pick up.

Flood was annoyed. But he picked up.

"Augustine Flood." At least he could be formal and aloof.

She was hyperventilating. The line sounded damp with her tears and breath.

"I need help." The last word, *help*, sort of shaking and collapsing. She couldn't put a sentence together.

Flood's heart rolled right over into his throat. God, it was her, finally, and goddammit. He was floored and mad and excited. *Now, she calls.*

"Kellee, what's the matter?" Flood caught himself being cautious. *She's playing you*, he thought. *Be careful. Don't be a fool.*

"Please," she said, desperate and strained, like he was already turning her down, like they were already beyond the cajoling and on to the begging. "I need help. Please, come get me."

"Settle down," he said. "Take a breath and tell me what's going on. You told me to leave you alone. I'm leaving you alone."

She cut in, talking over his last words, "He's going to kill me please. You have to come. You have to come."

"Who's going to kill you?" Flood realized that he had stood up, and was now talking loudly. People were turning their heads. "Who, Kellee?"

"This guy. This guy I'm with."

For fuck's sake, he thought, and almost said. *This guy. A boyfriend.* She couldn't bring herself to say the word pimp. I made him mad.

"Calm down . . ."

She screamed back at him, "I can't calm down. He's going to kill me. Why won't you listen to me?" She was sobbing now. Couldn't talk. A moment passed, and Flood was in a daze. He realized all the other people sitting at his gate were on their feet and moving into line. He wondered if she was losing her mind, the fallout from everything she had been through. Paranoia wa setting in. Skiddy and Melvin Runyon wanted to kill her, so now everybody wanted to kill her. She was lost. All Flood could think as he watched the people start to board the plane was, *God, this poor girl. She's already lost.* The gate agent called his group of rows, and he started to move into the line.

"Kellee, nobody's going to kill you," he said. "Calm down. If you want to come in, I can help. Tell me where you are and my friend Billy will come pick you up. He'll take you to Celeste, wherever you want to go."

Her sobbing intensified as he talked.

"I need you," she said. "You're the only one who can stop him. You stopped the other one. Please, help me. Please come."

He stopped. The image crossed his mind of that ridiculous piece of garbage, Pearl, hogtied with a clock radio cord in Vegas. The woman behind him peered around and gave him a look. The gate agent gave him a look. Flood stepped out of the line and said, "Listen, Kellee. Tell me where you are."

"The Prestige."

All the old favorites. Just ten minutes up Cicero Avenue from the airport.

"Why would he kill you, honey?"

The reality was that she was a gold mine to a pimp. She was still a child, a beautiful girl, who probably had two or three years of high-end tricks left in her before the abuse—mental, physical and substance—shredded and withered her. No pimp in his right mind was going to kill her. But then, why was he keeping her at a skid-row dump of a motel in Cicero?

"He chained me to a pipe in the bathroom. I got out of it and I was gonna go, but he's right outside. I can't get out. The pipe is broken. There's water everywhere in here, and he's gonna go nuts. Please, he's going to kill me. He's crazy. And I can't run. It hurts too bad."

He started to sweat a little. People were still watching him.

The last of them punching their tickets and filing on.

"What do you mean, are you injured? Kellee, what happened?"

"He's going to come back any minute. He took me to this house. Somewhere on the South Side. And all these gangbanger guys were there. I didn't want to, and he went nuts right there. He beat me up, and they were all just laughing. And then they dragged me into this room. And they took turns."

"Oh, God," he said, mostly to himself.

"He brought me back here in the trunk of his car. Then he kicked me and I can't move my leg. It hurts so bad. Please, Mr. Flood, please."

"Where is he now?"

"He went out to get dope. He's back. He's outside talking to some guy. And he's going to come in here to get high and he's going to see this and I know he's going to kill me."

The gate agent was looking at him, raising her pretty manicured hands and gesturing to the door to the gangway. She was about to close it. Flood thought of Jenny's words when she invited him. She didn't think she could relate. She didn't know if there was room in his life for her. How did this square with those thoughts? Not well. He thought about telling Kellee one more time, that if she'd just sit tight, maybe McPhee could come get her. In fact, he had no clue where McPhee was at the moment. Working somewhere. And would he really send his friend into this kind of situation blind?

The gate agent looked at him again. Her smile gone. Kellee sobbing, despondent, hearing nothing and giving up. Nowhere else to turn.

Flood reached down and grabbed the bag at his feet, turned and started running with the phone pressed to his ear still.

"Kellee, stay calm. I'm on my way."

ABOUT THE AUTHOR

David Heinzmann is a Chicago journalist and novelist. He has covered crime and politics for the *Chicago Tribune* for more than a decade. His first novel, *A Word To the Wise,* was published in 2009.